Bilge Rat - Pirate Adventurer

Remarkable Rascal

(Book One of a Series)

Kevin Charles Smith

Journey Publications

Journey Publications, LLC

© 2013, Kevin Charles Smith
This book is a work of fiction. All rights reserved and protected
under International and Pan American Copyright Conventions.
Published in the United States by Journey Publications, LLC

Library of Congress Cataloging-in-Publication Data
Smith, Kevin Charles
Bilge Rat – Pirate Adventurer / Book One, Remarkable Rascal
A novel by Kevin Charles Smith
LCCN: 2013922013
ISBN-10: 0979817188
ISBN-13: 978-0979817182

Printed in the United States of America

Journey Publications, LLC
POBox 2442, Warminster, PA 18974

www.piratetale.info

Film/TV/Subsidiary Rights: Mark B Miller Management. (markbmiller@aol.com)

Dedicated to my fabulous grandchildren, Rowan and Lia, who make all of my accomplishments seem trivial in comparison. I wish them a lifetime of fulfillment and happiness as they have provided me by their wonderful smiles and engaging personalities...

CONTENTS

ACKNOWLEDGEMENTS

With heartfelt thanks to all who assisted in making my dream come true. A special thanks to my wife, Patricia for her hours of typing, her patience with me and her encouragements throughout this long process. To my daughter, Kari for her invaluable advice and information on natural healing, herbology and witchcraft. To my daughter, Shannon for her knowledgeable insights on all things historical. To my son-in laws, Ryan and Clay for their continued encouragements and critiques. To all of my brothers, sisters, relatives and friends whose reassurances and optimism kept me focused and moving forward. To my dear mother, Dolores for her undying faith, belief and love.

I would also like to thank the writing professionals who enabled me to make this tale become an actual book. For the graphic work my appreciation to Rocio Amovadar, Mike Saputo and George Brigandi. To my editor, thank you to Ali Bothwell Mancini for turning my tome into a concise story. To my digital team Neil Harner and Melissa Cherepanya and the whole Inverse Paradox team for their continual efforts to see the work published, seen and read. Finally, my deepest thanks and utmost respect for my agent, publisher and long time friend, Mark B Miller, who never stopped believing in me and my work.

Regards and Thanks,
Kevin

AUTHOR'S NOTE

Without a historical guide to shed full light on pirate exploits, Bilge Rat... Pirate Adventurer is a fictional account of the true to life times of these merry reprobates. Chock full of whimsy and quirkiness, this trilogy is a rollicking tale of adventure and romance set in an age long-past but hardly forgotten. This saga is intended to capture the essence of the period...a hard and brutal epoch where life expectancy was woefully short and men and women were born to stations in life that rarely altered. Spiked with exciting sailor tales and stories, this action-packed trilogy attempts to relate a clearer understanding of those popular sea vagabonds in an entertaining and captivating way.

Book One: Remarkable Rascal

"Gulls Come a Flappin"
(Traditional Sailor's Ditty...Author Unknown)

Gulls come a flappin'
Waves are a lappin'
Tars afeared of dirty weather
While memberin the scent of heather
   Heave Ho...Heave Ho...Don't Let Go!
   Heave Ho...High and Low...Heave Ho
Behind are our loving families
Ahead lay unknown enemies
Captain bellows a call for all hands
While hoping to spot a spit of dry land
   Heave Ho...Heave Ho...Don't Let Go!
   Heave Ho...High and Low...Heave Ho
Time aboard moves far too slowly
A seaman's life is dull and lonely
Sweet liberty on all our minds
Wondrous dreams of rum and sweet wine
   Heave Ho...Heave Ho...Don't Let Go!
   Heave Ho...High and Low...Heave Ho
Strumpets willing to give us pleasure
Coins and gems traded as treasure
Their company costs a pretty penny
But offered readily to satisfy many
   Heave Ho...Heave Ho...Don't Let Go!
   Heave Ho...High and Low...Heave Ho
Pirates lurking in hidden shallows
Thieves bound to swing from the gallows
Our voyage fraught with pain and troubles
Our wake long and full of bubbles
   Heave Ho...Heave Ho...Don't Let Go!
   Heave Ho...High and Low...Heave Ho

PROLOGUE

The damned ship was sinking into the brilliant coral blue sea and there was nothing I or any of the remaining survivors could do to avert this final disaster. Well, perhaps not a completely blue sea since it was dotted here and there with bright red splotches, as if God's own paintbrush had been dipped into it. These red blemishes were a result of blood loss… serious blood loss! Perhaps this was our ultimate punishment…God knows we probably deserved it. Pirates never seemed to have really good luck, and this lethal predicament was just one more wretched example. The stygian black fins of the relentless sea predators were painstakingly making their assigned rounds in anticipation of a good day's meal. As the dead or severely wounded tumbled off the listing remnants of the ship, they were immediately ravaged by the savage gnashing teeth of *God's Welcoming Committee.* I've seen many ways in which a man can join the everlasting, and while many seem to me to be a lot worse, this current situation put me in a very foul mood.

The question was, *"Did I deserve this type of fate?"* This query has probably been asked by a host of forsaken souls. A far more relevant question was whether fate ruled our destiny. Was it predetermined that each human was subjected to an unchanging series of events that dictated the path of his or her life? If fate does not rule an individual's destiny, does each of us then have sole ownership over our own existence and outcome? Learned and wise thinkers have long debated these fundamental questions without reaching a consensus. Therefore, in the absence of definitive answers, I have come to trust in my own judgment to provide illumination on these salient queries.

In doing so, here are my thoughts on these age-old human preponderances. I believe that each individual has a multitude of choices to make throughout his or her life, which operate independently of all that fate decrees by the will of their choice of Supreme Being. Further, I believe a man's destiny is determined by the subtle mixture of these two elements, providing an individual with a final outcome that is partially based on individual choice as well as determined fate.

Sitting on the fire-torn scrap of this mortally wounded ship, I now think back to a good many of the choices that I have made over the course of my life. What I am attempting to understand is which of these many choices made should have been challenged in an effort to alter my present predicament. I know you are thinking to yourselves that this seems like a very bad time to recollect on my lifetime given that the maritime dinner bell is about to be rung. However, this is my life we are discussing, so you are just going to have to bear with me.

In spite of my precarious predicament, I will utilize what little time remains to examine in detail the various choices I have made throughout my life and the consequences they have caused…for I am William *Echo* Eden…rascal, scoundrel and pirate!

Chapter 1: Early Remembrances

Where should I start…a nagging question that faces us daily? I have heard travelers say that a journey starts with the first step. A seasoned sailor answers that a voyage starts with the weighing of the anchor. A man's start in life is easy to identify since it begins with his birth. But this is a bit misleading, because a man's early years cannot be truly remembered, at least certainly not by that individual! Rather the first several years of a man's life are remembered by others who have shared those experiences. In my case, any early remembrances are entirely unknown because I lost both parents to the plague in these early years. The truth is that if they were consumed by the plague, then you could say that I was lucky! Before you judge me harsh, callous or totally insane, let me explain. In my experience, I have seen many a young child simply buried alongside their parents when the *Plague Master* has seen fit to make an unexpected visit. Harsh and cruel you say…perhaps.

When it comes right down to the nub, human beings crave survival at any cost. While Toby, my younger brother, and I escaped the misery, pain and ultimate death at the hand of the *Plague Master*, we were left as helpless orphans in a cruel world that had no time or love to share with us. This was a death sentence pure and simple. You see, both Toby and I were born in London, England's largest city, to poor pathetic parents. They could hardly take care of themselves let alone a couple of squalling obligations. I cannot tell you very much about them…truthfully only their names. The year of their death was 1695. This means that Toby and I were born somewhat before this date, which placed me at the time somewhere in my early to middle teens and Toby several years younger.

London was a huge and fast growing city that had little or no time or care for a couple of filthy orphans. From the moment of our parents' cruel and untimely deaths, the fate my brother and I shared was not to be a happy or joyous one. While we were both lucky to be alive, the odds on the matter said that we would be joining our parents in the very near future. Yes, it is true that London had organized homes for orphans. The conditions of these homes left much to be desired. Many were poor substitutes for slave quarters, utilizing their innocent and helpless residents as laborers in the burgeoning work industries that were springing up all over the city. These institutions demanded a fresh supply of human fodder to be continually sacrificed in the effort of making the factory owners wealthy. Hard labor, starvation and harsh punishment were an orphan's daily companions, with no hope for salvation other than an early death.

Toby and I were spared this ugly fate by a distant relative. Our great uncle came to our rescue, the retired Arch Deacon, Williamson Archibald. He told that this kindness came as a result of his strong feelings for our mother, who he informed us happened to be his favorite niece. Later we both came to understand the real truth of the matter. But the fact was that we were both given shelter, food and care rather than face the brutal realities of the London streets. Our uncle was the appointed keeper of Saint Agnes of Agony Basilica. This hulking structure became our home over the next several long years. As to our great uncle, he was a very learned and pious man, who was almost blind due to an eye ailment that left both of his eyes covered by a milky white substance, making it very hard for him to endure any type of strong light. Toby called his condition *ghost eyes*, which in fact it did resemble. We both had a hard time adjusting to his extremely grotesque appearance. We came to call him the *Old Ghost* when not in his presence, and just Uncle Arch to his face. He was basically a good person, who spent most of his time in the bowels of the church, where there was no bright daylight to torture his suffering eyes. This also proved to be a positive for parishioners, who were genuinely disturbed by our great uncle's appearance and tended to avoid his eerie stare at any cost.

The *Old Ghost* was encouraged by his superior, Vicar Walters, to keep himself in seclusion so as not to alienate the congregation. Our uncle did have many duties to perform despite his eye affliction, including the general maintenance and upkeep of the basilica proper. Now all of this could have been handled by even an old man like our uncle, had he only been able to see. But having the curse of poor eyesight made even those simple tasks almost impossible for him. That is where Toby and I entered the grand scheme…we supplied the labor to ensure that our uncle kept his position at the basilica.

But that was not the only service Toby and I provided for our uncle. The old structure was subject to a very real problem that all of London suffered…rats! Yes these loathsome, furry little devils had virtually a free run of Londontown scurrying from one building to another…from basements to attics…from back alleyways to front streets. These black disgusting pests were a standard sight to citizens, and for the most part ignored with a shiver and a quick shift in sight. Daylight sightings were not all that rare. But these loathsome creatures became especially bold after sundown, when they exited their slime-filled lairs to prance and cavort throughout the city in search of food or adventure. The problem was not isolated to the poor downtrodden sections of the city, but it sure seemed like these hideous demons took a liking to the poor. Maybe it was a sense of brotherhood they shared with the starving and unwashed unfortunates, or maybe it was that the poor had little time to bother with their presence. In any event, these scurrying devils became the main reason both Toby and I were saved from an unhappy existence in a cruel and brutal London orphanage.

Rats also had a distinct negative impact around faithful churchgoers. You see a devout churchgoer was for the most part an highly superstitious type of person…trusting in all that was seen and certainly that which was not. Of all the superstitions that abounded at the time…and believe me there were a great number to choose from…the superstition that strongly stood out was the dreaded curse of viewing a rat in a place of worship. Only one circumstance was actually deemed worse…being touched by a rat in a church! It was firmly believed that any unfortunate rat contact in a place of worship meant that the individual was doomed to die in a most horrible way. Basically, rats kept people away from services, which meant less money for any religious institution. Rats literally *scared the religion* out of parishioners!

That was exactly why Toby and I had a solid roof over our heads and food in our bellies. You see no matter how many cats were on hand to protect against these creeping adversaries, there were never enough. Therefore, it was up to each institution to find a way to keep this crawling pestilence at bay. Traditionally, that meant hiring *ratters*, whose job it was to ensure that the rat population inside of church boundaries was kept in check by whatever means necessary. Our uncle, charged with this vital responsibility, settled on a very simple and convenient solution. Find a youngster that could serve as his arms and legs in the Saint Agnes rat war. Better yet, why not settle on a couple of lads who could not only perform daily cleaning assignments while at the same time keep the rats in check!

Therefore, the basement of Saint Agnes became both our home and our workplace. Our learned uncle also acted as our private tutor. The *Old Ghost* would send us up into the church during the day to perform necessary cleaning chores armed with an educational problem for us to ponder and solve as we went about our assigned duties. In this manner, he hoped to provide us with vital knowledge as we fulfilled his charge to the vicar. At the end of the day, we reported back to the *Old Ghost* on both our cleaning progress and to provide answers to his *problem de jour*. We would sit with our uncle after each long day and discuss the answers to these daily educational riddles. We were totally unaware of the gift of knowledge he was imparting to us.

Uncle Arch was a master of languages, mathematics, history and science. I never found these exercises to be troublesome or boring, while Toby struggled mightily. In my case, I guess learning came easy because I had the strange ability to remember all that our uncle would say by way of instruction. All I had to do was hear something once and I never forgot it! I became the star pupil, while my brother became the dunce of our tiny class. My brother's attempts at formal education proved to be nothing more than failure. I, however, learned a slew of new languages both in oral and written form. These included English, Latin, Spanish, Italian, French and Dutch. I also picked up great knowledge in mathematics, chemistry, geography, map reading, history and so much more. As you can imagine, this proved to be a great help later in life.

Chapter 2: Echo Revealed

The basilica was empty on most days after the morning mass ceremony, so we had the entire structure to ourselves. The design was very similar to any number of churches, but Saint Agnes of Agony was at least twice the size of any surrounding place of worship. The arches that formed the inner structure rose steadily upward to dizzying heights. Given the extreme height and its overall emptiness, Saint Agnes proved to be an almost perfect echo chamber. Toby and I would call out to one another and our voices would repeat and repeat themselves until they eventually died a soft death. Early on, this feature provided an amusing pastime. However, Toby and I soon became bored with our new game and concentrated on completing our given assignments.

One fateful day, I was in the process of studying some required Spanish translations. I spoke the words out loud to ensure that my pronunciation was correct, while I listened to these words echoing back to me. I realized this was the perfect method to learn new languages. Further, I began to experiment with my wondrous new toy. I wanted to mimic other people's voices like my dear uncle's, Vicar Walter's and many others'. All I had to do was hear a voice once and I could recall with perfect clarity the exact tone, pitch and cadence of that particular voice. Much to my surprise, I found myself able to duplicate each of these voices in very short order. More than once, I was able to stop Toby in the middle of a difficult cleaning task by imitating the one voice he knew best. I would speak out a command in our uncle's high and halting voice and order Toby to recite some inane bit of information that had been given to him earlier that morning. Sorry to say, my less attentive brother would become convinced that our uncle was somewhere near, hiding in the many shadows that inhabited the old church, demanding answers from him. Toby would dutifully stop whatever he was doing at the time, and respond to the best of his ability. I decided to keep my special ability secret and hastened to guard it at all costs. This meant that my mimicking practice had to be accomplished in a very secretive manner, so that the echoes that resulted were kept to a bare minimum.

I soon came to realize that I could do more with my talent than simply duplicating voices. I found I could actually duplicate a multitude of other sounds. I practiced whenever I got the chance at sounding like a dog, cat, sparrow, raven, cow, goat or even a rooster. Eventually, I could imitate virtually any sound that I ever heard. One minute I'd attempt the Vicar Walter's voice as he prayed in Latin, while the next I would duplicate the sound of the large church bells at the very top of the basilica. Each and every successful attempt made me more adept at my special skill, filling me with an insatiable hunger to add more and more sounds to my arsenal. From that moment on, I decided that my name would become Echo and no longer William. I would answer only to Echo no matter how many times either Toby or the *Old Ghost* used my old name. For me it was Echo or nothing! Does it sound like I had a big opinion of myself? Well you might be correct in thinking so, but remember I was just a lad at the time. Using the name Echo always put a smile on my face. You see, I really did not want anyone to discover the truth about my secret ability. But using the name Echo was like hiding my fabulous secret in plain sight!

There was yet another time when I tested this strange but wondrous ability with someone other than my brother. As it happened, Saint Agnes was undergoing some internal repair work aimed at shoring up the west wall of the structure. It was determined by experts that wind and rain had taken their toll on one of the major support arches on that particular side of the edifice. A team of masons and carpenters had been dispatched by the Vicar to reinforce the offending arch headed by Master Builder, John Block. His crew numbered twenty-three, and included men with unique building skills as well as junior apprentices, who fetched all the needed repair materials for use in this reconstruction effort. One of these junior helpers was nearly the same age as me. His name was Scarf Rockingham.

While Scarf was not his real name, it was the only name he would answer to. As a baby Scarf had suffered the same plague, smallpox, that devoured his entire family. Scarf was the lone survivor, but he did not escape the dreaded disease entirely. His face was marred with the extremely nasty scars that smallpox routinely bestowed on its survivors. His scars were angry, weeping wounds that made viewing his face almost impossible without retching. He hid his terrible deformity from the world with the aid of a louse infected, filthy red scarf, that in truth was almost as evil to look at as its owner's deformed face. Having been tormented his entire life by bigger and meaner children and adults because of this deformity; he became one of the nastiest bullies I had ever had the displeasure of knowing. He would go out of his was to ply extreme torment on anyone weaker or smaller. He never tired of this game, attempting to extract revenge for the shame and torment shown him by most everyone that laid eyes on him.

It just so happened that my brother was on Scarf's list of favorite victims. Toby's reminders of Scarf's viciousness included a broken arm that, while healed, grew slightly slower than his undamaged limb, scars from whip lashes on his back and legs, a right earlobe that was partially nicked off and a wandering right eye that had been the object of a severe facial beating. These past cruelties made Toby deathly afraid to venture alone anywhere outside of Saint Agnes for fear of running into this juvenile madman. He would only make this journey in the company of someone who could protect him from the pain and terror of Scarf's torment. For the most part, I filled this role, but even then Toby would constantly be on the lookout for his nemesis to appear from behind every open door or dark alley we passed. Imagine the terror that filled my brother's heart when he discovered that his most feared nightmare was actually prowling inside the church.

It was almost too much for my brother to endure; even though he knew that I would be very near should trouble arise. The problem was that Saint Agnes was a very large structure, and it became almost impossible for me to constantly keep an eye out for trouble while hurrying to complete my assigned daily chores. Several times early in the rebuilding work, Scarf had caught Toby alone and had just enough time to whisper gruesome threats of torture and pain. These whispered torments terrified my brother, forcing him to locate hiding places throughout the church, leaving the vast majority of the cleaning work for me to complete. I found the entire situation ugly and unacceptable, not only the continual frightful state in which my brother lived but also the extra duties I had to shoulder due to my brothers many absences. I decided for both of our sakes that something had to be done to stop this madness.

My first effort to cure this problem was to face the bully and demand that he stay away from Toby. I knew from past experience that this solution would not be permanent. In fact, once warned, Scarf became all the more determined to make good on his whispered threats to Toby. I decided that something more drastic was desperately required. I came upon an outlandish idea while scouring a very dark and seldom used side altar of the basilica...a dedicated altar to Saint Agnes herself. First of all, the altar's statue of Saint Agnes was old and in very poor repair. The wooden statue had been attacked over the years by wood gnawing insects that had transformed the once beautiful replica of our patron saint into a ghastly, disfigured monstrosity, who very few could tolerate. She truly appeared to be in utmost agony!

All I needed was the right circumstances to make my plan work. As it happened, I had to wait a slew of days before getting a chance to launch my attack. Hiding in the shadows of this altar, I kept a constant vigil for Toby's tormentor to wander by without anyone else in close proximity. Day after day the wait continued, but I learned that patience could become my friend if not treated as an enemy. Then one day my vigil finally paid off! Scarf came sneaking by my shadowed lair in search of my unfortunate brother. Quietly and menacingly calling out Toby's name, Scarf happened to step right in front of the shadowed altar with its decrepit image of our patron saint looking directly down on him. I used this opportunity to call his name slowly and menacingly from my hiding place using the voice of the old crone, who provided our uncle with fresh milk from time to time. I judged her voice to perfectly reflect the eeriness and horror that this shadowed abomination entailed. In this dark and isolated chamber, my voice resonated and croaked out a warning to Scarf that if he should as much look in a threatening manner at Toby, this visage of dread would pay him nocturnal visits and torment him with unspeakable pain and suffering for the remainder of his miserable life. I went further to inform this bullying brute that the saint represented by this hideous statue had also suffered the torment of smallpox. As a final curse, this nightmarish visage promised to transport the dreaded plague directly to Scarf's bed and deliver additional *pox disfigurement* to his entire body. Further, the statue of doom promised that there was no earthly scarf large enough to cover his entire pox marred body from the ridicule and jest he would receive by everyone.

A terrorized Scarf emerged from this dark alcove a different person when it came to my brother…at least for a short while. Scarf made a point of avoiding Toby for the next two full weeks. He actually ran away from my brother whenever he spotted him anywhere in the church. But as they say, all good things come to an end. As it turned out, Scarf made several specific trips back to the altar of Saint Agnes to inform the rotting piece of wood that her instructions had been followed faithfully. He also asked the statue for guidance on reaching a better life. For all his piety and groveling, Scarf received no response from the statue, and after a while decided that the whole encounter had simply been either a bad dream or one he imagined.

Soon after, the persecution of Toby renewed with great vigor, and I knew I had to attempt something more potent in order to keep the villain at bay. Once again hiding myself in the same shadowy alcove, I awaited Scarf's regular visit to his new patron saint. Upon listening to his silly pleas for wealth, women and fame, it took great restraint on my part not to lapse into uncontrolled laughter. Once again I intoned the crone's high and screechy vocal tone to admonish Scarf for his further attacks on someone as helpless as Toby. I demanded that Scarf perform penance for his sins, and decreed that he stab to death his employer's beloved pet dog, Brutus. The dog was huge, ugly, mangy and very, very mean… totally unapproachable! Anybody who came within an arm's length of the beast was treated to a vicious snarling growl followed by a savage snapping bite.

I watched from a distance as Scarf began preparations to complete his heaven-sent task. First he attempted to make friends with the beast, which resulted in nothing more than several vicious bites. Next he began tempting it away from his owner so he could conclude his business with the beast in private. The only bait that proved successful in this effort was his own meager daily food ration, which meant that for the next month Scarf went very hungry. This tactic only served to add a few extra pounds on the beast, while taking a number of pounds off Scarf's already thin frame. Futility and starvation forced him to come up with his next very devious plan. Knowing he had to somehow incapacitate the dog, he made a forced entry into a local doctor's office one night and snatched as many nasty smelling medicines as he could carry. Then guessing which noxious compound would prove to be the most lethal, he began mixing small doses into his daily rations. He would then feed these to the beast to decide which had the greatest desired effect on the monster. Finally finding the one combination that had the strongest effect, he mixed a generous portion into his next food offering and gave the entire dose to the animal. The dog did respond as Scarf hoped…lapsing into an inanimate helpless heap!

This positive reaction provided the bully all the opportunity he required to carry out his unholy instructions. He proceeded to viciously stab the dog again and again. Finally caught up in his holy bloodlust, Scarf was able to end the beast's life. To ensure that Scarf was caught committing this brutal deed, I imitated the dog's dying howls in the area where all the workmen sat eating their noon meal. They all came running upon hearing my deception to discover the cause of the dreadful howls. Scarf was literally caught red-handed, heaped across the dead carcass of his boss' pet by the entire crew, including a very angry John Block. The reaction of the group was hardly surprising given the barbarity of the crime. Scarf was immediately beat to an almost inhuman lump of meat by the entire crew. In addition, John Block made it clear to the bleeding blob on the floor that he would never again work for any building crew in the entire city. Block then had one of his bigger crewmembers carry the boy's bruised and battered body to be dumped in the Thames River for the fishes and the monsters of the deep to feast upon. Thus, I finally rid Toby of his most feared nightmare, but in the process unknowingly made a very terrible and real enemy. You see, Scarf would somehow recover from his terrible beating and the attempted drowning. From that day forward, he would blame both Toby and I as the reason for all of his misfortunes…whether real or imagined. The brute had a very unforgiving streak in him, and he was intent on getting even with us both no matter how long it took.

Chapter 3: A Ratting We Will Go

After Scarf's justified end, Toby and I turned our attention back to the ratting. Our instructions from our dear uncle were very simple: bring back twenty-five rat tails each morning in order to earn a very meager breakfast as reward. Many days, breakfast was our one and only meal. Missing it meant going hungry for the entire day…a fate any growing boy does not look kindly upon! Now twenty-five tails does not seem like an extraordinary sum. However, if you stop and think about it for a moment, you will start to realize the enormity of our assignment. We were two inexperienced lads, with no knowledge of capture and with no tools of the trade, pitted against a savvy and experienced competitor. Are you starting to understand the daunting task that had been bestowed upon us? We were being challenged to destroy this wily bunch of rogues or face starvation.

Additionally, we had to learn all of the subterranean nuances of the old church. The vast majority of the basement of Saint Agnes was composed of a jumble of old rooms and an extraordinary abundance of burial crypts. Many of these last resting places had long been forgotten by any living soul. The church's basement was also a repository where unwanted goods were commissioned for burial. Items like ancient records, old furniture and other assorted trash were piled everywhere to the keeping of the darkness and gloom. Were we scared you must be wondering? Of course we were! I dare you to perform a quick experiment to gauge the extent of our fears. Find any solitary, dark and unfamiliar space and extinguish all lighting. Then I command you to remain motionless for an hour or so listening to the mysterious sounds that your new hell has to offer. I am quite sure you will begin to imagine yourself surrounded by all sorts of monstrosities. I am also certain that it will not take long before you flee your unholy Hades in favor of safer surroundings. Believe me, all you have to do is attempt this experiment once to begin to appreciate the mortal fear experienced by Toby and me.

Nevertheless, these dark scary rooms proved to be a perfect habitat for our four-footed quarry, whose droppings and gnaw marks were the only real clue to our enemy's presence in this dirt encrusted hell. Many rooms were dead-ends, while others led to larger junk-filled spaces. In all, it made for a very devilish maze that was very easy to get totally lost within. Our first attempts at capture were clumsy and totally inefficient. One of us would act as a *catcher* staying by a well-used rat trail, one that had plenty of fresh rat droppings. The other partner would act as a *beater* to force these odious critters to run toward the stationary *catcher*. The role of *beater* was simply to make as much noise as possible in order to move the residing rat hordes in the direction desired. You see a rat has an extremely fine sense of both hearing and smell, while having the visual acuity about equal to the *Old Ghost*...virtually blind! The role of the *catcher* was also very simple. His job was to grab as many of the fleeing rats as he could, and stuff these squealing forms into a burlap sack for later killing and detailing. Neither role was optimal, but the role of *catcher* would prove quite hazardous due to the numerous bites given by the panic-stricken stampeding rodents.

At the start, we were able to capture and kill only a handful of rodents each night, forcing us to endure long days of starvation while we cleaned the main floor of the basilica. We realized early on that this method was totally inefficient, and that we needed to revise our capture techniques in order to avoid outright starvation. Our next futile attempts involved various hastily invented traps, of which some had limited merit. Probably the best of these involved digging pits a little over an arm's length in depth situated along well-used *rat roads*. We then filled these holes about half full with water. The other vital necessity of our homemade rat traps was to ensure that these holes had very smooth sides so that our furry adversaries did not simply leap or climb their way out of our drowning pools. The beauty of this simple trap was it required very little work in order to create a number of rat *hell holes* throughout the basement. It also allowed us the luxury of operating our rat catching duties at all times of the day and night, since our rat *hell holes* never closed for business. By this method, we were able for the most part to satisfy our daily twenty-five-tail bounty, while avoiding the painful bites we were accustomed to receiving. These traps also allowed Toby and I to manage our daily rat harvest by allowing us to stockpile any additional tails over the required number for times when the harvest was not as good.

Since a rat's sense of smell more than makes up for its vision shortcomings, we also quickly learned that each trap had to be cleaned of dead rats and water regularly, if we expected to keep these *hell holes* functioning efficiently. This duty became our most difficult and certainly our most tedious chore each evening once our harvesting was completed. It also became apparent to both of us that the rats seemed to be getting smarter over time and tended to avoid our numerous traps more and more often. We both knew it was time for a new strategy…one that would require less work and effort while still providing our daily rattail bounty.

This is where my special talent once again came into play. Over the numerous months that Toby and I had been ineffectively going about our nocturnal duties, we had come to understand quite a lot about our cunning adversaries. We came to know their habits and haunts, their movements and patterns and most importantly their sounds. It occurred to me that one particular piercing screech that any excited rat would elicit would draw a number of its fine furry friends to that particular locale. I was never quite sure of the actual meaning of this particularly shrill call, but I did come to appreciate the results it delivered, bringing hordes of these loathsome hairy monsters directly to me.

My role was to lie on my stomach holding a burlap sack open in front of me in any dark recess while using this special rat call over and over, echoing through the vast underground basement. The effect of this mournful screech was simply amazing, as I watched the parade of victims casually entering the sack that I held open just in front of my face. So that Toby did not catch on to my secret, I would use a small crumb of food placed in the sack to be seen by him as rat bait. This ruse provided Toby with a plausible reason for my success. At the same time, I would equip Toby with a similar baited sack so that he could duplicate my efforts in a different part of the church's basement. It never ceased to amaze Toby that my bag was always full of these horrid squealing pests, while his was always empty. The rationale I provided him for my success and his failure was his inability to remain completely still and silent. As I related earlier, Toby was a good lad but not very bright, so he never really caught on to the real reason for my success. It was only necessary to carry out this nightly chore once a week in order to provide us with the total number of tails we needed for that entire week! This highly successful method left us with extra time on our hands to explore the sights, sounds and activity of a totally new and wondrous playground... nighttime London.

Chapter 4: London at Night

Toby and I now had the opportunity to prowl the dark, fog-laden streets of London by weak lamplight...far too few or effective to provide either good visibility or safety. You see, the nighttime streets of London were indeed very dangerous to any individual's health.

However, these nightly wanderings provided us an entirely new form of informal education that went beyond our uncle's daily lessons. Given the significant hazards and dangers we routinely encountered, we became quite *street savvy* in our effort to simply survive. While London was considered by many as the most civilized city in the world, it was certainly rife with all manner of crime, violence and wickedness. As we conducted our customary explorations, we were forced to develop a few life-saving tools to keep us alive and out of harm's way. In short, we became quite versed at relying on our wits, developing special skills and utilizing our fast feet to avoid or flee perceived perils.

The first major hazard to venturing out on the night streets came in the form of the seemingly supernatural fog, which snaked its venomous tongue throughout roadways, lanes, courtyards and alleys. This furtive intruder coupled with the lack of any decent lighting made visibility virtually impossible. Prohibitive for normal humans perhaps, but remember Toby and I had spent the past several years in lighting conditions far worse in the basement of Saint Agnes chasing an elusive and crafty villain. Our rat-catching night vision allowed us just enough visibility to navigate the narrow and filth-encumbered streets and alleys. This specially honed ability enabled us to avoid many a trouble spot along our paths of discovery. We also became grand experts in the art of *snatching*. This act involved grabbing bits of food from the carts of the many city street vendors, while they were preoccupied or just night blinded by the fog and overwhelming darkness. You see, theft was a way of life in our town. To merely survive everybody stole from everyone! Our purloined bits of food went a long way to keeping us energized and alert in order to continue our nightly patrols. We became masters of the streets and alleys; running and hiding from the many dangers while constantly on the lookout for new and interesting diversions.

The second danger we encountered on the nighttime streets was the many breeds of criminals and murderers who also occupied our nightly realm. Pickpockets, beggars, prostitutes, drunks, muggers, vagabonds and fiends of all sorts were our nightly companions. Two small boys posed little threat, but were very enticing bait for these lawbreaking scum. It became paramount to our continued longevity to identify these criminals and their intentions before they had the opportunity to do us any harm. Again our nightly *ratting* duties came into special play here. As I have related, rats have an exceptional sense of smell. In our quest to capture these wee beasts, we also developed a bit of this unique talent. We could smell trouble from the myriads of nightly opportunists, before they were aware of our presence. How? you may ask. Well, most Londoners did not bathe on any kind of regular schedule. It was simply not done for fear of inviting disease. These unwashed masses were foul-smelling characters; more like *filth slugs* than human beings. Our quick reflexes and hard-earned knowledge of London thoroughfares, coupled with our unique sense of smell, kept us well clear of these mortal dangers. To avoid certain disaster, we simply were forced to make numerous detours in our nightly excursions.

As illustration, I submit a brief reference to an occasional nightly cohort, named Filching Teddy Finnigan. Filching Teddy was a seasoned street-prowling veteran, who had also mastered the ability to detect potential danger using his nose. Regrettably, he had the unforgivable misfortune of being nabbed one evening by a vile gang of cutthroats, who beat the poor lad to death merely for sport. Just prior to the tragic accident, Teddy had contracted a nasty illness that caused him to snivel and sniffle his way around town. With this critical sense dulled by the ailment, he unfortunately blundered into the sadistic grip of his murderers. You could say that his runny nose had cost him his life!

Given Teddy's tragic demise, I realized that we needed more than an acute sense of smell to identify potential threats. The other crucial advantage I counted on was my exceptional hearing ability. Since every night spent in Saint Agnes' basement was done in total isolation, I became adept at identifying all manner of night sounds. My sense of hearing became so superb that I could fix on any offbeat noise and identify its source long before it could become any sort of problem.

The last mortal danger we faced was the sheer madness of activity occurring on the streets, lanes and alleys we traveled. Horses, carts and drays jammed the lanes at all hours. Stepping out in front of any of these hurried transports was a good way to be flattened into the mire for eternity. Additionally, feral and vicious dogs roamed the alleyways and courtyards constantly in search of meager meals. Running afoul of a pack of scavenging mongrels was also a good way to end one's earthly existence, since these creatures were not very particular when it came to nourishment. These ravenous creatures would eat almost anything!

On top of these hazards, we faced the ankle deep quagmire that made up almost every busy thoroughfare. Getting bogged down in this mixture of human and animal sewage was a sure way to be run over by a wagon, or worse yet risk capture by any one of the undesirable criminal elements roaming the night streets. Therefore, we had to be constantly aware of our footing as we trudged along in our nightly wanderings. In truth, one night during a sudden and ferocious rainstorm, Toby was swept away in a fast-forming river of sludge and raw sewage that transported the poor lad directly into the path of a speeding carriage spelling his everlasting doom. Acting quickly, it took a super-human effort on my part to drag my much-covered brother to safety, suffering only a myriad of nasty cuts and scrapes as a result of this grisly encounter.

Have I painted a very grim picture of London in all of its putrid and sordid ways? Probably so, but Toby and I never saw it as such. Instead we delighted in all that our wondrous city had to offer, disregarding all the ugly, smelly and dangerous aspects as mere trifles as we honed our critical survival proficiencies. We made it our nightly duty to enjoy all that our London had to offer, while never letting down our guard on the pain of losing our very lives.

Chapter 5: Slugger O'Toole's Sport Emporium

One of our many wondrous discoveries on our nightly excursions was that of Slugger O'Toole's Sport Emporium. Nestled on a small backstreet off the beaten path,

Slugger's was a rare treasure for those interested in a endless variety of nighttime pleasures. While the building housing this temple of depravity was relatively small, it was designed to take full advantage of the minuscule footprint it created. The building itself was only two floors high, with easy access from front or rear. Since youngsters at the time owned very little in terms of wealth, the back alley access became a regular revolving door for Toby and me…revolving since we were both thrown out of this fine establishment more times that I care to remember. This did not deter us from partaking in the many delights the unique province provided.

The first floor of Slugger's was a vast ginhouse with mismatched tables and chairs strewn from one end to the other. Additionally, an ancient oak bar dominated one side of the room, providing gin and ale to its decadents at less than fair pricing or measure. Women of the night prowled the dusty straw-lined floor in search of companionship, while games of chance dominated almost any table in the place. At Slugger's, drunks, criminals and the creeping poor cavorted and mingled with wealthy knobs in an eternal search for fun and entertainment. Pickpockets snuck through the narrow lanes created by its patrons in search of easy pickings from drunks or preoccupied souls. Mangy dogs and cats roamed the floor sniffing and scrounging for any fallen or discarded scrap of food. In all, it was a madhouse of fun and activity, certain to satisfy the vilest of human vices.

The upper floor of Slugger's was reserved for lodgers who wished to sleep off a nightly excess of gin, or find solace from one of the painted ladies always ready to be of service for the right price. Huge bouncers roamed this area evicting anyone who was not good for business; be they drunk, querulous or simply without funds. While we could remain somewhat inconspicuous on the main floor, it was impossible to slip by these sharp-eyed minions in order to get a closer peek at the activity on the upper floor. Given the danger of being badly bruised for our efforts, we tended to ignore this second level of hell entirely.

The basement, however, was the real shining gem to this exciting den of sin. The basement was basically one large room...bright toward the middle and dark and shadowy in the corners. A boxing ring dominated the middle of the room with overhead oil lamp lighting to give the combatants some sense of sight. The ring was nothing more than a roped square with rough-sawn pine planks serving as a floor. The boards themselves were a rusty, dark reddish-black color attesting to the gallons of blood that had been shed by fighters over the course of time. Anytime a fighter was knocked to the *pines* by a competitor, he would rise with huge nasty, jagged wood splinters as a painful souvenir of his trip. The events held here were bare-knuckle brawls. These barbaric matches would last until one fighter could go no more...whether he was unconscious or dead. There were no rules in the ring, so fighters could employ an arsenal of weapons from fists to elbows, knees, teeth and feet.

Crowds of villainous and overheated swine encircled the ring during each bout and placed wagers on their favorite fighters. The betting syndicate was run exclusively by Slugger and his cadre of bet takers. Odds were announced prior to the onset of the battle and bets were placed accordingly. Since space around the ring was at a premium, it behooved Slugger to employ fast, agile and very small bet takers, who could negotiate the narrow confines with speed and efficiency to glean the maximum amount of wagers possible. This is where Toby and my usefulness paid off. After time spent observing these brutal battles from shadowy corners and being rudely evicted whenever caught by Slugger's bouncers, we somehow became known to the man himself. One night Slugger asked us if we would like to earn the right to keep watching each evening's bloodfest. He explained that we could have a sort of official status in his emporium on any given night, if we agreed to be his *wage runners*. He even hinted that we might make a few pence in tips for our efforts by also serving as drink runners for his inebriated audience. Since we had very little choice in the matter, we readily agreed, and thus became an official part of the festivities.

The work was not difficult and it entitled us to watch the bloody events from a much closer vantage point. The daily lessons of the *Old Ghost* also came in very handy in our new employment. You see, part of our ringside responsibilities meant counting and ensuring proper payments for each wager we collected, along with doing the right calculation of winnings for those fortunate few. To be wrong in our calculations meant much more than being released from duty…it could result in very serious injury as reminder that exactness was a life-threatening necessity. Thus, we would work among the hostile screaming crowds, who were anxious to place various-sized wagers prior to the start of each battle, in an extremely precise manner. Once the fight was under way, we were free to observe the battle or run upstairs to fulfill drink requests from drunk, preoccupied patrons. For me it was just another form of education… one of self-defense. In watching the fights, I learned very quickly how to defend myself in close quarters with no other weapon than those that God had granted me. I learned by example how to throw punches that would knock men unconscious as well as other more dastardly techniques like elbowing, kneeing and biting when fists were simply not enough. I learned that hitting first and hitting hard had the most chance of success in a fight. I also learned how to measure an opponent and anticipate his attack, along with the best ways to defend myself in the process. All of this would come in very handy in later life, but at the moment I was just having a grand time.

There was yet another bloodthirsty treat available to the good patrons of Slugger's. Under the gore-soaked pine planks of the bare-knuckle ring was a special place of death reserved exclusively for animals…not that the fighters dominating the upper ring could be excluded from this classification. You see, under the ring was a deep pit that was used to wage animal wars, dogfights, cockfights and the crowd pleasing favorite, rat baiting. The pit below was as deep as the height of a normal man, painstakingly hewed out of the dirt and stone floor of the basement itself. Because a rat or dog can leap vertically quite a distance, the extra depth ensured that none of the sacrificial animals had any chance of escape. The crowd always cheered and jeered the efforts of these high-jumping would-be escapees, calling them *leaping lizzies*.

When the time was right and the crowd's bloodlust was at its upper limit, the pine planks were slid back to reveal this shadowy rank hole, which never failed to bring a roar of support and encouragement from the gin-soaked mob. In this modern day Roman Coliseum, animals were given the chance to savagely attack and slaughter each other for the exclusive delight of Slugger's patrons. As was the case with each bare-knuckle contest, patrons could bet on the outcomes of these poor creatures. Usually cockfights started these death matches. Once the festivities were well under way, dogs became the next level of bestial butchery. To round off the evening's slate of savage sadism, dessert was served in the form of the rat baiting skirmishes. In these bloody affairs, specially trained rat killing terriers were pitted against an army of grey and black vermin in timed battles. The winning *ratters* were those blood hungry mongrels who could kill the greatest number of rats during the prescribed five-minute bloodbath. Up to a hundred squeaking and squealing rats were released into the pit already occupied by the lone canine contestant, and then the real fun would begin. The dogs, trained to dispatch their furry rivals in as short a time as possible, went from one rat to the next leaving a trail of rodent bodies in their wake. I cannot express the utter joy this event brought to the drunken crowd every time this blasphemy was performed. While the death of any one of the combatants…human, cock or dog…could bring a sudden sadness to the madness of the evening, the wholesale slaughter of a multitude of rats brought nothing but happiness and pleasure from the mob. Therefore, it naturally became the traditional combative finale to any evening's sport and entertainment.

Again, Toby and I had the opportunity to be of great service during this savage animal horror show. During any animal fight, we served the same role as bet runners, allowing us a ringside view of each and every contest. In addition, we were called on to be the dead rat counters at the conclusion of a rat baiting slaughter. There was even a name for this service; we were christened *yellow callers*, because the majority of dead rodents had their yellowish-white undersides exposed as they lay in ruin. We were also given the opportunity to supply as many live rats as we could catch each night for this traditional unholy sacrificial rite! We quickly realized that to achieve capture of a larger number of rats, we would have to go beyond Saint Agnes' walls. The question became, *"Where could we find a location that offered rats in great multitudes and at the same time minimized the dangerous elements of London's streets, so we could continue to enjoy the fruits of our labor?"* The answer came to me in a flash on one of our nightly patrols. This specific jaunt brought us to the famous London shipping docks. Here ships of all types and nationalities anchored to load or unload their precious cargos in the world's busiest trading center. It seemed that these great ships were a natural breeding ground for our loathsome furry friends. In addition, the docks provided a suitable playground for rats given the copious amount of rotting and discarded food scraps that was a natural by-product of the shipping industry. Thus, the docks themselves became our new hunting ground for our wily adversaries.

These same filth-strewn docks also became our new school for further knowledge and learning. On nights that offered poor weather, hard rain or cold snow, Toby and I would sneak aboard various ships in port to do some exploring, safe and away from the nasty weather. We used the *rat roadways*, the ship's mooring ropes, to gain the easiest access. The poor visibility of the docks enabled both Toby and I to get on and off these idle ships without notice in the same manner as we negotiated the squalid London streets. Usually these ships had a few crewmembers left on board to guard against unwanted theft and vandalism. Since this duty was normally exceedingly boring by nature, most times we would find these ship watchmen sound asleep or dead drunk. If we ran into one of these watchmen who was actually awake and vigilant in his duties, all I had to do was create a small diversion by using my *special voice* to project some strange or mysterious sound that would send this would-be protector scurrying off in search of the source of the commotion.

On one particularly nasty night, with rain falling hard enough to wash away the city's perpetual layer of coal soot and filth, we took shelter on a merchant class vessel called the *Amafata*, a strange name indeed. The ship itself was in rather poor condition, and looked to us like it would be in port for a while making a multitude of necessary repairs. The one main attribute that drew our attention to this particular ship was its masthead. It was the image of a mermaid bare from the waist up, which obviously held the complete attention of two young and curious lads. Later in my travels, I would learn that just such a figurehead was not uncommon since sailors believed in an old superstition that a raging storm would calm at the sight of a woman's nakedness. Whether this nautical trick actually worked was immaterial to scared, superstitious tars who believed in its powers implicitly.

We had not encountered a single soul since our unlawful trespass, but kept a sharp lookout for the ship's watchmen. Two decks down, we came upon the ship's galley. Being as quiet as we were capable of being, we prowled through the entire area finding bits of cheese and the remnants of hard biscuits. Unfortunately the discovery of these small morsels kept us very preoccupied. Out of the darkness emerged a very scary specter whose position completely blocked our only avenue of escape. Upon sensing this new arrival, both Toby and I were so startled that we found ourselves paralyzed with utmost fear. The ghostly figure understood our plight and issued a loud bark of laughter at finding two young scoundrels caught in the act of thievery. As soon as we heard his course cackle we began to relax, sensing that the figure really meant us no real physical harm. Years at sea had prematurely added age to our hunched, wizened captor. He was missing his left arm and navigated with a noticeable limp. His hair and beard were dark grey in color, both wild and bushy to the extreme. His face was fully weathered but softened by the wide grin he sported for our behalf. He introduced himself as Jedediah Potts, but told us that most men called him Handy…a tribute to his lost aperture no doubt. Handy informed us that he was the cook and keeper of the very galley we were raiding. Rather than seeming upset with our presence, he seemed very glad for our company.

He asked for our names, which we reluctantly provided, and questioned us as to our reason for our unlawful trespass. We explained that we were *ratters* by trade and that the foul weather had driven us to find shelter and perhaps a chance to capture our quarry on his ship. We further elaborated on our role of providing fresh prey for Slugger O'Toole's rat baiting pit, which brought a big smile to Handy's face, since he was very much aware of our place of employment. He told us that the *Amafata* was indeed burdened with its fair share of these cunning creatures, who were constantly challenging his authority over the galley given their voracious appetites. He made it very clear to us that we would be more than welcome to ply our trade on his vessel any time we were in the vicinity. So began our friendship with this seasoned veteran of the sea.

We spent the next several hours filling Handy in on our brief lives and he would stop us every once in a while to ask for clarification or further details to our narrative. After a few hours of talking, we realized that our time was short and that we needed to return to our nightly bet running duties but promised a return visit soon.

We did return to the *Amafata* the following evening to continue our discussions. Handy was more than accommodating in welcoming us back, and had even prepared a light snack for our enjoyment! While we greedily wolfed down the food he had prepared for us, he took this opportunity to relate the story of his life and the many adventures he had experienced. Handy told us that in his younger days, he was a damn good pilot for another trading merchant ship named the *Achilles*. His duty was to provide navigation for his ship as it went about its trading routes from London to ports in the New World as well as those of darkest Africa. He was an accomplished sailor having spent all but a few years of his life at sea. He had been taught the art of navigation by a kindly old, half-blind navigator, who required the lad's keen eyesight to compensate for his own poor vision. For the most part, Handy told us that this training came very easily to him since he was a rather bright lad blessed with a good memory for details. He confessed that he did have a deficiency that would later lead the *Achilles* into serious trouble...an extreme difficulty with mathematics. While he could read charts and use all the necessary instruments of navigation, he would sometimes make erroneous calculations due to his poor skill with numbers.

As time went by, he informed us that his mentor eventually became sick at sea and passed away, leaving the duties of navigation solely to him. After several years faithfully performing his navigational duties, Handy and the *Achilles* found themselves in a raging tempest just off the Ivory Coast of Africa. Having limited visibility, the Captain of the *Achilles* called on Handy to plot a course to safety, navigating the ever-present reefs and treacherous shoals of the African Coast. In the process of doing so, Handy made a very serious math miscalculation that proved to be the undoing of both the ship and its crew. His erroneous computations led the *Achilles* directly onto a shallow but deadly reef, which ripped the hull out of the trading ship and sent it directly to the bottom.

The result of this disaster forced the crew to abandon ship and face the full fury of the wind and waves. Yet another danger awaited the helpless crew as they fled from the ship into the dark, wave-tossed water. It seemed that this patch of ocean was infested with savage, man-eating sharks, which made very short work of the floundering crew. Handy lost his arm to one of these hungry predators. However, he was lucky to survive this lethal encounter by being washed to shore along with the First Mate, who saved his life on shore by using Handy's own belt to staunch the copious amount of blood lost due to the severed arm. Handy would recover, but news of the disaster spread throughout the maritime community, never again allowing him the chance to pilot a ship of any kind. Since Handy's first and only love was the sea, he accepted a less prestigious role as chief cook and galley master after successfully recovering from his ordeal. For ten long years since the time of the *Achilles* disaster, he had been fulfilling this role on a variety of merchant ships, including his current position on the *Amafata*. Handy told us that he was convinced that fate had dealt him a very cruel blow, but was gratified that his life had been spared so that he could continue to function as a sailor no matter the role. At this point in the tale, I sneezed my customary three times which brought a halt to his narrative. You see, Handy saw this as a good luck sign…any sailor will tell you that sneezing three times is a blessed omen of good fortune! It seemed to me that Handy decided right there and then to make both Toby and I his trusted confidants and friends. He made it clear to us that we would always be welcome in his company and on any ship on which he was serving. We had successfully found a true friend and someone we could trust, which was very rare for us indeed.

Chapter 6: Scarf's Return

Imagine our shock and fear upon returning to Slugger's that very evening to find our bitter enemy of the past had once again returned. Scarf, in all his viciousness, had been newly hired to provide fighting dogs for the death pit matches. It appeared that Scarf had somehow survived both his brutal beating and his subsequent swim in the Thames River. He had been found by a kindly old washerwoman, who took it upon herself to nurse this poor child back to health. The rumor we heard was that when he gained back his physical well-being, he rewarded his savior's efforts one evening with a knife to the throat. While all of this was whispered rumor, I found the story very easy to believe. After taking her life, Scarf appropriated anything of value and later found employment with a fighting dog breeder, who was especially drawn to this young criminal due to his vicious and cruel nature. Upon spotting us entering the basement, I imagined that a savage smile formed on his hideous face under his ever-present scarf in delirious anticipation of getting his just and long overdue revenge.

It was Scarf's assistant, Lipless Billy Winder, who filled us in on the recent history of our feared enemy. Lipless was a cringing, cowed little street urchin who we had met several times in the past. His nickname was wholly justified, since he sported a mangled mass of flesh in place of his actual lips courtesy of Scarf. He had found his new protégé Lipless on the streets both starving and disease-ridden. Once Lipless was able to regain his feet, Scarf forced him to become a pickpocket, a *dip* in criminal terms, and ply his trade on crowded noxious lanes both day and night with no regard for his welfare. Lipless would spend most days roaming the thoroughfares in search of prey. Returning to his master, he would dutifully hand over all of his stolen loot as payment for being allowed to live. At the end of one very successful day, the lad held back a small portion of the day's take so that he could purchase a pair of miserable second-hand boots. Scarf discovered these boots hiding amidst his assistant's straw bed and questioned the boy on their source.

A terrified Lipless attempted to lie about where the boots had originated, but was unsuccessful at convincing his tyrannical boss of the deception. In the end, he broke down and confessed the truth. The consequences were both swift and brutal. Scarf secured the terrified lad to a chair in the kennel, insuring that no part of him could make the slightest twitch. Scarf then placed live leeches, purloined from a nearby medical facility, onto the panic-stricken child's lips. Unable to shake off the hungry little monsters, all the unlucky imp could do was scream repeatedly as the leeches ravaged and mauled their way over his sensitive lips in search of a fluid meal. His torment went on for hours and went unheard due to the incessant barking of the kennel dogs.

Well, it didn't take very long for Scarf to resume his reign of terror on Toby. Sure signs of his evil bullying started to manifest themselves on my brother...a broken nose, a crushed finger, a blackened eye and more! I could not always be there to protect Toby from this onslaught. One night, Toby confided to Handy and I that Scarf had threatened him serious harm from the vicious beasts he managed nightly at Slugger's. This type of threat would just about terrify anyone. For Toby it was indeed effective, because my brother had always harbored a secret fear of these blood-maddened monsters.

Listening to Toby's plight gave Handy an idea. Scrounging through the *Amafata's* medical store, Handy delivered a lethal poison that he hoped would put an end to Scarf's reign of terror. All Toby had to do was get the bully to ingest this poison, and his problem would be over once and for all. Later that night, Toby added Handy's potion to a fair-sized hunk of cheese provided by our friend from his galley. Since Scarf constantly stole Toby's meager rations, all my brother had to do was get the bully to steal this one specially tainted morsel. All seemed to be go according to plan as Toby dug out the tainted cheese from his pocket right in front of his tormentor. Tempted by this tasty morsel, Scarf instantly snatched the bait from Toby. He was about to devour it, when instead he collided with a stumbling drunk who knocked the poisoned cheese from his hand. The cheese fell to the ground, and was instantly swallowed by one of his fight crazed hounds that was being escorted to the death pit for the next match. Initially the poisoned beast showed no real signs of trouble as the battle began. Not long after, the poisoned dog lapsed into a series of uncontrolled seizures taking him completely out of the match.

The maddened crowd was instantly silenced by the dog's strange behavior, and the boldest of them began to clamor for their bet money to be returned, since the match had surely been sabotaged. In the meantime, the unfortunate hound simply tumbled over on its side and expired. Now the entire throng shouted their inebriated disapprovals and demanded the return of their wagered money. Slugger, at a complete loss as to the reason for the beast's sudden death, had no option but to rule the fight a *no contest*, and reluctantly returned all money wagered. Sensing something woefully amiss, Slugger's patrons hurriedly collected their money and began to exit the basement, disappointed with the night's entertainment to say the least. Slugger was powerless to stop this exodus of his fickle patrons, and in total frustration turned his anger full force on Scarf. Intending immediate revenge for the disastrous situation, Slugger unleashed his largest and meanest bouncer, Big Jack Masters, to teach the offending dog handler a hard, painful lesson. Big Jack escorted Scarf into the back alley where he proceeded to beat Scarf totally senseless, breaking a number of the young tyrant's bones in the process. He did not kill Scarf, but after seeing the victim I knew it would surely be a very long while before that intimidating menace would be resuming his dog handling duties for Slugger. While the plan did go awry, Toby and I experienced gleeful joy at its results. We both knew that we were safe from our enemy for the time being from our sworn enemy.

Things went back to normal with the temporary absence of Scarf. We were spending a lot of time aboard the *Amafata* visiting Handy, so that we could listen to more of his exciting nautical tales. As we promised, we also made forays down to the lowest decks of his ship to hunt down his elusive bane. As usual, my rat-capturing squeal worked flawlessly, providing us with a glut of victims for Slugger's contests. Handy was so thrilled with our results, that he rewarded our success with the very first gifts we had ever received…small pocketknives. Toby and I were absolutely thrilled with these new playthings, and whittled hour after hour to Handy's exciting sagas of life at sea. We even carved our names into each of the handles as proof of our proud ownership. For the first time in our lives, we were happy, but it was not to last.

I can report that Scarf, healed from his wounds, had wormed his way back into Slugger's employ. The torment resumed very soon after.

Toby again took the brunt of the attacks, and by their vicious nature my brother was being driven right out of his mind. He imagined Scarf's presence everywhere…in a back deserted alley, on the lower decks of the *Amafata*, in the basement of Saint Agnes…anywhere and everywhere! Scarf's first depraved act of vengeance was to force Toby to partake in a slice of *maggot pie*, a treat fit for Satan's palette alone. Toby was coerced by Scarf to actually ingest a fistful of live maggots, rather than facing being literally torn apart by his canine champion, the *Bloody Beast*, his most vicious and brutal killer. I know that sheer desperation alone was responsible for driving my brother's next plan of attack as Toby convinced Scarf's assistant, Lipless, to join him in attempting to rid both of their lives of this evil menace.

Their plan was really very simple in nature. They realized they required assistance from Slugger and his hired goons to take care of their mutual problem permanently. They needed to give Slugger a good reason to lose his legendary temper at Scarf's expense. In the end, they decided to snatch Slugger's pocket watch prior to the start of an evening's festivities. Lipless would then turn it over to Scarf as was customary with any pickpocket swag he collected. The act itself was easily perpetrated with Toby acting as a diversionary decoy, while Lipless performed the dirty deed. Slugger was oblivious to his missing watch amidst the noise and chaos preceding the evening's entertainment. With the pocket watch in his possession, Lipless hastened back to his depraved master to turn over this recently stolen booty. Scarf greedily snatched the watch from the trembling hands of his cowed assistant, and sent him back into the fight crowd for more of the same. Without the watch, Slugger was unable to keep time in the official manner required for each vicious match. A short delay in the action was immediately announced to allow Slugger time to find an alternate timepiece. Consequently, Slugger put out word to his muscled henchmen to keep a sharp lookout for the missing watch. Scarf, oblivious to these developments, was far back in one of the darkened corners of the room admiring his most recent possession. Big Jack Masters spotted the little thief and in a flash, Scarf was hauled in front of Slugger to explain how the watch came into his possession. Taken completely by surprise, the scurvy little delinquent could not manufacture a plausible explanation for the watch coming into his possession. Slugger was furious and in a fit of rage sentenced the thief to yet another vicious and brutal beating by none other than Big Jack. However, before this likely death sentence was carried out, the untrustworthy cur was first condemned to spend a full week's time in a standing pillory.

The standing pillory was an age-old torture device usually reserved for drunkards. The device was simple in construction, utilizing an empty beer barrel fitted over the victim's head preventing normal use of arms or legs. The victim's head was secured by a barrel top that had been severed in two with a hole cut out to accept the victim's neck. This sliver-inducing collar was then secured to the barrel prison providing complete immobilization and helplessness. To add even more insult to the punishment, Scarf's trademarked face scarf was stripped off prior to his incarceration, so that his pox marred face was on full display for everyone to scorn and deride. Toby and Lipless couldn't have been more pleased with the outcome of their plan, reveling in the misery and degradation heaped on their relentless tormentor. Both joined the vicious mob in its full measure of continual taunts and abusive acts on the now helpless convicted thief. Toby and Lipless totally missed the revengeful, demonic stares that Scarf gave them. Meanwhile, I prayed that Scarf would not survive so that we could be free of his unending cruelties once and for all!

How is it that just when you desire something to occur with every fiber of your being that fate always has the nasty habit of interceding so that your vitally urgent wish is not granted? Once again, Scarf virtually rose from the dead to exact his evil revenge on Lipless, Toby and me. After Big Jack punched, kicked and beat the unfortunate thief senseless, he once again hauled the boy's mutilated body back to the Thames for a final burial. But Scarf survived with the sole purpose of getting even with us for causing him to unjustly endure total and complete humiliation, suffering and excruciating pain. Lipless, the first victim in this unfolding tragedy, suddenly disappeared from sight. Months passed by without any word on his whereabouts until the mutilated and half eaten corpse of our friend was discovered early one morning on the steps of Saint Agnes, serving as a woeful omen of our own doomed future.

It appeared that Lipless had been dealt an incredibly savage beating prior to being nearly disemboweled. When Scarf finally made his appearance, he told us that he was responsible for our friend's dreadful death. He crowed about slitting the lad's stomach open and dumping him in a deserted courtyard frequented by a pack of feral hogs. These hungry monsters made short work of the boy's stomach, intestines and all manner of soft tissue and organs available to their frenzied foraging. Scarf bragged that Lipless' screams were long and harrowing as the swine went about their feeding while the imp was still alive, utterly powerless to arrest the beasts' manic activity. After hearing this, Toby and I spent the next several months living in abject fear. It's a wonder that we were able to get any sleep at all fearing the same fate or one potentially worse would happen to us. But as time moved slowly on, we both started to believe that perhaps Scarf's burning desire for revenge had been appeased by the pain and suffering he delivered to Lipless. It would not be long before we realized just how wrong we were!

Chapter 7: Toby's Disappearance

Now that Lipless had been murdered, our dilemma was finding an authority figure that would believe the story of Lipless' murder and act on this information, while not laying the blame on Toby and I. After hours of discussion and arguments between us, we determined that the only adult who was familiar with the participants in this gruesome tragedy was Slugger. Therefore, we approached him the very next night and pored out the ugly details to him. There was really never a question or hint of doubt on Slugger's part, since he was very much aware of Scarf's reprehensible nature. Slugger did warn us that the entire episode was based on Scarf's confession to us, and that higher authorities might choose to not pursue the matter based solely on the words passed between a few street urchins.

However, Slugger continued to harbor a very serious grudge against Scarf for past infractions. Because of this, Slugger was more than willing to bring the matter to a few of his friends in authority to see if anything could be resolved in Lipless' murder. We heard no more on the matter other than Slugger informing us that certain authorities were looking into the murder and answers should be shortly forthcoming. However, very little was accomplished in the resolution of the crime, since Scarf had taken it upon himself to go into hiding. While Scarf continued to go unpunished for his dreadful act, we knew that our best chance of remaining safe was to spend as much of our time as possible in friendly public places among people we trusted. Since we already had assigned duties at Saint Agnes and at Slugger O'Toole's, we began to spend any remaining time aboard the *Amafata* listening to even more of our new friend Handy's yarns of past sea adventures.

A few nights later, Handy questioned both of us as to why we seemed to be so nervous and Toby and I decided it best to be honest with our friend. After listening to our sordid tale, Handy said he understood our predicament and promised to help us in any way he could.

Further, he informed us that our situation reminded him of a story of a past crewman. Both Toby and I shared a brief knowing glance because we knew this to be the signal for yet another of Handy's *sea tales,* as we had come to call them. The story began with a simple sailor and friend of Handy's named Edmund Spriggs. This particular tar was a very timid and superstitious fellow who seemed constantly on the lookout for trouble headed his way. Handy informed us that Edmund was a cautious individual and avoided dangerous situations at all cost. However, Edmund was convinced that something bad was headed in his direction, and that it could be avoided if he kept a sharp lookout for signs of this approaching calamity. Edmund was also a bit dimwitted and was quite clueless as to what danger signs to look for. Because of this, he took any sign as a precursor to evil…a sudden rain, a seabird soaring toward the sun, a dolphin following the ship on the portside, a day without wind… virtually sensing evil in anything that occurred around him.

Edmund, living in absolute terror of normal everyday occurrences, was continually edgy and jumpy while seriously getting on his mates' nerves with his paranoid fears. The crew decided en masse that something had to be done to rectify the situation. Their plan was to convince Edmund that his next evil omen was the true sign he had been awaiting, and thereby put an end to his suffering and anxiety. As it happened, Edmund spotted a black cat on a lower deck and instantly knew that this was the harbinger of doom that he had been anticipating. In relating this discovery to his mates, they agreed with the lad that the sighting of the black cat aboard their vessel was a very bad omen indeed. The entire crew vowed to assist him in locating and ridding the ship of this nasty omen. Search parties were sent to every part of the ship to locate Edmund's black cat. After six long days of searching, no sign had been found of the elusive ebony creature. The majority of the men actually believed that the phantom feline was a figment of Edmund's tortured mind and did not exist at all.

The frustrated crew was successful at convincing the skeptical sailor that his black cat was actually a *sea mirage,* and posed no real threat or danger. The next several days were spent without incident, and Edmund's sighting was put behind them for good. Under a sky full of stars and a calm westerly breeze, Edmund and his mates settled into their bunks for a peaceful slumber. No sooner than the snoring began, a dreadful crunching noise sounded from below, followed by the entire ship shuddering to a complete stop. Edmund took a particularly nasty spill and banged his head on a water barrel causing a huge knot to rise on his noggin. His mates flew out of their bunks amid the chaos, and raced to the maindeck to discern the cause of the commotion. They were told that the ship had encountered a nasty reef that had ripped a huge gash in the hull causing the vessel to take on a prodigious amount of seawater. The Captain ordered all hands below to staunch the leak and to affect temporary repairs so that the ship did not sink to a watery grave. Edmund was ordered to stay in his bunk and nurse his head injury.

During their crazed and hurried efforts on the damage below, the crew was treated to an unholy wailing and screeching emanating from somewhere above them. They dared not stop the repair work for fear of sinking, so all they could do was listen to the satanic clamor that seemed to steadily increase in volume. Once finished with all the necessary repairs, the crew branched out to search for the source of this evil noise. What they eventually found shocked and frightened them more than the hidden reef's damage. They discovered Edmund alone in his hammock virtually ripped and torn into shredded chunks. Blood spray had splattered everything in the vicinity of the poor unfortunate, while his body parts were decorated with a series of deadly scratches and lacerations. The horrific glaze on Edmund's face foretold an even more eerie story.

The ship's doctor was called to examine the victim's remains, and his conclusions once again sent a wave of fear throughout the entire ship. The doctor promptly announced that Edmund had been attacked by a bloodthirsty creature intent on causing his ruin. While the scratches and lacerations resembled those of a feline, the doctor had a hard time explaining that any ordinary cat could have caused the wholesale destruction of their friend. Further, amidst the blood and scraps of flesh, there was a distinct trail of feline footprints that led directly to the ship's outer hull and ended there. The entire crew knew what had cased Edmund's death, since they had all participated in the search for the elusive creature. The crew also was sure that this monster had sought out Edmund as its unlikely victim, and had proceeded to rip him apart piece by piece. While a renewed search was organized to find the black demon, many crew members silently crossed themselves to ward off danger. A full two days were spent searching the ship from stem to stern but no feline was found. Once the ship reached a safe harbor to affect needed repairs, many of the crew took their leave and never returned. The Captain was forced to recruit a completely new crew to replace the deserters, including Handy who confessed that he had also fled the cursed vessel. While my brother and I listened in terror to Handy's dark tale, we began to wonder what the story had to do with the predicament facing us. Handy was quick to read our troubled expressions and informed us that the moral of his story was very relevant to our current woes. I can still hear his prophetic words today as he said, *"Do not ever ignore evil and trouble because you simply cannot see it, because it is more than likely very close and poised to strike when you least expect it."*

After listening to Handy, we both realized that our trouble was very real and would find us very soon no matter how diligent we were in our attempts to avoid it. As it turned out, all of our watchfulness and caution did little good in thwarting the maniacal plans of Scarf. One day while we were both completing our cleaning tasks at Saint Agnes, we were shocked to find that a fire had sprung up in the back of the church, which, while minor in nature, still demanded immediate response to prevent the blaze from getting larger and destroying the entire basilica. I immediately ran for the water buckets left in the basement, while Toby was busy stamping out the small fires that surrounded the main blaze. Upon my return I found the fire had not gained any momentum, but my brother Toby was nowhere to be found. After putting out the fire with a bucket of water, I went in search of my wandering sibling. I searched Saint Agnes from the top to bottom with no success and then took my search outside.

Once again, I had absolutely no luck in locating Toby in the general area surrounding Saint Agnes. Perplexed and starting to feel real concern, I widened the search area again and again in vain. I searched for an entire week, both day and night, without finding a trace of my missing brother. I even convinced Slugger and his minions to assist me in my search. In all, I spent the better part of six long weeks on my quest to find my brother, and in the end had nothing to show for my prolonged efforts.

The *Old Ghost* was convinced that Toby had simply become lost in the chaos caused by the fire, and had been taken in by some good soul who was tenderly caring for the poor lad in his moment of need. While I wanted to believe this fanciful story, I had a very strong feeling of dread believing Scarf had abducted Toby. After six weeks had passed, I knew with certainty that Toby was in either grave mortal danger or was no longer alive. Giving up my fruitless daytime searching, I resumed my church cleaning chores but utilized the nights to continue the hunt for Toby. Even Handy lent a hand, abandoning his beloved galley to assist in my quest to locate my brother. All of this searching proved totally useless and extremely frustrating, but I was all the more determined to never give up hope for my brother's safe return.

Returning from a frustrating night of failure, I launched into my cleaning duties at Saint Agnes and discovered something truly startling. Hidden in one of the rear holy water founts was Toby's prized possession... his pocketknife! Reeling with my discovery, I quickly scanned the entire church in search of anyone who might have deposited the knife in the fount. To my utter amazement there was absolutely no one else in the church except me. I knew by my cleaning schedule that Toby's knife had recently been placed in the fount for me to find, since I had added fresh water to that fount very late the previous day. What I could not deduce was the intended message. Was it to let me know that my brother was still alive and in need of my assistance? Or was it to inform me that my poor brother was dead and far beyond my help?

I approached the two servers who assisted with morning service and inquired if they had seen anything suspicious at the service. While one young boy was totally clueless, the other boy did remember an odd sight from the morning's ritual. He remembered a big lad at the far back of the basilica, who seemed to be playing with something throughout the entire service. He went on to describe the lad as having a red scarf covering most of his face, but could remember very little else. At the sound of his words describing my hated nemesis, my heart stood still for a very long moment. In his cruel and hateful way, Scarf had sent his nasty message. For me, however, it provided a new ray of hope that my brother was yet alive, although I did not want to spend time imagining what kind of perils he faced.

That day I finished my chores in record time, and ran all the way to the docks to inform Handy of the good news. Once I relayed the complete story of the morning's discovery and the sighting of Scarf at the Saint

Agnes' service, I glanced up to find my friend in a deep and serious mood. Handy sat me down and patiently explained the source of his new concern. It seemed that a man's knife resting in a pool of water had a very special meaning for seamen, especially because it was found in a pool of sacred holy water. The meaning of such a portent was to let all know that the person who owned the knife was indeed dead. I refused to believe the words issued by Handy. Running away from the *Amafata*, I was teary-eyed but staunch in my belief that my brother was indeed alive and in desperate need of my assistance. I knew that if I could locate my adversary, he would lead me to my brother.

Over the next several weeks, I resumed my hunt for both Scarf and my brother with equally empty results. Then one night I ran into an old gin-soaked hag who gave me a completely different answer to my queries. Her name was Gwen Corder, and she seemed to remember seeing both of the boys that I had described in detail not very long ago. I was extremely leery at first, because I believed this was her way of tricking me into giving her money to support her gin habit. But the more she talked about the episode, the more interested I became. She recalled seeing the pair I had described walking together through the early hours of the morning just a few days past. She remembered that they seemed in good spirits, but then again she informed me that she had drank a snoot full of gin and could vaguely remember anything else pertaining to the incident. After several excited prompts from me, she did seem to remember that the taller of the two boys was indeed wearing a red scarf over his face, which seemed very odd to her at the time. She also remembered the saddened face of the younger lad. She clearly remembered this because at the time she asked herself what could cause such anguish in such a small child!

This was finally some positive news after all the exhausting searching of the past two months. One thought hammered in my head, my brother was still alive and was hidden somewhere in London! I gained a new surge of confidence, and vowed to continue my efforts until I discovered where my brother was being kept. Finally, in the dog training kennels that Scarf used to manage, I found a bloody torn remnant of my brother's shirt. The blood had dried on this tiny cloth scrap, so it was virtually impossible to tell how long it had been lying in the kennel. At the same time, I knew that my brother was deathly afraid of the killing beasts that

Scarf trained, so it would be a natural place for Scarf to bring my brother to elicit pure fear and terror.

I redoubled my efforts yet again, but as before found no further clues to Toby's whereabouts. As I was wandering the alleyways one night, I thought I spotted a familiar figure making the turn at the next street. It appeared to be someone with a covering over his face. I ran the length of the alley and turning the corner, spotted a male figure gliding along ever cautious and guarded in his every movement. Again, it seemed in the very dim light that the figure was either masked or had his face covered, but I was still too far away to judge for certain. Running with all my energy, I closed the gap between us and to my surprise found that it was indeed Scarf. I must have taken him by surprise because neither of us was able to speak for what seemed like an eternity. At that point, I regained my voice and demanded to know where he was keeping Toby. The only answer I received from my breathless enquiry was a cold cruel laugh from the veiled monster. His wicked laugh continued on for a long time before he stopped and regarded me in the predatory way a cat does before pouncing on a rat. He told me that I could search the remainder of my life, but would never find my brother. He said that Toby was beyond finding and that I was wasting my life in a vain search that would serve absolutely no purpose. Then he whispered the following words that made my blood run cold and my anger swell beyond the boiling point. He said, *"He got exactly what he deserved!"* These words sent me over the edge of sanity, and I attacked the fiend with the sole intent of murder. Scarf, being no fool, used a discarded barrel stave that he was carrying by his side, and delivered a series of vicious thumps to my head that knocked me unconscious…at least that was as much as I remembered of this brief scuffle.

I awoke a while later numbed by his onslaught and at a complete loss as to my whereabouts. The blood inside my head hammered at the walls of my skull. Some of the blood that I had lost ran down my face and neck and covered a good portion of my shirt. While I was thankful that I was still breathing, I could not be certain that I was actually alive given the eerie landscape that surrounded me. I was in some type of ominous cemetery, laid out on a small gravestone with absolutely nobody else nearby. It must have been one of the older cemeteries of London for it seemed filled to capacity. As I sat up, I noticed the name on the burial stone where I was sitting. The name read just Toby, but it was the crude inscription underneath that really caught my attention. It read, *"He got exactly what he deserved."* With an anguished cry I bounded off the gravestone to inspect it more carefully. There were no other clues to the identity of the interred, other than the cryptic inscription and the haunting name similarity. Was this a very twisted joke being played by my adversary, or was there a real message being conveyed?

My only choice as far as my reeling mind could conjure was to make certain that my brother was not buried directly beneath me. I did not relish the thought of digging up this gravesite, but knew deep in my heart that it was an unpleasant task that I needed to accomplish. I found a shovel on the back of a nearby manure wagon, and began the ghoulish task of unearthing the denizen of this grave from his final rest.

I was finally rewarded for my maniacal labors when my shovel struck something solid. Digging even more frantically, I unearthed a small wooden coffin. I used the shovel to pummel my way into the final resting place of Toby. What I found was the worm-ravished remains of a small child that was far too small to be my brother. Part of me was elated that my brother was not buried in this coffin, while the other part of me was nauseated by my callous attack on a stranger now known to me only as Toby. Completing the ghoulish task of restoring this stranger's gravesite to an inexact replica of the original took an hour or two more of fevered work. Eventually the deed was done, and I ran all the way back to the *Amafata*.

Handy noticed the dreadful expression on my face. I accepted his offer of ale, but declined any food since it would take a long while to forget the graveside horror I had just witnessed. I related the entire gruesome story and his advice was that I needed to locate Scarf and try yet again to reason with him for my brother's release. Should this effort prove unsuccessful in gaining my brother's release, Handy offered to have a long discussion with Scarf. He was convinced that Scarf would divulge all that he was keeping secret with a little painful attention sent his way. He simply said to me, *"Give me and my boys a chance at him and he'll be singing long before we're through with him."* Either way, I felt a flood of relief at finally having some assistance in discovering what Scarf had done with my brother. In fact, I felt so much better that I fell into a deep sleep right there in the galley, and did not awake until the first rays of the morning sun entered the ship.

The streets of London were coming fully alive by the time I reached Saint Agnes. Upon approaching the basilica, I was surprised to find the early morning parishioners crowded around the outside of the church, rather than inside attending the service. Shockingly, I was told that the old curator of the basilica, Williamson Archibald had been cruelly murdered in his own bed. He had been stabbed at least one hundred different times, so that his own bed resembled nothing more than a slaughterhouse. Further, I learned that the poor victim had been unmercifully stabbed to death by his own nephew. *"How was this determined?"* I asked an old gent who seemed to be most aware of the horrid details of the crime. The old man informed me that the victim had been found dead that very morning with the perpetrator's knife still wedged in his body. My hand involuntarily went to the pocket where I kept my knife, but felt no surprise at not finding my prized possession there. The old man also told me that the knife handle bore the killer's name and the authorities were now in search of the victim's nephew, who was believed to be the evil murderer. The name of the nephew was none other than Echo Eden.

The old man also informed me that the church had been robbed of valuable treasures, like the gold candlesticks from the altar, the donation fund for the poor of the parish and most importantly a sacred silver chalice once used by none other than Saint Peter. Deciding that it was very dangerous for me to spend anymore time asking questions, I turned and walked quickly away from the scene in mortal fear of being recognized. I wandered the London streets that entire day in a state of confusion and shock. All I could piece together was that Scarf must have taken the knife from me while I was unconscious. He then used it to murder my helpless old uncle as a means to get me into serious trouble with the authorities.

At this point, blind fury now possessed me. I was actually spotted by roving bands of vigilantes several times, but quick thinking and fast feet kept me out of their clutches. I decided to use the basement of Slugger O'Toole's to hide myself during daylight hours so I could plan my next move. As the day slowly progressed, I started to lay out a plan of action that would enable me to rid myself of my evil nemesis once and for all. By the time early evening came, I had formulated a workable plan, and was ready to put it in motion.

That evening I came out of hiding and found my way upstairs to visit my old boss. At first glance, Slugger looked like a man who had just seen a ghost. He asked me exactly what I was doing there and what I wanted. I told Slugger that I wanted revenge for the death of both my brother and uncle, but this statement seemed to confuse him all the more. It was then that I decided to tell him all that had happened to me since he had last seen me. Upon completion, I then laid out my plan of revenge to Slugger, and he listened without comment until I had finished. I told him that I suspected Scarf as the real villain, who had waylaid me and taken my pocketknife in the process. I reasoned that Scarf had used my knife to murder my uncle and lay the blame directly on me. All I wanted was a chance to even the score with the malicious little demon, and I needed Slugger's help to do so. I planned on confronting Scarf that very evening for his crimes against me and my loved ones. As such, I intended to challenge Scarf to a bare-knuckle fight from which I knew only one of us would survive. To do so, I needed Slugger's agreement to allow this fight to occur in his basement ring. Slugger hesitantly approved and gave me a tip on where to locate Scarf.

With Slugger's information, it did not take me long to track down my mortal adversary. He was hiding in a back alley very near his old place of employment torturing a slew of cats. As I came upon my adversary, I stopped my advance and found a space between the mounds of debris in order to maintain my silent vigil. As he continued with his unholy work on the innocent felines, I once again reached out to him in the voice I had used in the basilica so very long ago. I told him in that same old crone's voice that he would soon be facing the possibility of a challenge from a long time foe, and that this opportunity must not be ignored. Further, I croaked out that this was the opportunity he had been hoping for and would end his long wait at gaining the satisfaction he so desired. Well, the pump was primed, so I glided out of my hiding spot and confronted my archenemy. Having spotted me making my way toward him, he took a moment away from his devilish work to confront me face-to-face. I calmly challenged him to a bare-knuckle fight that very evening to prove once and for all who the better lad was. His eyes shone with a sort of smirking awe at my challenge, as if he had expected this new development all along. He told me that he would be honored to do battle that evening, but expressed some concern about his prior relationship with Slugger and the threats made on his life a number of times in the past. I assured him that I had Slugger's solemn vow that no harm would befall him that evening if he agreed to meet me in the basement ring to do battle. A sly smile came to his face as he told me that he yearned for this kind of opportunity for a very long time. As I turned to head back out of the alley, I heard his sinister laughter follow my every step.

Chapter 8: Fight of My Life

Upon returning to Slugger's, I filled my boss in on the agreed bout and my promise to Scarf that he would not be harmed in any way. Slugger reluctantly agreed and I retired to the lice infested, downstairs' locker room to prepare myself mentally for the fight of my life. I was fully aware that Scarf was a much stronger opponent, and that I would have to rely on many of the tricks and ploys that I had learned observing previous fights. As the evening's events began, I was aware of the crowd noise for the first time, so I knew that my long wait was nearing an end. Several of Slugger's men stopped by as the evening progressed to wish me luck. Either way I knew that the betting odds would be totally stacked against me, and that it would take nothing short of a miracle for me to walk out of the ring alive.

A little while later, Scarf made his grand appearance to a chorus of boos from the crowd, who by that time were maddened with bloodlust for our upcoming bout. My opponent was escorted to the locker room by Slugger's men so that he too could prepare for battle. Stopping near me, he made a sly comment or two about Toby's disappearance. He went further by telling me that my brother would be spending another night alone, scared and injured. He also informed me that he was sick of listening to Toby's wailing and moaning. From my sitting position, all I could see was a cloud of bright red along with a burning desire to rip this evil fiend asunder piece-by-piece. I knew that I had to remain calm and not give in to these primal desires if I hoped to survive the evening. Finally, the time had arrived, and we were both escorted to the ring so that proper introductions could be made.

Upon entering the ring, Scarf undid the filthy red rag that covered his face. His leering mutilated appearance gave me pause, but I was determined to extract my revenge at whatever the cost. The bell starting the first round was finally rung, and I attacked Scarf in a blur of motion. I kicked, punched and elbowed my opponent as if the end of the world was on hand. Scarf merely weathered all of my aggression with a calm demeanor as he continually laughed at my actions. His laughing only incensed me all the more. The first several rounds were spent in much this same manner, as I scored some direct hits on Scarf in between his taunting laughter and smart remarks. During the fourth round, I saw an opening and was able to send a short right hook directly into his throat. The blow was massive and caused Scarf to reel back in an attempt to catch his breath, which was ragged at best given the damage I had done to his throat. As he was gasping for air, I converged on him sensing the opportunity to end the battle in my favor.

Unable to breathe normally, Scarf took a very defensive position that I immediately recognized. I felt it was time to unload everything I had and did so to the delight of the crowd. Scarf actually went down to the *pines,* but I never stopped my unwavering barrage. It seemed like all was going to end well on my account, and that the match was very near its end. However, the bell signaling the end of the round was rung, and I was pulled off my opponent by the referee in charge of the match. Back in my corner I delighted in the damage I had inflicted on Scarf. He was still having difficulty catching his breath, but I could see that he would recover from my blows and would be ready to resume the fight once the bell was struck. I also noticed that the swagger was now gone from his face, replaced by the same cold hard look of hatred that I had long since come to know. With the start of the fifth round, he was ready to attack with pure bloodlust in his eyes.

I moved across the ring ready to resume the war, but Scarf was now angry beyond reason and quite prepared for this advance. He went virtually crazy and proceeded to pummel me with blow after blow, staggering me with each strike. I attempted to deliver an elbow once again to his throat, but he was more than prepared for this tactic. Shifting his weight, he slid by my flying elbow and punched me directly in the nose. I saw a whole sky full of stars, and I tumbled to the pine floor amid his continued murderous assault. As I was down, Scarf was able to land several swift kicks to my head, which by then was already spinning. Just before I was about to pass out from the tremendous blows that Scarf had landed, I heard the sweetest sound in the world…the bell ending the fifth round! Helped to my corner by several of Slugger's men, I began my slow assent into consciousness. My face was now a bloody mess with rivers of red pouring out of my broken nose. I had a serious cut above my left eye. I was also quite groggy and unprepared when the bell struck once again signaling the renewal of savagery.

At the start of the sixth round, I found the entire room spinning, and it was very difficult to keep my balance. Scarf realized my dilemma and closed in for the kill. As he advanced, he was back to his usual antics, taunting me that my brother and my uncle had put up a better fight than I was giving. For a brief moment anger replaced my pain, and I was able to land a solid kick to his right knee that gave me a brief respite from his pummeling. This rest did not last long as my opponent was back on the attack before I could get any more of my senses back in line. The crowd knew that the end was close, but continued to cheer me on in the hopes that I could somehow rally from my pain and dizziness. Finally, the bell rang ending the round, and I weaved my way unsteadily back to my corner. Slugger made his way over to my corner to check on the extent of my damage. He pleaded with me to end the fight right there. My anger and stubbornness kicked in, and I told him that I was still game to compete and did not want the fight to end this way. He cautioned me that it would be far wiser to end the fight this way than to see me killed in the ring. I promised him that I was still able to fight so he reluctantly gave the signal to the bell keeper.

As the seventh round began, I made a mental inventory of my injuries. My nose was plainly broken, which made breathing difficult. The cut over my eye continued to leak volumes of blood so that my vision was completely blurred. My legs were very wobbly and having a difficult time keeping me erect. In short, I was a mess and had very little energy left even to defend myself. I knew that if I did not do something drastic soon that I would not have a prayer of living beyond the night. As I once again weathered Scarf's savage barrage, a thought came into my woozy head. I remembered a fight almost a year ago when a contest that should have been won by the stronger opponent was lost due to an ingenious tactic on the part of the underdog. I realized that the time was now or never, so I began to maneuver myself closer to my own corner so that I might execute this one last lifesaving ploy. As I made it to the desired spot in my corner, I knew that I needed just a brief diversion so that I could affect my last stand. Summoning every last bit of energy and willpower that I had, I used my *special voice* to once again call out to Scarf. In the old crone's voice I croaked out his name and the result was a brief but welcomed interruption to the brutal beating I had been receiving. In the same haunting voice I had used successfully on this nasty villain in the past, I told Scarf that his final victory was moments away.

The crone's voice worked its wonder one last time as Scarf momentarily stopped his attack to listen attentively. This was the opportunity that I needed, and I reached my hand into my corner and grabbed the stool that I sat on between rounds pulling it into the ring. Having no time to waste, I began climbing onto the stool and in turn proceeded to frantically climb up the corner post making it look like I was trying to make my escape from the ring. In reality, I had no such plan! Scarf, now wearing a delirious smile of anticipation, closed on me to stop me from running away. I appeared totally helpless as I remained clinging to the top of the corner post with my feet firmly planted on the second row of ropes. I wore a face of abject fear and apprehension for the benefit of my adversary, while I calmly waited for his advance. As his grinning face appeared directly behind me, I unleashed my secret move. Rearing back and putting all my remaining strength into my right leg, I delivered a perfectly timed blow to his face. My right foot acted like a well-aimed lance as it parted the distance between us and landed a perfectly vicious blow to Scarf's unprotected face.

Scarf was felled like a great oak and hit the *pines* almost as hard as the kick I had just delivered. There was absolutely no movement from my opponent and someone in the crowd called out that he thought the young man was dead. I did not wait to find out. I quickly climbed back down the corner ropes and proceeded to send a series of determined kicks to the scoundrel's head as viciously as I could possibly deliver until the entire pine floor was a huge lake of blood. I continued this savagery for Toby, my uncle and myself. Curled into a fetal ball now, Scarf was subjected to my full fury. It took Slugger and three of his burly assistants to pull me off the devastated form that had once been my evil enemy. Scarf meanwhile was being examined by the attending doctor, who made it known that Scarf was still alive but just barely. His blood and teeth were scattered all around the ring, as my right arm was raised by the referee to signal me the victor. I took a moment to look down at the pitiful lump of flesh on the floor, but found no sympathy in my heart for my tormentor. Slugger entered the ring and gave me a huge hug in celebration of my victory, while whispering in my ear that this would be the very last the world would ever see of the evil Scarf Rockingham. With that he signaled to his largest three henchmen to drag the bully's beaten body out of the ring and dispose of it for good. In fact, he instructed his men to be sure to tie a very weighty anchor on to the body this time before giving the monster his final send off. This was to be Scarf's last swim in the Thames, and Slugger wanted to be certain that all was done properly.

It took me a while for the realization that I had won to sink into my addled brain. For a very brief moment I felt utter joy, but quickly came down to earth when I remembered all that Scarf had taken from me. I was now quite alone with absolutely no place to call home. I had no family remaining to turn to with the death of the *Old Ghost* and the disappearance of my brother. I realized that my desire for revenge had been driving my actions over the last few days and now that it was done, I had nothing to live for anymore. Sadness and melancholy filled me while I tried to reason what I should do next. While revenge is a great motivator, I realized an important lesson that evening: the act of revenge never satisfies completely. Too bad hard lessons like this are so soon forgotten!

As his men dragged the unconscious body of Scarf from the ring, Slugger reminded me of my current predicament. I was still a wanted man by authorities for a murder I did not commit. I was in need of immediate medical attention. Infection would probably set in if I was not medically treated, since the *pines* were far from being considered sanitary. In addition, several members of the crowd had recognized me and had made their way to the exits upstairs in order to alert the proper authorities. Slugger jumped to my assistance and quickly carried me to his own lodgings on the top floor of the establishment. He bandaged the worst of my wounds to staunch the bleeding. He then had me don a woman's outfit complete with a wide-brimmed bonnet to hide my injuries. Having prepped me for a hasty escape, he took me down a private set of stairs to the back alley. He wished me the greatest of luck, congratulated me again on my momentous victory and quickly sent me on my way.

It was none too soon, for as I weaved my way away from Slugger's, numerous loud groups of torch-wielding men stormed down the street directly to the establishment's front door. I could still hear them shouting my name as I quickly made my way toward the safety of the *Amafata*. I knew that the ship was scheduled to sail in a day or so, and that it was my only real chance to leave the troubles of London far behind. I was also aware that sailing ships were continually short of manpower so that my chances of signing on as a new crew member were very good. My biggest problem was now getting safely to the ship before my disguise was discovered by the enraged mobs in search of me.

I started toward my destination at a slow trot due to the severity of my injuries, and the fact that I was wearing a dress. My disguise worked admirably well in getting me past a number of hot-headed patrols. As I progressed, I stumbled into a trio of drunken sailors looking for female companionship. Launching into a fictitious story, I explained that I was the wife of a criminal who had been caught stealing food for our family. I told them I was on my way to visit him, and asked if the trio would serve as my escort. I promised them a reward for their services, but never went into further detail. I kept my tale simple because I knew that the more a liar embellishes his story, the easier he is discovered. My ploy worked to perfection. When we neared the docks, I announced that I was now willing to repay their kindness. However, I informed them that it was only fair to warn them that my husband had recently been diagnosed with a sinister case of the pox. I had remembered Handy's proclamation that sailors lived in abject fear of contracting this dastardly disease. My deception worked as my companions made a very hasty departure after I had delivered my frightening news!

At last, I reached the *Amafata* tired and completely worn out but elated to still be alive. I believe I gave poor Handy the shock of his life when I entered his galley in full female dress. My ruse was short lived as my friend recognized me. I filled him in on the entire story of the evening. As soon as I divulged all, he rushed off to find suitable clothes for me to wear aboard the ship. He prepared a veritable feast in honor of my ring victory over Scarf, and we ate and laughed as we wolfed down the sumptuous meal. He agreed that my best option was to vacate the city of London as fast as I could. He further agreed that a ship soon to sail like the *Amafata* was the perfect method of escape for me now. He promised that he would speak personally with the Captain of the ship the following morning to secure a place on the voyage for me. He told me that I was now his long-lost nephew, who he had reunited with while on shore leave. Further, he told me that my parents had just recently died in a tragic fire, and that I was now an orphan with nobody to care for me. In this regard, he would petition the Captain to allow me to sail with them acting as the cook's assistant and chief ratter. It all sounded very good to me, but then again what choice did I really have! If all went well, we would be sailing for our next port of call in less than a few days time, and I would be safely away from the vigilante mobs now searching the city for me.

As promised, Handy approached the Captain the very next morning and explained my presence aboard ship. The Captain was delighted at the prospect of adding an additional hand to his crew, especially one who could prove very useful at keeping the ship's rats in check. So the very next day with a new dawn breaking, the *Amafata* slipped its mooring lines and headed slowly out to sea. While a number of divergent thoughts assailed my overworked mind, the most prevalent centered on my brother. I could not mentally accept the notion that he was no longer among the living. However, after my long and exhausting searches, I had no idea as to his location or his condition if found. I also knew that his mysterious disappearance would continually haunt me until I successfully uncovered the truth. In my musings, I realized that it might be a very long time, if ever, before I would be revisiting London. However sad this notion made me, it was more than offset by the excitement building within me as we set sail on a whole new adventure and a whole new life!

Chapter 9: Life at Sea

While I have spent a fair amount of my life as a sailor, I will not bog you down with a litany of detailed sailing instructions or terminology. After all, I am not conducting a school for untested tars. Therefore, I will attempt to limit the preponderance of sailing information in favor of relating my story in the simplest terms possible. That is not to say that I will not lapse into a nautical mindset from time to time, so I ask your patient indulgence in advance. In many instances, it will be far easier to communicate my story with a sprinkling of nautical language rather than being a stickler for terminology that only a *landlubber* would understand. As I continue my recollections, I will attempt to provide a decent understanding of any nautical expressions utilized.

The best place to start describing my new life was with the *Amafata* herself. As I told you earlier, the ship was a merchantman not unlike any one of her trade-laden sisters plying the oceans of the world at the time. She was neither enormous nor small in size. She was, however, designed to hold an ample amount of cargo to successfully compete in the shipping trade. At the same time, she was outfitted with all the required masts, yards, sails and lines that would enable her to travel from one port to another very competitively. While she was not the fastest ship on the ocean, she had the ability to travel the sea lanes almost effortlessly. While the external appearance of the *Amafata* was rather ordinary in comparison to her sister transports, I soon realized that this illusion was intentional on the part of her owner. She was designed to not attract attention whether she was in port or sailing open waters. By doing so, her owner hoped to avoid making his merchant ship a target for trouble of any sort.

The *Amafata*'s internal structure was also very unremarkable both in style and design. Most of the spaces below were low, cramped and damp at all times. Internally, water continually leaked and dripped downward from the waves and weather occurring on the top deck. Given this, the lower decks were continually wet no matter the weather...basically a dripping damp and utterly cheerless prison! The other feature of this subterranean space was the total absence of light. Because our ship was fashioned out of wood, fire was a continual threat so an open flame was strictly forbidden below decks under severe penalty. Naked candles and tobacco pipes without caps were a sure way for a sailor to earn a nasty punishment regardless of the situation. The end result kept the underbelly of the ship in almost complete darkness day or night. Believe it or not, these conditions suited me perfectly. I had no trouble adapting at all. Again, my excellently developed night vision, acute hearing and fine sense of smell helped to acclimate me quickly to my new life aboard the *Amafata*.

I could handle everything onboard except the sleeping arrangements. We were forced to sleep in hammocks hung from internal beams with as little as a forearm of distance between your nearest neighbors. This tight situation proved very difficult for sleep given the constant level of noise generated by my exhausted crewmates. Snoring, talking, groaning and grumbling made up the norm, preventing me from dozing off into restful sleep. Taking into account the constant groans issued by the ship, its continually noxious atmosphere and the changing of the crew every four hours, it was a small wonder any one of us was able to achieve peaceful sleep at any time. On top of these disruptions, friendly cockroaches would boldly gnaw at our unprotected toenails if left unmolested. I found sleeping under these conditions almost impossible and labeled the time spent in my hammock as a *period of exhausting rest.* In heavy seas, these same hammocks would *dance a dead man's jig.*

The crew numbered twenty-seven in all. They were for the most part a very sorry lot, due to the persistent shortage of seasoned sailors to choose from in any port a ship might anchor. The majority of these unskilled sailors consisted of failed landlubbers, farmers and merchants, ne'er-do-wells with no other choice but the sea, prisoners and criminals, drunks and thieves and all other manner of idlers gravitating around the shipping docks. They were a grumbling and complaining lot of social incompetents, whose previous failures left them malcontented, bitter and conniving in nature. For the most part, the ship served as a sort of *floating prison* for these rough and tough characters. The food was decidedly poor and the work was both exhausting and harsh. Punishment was brutal and swift with the pay relatively insignificant. In all, life at sea was extremely austere, disagreeable and overly nasty in nature, but since I had been dealing with almost identical conditions on shore, I felt very much at home among this seagoing rabble.

The crew was divided into three basic categories, officers, crew and idlers. Officers numbered six including the Captain, First Mate, Sailing Master, and other assistants. The crew was made up of sixteen men divided into two watches. Each watch served four hours at a time followed by four hours of rest. The final group was the idlers, a misnomer at best for we were far from idle anytime onboard. This group included Handy as Chief Cook, me as Cook's Assistant, Sailmaker, Carpenter and Doctor. The important point was that I, as the Cook's Assistant, was very low in the crew's ranking, to say the least!

The standard clothes, called *slops* consisted of loose-fitting, wide-bottomed breeches that enabled us to quickly roll them up to avoid getting them wet. Also mandatory was a loose-fitted shirt, a short coat for heavy weather and a neckerchief that served as both a sweat rag and a head covering to keep the raging sun from frying our brains. The more seasoned men brought all manner of hats aboard to also serve as a protection from the sun's penetrating rays. We were barefoot since no shoes were issued. The seasoned sailors, called *salty tars*, wore their hair in pigtails greased with tar. This fashion statement served to keep their hair out of their eyes while aloft in wind and weather. Additionally, these individuals also coated their breeches, shirts and coats in tar to keep them as waterproof as possible. In all, we were a very pale bunch having spent the majority of our lives out of the sun. Handy told me that as the voyage ensued I would develop *sea color,* a rich mahogany shade resulting from a combination of suntan, salt spray and filth!

As the voyage began, I happened to mention to Handy that I could swim, but with so much water surrounding me I was concerned about drowning should something go terribly wrong. Handy halted my admission and lectured me that the word drown was not to be used again at any time during our voyage. He explained that most sailors did not actually know how to swim, and lived in mortal fear of actually drowning. Handy said, *"Sailors live on the sea, but also die in it!"* Now do not take me wrong when I claimed to be able to swim. You see, my past experience at this art was conducting a *Thames Treasure Hunt,* which consisted of swimming out to floating corpses traveling down the river to search of any valuables remaining on these bloated cadavers. To participate in this gruesome hunt an individual was required to brave the swirling river currents as each body was thoroughly searched for treasure. If one was not a proficient swimmer, he would soon join the caravan of floating corpses!

Handy was the king of the galley. Like the rest of the ship's lower decks, our galley was cramped, dark and damp. The main feature of this space was the wood-burning stove that was used to cook all meals. The tables were actually a pair of doors hinged on one end to the hull of the ship about waist high and kept in place on the other end by cables suspended from ceiling beams. This allowed the tables to be raised out of the way once any meal was over. Benches and barrels served as seating for the diners, who ate in two shifts during the dogwatch…a period from four in the afternoon to eight at night. Mealtime for each shift lasted about an hour and a half, leaving enough time in between to clean up the prior shift's mess and prepare food for the next shift's meal. All the food had to be consumed in a stinking, hell-like atmosphere. The first source of the stench came from the unwashed, sweat-soaked, vermin- and filth-infested bodies present at the tables. This was coupled with the *perfumed bilge water aroma* wafting up from the hold. Needless to say, the cramped, crowded and smelly conditions of the galley led to many nasty skirmishes from hungry, weary crewmembers, but for the most part evening mealtime was the happiest time on the ship. The crowded and miserable conditions of the galley would have gladly been ignored by the ravenous crew had the food been delicious and satisfying. As my crewmates were prone to say, *"God made the vittles but the Devil made the cook!"*

While my title was officially Cook's Assistant, a better descriptor might have been *galley slave.* First and foremost, I was responsible for the general upkeep of the entire galley, which included galley cleaning, serving food, after-dinner clean up, dish washing, garbage removal and the retrieval of food stored in the hold for use at mealtimes. Additionally, I was responsible for starting, maintaining and extinguishing the fire in the galley stove. This also meant that I was responsible for ensuring that there was a constant wood supply for the stove from the inventory stacked down in the hold. In all, I had the pleasure of furious exertion and toil for four full hours during meal serving time! At the end of this period, I was usually dead on my feet and retired to my hammock for a few hours *exhausting rest* prior to tackling any other chore.

My time spent as *galley slave* did have a positive side to it. As I traversed the scullery fulfilling my duties, I had the opportunity to listen in on all that was said during both dinner periods. It was a splendid way to stay abreast of all shipboard news or *scuttlebutt* as the crew referred to it!

For one thing, the crew was incredibly superstitious. From Handy's previous stories, I was aware that black cats were particularly feared. Because of the raw power that this superstition seemed to inspire, I decided to create my very own demonic black cat aboard the *Amafata* as a method of inventing a useful future diversion should the need arise. I delighted in the haunted faces of my fellow superstitiously frightened crewmen when I issued my first rendition of this demon cat howl, and then continued to utilize it every so often at my whim. I was also amazed to discover that several of the crew also reported sighting the elusive curse-laden creature as they went about their normal duties aboard the ship. My ruse worked perfectly and would prove very useful indeed as our voyage continued.

The food brought aboard prior to sailing tasted and smelled good only in the very early stages of the voyage. As time passed, the beef, pork and fish salted and packed in barrels began to spoil leaving the meat and fish shiny in appearance, smelly, rotting and blue with mold. Sailors called this fare *salted junk* for obvious reasons. The biscuits were notorious for the large black weevils they contained. The experienced tars taught the less experienced seamen to rap the biscuits against anything hard in order to knock out the worst of the weevil offenders. The hens brought on board for meat and eggs did not last long in the hold. They were constantly attacked by the hordes of voracious rats looking for anything to satisfy their ever present hunger. Therefore, a good cook used these precious resources early after sailing.

Water was stored in barrels in the hold. Not long after sailing, it began to stagnate turning brackish and green with the distinctive taste we called *marsh water*. The beer brought on board was also in barrels. It was preferred over the water, and rationed to the crew at no more than a quart per man per day. Eventually it too became spoiled tasting very sour and acidic, forcing us back to consuming the *marsh water*. Cheese brought on board also became hard and green with mold over time. The only foodstuffs not really affected by time were the dried goods like peas, rice and beans used for soups and stews. Handy made a batch of hardtack every morning. This staple was basically a large hard cracker without salt. As time went by and other stored foods soured, staled or rotted, hardtack became the food of choice for all of us. Given any of the odious alternatives, only an utter fool or a *salt-crazed gob* would chose otherwise. In addition to the beer ration, we were also allowed a small ration of rum each day. Each of us was allotted a tankard of rum daily, which most mixed with water to make a drink called *grog*. *"Splice the main brace"* was Handy's call to announce that the daily rum ration was about to be served. While I never really developed a taste for hot spirits, the same could not be said of my crewmates. They would eagerly push and shove their way to the front of the rum line to get their fair share.

In addition to assisting Handy in his galley duties, I was once again thrown into an old familiar role of *ratter*. But this was no real hardship. Water collected in pools in the hold's lowest levels as a result of the continual drip from above. This water became a perfect breeding ground for rats, lice, cockroaches and other assorted nasty vermin. In all, it was a dark, damp and dreary place not unlike the basement of Saint Agnes that had been my home for the past several years. The terrible smell that emanated from the sloshing, filthy, pest-ridden bilge water was also very much like the noxious odors found on any of London's streets during the height of summer. I was very much at home in this dark, loathsome place and quite content to spend many an evening there. The nastiness of the lowest deck also guaranteed that very few of my crewmates would venture this far down in the bowels of the ship. Hell for most others, heaven for me!

As for my ratting duties, I simply relied on my special rat screech to entice my adversaries into an empty bag for later burial at sea. Since there were a limited number of rodents populating the hold, it was only necessary to utilize my abilities once a month or so. I carefully guarded this secret. I utilized the spare time that I had to sleep and rest in the tomb-like solace that the hold provided. In addition, the hold was a great place to hide from troubles and tormentors whenever I required the need to disappear.

Handy was called a *soft toad* by the crew because of the compassion he demonstrated. Handy acted as father confessor for most of the crew because of his approachable demeanor. He was without a doubt the informal leader among the crew. But his role as trusted advisor did not end solely with the crew. It seemed that the Captain also utilized Handy as a chief confidant. I would eventually work out the reasons behind this extraordinary trust on the part of the Captain, but for now I was amazed and awed by the sight of the Captain and Handy in deep, serious conversations meant for their ears only.

Handy was not loved by all. In fact, he was at odds from the very start of the voyage with the First Mate, Mr. Bass. I am sure the rationale behind this unfriendly attitude on the part of Mr. Bass was a jealous reaction to the special relationship Handy shared with the Captain. Added to my rationale was the fact that the entire crew, save Mr. Bass, paid honor and utmost respect to Handy, which is far more than they showed the jealous First Mate. Known as a bully of the worst sort, Mr. Bass would go out of his way to discover or invent rule infractions made by Handy, so that he could reward the likable tar with swift and harsh punishments. Because Handy was my friend and confidant, I was an instant enemy in the eyes of Mr. Bass. I had to be on constant guard whenever Mr. Bass was present for fear of making any kind of mistake that I would surely pay for in terms of a harsh punishment. The questions I had to ask myself were, *"Why was I continually plagued by bullies?"* and *"What did I do to deserve the company of such evil, odious individuals?"*

Chapter 10: The Captain and First Mate

The Captain, Samuel Conway, was an aloof, well-educated and introspective individual. He spent the majority of his time sequestered in his own quarters away from any real contact with his crew. From afar, the Captain seemed very much alone and saddened. The Captain was also a navigator of renown and fulfilled this vital duty with both vigor and pleasure. His cabin, albeit small in size, housed a substantial seagoing library that was his other major passion. Holding the title of Captain made his word law while at sea. He had absolute and complete authority over the ship and all of us serving as crew. Being a solitary soul by design, he opted to delegate this all important authority to his First Mate, Mr. Bass.

My diligent pestering finally provided the reason for the strong bond between Handy and the Captain.A fellow crewmate named Creeping Jeremy confided in me that the Captain was the First Mate on the *Achilles* and was the individual who saved Handy's life when their ship floundered and sank on the hidden African reef. It was the Captain who used his own belt to staunch Handy's shark amputation before he had the chance to bleed to death. From the moment I learned about this prior association, I began to truly understand the strong bond shared by these two men.

Mr. Bass was a polar opposite to the Captain. As the old tars said, Mr. Bass was a *hard man to shave*, which meant he was a very rough and tough sort of individual. He was arrogant and extremely strict in both his manner and actions. Since the Captain abdicated absolute authority directly over to him, Mr. Bass' word was the law to us while we were at sea. He had a fiery temper and was forever in a perpetual foul mood. For the most part, his continence was evil, dark and brooding. Tall and athletic in frame and stance, Mr. Bass was prone to quietly stalking the ship environs to ensure the ship's operation met his more than high standards at all times. It appeared to me that this activity enabled him to easily identify unfortunate sailors who required punishment. His favorite pastime was *walking the cat*, which was a nickname he used for lashing a guilty party with his favorite toy, the *cat-o-nine-tails* whip. This vicious device was a whip with nine knotted and braided leather strips that attached to an intricately carved ivory handle that when wielded properly would produce massive amounts of damage.

Rather than describing this weapon, I believe it would serve better to provide an example of the cruel and painful results of *walking the cat*. The victim in this tale was named Matt Pyewicket, but known to all as Stuttering Matt due to an unfortunate speech impediment. For the most part, Stuttering Matt was a likable rogue but a known thief. There was no reason for the crew to dislike Stuttering Matt; we just had to keep a close watch when he was around. Upon sailing, Stuttering Matt took it upon himself to toast the onset of the voyage with a bottle of rum he had wrongfully liberated from the locked liquor cabinet in the galley. Stuttering Matt easily consumed the entire bottle while Handy and I dozed. Wandering the ship in a drunken haze, he was so inebriated that when he accidentally stumbled into Mr. Bass, he offered him a drink from his private but then empty stash. Needless to say, the drunken tar was in serious trouble and Mr. Bass was quick to judge him guilty of theft and drunkenness, sentencing him to *twelve lashes and a bath*. Normally the *cat-o-nine-tails* whip was more than enough punishment but the addition of a bath of salty seawater after each lash made the punishment inhuman. Because of Mr. Bass' sadistic nature, the bully utilized filthy, slime-infected bilge water in place of fresh seawater in the hope that a serious infection would result from the whipping.

The brutal punishment was carried out to the First Mate's delight and the unconscious thief was carted to the doctor's surgery once the cat's job was done. Witnessing the torture, mandatory for all hands, made the majority of us physically ill and disgusted. Delirious and suffering extreme torment, the poor, pain-crazed creature spent the entire night in unholy moaning and wailing agony.

It did not take long for Stuttering Matt's brutalized back to turn gangrenous…the gory mess of savaged flesh turned a green-grey hue and stank of rot. The doctor, who was equipped with few medical supplies, was forced to administer meager portions of laudanum to ease the lad's suffering and torment. The massive infection caused Stuttering Matt to lapse into a delirious fever state hovering between life and death.

Until his final demise, the poor thief issued stuttering moans, howls and screams to unseen gods for his deliverance from the mortal suffering he was enduring. These pain-induced stuttering wails proved to unnerve most of the crew, who would make the sign-of-the-cross on their chests upon their issuance. Since these dreadful wails were too awful to ignore, I decided to listen to them closely and add them to my arsenal for future use. While I was no ghoul at heart, I was an opportunist who recognized them as a potential weapon!

Mr. Bass had a young lad assisting him by the name of Jemme Buttons. This lad was a friendly red-haired child probably four or five years my junior. Because all novice assistants were labeled with the moniker of grommet, it was not long after setting sail that Jemme Buttons became simply Grommet Jemme. To say that the lad was stupid to the extreme would have been a fair compliment in his favor. He was extraordinarily dull, as if he had been beaten senseless too many times in his childhood and the condition took hold permanently. For the most part, Grommet Jemme was a shy and retiring child with an ever-present sad smile adding to his overall unremarkable demeanor. The one defining attribute of this wee tot was his almost comic crossed-eyed appearance!

Well, it didn't take Mr. Bass long to begin his rule of terror and torment on this helpless lad. Grommet Jemme was punished repeatedly for all manner of minor infractions, be they real or imagined. His first round of punishment came as a result of his oversleeping on his scheduled watch period by just a short time. His cruel punishment for this minor infraction was to digest ten live cockroaches without the luxury of disgorging them at any point in the process.

Yet another time, Grommet Jemme's two front teeth were knocked from his head as a punishment for not performing his listed chores to the total satisfaction of Mr. Bass. Added to this list of punishments were a variety of minor but painful and frightening tortures like broken fingers and toes, black eyes, a bloodied nose and a whole lot more. It seemed a day did not pass without Grommet Jemme being punished for some insignificant transgression. The entire crew felt sorrow and pity for Grommet Jemme, but we were all very powerless to stop the torment at the hands of the master and ruler of the vessel. Secretly, I believe we were all very grateful that we were not the unlucky punishee like Grommet

Jemme…an emotion that sickened me to my very core!

To add to his misery, many of the crew began to whisper that Grommet Jemme was nothing more than a *jonah*…a name given to an unfortunate individual capable of bringing bad luck to a ship. The crew did so for a number of reasons, none of which made any kind of rational sense! He had red hair and several sailors were quick to point out that this was a sign of a *jonah*. He was cross-eyed, which also meant that his dealings aboard the ship would lead to ill luck. Additionally, he seemed to be the constant source of problems and issues aboard no matter how he behaved.

Finally, a very innocent act took away any doubt in the crew's minds that he was indeed a *jonah*. One day at sea, Grommet Jemme hooked onto a sizable fish and fought the creature for hours before finally landing the monster. It was not long before the entire ship was alerted to this exploit and the fact that he had mistakenly landed a porpoise. As fate would decree, it was yet another nautical superstition that this type of fish was considered good luck and that they should never be killed for any reason. To prove the point, that very night an unexpected tempest erupted right after dinner. The wind howled like a maddened banshee and the ship rocked like a well-paid trollop preventing all from any sort of rest.

Just an unlucky event you might say, but the crew did not agree! Rather they blamed Grommet Jemme for the weather because of his slaying of the porpoise. He was instantly deemed a *jonah* by all. Mr. Bass thought long and hard about a fitting punishment for the lad's actions. In the end, he devised a particularly nasty chastisement. He decreed that since the *jonah*'s fishing exploits were responsible for the storm, his castigation would be related. He ordered two large fish hooks inserted at right angles in the lad's cheek, which would remain in place for an entire month. He named this particular form of punishment *face jewelry*, and snickered whenever Grommet Jemme crossed his wake. The cursed urchin with his mouthful of metal was certainly very difficult to understand given his continual mumbling. In addition, he found it impossible to eat normal meals due to the *face jewelry*, and reverted to eating mushy foods that could pass beyond the metal encumbrances without too much pain or difficulty.

In any event, I had a soft spot in my heart for this tortured adolescent because he reminded me of my lost brother. While he bore no physical resemblance to Toby, he was the mistreated victim of a nasty bully. After his unfortunate fishing exploit, I became the only person onboard willing to come to his aid, as I diced and mashed his food into palatable portions so the miserable waif did not starve to death. As bad luck would prevail, it did not take the lad long to land in even deeper trouble with his overseer. As he was conducting his daily deck swabbing duties, he managed to lose his bucket overboard. This simple mistake provided the crew with yet another example of his cursed bad luck. Yes, there is a sea superstition that the loss of a bucket overboard is a sign of impending bad luck. Approaching me in a state of near hysteria, he related his latest misfortune and expressed the abject fear of the punishment that would result. Sensing his extreme terror, I told him that I would take the blame for the loss of the bucket. Further, I told him that the punishment would probably not be as severe as those that he had experienced in the past, but that I would take his place as a matter of friendship. His relief was overwhelming as he folded down on the deck in front of me in real tears of joy.

When I reported the missing bucket to Mr. Bass, he gave me a very odd look as if he really did not believe me. Regardless, he was quick to dole out a harsh punishment of a full night in the hold. For anyone else, this punishment would have seemed terrifying and extremely severe. Since the hold was my second home, I had a very hard time not smiling at my good fortune. For fear that Mr. Bass would change his mind in favor of a much harsher punishment, I was sure to play the role of a frightened and totally panic-stricken offender. Privately, I vowed to get even with the autocratic despot for all of his vicious bullying of the entire crew... especially Grommet Jemme.

I was led personally to the hold by Mr. Bass, who was all smiles and giggles at my upcoming confinement. For my part, I continued the ruse of playing the frightened little waif. As soon as Mr. Bass had seen to my incarceration in the hold, he quickly departed with a parting warning to be wary of the evil spirits that dwelled in my new hellish domicile. Sitting down on an empty water barrel, I began to plot my revenge. Remembering the success that I had with Scarf utilizing my *special voice*,

I decided that the same course of action would serve me well with my newfound enemy. My challenge was to identify the best way to attract Mr. Bass' attention without directly involving myself in the process. I settled on the haunting, stuttering moans and wails of Poor Stuttering Matt. I rationalized that the awful and grisly wails and moans of a dying sailor would surely frighten my tormentor to his very roots, while serving to remind the rest of the crew of the unusually harsh and unfair treatment Poor Stuttering Matt experienced at the hands of a sadistic bully. With a plan in place, I intoned the same eerie, mournful stuttering wails and moans that I remembered all so well.

So as to not overdo it, I issued these dreadful sounds for a short while, but was sure that they were loud enough in volume for the entire ship to hear. Having set my plan in motion, I settled down to get some rest and relaxation. The next morning, the first question that was asked of me was whether or not I had heard Poor Stuttering Matt's ghostly caterwauling during the night. In a feigned frightened voice, I was quick to respond yes to this question. I also pressed the seasoned sailors, who were questioning me about the ghostly racket, as to whether or not the ship was haunted. White-faced and bug-eyed, the crew felt the ship was indeed haunted by Poor Stuttering Matt's spirit. Further, they felt that Mr. Bass had issued a truly unfair punishment to the unfortunate sea dog, resulting in the terrible haunting we now all faced. Mumbling and cursing by a terrified crew followed Mr. Bass that entire day as he went about his normal shipboard duties. Again I kept my smile hidden well as I realized that my new scheme was working even better than I had hoped. Only time would now tell whether or not I would succeed in my plot to gain the revenge that I truly craved!

Chapter 11: Ajax Rowe, Navigation Assistant

Aboard ship we also had another junior assistant by the name of Ajax Rowe. He was a nasty mean sort of youngster, who excelled at backbiting and snitching on his fellow crewmembers for all manner of infractions he observed. He was definitely a *cuddle up* to anyone representing authority over him. This odious talent of snitching was soon discovered and put immediately to use by Mr. Bass. Ajax's first responsibility aboard the ship was to assist the Captain with navigational duties. However, being totally pathetic at mathematical calculations and having absolutely no knowledge whatsoever of map reading, he was quickly dismissed in this role by the Captain. Rather than go through the lengthy education process necessary to make the lad marginally effective, the Captain decided that Ajax would serve far greater value reporting to Mr. Bass in a general assistant's role. This new role really suited the mean-spirited dullard. He ached with anticipation for every punishment session conducted by Mr. Bass. Additionally, Ajax was allowed to actually carry out some of the lighter punishments doled out by his newly appointed master. Several crew members noted that Ajax seemed to take extraordinary delight in the torment and pain suffered by any transgressor. Given these detestable actions, this sniveling squeaking puppy was hated and despised by the entire crew! Because Ajax was a tattler supreme, we coined a new name for the sneaky brat…Bigmouth Ajax.

During one particular meal, Handy had made several disparaging comments about our mean-spirited First Mate and his delight in inflicting serious punishments for the most trivial of misdeeds. Handy was unaware of the presence of Bigmouth Ajax, who was feigning sleep in his hammock, but in reality listening intently for any interesting news to convey to his superior. Well, it sure did not take long for our shipboard tattler to report these comments to Mr. Bass. Handy was called out by the First Mate for the minor transgression of smoking his pipe without a cap below deck. In reality, Handy was simply in the process of lighting his pipe tobacco prior to applying the regulatory cap once the pipe was well lit. Well, Mr. Bass would not hear any excuse for the action, and sentenced Handy to receive five lashes from his trusty *cat-o-nine-tails* whip. Handy, incensed over this unfair treatment, appealed to the Captain, who commuted the sentence to a less serious punishment of not being allowed to smoke his pipe for a full week. Mr. Bass was enraged with the Captain's decision, but was forced to abide by the ruling causing yet further hard feeling between him and Handy. Plotting his method of revenge, Handy asked me for my thoughts on how he might teach this sneaky little busybody a real lesson. Thinking the situation over, I came up with an insidious method of getting even without having the blame revert back to us.

The plan I devised involved the *seat of easement* as a way to instill a stern warning to Bigmouth Ajax that his eavesdropping habit was detrimental to his health aboard the ship. You see, the *seat of easement* was the device the crew employed to conduct their biological needs while at sea. The *seat of easement* was located at the bow of the ship and consisted of a pine plank that was anchored to the ship by way of two strong ropes securely threaded through each end of the plank. A sailor needed to sit bare-bottomed on the plank and then swing the device over the ship's side to conduct any natural defecation. My plan was to prepare a special greeting for Bigmouth Ajax while he was in the process of utilizing this very necessary device. As it turned out, the weather cooperated with my plan by becoming very windy and rough the night of my choosing. Waves and wind lashed the upper deck that night so that any chore performed on the main deck became extremely hazardous to complete. As Handy and I had observed, Bigmouth Ajax habitually utilized the *seat of easement* each evening as soon as our supper was completed regardless of weather conditions. Aware of his routine, I slipped out of the galley prior to the end of supper to prepare a real surprise. Toting a bucket of lard from the ship's store, I very carefully made my way to the ship's bow and proceeded to lather the *seat of easement* with the slippery substance. Once I was done with my preparations, I found a nearby place of concealment to await the unsuspecting victim.

As predicted, Bigmouth Ajax appeared on deck to attend to his nightly ritual not much after I had made my concealment. He moved very cautiously toward my hiding place and dropped his breeches to his ankles. Being a dark, nasty night, he did not take any time at all to inspect the device and proceeded to hop aboard and swing the seat over the side. Well it didn't take very long for my ministrations to come into play, as the lad began to slip and slide furiously on the seat as the wind and waves caused the ship to lurch almost uncontrollably. Hanging on to the cables anchoring the seat, Ajax slipped and slid from side to side while all the while screaming for someone to come to his immediate assistance.

Observing his extreme terror and weak calls for help was so deliciously humorous that I broke into a hysterical fit of laughter that would have given away my hiding location had it not been for the sound of the raging storm that tormented us. To complete my revengeful act, I utilized Poor Stuttering Matt's suffering voice to call out loudly to Bigmouth Ajax that the damned spirit had observed the *cuddle up*'s sinful spying on his own crewmembers. Further, I informed Bigmouth Ajax in Matt's familiar stutter that hell would surely send its worst denizens in pursuit of the lad's own soul if he ever tattled on any of his fellow crewmates again. Shrieking now in absolute terror, Bigmouth Ajax screamed for assistance again and again. Eventually, the delirious lad was rescued from his precarious perch by one of the watch crew, but not before he experienced the ride of his life! The unpopular waif was escorted below deck to regain some of his sanity. In the meantime, I came out of hiding and proceeded to carefully clean all of the offending lard off of the *seat of easement* so that the entire episode would be blamed on the stormy conditions and not a calculated act of sabotage. Then I made my way back to the galley to report the hilarious details to my co-conspirator, Handy. Relating the full story of Bigmouth Ajax's adventure brought tears of hilarity from Handy for the next hour or so. The results of our venture were mildly successful. While the entire episode was deemed a natural occurrence and no blame was ever leveled at any crewmember, the episode slowed our adversary down from his habitual eavesdropping but really did not cure him of this nasty habit. However, the experience did scare the senses out of the unpopular rascal and his nocturnal visits to the *seat of easement* were curtailed leaving the little villain in an obvious uncomfortable state for the next month or so. It was decidedly difficult for either Handy or I to not break up in uncontrollable mirth every time we noticed the extreme discomfort displayed on the face of our mutual adversary!

Chapter 12: The Azores' Our First Stop

We had been at sea for an eternity in my estimation when we made our first stop...the Azores. A Portuguese-controlled group of islands out in the middle of the Atlantic Ocean, the Azores were a traditional stopping place for sailing ships on their way to many Caribbean ports of call. For our sakes, this tiny group of islands provided a much needed opportunity to freshen our food stores and water supply. The fresh food that we procured included salted beef and fish, fresh sea turtles, vegetables and fruits of all types. We planned on storing the live turtles in the hold where they would exist quite contentedly in their new surroundings. I was told by Handy these creatures would be slaughtered sometime later and used as fresh meat for stews and soups when the vast bulk of our beef and fish either ran out or went completely rancid.

To my dismay, no crew member was allowed off the ship during this stop. Handy explained that these islands had an evil history of sickness and disease that the Captain wanted to avoid at all costs. Whether or not these superstitions were based on fact or just old sailing tales made no real difference to the Captain, who could not afford further crew loss on our voyage. Made to wait on the ship while the procurement process was conducted by the Captain and Mr. Bass, we became very restless and needed a source of diversion. Handy decided the matter for all by proposing an impromptu concert on deck. The enthusiastic response by the entire crew was astounding. A makeshift band gathered on the top deck led by Handy whose instrument was the triangles. Other members of our shipboard ensemble included Nasty Cornelius Marr on the squeezebox, Fighting John English on the fiddle, Muttering Moses Hart on the fife and Grommet Jemme on the spoons. In just a short while, we were being serenaded by the finest musicians our ship could offer. And you know what...they actually sounded very good!

Since I had a gift with my voice, I volunteered to sing along with our newly constructed band. Using a deep tenor voice copied from a stage performer that I had once witnessed at Slugger's, I joined the ragtag ensemble that had been gathered on deck. Singing several particularly sad and well-known English ballads, I was an instant success with the entire audience. Upon completing one particularly touching song about lost love, I happened to notice that my voice had a very pronounced effect on all gathered. In fact, the vast majority of these hardened men of the sea actually had tears in their eyes upon listening to my rendition. I was both gratified and shocked at the results that I could achieve utilizing my *special voice* in public. I found that I enjoyed entertaining my fellow mates, and marveled at the stunning effect it had on them.

After the concert reached its conclusion, there was a call from the crew to participate in a very popular gambling contest called *Rats-o'-flame*. This gruesome pastime involved catching ten fresh rats from the hold to be used as very unwilling participants for our idle time diversion. Since I was the ship's *ratter*, it became my immediate duty to scuttle down into the hold and capture the required rats for the afternoon's festivities. This proved to be of no real difficulty for me and in no time at all I was back on deck with a sack containing ten squealing, squirming vermin. Each of the rats I captured was taken by a different crew member and held firmly while identification marks were painted directly onto their backs. Once done, the entire lot was doused in whale oil and they were now ready to be set aflame. Prior to their release, bets were made by each crew member on which rat would last the longest in the hellish inferno that was about to engulf them. Handy and I made our rounds of the deck noting each individual and the rat they chose to be the winner. In many ways, I was reminded of my bet taking duties in Slugger's basement prior to any fight!

Having completed our task of accounting for each and every bet, the rats were ignited and the real fun began. I was shocked at the unearthly squealing and screeching that my prisoners made as they scampered round and round the deck in utter agony and pain searching for an avenue to escape their hellish condition. Beyond observing this bizarre spectacle, our jobs were to ensure that the flaming rodents did not sneak their way down into the ship's lower levels where they could easily spark blazes and end our fun. Ultimately, it was Grommet Jemme who had chosen the lone scraggly competitor who outlasted its unlucky brethren. Grommet Jeeme's victory claim was challenged by none other than Bigmouth Ajax, who supported his own rat as the certain winner of the contest.

About the same time, Mr. Bass returned to the ship to secure money to pay for the fresh supplies. Stopping momentarily to enjoy the cruel sport, he immediately sided with his underling, declaring Bigmouth Ajax's rat to be the winner. Although the entire crew knew the truth of the matter, they remained very still for fear of incurring the ill will of the ship's vicious bully. Grommet Jemme, in a moment of foolish rashness, decided to contest the decision of Mr. Bass, and could not be dissuaded from altering his take on exactly who was the actual winner. He was warned sternly by Mr. Bass of the ugly consequences of following this unwise course of action. Nevertheless, Grommet Jemme did not back down from his feared nemesis, even after being threatened several times by both Bigmouth Ajax and Mr. Bass. It was as if Grommet Jemme couldn't bring himself to stop challenging the decision. The matter was finally decided by Mr. Bass who promised Grommet Jemme that the child's lips would be sewn together for a week as punishment for his insubordination if his confrontation continued.

I knew immediately that something needed to be done to save my friend. I needed a significant diversion to occur to take the heat out of the escalating disaster that was occurring right before all of our eyes. Stepping to the side away from the eyes of my fellow crewmembers, I began issuing the low stuttering wail that I had used the night of my imprisonment in the hold. With the issuance of Poor Stuttering Matt's agonizing moans seemingly arising from somewhere in the bowels of the ship, the entire proceeding halted at once.

Having captured the attention of everyone onboard, I decided that I would go one step further in my efforts. After a ghostly burst of muted stuttering wails and moans, I announced that Grommet Jemme was indeed the winner of the contest. While the crew was totally frozen in supernatural awe, they immediately focused on Grommet Jemme and nodded their own agreement. Bigmouth Ajax and Mr. Bass were absolutely powerless to counter the decision handed down by the ship's newly acquired ghost. Instead Mr. Bass ordered an immediate search of the lower decks by all those present in order to discover the source of the ghostly utterances. With the troubled situation totally diffused, I joined my fellow sailors in what I knew would be a fruitless endeavor.

It was not too long after that the Captain returned to our ship. He commanded Mr. Bass to oversee the loading and storage of the fresh stores garnered on the island. Once done, we weighed anchor and unfurled all sails to hasten to our next port of call. In a state of jubilation over my treatment of Mr. Bass, I failed to notice that a passing gull had unceremoniously dropped a present on me. Some present indeed for the bird had just defecated on my head. This event brought me back to reality as I returned to the galley. I told Handy of my unfortunate bath from the dirty seabird and was quite surprised by his reaction. He immediately brightened and clasped my shoulder with his remaining arm, informing me that the bird incident was a wondrous omen. This revelation stunned me for it was hard to believe that anyone could judge the episode as fortuitous. Nevertheless, that was the exact reaction I received from all upon my admission to the filthy shower. The entire crew took heart at the fact that signs now pointed in a positive direction for the continuation of our voyage. All I could do was wonder what sailing lunatic had devised painting such a disgusting act as a sign of good luck!

Chapter 13: In the Name of Italian Medicine

The doctor aboard the *Amafata* was named Geovanni Perilli. Italian by decent, Doc Perilli was a very accomplished drunk. Small, dark and intense by nature, Doc was for the most part a very easygoing individual whether drunk or sober. Doc spoke in his native language and had a very marginal understanding of English. When excited, Doc would become quite animated spouting foreign words that he believed everyone understood. This sadly was not the case at all. I easily understood these manic rants because of my early language lessons taught by my deceased Uncle Arch. The remainder of the crew, however, could not understand a single thing this manic little sot was yelling. All this accomplished was to infuriate Doc all the more when he was in one of his moods.

When it came time to remove the *face jewelry* from Jemme's mouth, Doc was called to handle the operation. Seated in front of the lad, Doc kept demanding that he turn starboard or larboard so that the removal of the hooks could be accomplished with a minimal amount of damage. Jemme, having no understanding of Italian, had no idea what was being asked of him. All the lad could fathom was that the Doc required further tools to assist in the exercise. Because of this, the lad kept attempting to stand so that he could fetch whatever Doc required. His constant attempts at flight only frustrated Doc all the more. Losing his patience, Doc began to jump up and down swearing furiously in his native tongue. Convinced that something dreadful had gone amiss, Jemme began to sob uncontrollably, convinced that the hooks had caused mortal damage. This farce continued for a while longer before Doc finally abandoned the removal attempt due to his patient's disruptive actions. In the wake of the Doc's exodus, Grommet Jemme remained rooted in a confused and sorrowful state convinced that his end was very near. He lamented loudly that he was far too young to die. Finding the entire farce hilarious, I had a very hard time stifling my mirth at the poor lad's expense. In the end, Handy performed the necessary actions to free the boy from the wickedly sharp hooks.

The shipboard rumors on the Doc were certainly mixed and confusing.

What remained consistent was that the Doc was running from something that occurred in his past life. The most consistent story that I heard was that he was responsible for the care of a very important individual in the Italian city of Rome. This individual was the first and only son of a very prominent city leader, who had entrusted the Doc with the responsibility of healing his beloved child. It also was rumored that the family was one of the wealthiest and most powerful in all of Italy. In the process of caring for the boy something went terribly amiss, and the son died. The boy's father, as well as the entire family, blamed the Doc solely for the boy's death. Intent on getting revenge for the Doc's incompetence, the family hired a group of assassins to eliminate him. The Doc was made aware of this dilemma and fled both the city and the country in an effort to elude his murderous pursuers. The Doc absconded across several different countries seemingly one step ahead of the hired assassins. However, the paid killers were very intent on their mission due to the promised reward. Realizing the utter futility of making a successful escape, the Doc decided that a long sea voyage might actually rid him of his tireless hunters. So he signed on for our voyage, never accounting that his language deficiency would prove to be a problem. But it certainly became a huge issue when he eventually discovered that no one aboard could actually understand his strange mutterings.

One fateful day, the Doc was preparing a mug of tea in the galley when the ship lurched to starboard causing him to spill his newly made beverage all over himself. Jumping up and issuing a long string of Italian curses, the Doc called out for a galley rag to clean up the mess he had made. I responded immediately, providing the necessary implement and the Doc thanked me profusely. Without thinking I answered him back in his native tongue, which shocked both the Doc and those present in the galley into total silence. The Doc was the first to regain his senses and questioned me on the language ability that I had just displayed. I answered that indeed I did speak Italian having been taught the language as a young boy. The Doc was extremely gratified that someone on the ship actually could communicate with him. He then launched into a hurried conversation as to his background and his rationale for making this voyage. We continued our talk for a few minutes more before Handy interrupted us…sending me on an errand to fetch more firewood for the stove. Promising the Doc that I would visit his humble surgery to continue our conversation, I made my hasty retreat into the bowels of the ship to execute the order given by Handy. From that day forward, I became a regular visitor to the Doc's surgery. We spent many an afternoon deep in serious conversation on various subjects concentrating especially on medicine. During the time spent with my newfound friend, I was instructed on a variety of medical knowledge and information so as to serve as an assistant should a complicated medical problem arise. Now do not get me wrong about the extent of knowledge imparted to me. I was in no way qualified to practice medicine in any meaningful way, but did have a strong understanding of basic medical procedures that would one day become very opportune. My extended visits to the Doc's surgery also kept me out of the way of Mr. Bass' temper and punishments. All in all, it was a very beneficial arrangement that I had made for myself!

The Captain was informed about my ability to communicate with the foreign doctor and asked that I come to his quarters to explain. Awed by the prospect of being summoned by the Captain, I made my way nervously to his chamber unsure of exactly what the outcome of this visit might spawn. The Captain greeted me in a very friendly manner and immediately launched into a series of questions concerning my language abilities. The Captain was very much intrigued by my educational background and pressed me with further questions on what other knowledge I had been taught. I told him that in addition to being fluent in a variety of foreign languages that I had also been taught mathematics, science and map reading. Upon hearing this, the Captain became very excited. He quizzed me on the extent of my knowledge in several of these disciplines especially mathematics and map reading. Listening closely to the answers that I provided to his many complicated question, I could see that he was highly impressed. Like Doc, the Captain made me promise to visit him on a daily basis in order to assist in the navigational duties of the voyage. Since this was an entirely new area of knowledge for me, I gladly agreed to his request and promised to visit him regularly. I also knew that having the Captain as a confidant could prove totally worthwhile in aiding my determined efforts to avoid Mr. Bass' *cat-o-nine-tails* whip. In just a short period, I had made friendly acquaintances with two of the most important members of our ship's company, and I intended to utilize both of these to gain further education and instruction. I quickly made my way back to the galley to inform Handy of the latest developments. As I suspected, Handy was overjoyed with my news, and promised to make sure that my galley duties would not interfere with the time I would need to spend with both the Captain and Doc. All seemed to be going my way, but I was soon to learn that things have a habit of changing at a moment's notice!

Chapter 14: Moses "Chips" Hayes' Plight

Another key member of our crew was the ship's carpenter, Moses Hayes. Nicknamed Chips by the crew, he was in charge of everything made out of wood on the ship…which just about included everything. He was an absolute wonder when it came to all things wooden and could fix, maintain or create damned near anything. Chips was a friendly and amicable sort who always seemed to have a smile on his face and went out of his way to keep everyone on the ship smiling with him. Now, our ship was large, which meant that Chips needed to take extraordinary measures to keep the rest of the crew smiling with him. He seemed slightly daft to me but was *merry as a cricket*. The crew also believed him to be crazy and in all likelihood fodder for the many London asylums for the insane. Like my crewmates, I tended to totally enjoy his presence and found that I could not stop myself from laughing at his inane jokes even though they made very little sense to me. Drooling and slobbering while spinning his nonsensical tales, he was a very hard man to ignore. Chips sported a wicked looking scar that started at his wrist and ran all the way up his arm. The scar bore the strange resemblance of a large snake or sea serpent depending on the angle you viewed it.

Being naturally inquisitive, I approached Handy and questioned him on the strange behavior on the part of our happy but delirious carpenter. As I suspected, Handy did have the answers to the questions about Chips that had been plaguing me for some time. It seemed that Chips once held the exalted position of Chief Gallowman for the Crown. This important position required him to oversee the construction and operation of any gallows serving as the last port of call for the Crown's prisoners. Because our King was very aggressive in his pursuit of political and treasonous adversaries, Chips' services were constantly in very high demand. Chips led a life of leisure and ease since he received a significant second source of income from the condemned relatives and close friends paying to ensure a swift and humane execution of their loved ones. All was good in his life until the day the Crown sought to execute the notorious traitor, Baron George Wren. The Baron had been convicted of conspiring with foreign nationals to overthrow the King. This heinous crime earned Baron Wren a swift and early retirement from all things political.

On the day he was to be executed, Chips was suffering mightily from an overdose of medicinal gin and was in no means capable of ensuring that the gallows erected for the Baron's pleasure was in top working order. As it turned out, the gallows construction was indeed faulty and during the execution collapsed, failing miserably in its efforts to end the Baron's life. Now it also just so happened that the King was in attendance for the execution along with a majority of the London populace gathered to enjoy the spectacle. All were disappointed with the disastrous outcome of the proceeding, laughing and scorning the King for the failed execution. Our proud and haughty ruler was totally embarrassed by the botched execution, blaming Chips for the entire travesty. Immediately stripped of his title and position, Chips was relegated to enduring the continual scorn and harassment from the London populace for the key role he played in this comedy of errors. To escape this unceasing torment and persecution, Chips had long ago enlisted to serve on various sailing ships as their much needed carpenter and repairman.

What seemed very strange to me was that Handy and Chips were very close friends. In fact, Handy was forever laughing hysterically at the strange mumbled jokes of this bizarre creature. Further, it appeared to me that Handy could actually understand all that Chips was saying in his mumbling and drooling conversations. One night, after the two of them had shared an extra ration of rum, Chips launched into one of his strange soliloquies that Handy translated for those in attendance. The tale concerned a former shipmate of Chips, who, like Grommet Jemme, was judged to be a *jonah*.

The story took place several years prior on a ship christened the *Flying Dutchman*. While the vessel was in the port of Havana on the Spanish isle of Cuba, a fellow shipmate brought a new recruit onboard for their return voyage to England. This individual's name was Pablo Cruces and he claimed to be a deserter who hungered to flee Cuba to escape the cruel and rough treatment he had received from the locals. While his story seemed rather strange, he was graciously hired on due to a temporary manpower shortage. Totally unaware of the problems that their new recruit represented, the Captain ordered the anchor weighed and sails set. From the start of the voyage, the ship experienced a series of unfortunate disasters. The first was the unexplained disappearance of a seasoned crewman presumed lost in a violent storm that arose without warning. The ship itself had also been significantly damaged as a result of this *dirty weather.*

With the vessel in immediate need of repair, the Captain was forced to anchor off of an uncharted and seemingly uninhabited isle. The truth of the matter was that the island was indeed inhabited by a very unfriendly tribe of natives, who remained hidden while the work crews were sent ashore in search of materials to affect the necessary repairs. Once ashore, these unwary unfortunates were attacked and slaughtered, ending all repair thoughts as the ship headed back to open water. Beginning to suspect foul play, the crew pointed out to each other that their string of bad luck seemed to initiate as soon as the new sailor came aboard. Anxious and frightened, they blamed Pablo for their misfortunes and dubbed him a *jonah.*

Still in need of repairs, the Captain plotted a course for the island of Bermuda. As they approached their destination, the *Flying Duchess* ran aground on a hidden reef and began to take on seawater. Able to extract itself from the reef, the ship limped into the Bermudian port. While repairs were being completed, an unknown epidemic swept through the vessel claiming even more lives. At this point, everyone was convinced that Pablo was a *jonah* and begged the Captain to offload the Spaniard before any more calamities could occur. The Captain dismissed this plea as sheer folly and continued the voyage as soon as the ship was repaired. In a matter of days, the vessel was attacked and taken by a band of savage pirates, who in their lust for booty slaughtered the Captain and most of his brave officers. Pillaging and ravaging continued until the ship was stripped clean. The survivors were transferred to the pirate ship and their beloved transport was fired and destroyed before their eyes.

These survivors were then marooned on an uncharted spit of land. As luck would have it, these same pirates returned shortly to the isle with the vital intention of finding a replacement carpenter for one who had had been lost in a freak onboard accident. It was now the marooned crew's chance to extract some revenge. En masse, they conspired and convinced the pirates that Pablo was indeed an experienced and exceptional carpenter. The pirates, totally taken by the ruse, hauled a hysterical and sobbing Pablo back to their ship.

With their *jonah* gone, the survivors prayed for a stroke of good fortune to come their way. Their prayers were answered when a Dutch merchantman rescued them and brought them to the English island of Barbados. Once arrived and having related their sad luck story, they were informed by the island authorities that word had reach the isle of a similar sounding band of rogues who had experienced some very bad luck of their own. They were told that these pirates had blundered into a Spanish *Man-o-War*, which promptly attacked and destroyed the villains save one. The lone survivor was said to be of Spanish decent by the name of Pablo Cruces! Amused by this strange turn of events, the survivors of the *Flying Duchess* had to laugh at the fate of their persecutors once their unlucky *jonah* had been forced upon them!

As the story concluded, the moral to the tale was quite obvious to us all. Certain star-crossed and unlucky individuals could bring unfavorable fortune down on those around them. They were indeed *jonahs* and could surely spell disaster for any unsuspecting ship that they signed on to serve. At this point in the narrative, all eyes seemed to turn and focus on Grommet Jemme. Sensing sudden ugliness in the mood of his fellow crewmembers, Grommet Jemme abruptly jumped up to flee the angry and accusing stares that were now leveled in his direction. Hastily making his was out of the galley, he accidentally bumped into Chips, who had inadvertently blocked the poor lad's escape route. Chips, unprepared for the jostling, was thrown into the galley stove which held a very large boiling cauldron of Handy's latest culinary creation...*Brisket of Blue Shiny Beef*...a crew's distinct appetite nemesis! The cauldron was knocked from the stove, severely scalding a number of sailors in close proximity to the stove. Being the closest, Chips received the very worst of the damage! In fact, his hands were singed by the fiery concoction to such a degree that we all knew that he would be unable to hold any of his woodworking tools for a very long time!

Needless to say, the rest of the gathered crew fresh with the memory of Chips' *jonah* tale, decided unanimously that something had to be done immediately to rid the ship of this potentially lethal influence. Grommet Jemme was roughly grabbed by the closest conspirators and hauled toward the maindeck, where they planned to dump the poor lad overboard, thus ridding the ship of the cursed bad luck he brought down on us all. In my vain attempt to stop this mob from ending the life of my friend, I was rewarded by my enemy, Bigmouth Ajax, with a savage blow to the head from a pistol he had been cleaning while listening to Chips' saga. In my groggy and stunned state, I could offer little help to my hapless mate, who was now on his way to an early death! Screaming and wailing in protest, Grommet Jemme was hauled hurriedly to meet his grisly end. As the procession reached the maindeck, they were met by a curious and questioning Mr. Bass. Taking full measure of the situation, Mr. Bass made the decision to not interfere in the vengeful proceedings. With a whoop of joy, the murderous mob prepared to launch Grommet Jemme into the dark and angry sea. All at once, the entire ship was filled by the mournful and ghastly wails of Poor Stuttering Matt, which put an immediate halt to the proceeding. Stunned into silence and inactivity, the guilty crewmembers realized the folly of their actions. To a man, it seemed like the ghost of Poor Stuttering Matt was very unhappy indeed with the prospect of the innocent lad's murder. Each of the offending crewmembers further realized that they risked terrible consequences if they proceeded in their heinous act.

With the ghostly racket as a constant deadly reminder, the mob diffused and Grommet Jemme was placed gently on the deck. Having forgotten their original murderous intent, the crew was immediately organized by Mr. Bass into three separate search parties intent on discovering the source of the ghostly clamor. However, as with previous searches, no evidence was ever found that would identify the source of the unearthly racket. I, on the other hand, was quite taken aback by the whole incident. I was totally shocked and disgusted in my fellow crewmembers' actions regarding Grommet Jemme. At the same time, I was quite disturbed and totally frightened by the ghostly clamor since for the very first time I was in no way responsible for their issuance! In fact, the small hairs on the back of my neck seemed to stand on end as I realized for the first time that our ship was indeed haunted!

Chapter 15: Man Overboard

The very next day, two of our top men, responsible for sail management and lookout duty, developed a very strange fever. These men awoke to find that they were sweating profusely and running a very high temperature which meant an immediate visit to the Doc's sickbay to affect a cure and to keep them away from the other sailors. The Doc was very perplexed by the symptoms. We all felt that it was probably something that they ate since the shipboard stores were once again running low and what was left in stock was moldy to the extreme. In any case, the absence of these two crewmembers left a serious shortage of hands to carry on the required work. Mr. Bass made a quick decision that Grommet Jemme and I would fill in for the sickly tars since in his opinion neither one of us would be missed in our daily duties.

I can tell you honestly that both of us were deeply frightened thinking about the dangerous task that awaited us. We knew how easy it would be to slip while aloft and hurtle down to either a serious injury or a painful death. Realizing we were totally terrorized, Handy stepped in to give us some much needed advice and encouragement. Handy told us both that we needed to *know our ropes* whenever we went aloft. This knowledge was both simple and easily understandable, and if followed religiously could prove to keep us out of harm's way. The first rule of working aloft was that we should always use the windward side of the ship to climb the riggings but never the leeward side. When we had reached the desired height in any climb, then and only then should we ever attempt to crossover to the leeward side given that was our destination. The reason for this rule was pretty obvious. Climbing the ratlines on the windward side of the ship would keep Jemme and me out of the direct forces of nature like wind, rain, sleet, hail or other nasty and dangerous conditions. The second rule also seemed pretty elementary but wise in practice. As we made our way up the ratlines, we needed to be in the constant habit of always giving a firm tug on the next handhold to ensure it would support our weight. Weather and rot were a constant plague to the rigging and taking this small precaution would ensure that we could locate any of these spots before they posed a danger. The third rule of thumb in climbing was to never relinquish a handhold until you had a very secure grip established with your other hand. To any sailor this rule was simply stated as, *"one for the ship and the other for yourself."* The last and final rule issued by Handy was, *"for God's sake be very careful!"*

Mr. Bass took Grommet Jemme and me aside in order to fully explain what he expected of us. He told us that we were to climb to the top of the mainmast during the first watch following our supper. While aloft, we were responsible for keeping a sharp lookout for any type of danger that might be headed our way, including, but not limited to, floating debris, another ship, hidden shoals or reefs or even sea monsters. Upon hearing the last few words, both Grommet Jemme and I gave each other a nervous glance. At the same time, I happened to notice Bigmouth Ajax, who had been conspicuously absent at suppertime, make a sudden appearance and he seemed to be wearing a very sneaky smirk. I never gave Bigmouth Ajax's absence any thought other than musing that maybe he had finally worked up the courage necessary to resume his use of the villainous *seat of easement.* I was about to find out just how wrong I was in this presumption!

Since I had never really been aloft on this or any ship, I decided it prudent to follow Grommet Jemme who had limited experience in making his way aloft. Terrified and shaking, we prepared to begin our arduous climb upward to the utter delight of Mr. Bass and Bigmouth Ajax. As we were about to begin, I noticed that a curious crowd of fellow crewmembers had gathered on deck to monitor our progress. With the signal given by Mr. Bass to go aloft, Grommet Jemme grabbed the nearest ratline and began his assent. With my friend in the lead, I followed closely behind matching each and every one of his movements in very careful and deliberate manner. Behind me was Phillip Watson, who had been assigned *crow's nest* duty, while Grommet Jemme and I were supposed to closely inspect all the upper sails for rips, tears or weather damage. Phillip, an old hand of climbing, seemed frustrated at the slow progress being made by Grommet Jemme and me. Anxious to reach his assigned position as lookout, Phillip passed both Grommet Jemme and me on his hell-bent climb to the top, making use of the less secure and sturdy ratlines that Grommet Jemme had avoided so far in our climb.

About three-quarters of the way to his position, Phillip seemed to encounter some type of problem, calling down to his gawking crewmates that the main ratlines seemed unusually slippery for whatever reason. In just a few moments, both Grommet Jemme and I heard Phillip call out in a panic stricken voice for assistance. The next moment, Phillip seemed to lose his precious handhold and was twisting and turning in a frantic manner above us attempting to regain contact with the lines. All at once, he let out a hysterical wail and plummeted directly down into the churning sea alongside our ship. Watching in absolute horror, Grommet Jemme and I kept a steady eye on the sea's surface waiting to announce the exact location of our fallen comrade to those standing below us. As we stared transfixed into the darkening water, we were not rewarded with the sight of Phillip's head bobbing to the surface. He just never surfaced!

Meanwhile the panic-stricken crew ondeck went into emergency mode. Someone was immediately dispatched to inform the Captain of the situation. In virtually no time at all, the Captain arrived on deck and surveyed the scene with no sighting yet of Phillip. As I continued my vigil looking down in hopes of sighting the lost tar, I happened to notice that both of my hands kept slipping off the ratlines I was using to support myself. The source of the slipperiness seemed to be the actual ratlines themselves.

Upon more careful examination of neighboring ratlines, I discovered that there appeared to be a foreign slippery substance on the lines at varying intervals. Taking the time to further scrutinize the actual substance, I discovered to my absolute shock that the substance resembled and tasted exactly like the cooking lard Handy employed in the galley. In making this discovery, I could not for the very life of me figure out how this substance could have found its way onto these upper ratlines. Then a very frightening thought occurred to me. Remembering Bigmouth Ajax's unexplained absence at dinner along with the conspiratorial smiles and manner displayed by both Ajax and Mr. Bass prior to our ascent, I questioned whether these sworn enemies would actually resort to such a dastardly act in order to cause serious harm to Grommet Jemme and me. The answer I quickly reached was an obvious yes.

At that moment, the Captain issued orders to launch our small dingy to search for Phillip, while Grommet Jemme and I were told to descend to the maindeck. I realized that given the slippery conditions of the ratlines, I had to be doubly cautious in executing my climb back down the ropes. As I began my return to the deck, I warned Grommet Jemme as well. I made the arduous trek back to the safety of the maindeck totally frightened and shaken to my core! Upon the warm greetings I received from my fellow crewmen, I could not help but notice the visage of total disappointment on the faces of Bigmouth Ajax and Mr. Bass! A few moments later, Grommet Jemme also reached the safety of the maindeck to stand beside me. He immediately began questioning me as to the source of the danger we both encountered on our fateful climb. I told him to remain quiet about the cooking lard we had discovered, so as to not alert our enemies. Understanding my message, Grommet Jemme lapsed into silence and joined the rest of the crew making preparations to launch our rescue dinghy in search of Phillip.

The dinghy was finally launched and an exhaustive search was made for our lost crewmember. It almost seemed like the sea had swallowed him up following his disastrous plummet. After a more than two-hour search, the Captain realized the utter futility of continuing this useless endeavor and ordered the dinghy back to the ship. The Captain took a few minutes to say a few prayers for the deliverance of Poor Phillip's soul into eternal peace and ordered us to make ready to resume our voyage.

The first step in my plot for revenge was to ensure that I had the right culprits. I sought out Bigmouth Ajax's location and proceeded to shadow him as he made his way around the ship. I was looking for the perfect opportunity that would enable me to get this sneaky little monster alone and isolated.

My efforts finally paid off when Bigmouth Ajax was ordered by Mr. Bass to take an inventory of the fresh water supply barrels in the hold. As Bigmouth Ajax went about his inventory duty, I made my way to the darkest recess of the hold so that my presence would not be detected. Utilizing the now familiar voice of Poor Stuttering Matt, I called out to Bigmouth Ajax in a tortured voice that I knew exactly what he had done to cause the death of a fellow crewman. I further told Bigmouth Ajax in my finest ghostly rendition of our dead stuttering mate that Phillip's recent death was now a black mark on his soul and that the death would surely be avenged. Bigmouth Ajax, caught completely by surprise, whirled around in circles in search of Poor Matt's ghost. When he finally resigned himself that finding the source of the ghost was impossible, he broke down completely into a sobbing, wailing state claiming the whole act was simply a harmless prank. He further blubbered that he intended no harm to come to anyone by the actions he had taken. Lastly, he beseeched his haunting specter to forgive him of this crime, since it was really Mr. Bass who had forced his actions in the first place. It seemed that Mr. Bass planned the entire episode in order to scare the hell out of the arrogant galleymate, Echo! I reiterated in Poor Stuttering Matt's voice that regardless of who had put him up to this evil deed he was certainly guilty of murder. I further voiced that Bigmouth Ajax had better keep sharp eyes out for retribution from the revenge-minded spirit. With my threat voiced, I launched into a loud issuance of Poor Stuttering Matt's last mournful wails and moans that literally drove Bigmouth Ajax scrambling out of this dark, solitary hell into the safer environs of the upperdecks. Completing a last series of the frightful caterwauling, I made my own way up to the maindeck to view the results of my plan.

I discovered Bigmouth Ajax, who was terrified and groveling, on the maindeck in deep, heated conversation with Mr. Bass. It appeared to me that Mr. Bass was doing his very best to calm his co-conspirator down. My rat-like hearing proved more than enough to catch the majority of the conversation passing between them. Finally, frustrated by his use of soft encouraging words, I was able to hear Mr. Bass threaten his partner-in-crime with a taste of the *cat* should he not begin to shape up and resume normalcy. I also heard Mr. Bass use my name in a very unkindly manner. Mr. Bass reminded Bigmouth Ajax in no uncertain terms that I was the person responsible for all of his problems. Mr. Bass went on to tell Bigmouth Ajax that he needed to figure out a way to *"take care of Echo"* in order to set all things right! Listening closely to these words and with the threat of the *cat* hanging over his head, Bigmouth Ajax began to calm down and begged his mentor to provide a solution to ridding him of his tormentor…me! Risking imminent discovery, I turned my back on the evil pair and began to make my way back to the galley so I could inform Handy of these latest developments. As I started to drift away, I distinctly heard Mr. Bass tell his now cowed and fearful assistant to be on a constant watch of each and every one of my movements. Bigmouth Ajax was further instructed to keep this vigil up until such a time when opportunity would present itself to allow him to achieve complete and utter vindication over me!

Handy was not the least bit surprised at the details of the plot to kill me and Grommet Jemme. As he suspected from the start, his hated rival along with his tattling minion were both guilty of murder and deserved to be hung as a result. However, he was also quick to realize that little proof existed in order to formally charge these two criminals with murder. Handy instructed me to simply stay calm and wait for the right time to seek the justice we both desired. In the meantime, he was extremely worried about me. He knew these two murderers were also biding their time, watching for an opportunity to cause me more harm. Sensing his concern, I promised him that I could certainly take care of myself. I further pledged that I would keep a sharp lookout for any potential danger. At the same time, I vowed to myself to watch for my opportunity to take the initiative on this matter and not simply wait for my own doom to occur.

I spent the remainder of the night and the following day making preparations for my next move. I had already had a rough plan, but needed a little help from the weather to see it through to completion. With the scheme in mind, I began my detailed preparations. Borrowing a much needed item from the galley, I found a perfect hiding place for it on the maindeck, and stowed it until such a time as it was needed. All I had to do in the meantime was relax and wait for some nasty weather!

Three days passed without any new developments. At last, the weather took a decided turn for the worse. We had sailed directly into the path of a storm that brought high-rolling waves, gale force winds and plenty of sleet and rain. As part of the plan, I feigned a sudden sickness at the first supper hour. Looking dreadful and pretending disorienting shivers and shakes, I pleaded with Handy in a very loud voice for leave to go up on the maindeck to get some fresh air. I also told Handy that I was going to be sick to my stomach, and would require the ability to use the ship's side to heave my unwanted stomach contents into the sea. Avoiding the watch crew, I began making all my final preparations. Once ondeck, I stripped down to my breeches and retrieved the special item I had hidden just a few days prior. Almost ready, I made my way to an isolated section of the deck to make one last preparation. Once this step was accomplished, I leaned precariously over the ship's rail pretending to vomit again and again from the illness that had suddenly overtaken me. For the benefit of my enemies, I appeared to be a helpless target with too much on my mind to pay attention to anything else going on around me. Retching and hanging on weakly to the rail, I calmly awaited the arrival of my assassin. I made sure that it would appear to Bigmouth Ajax or Mr. Bass that I was now in a very precarious position, and could easily be heaved over the deckrail. However, the first of my preparations was a block of wood that I had nailed to the outer hull to provide a strong and anchored handhold. The second involved using the special galley item I had borrowed. This item was a tub of cooking lard that I utilized to cover my entire upper torso. Now with everything ready, I waited for my opportunity with darkness continuing to descend around me.

It was not very long before I heard the faint, stealthy footsteps of someone directly behind me. With this warning, I tightened my grip on the wood handhold in anticipation of an imminent attack. Ajax launched himself at me just a moment after I had detected his presence. His hands reached out for my back in order to push me over the side of the boat. What he found as he tried to gain purchase on my back was nothing but a slippery surface…a veritable *human eel.* As he struggled to complete his murderous task, I utilized my secret handhold as an anchor. I then pivoted my entire body in a lightning-fast move to put me sideways to my attacker. This quickly executed action left Bigmouth Ajax clutching at air as his forward momentum went totally unchecked, carrying him completely over the ship's rail in a blink of an eye. I heard him make a small muted exclamation of total surprise just prior to the sound of the splash announcing his taste of seawater. Knowing he could not swim by his own admission, I knew that my job was finished. I disposed of both the newly constructed handhold and the remainder of the cooking lard in just a few minutes' time. Using an old rag that I had stowed in my secret cache, I wiped the lard off of my upper body so that nobody would notice anything at all unusual. This rag joined both the excess lard and the wooden handhold in the black and nasty sea so that no evidence remained. Locating and putting on my shirt took another few precious moments so that all was back in order in less than a five-minute span of time. Feeling pretty good about the flawless execution of my plan, I made my way back to the galley to resume my chores, bringing little attention to myself.

Bigmouth Ajax was not even missed until the next morning when Mr. Bass started asking about his whereabouts. When Mr. Bass approached me to ask about Ajax, I answered in a clear and calm voice that I had absolutely no idea where Ajax had gone or where he was hiding. This same answer was also voiced by everyone else on the ship. A full search of the ship was conducted without finding a trace of the missing lad. The majority of the crew was convinced that the ghostly spirit of Poor Stuttering Matt had a hand in this mystery. While Mr. Bass suspected my involvement in Bigmouth Ajax's disappearance, there was absolutely no evidence of any kind to support his theory. In the minds of my fellow crewmates, the disappearance of Bigmouth Ajax became just another intriguing puzzle which in all likelihood would never be solved.

Imagine my delight at utilizing my *special voice* to imitate our lost crewman, Ajax, crying for help in every section of the vessel. I led Mr. Bass and his volunteers on a merry but fruitless chase in the vain search for his wretched assistant. At the end of a week, Mr. Bass, appearing totally haggard and spent, announced that all searching would cease since Bigmouth Ajax must have somehow fallen overboard. Since we all knew that the lad could not swim, we were silently convinced that he had suffered the sad state of drowning…although this word was never mentioned!

Once again we need to visit the subject of choices. In the case of Bigmouth Ajax, I did have a distinct choice in dealing with this tattling scum. I could have ignored his attempt to murder both Grommet Jemme and myself. The choice I made in this matter was merely one of survival. While I was not fond of killing, I was totally prepared to take the actions necessary to protect my life. If faced with this type of situation again, I know with certainty that I would once again opt for the same solution! But my fight was not over. I had merely dispatched a pawn.

Chapter 16: Jonah Jemme

Well, not much more time passed before Grommet Jemme got in deeper trouble with Mr. Bass, and for that matter the entire crew! While he was below deck on a meaningless errand for Mr. Bass, he accidentally toppled a lantern he had brought along for light.

The dropped lantern burst in a hundred pieces drenching the surrounding cargo with flaming whale oil, which proceeded to hungrily devour any stowed cargo in its path.

Grommet Jemme made a very hasty retreat from the hellish inferno he had created looking to find assistance to put out the blaze. As soon as he found help, he made his immediate return to the scene of the crime to find that the flames had spread even further. Slowly the blaze was brought under control and extinguished with help from just about all of us aboard. However, as much as a quarter of the goods stowed in the hold for trading were now destroyed by this accidental fire. Grommet Jemme was in serious trouble and he terrifyingly well knew that the punishment for such a crime would be severe indeed.

Mr. Bass needed no encouragement to levy a harsh sentence on his poor assistant. Rather than face the deadly strands of the *cat*, Mr. Bass decided on a much harsher form of castigation. Grommet Jemme, now christened Jonah Jemme, was sentenced to be keelhauled the very next morning. Keelhauling was an age-old nautical discipline used sparingly because most victims never survived its scathing brutality. The condemned sailor was tied by a stout rope around his middle. Another rope was used to tie his ankles together to strip the victim of any navigational abilities. He was then to be flung over the side of the ship's bow and dragged the entire length of the ship to the stern where he would be hauled from his watery surroundings. Along the way, the punished tar would be subjected to a slow terrifying drowning. But there is more to this chastisement than a simple act of drowning. Tiny stowaways called barnacles invariably clung to any ship's bottom slowing the progress of that ship if left untouched. These freeloaders served as tiny razors when they encountered the frailties of human skin. As the victim was dragged on his torturous path, barnacles ripped and sliced skin as the victim was towed across them. A keelhauled sacrificial offering was usually hauled on board sliced and bleeding with his lungs filled completely with salt water. The majority died right on the spot from both the extensive loss of blood and the copious amount of seawater ingested. This was the cruel fate that awaited my friend, Jonah Jemme!

Early the next morning, all hands assembled on the main deck to witness Jonah Jemme's punishment. Crying and weeping, the poor lad was bound tightly around his middle by Mr. Bass with a stout length of rope. While the majority of onlookers shivered at the pain and suffering Jonah Jemme was about to receive, I alone held my fears in check so as to not incite my friend into total panic. At a signal from Mr. Bass, Jonah Jemme was launched screaming into the sea from a position at the bow and the punishment began in earnest. Dragging the poor unfortunate toward the stern of the ship, Mr. Bass seemed almost ecstatic in anticipation of the death his sentence was sure to cause. Because Jonah Jemme weighed very little, he was dragged quite quickly and , as such, was spared slightly from the unseen barnacles waiting below to rip him apart. However, as the rope was dragged toward the stern, it made contact with these insidious freeloaders and was literally torn apart. The result of this was totally unexpected as Jonah Jemme was cast adrift no longer secured by his rope lifeline! Racing to the stern, the entire crew now spied Jonah Jemme surface screaming and wailing for assistance. The Captain immediately ordered a dinghy to be lowered in order to pick up this wayward flotsam. I knew by his terrific struggles that Jonah Jemme would not last until his rescuers arrived to pluck him from his watery death.

From the stern, I executed a flawless dive into the sea in order to save my friend. Totally shocked by my dire actions, the remaining onlookers called encouragement to me as I made my way toward my now drowning friend. In just a few short minutes, I had reached my objective and wrapped my arms around Jonah Jemme to keep him from swallowing any more seawater. Managing to keep his head above water, I clung on with dear life while I awaited the arrival of the rescue dinghy. As I suspected, the arrival of my fellow crewmembers took what I believed to be a lifetime to reach us. We were hauled aboard the rescue boat, sputtering and choking on the water that had entered our lungs. As we made our way back to the ship, I could hear the boisterous cheers from the remaining sailors for the selfless act that I had attempted.

Once aboard, Jonah Jemme was rushed off to the Doc's surgery for resuscitation and first aid while I was congratulated heartily by everyone onboard, with the distinct exception of a brooding Mr. Bass. Both the Captain and Handy were quick to come to my side and whisked me away to the Doc's office to ensure that I would survive the ordeal unscathed. Handy kept slapping me on my back telling me that he had never before witnessed such a brave and heroic deed. I accepted his compliments humbly as I sputtered and spat out unwanted seawater. This small act of kindness brought me huge rewards with the rest of my crewmates. The only member of the crew who was not elated by my rash action was Mr. Bass. Having failed once more to rid the ship of either Jonah Jemme or myself left our vicious First Mate in a very foul mood indeed!

Chapter 17: Pirates... Mad Sea Mongrels

Just when I believed that things could not get worse, fate intervened and things took a decidedly bad turn. You see, it is a very bad habit to believe that your present situation cannot get any worse…because it always does! We were now short three crewmembers so the extra workload was shouldered by the rest of us. It kept us constantly busy and many times, because we were all overworked, at each other's throats. I continued my daily visits to both the Doc and the Captain, but had to shorten the length of stay due to the work that was always awaiting my return. While the Doc was providing a valuable education in medicine, the Captain was in the process of making me into a navigator. As I experienced in my earlier studies, I had no trouble at all absorbing a vast amount of knowledge in a very short time. I could easily calculate the ship's position and course with all their intricate calculations almost as quickly as the experienced navigator, who acted as my tutor. Should I have any questions or further need of knowledge on any nuance, I could rely on my friend and ex-navigator, Handy. It seemed to me and my tutor that it would not be very much longer before I could actually fill the role of ship's navigator.

Due to my proficiency of study, the Captain began to rely on my opinion as to the best course to ply. He learned quickly to both trust and value my thoughts and opinions on all navigational matters. Having picked up this knowledge so quickly allowed us a little spare time each day in which the Captain began to instruct me in a whole new game…chess! When our navigational instructions were concluded each day, he would pull out his well-used chessboard and a bunch of strange looking playing pieces. Providing detailed instructions on each of these pieces and their movement along with a variety of tactics and ploys, we would sit each day and play a game or two before I was called away from his quarters to attend to my regular duties in the galley. At the start, I lost every game we played but patience, strategy and clear thinking made each contest closer and closer. I felt that it was only a matter of time before I would eventually prevail. For now, I was content in the new knowledge and the strategic thinking that this game instilled in me. I was truly a thinking man and chess was quickly becoming my game!

During this time, I had very little contact at all with the jealous First Mate. I was now operating as the unofficial Assistant Navigator. Every order issued by the First Mate aimed at curtailing my time spent with the Captain was immediately countermanded, leaving my sworn enemy all the more frustrated and angry. One day during an exceptionally close chess match, we were interrupted by a call from the lookout posted above that a ship had been spotted in the far distance. With absolutely no reason to panic, word was sent up to the lookouts to keep a close watch on this vessel. The Captain utilized his telescope to attempt to discover the trailing ship's nationality, but was indeed surprised to find that this strange ship flew no flag whatsoever. This situation of not flying a national flag was certainly not unheard of given the number of armed conflicts happening all across Europe. France, Spain, Germany, Italy and England were at war with each other one minute, while the next they were allied with each other to oppose the other contending nations. The practice at sea, therefore, was to possess a variety of different national flags onboard so as to be able to display the proper nation's colors depending on each situation's need. Additionally, it was wise to sometimes post no colors until an exact determination was made for any particular situation.

Now there was also another possible reason for a ship not to flying a national flag. During this time, pirates also roamed the sea in search of easy targets to plunder and rob. Many horror stories abounded of all the evils and atrocities that these savage, voracious scoundrels could inflict in their unending quest for booty, especially gold, silver and precious gems. Since we had no idea at all who was crewing this mysterious ship nor did we have any clue as to their intentions, we played the watch and wait game as we continued along our charted course. Being an important part of the navigational duties, I knew that we were at least a few weeks or more away from our next intended stop. I was also aware, from listening closely to the Captain's conversations, that he had several friends on this island that would surely allow us to replenish our food, water and medicine supplies while in port. Additionally, we now had room in the storage hold for replenishing all the trade merchandise lost to Jonah Jemme's carelessness.

For the rest of that day and night, we kept a sharp eye on the mysterious ship we had spied. During this time, we were not able to learn very much. The quirky ship seemed to be staying at the same distance away from us during the days we spent monitoring its progress. In fact, our mysterious neighbor stayed in the same relative position for the next several days without any change at all. This situation brought nervousness and anxiety to all onboard. Many of the crew were absolutely convinced that this ship was indeed pirate. They reasoned that like a shark, which swims behind a ship for days on end waiting for a chance to fill its belly from refuse thrown overboard, the pirates who crewed this tailing ship were doing the very same thing.

Mr. Bass and the Captain debated for several hours on how best to handle this strange predator that seemed to be stalking our every move. Mr. Bass argued for more speed to flee our pesky shadow. The Captain retorted that the *Amafata* was a trading not a racing vessel and making a run for it would surely signal weakness. The Captain was absolutely sure that our trailing friend had enough speed to overtake us at any time they chose regardless of whether we opted to run or not. His thought was to continue our charade of normalcy until a clear avenue of escape presented itself.

While the Captain and Mr. Bass argued the merits of each of their strategies over the next several days, I had the opportunity to ponder a solution to our predicament with Handy. Actually it was Handy's own unique idea that won the day. Handy was certain that the ship following us was up to no good. He believed that this mysterious ship was just biding its time waiting for the perfect opportunity to attack. Handy was also aware of the *Amafata*'s capabilities, and the one thing he was sure of was that we could not outrun our new sea neighbor no matter the situation. Handy argued that we should drag a heavy door directly behind us that would be dropped strictly under the cover of darkness. Dragging this heavy object behind us would slow our speed down considerably. We would be sending the impression that we were a prodigiously slow trading vessel that could certainly be easily overtaken at any time by our adversaries. We needed to keep this ruse up for a few days…if we had that much time…while we set the second part of the plan in motion.

The second part of his plan was even more devious. As we proceeded on a very slow pace, Handy suggested we continue until we met with *dirty weather*, a fortuitous storm, fog or strong winds. When such an ideal opportunity arose, hopefully during the cover of darkness, he proposed launching a well-lit dinghy into the water that would be towed directly behind us with enough cable to allow us to extend some crucial distance away from our enemies. He named this ploy a *Judas boat*, and it would serve as a method of misdirecting our trailing hunters just enough to allow us to make a hasty escape. To succeed, all of the lights aboard the *Amafata* needed to be doused at dusk and would remain unlit throughout the night. The *Judas boat* would act as a replica of our dear ship and hold the attention of the trailing ship. It would be equipped with its own sail to further add to the ruse. When we had extinguished our cable supply and put as much distance away from the potential trouble following us, we would release the cable on the *Judas boat* and allow it to continue sailing under its own hastily rigged sail. At the same time, we would retrieve the door drag so we could have a fighting chance of utilizing added speed in order to slip away into the night. Lastly, we also needed to plot a course away from our intended destination to further confuse and addle our followers.

Now it was up to the Captain to decide our next move. While he seemed inclined to follow Handy's plan, Mr. Bass was in total disagreement. Mr. Bass believed the entire plan to be folly on the part of his enemy. At this point, I entered into the discussions. Reminded of a similar misdirection tactic used in chess, I approached the Captain to inform him of my thoughts. I reminded the Captain that the proposed plan by Handy seemed very similar to the chess move called a *castle*. In this ploy, a player simply switches the position of his most valuable man, the king, with a less valuable and more mobile man, the rook. This move allows the king freedom to move away from a potentially troubled spot in favor of a safer avenue. Once he heard my chess analogy, the Captain gave me a sly smile and told me that he agreed with my thinking. He made the decision on the spot to attempt this *castle* move utilizing the *Judas boat* as a decoy. Mr. Bass was infuriated with my interference and made several attempts to dissuade the Captain from this course of action. The Captain was adamant and shrugged off all dissuading arguments.

With our unconventional plan agreed to, we dropped the door and waited for *dirty weather*. Preparations were made to the ship's dinghy, including adding a small sail so that we would be ready to execute our ruse. After two long and stressful days, it seemed that our silent prayers were answered. In the distance, we all spied the building of black ominous clouds that heralded the onslaught of stormy weather. The wait for darkness that evening was excruciating. Buoyed by the presence of dark, wicked storm clouds, we all knew that our time for action was very near.

As the waves got larger and larger, we began our final preparations. We extinguished our lights and launched the *Judas boat*. We had been deceivingly headed in a due south direction for the last few days in order to mask our true destination. The storm we all prayed so very hard for came later that evening. We stretched the distance between our ship and the *Judas boat* to the utmost degree by using as much of the spare cable that was available to us onboard. Blessedly the storm did not include lightning in its repertoire, which could have foiled all of our careful preparations. Finally, in the midst of the raging sea, we had extinguished all of our spare rope so we merely sliced the tow rope and set the *Judas boat* free to continue under its own sail. We had purposely jammed the rudder of the boat to ensure that she remained headed in the same southerly course that we had been following for the last several days. At the same time, we chopped through the cords that held the heavy door drag and freed ourselves to make a run to freedom. We immediately changed our course to the west and watched as the *Judas boat* drifted steadily away from us.

The mood and the nerves of my crewmates were very taught and anxious for the next several hours. We finally lost sight of our well-lit *Judas boat*, but we still had no idea if our plan had worked. As dawn finally broke and the raging seas calmed, we were all very relieved to find no trace of either our *Judas boat* or our mysterious prowling guest. We had really done it! We were all in a celebratory mood, so the Captain issued an order for an extra ration of rum for all. With the danger far behind us, we resumed our course for the isle of Saint Domingue.

Chapter 18: Scurvy...the Scourge of the Sea

The very next day, however, a new and different plight arose and began to take its toll on our unsuspecting members. While we had been at sea for almost two months, we had for the most part avoided the danger of serious illness. That situation was about to change drastically. I was summoned by Handy to the galley early the next morning to find my friend in a dreadful state. It seemed that Handy had spent the vast portion of the previous night suffering from a vicious case of violent diarrhea along with bouts of vomiting. He looked extremely weak and truly awful as he gave me instructions on fulfilling the galley chores he normally handled. He believed that something he had eaten recently was the cause of his malady, and that it would pass just as quickly as it had come. However, he got progressively worse and worse.

I managed to assist Handy to the Doc's surgery so that he could be examined. The Doc took one look at Handy and declared that he was suffering from a disease called scurvy. The Doc asked Handy if he was experiencing any cramping of any of his limbs to go along with the stomach issues. Handy answered yes to this query with a look of fear and dread on his face. The Doc finally questioned my friend as to whether or not he was also experiencing unquenchable thirst. Again Handy answered this question with a knowing nod of his head. Yes, the Doc was almost certain that the dreaded sea curse, scurvy, had made its presence known aboard our vessel. In fact, the Doc was not all that surprised by Handy's sickly condition because he had previously attended to three other crewmembers with much the same complaints. It seemed to the Doc that we had a full-blown scurvy epidemic on our hands that would eventually lead to death if not properly treated.

Pulling me aside, the Doc began to issue instructions on what needed to be done in order to battle this cursed illness. A temporary hospital room was made in Mr. Bass' quarters to house the scurvy patients. This situation made our First Mate highly irritable and mean-spirited. The thought of giving up his bed to his most hated rival made him furious and indignant. However, the Doc was staunch in his orders and the room was cleared for the four suffering patients. The Captain ordered me to assist the Doc. I spent day and night in this cramped, vomit-reeking room ministering to the needs of the sick. While at first I was in fear of catching this malignant malady from one of my sick brethren, the Doc relieved my worries by informing me that scurvy was not believed to be passed from one patient to another. He went on to inform me that very little was actually known about the disease other than it seemed to strike sailors who had spent a long time at sea. He told me that a physician friend in Sicily had done some research on scurvy. It seemed that this friend was told by trusted Sicilian fishermen that lemon juice could prevent as well as cure the patient of this deadly menace.

While procuring a source of fresh lemons was impossible at this stage of our journey, I suddenly had an idea. Remembering my many nights spent in the deep solitude of the hold, I had ample opportunity to explore every nook and cranny of my private domain. I now recalled that my explorations included doing a thorough inspection of all of our trade goods. I clearly remembered taking stock of the different vials that were located in a separate box for use in dying cloth fabrics. Included in these many different bottles was a bottle of lemon juice that when mixed with several different ingredients would act as a lightening agent for any dyed fabrics. Hastily making an excuse to the Doc, I scrambled my way below deck to see if this precious commodity still existed after the fire. My luck held as I was rewarded by finding the box that contained the precious liquid. Snatching the lemon juice from the box, I quickly made my way back to the sick bay. Informing the Doc of my discovery, we immediately began issuing teaspoons of the precious lemon juice to our suffering patients.

Both the Doc and I expected miraculous results after we had administered our first dose of lemon juice. We were soon disappointed as the patients in our care seemed to only worsen. Handy's skin became extremely dry to the touch, and he turned a very scary dusky blue color. Handy's eyes seemed to be actually shrinking, and his voice was hoarse and barely audible. He, along with the other stricken sailors, seemed very close to death, but that did not stop our efforts of the lemon juice doses. Continuing to administer to my friend's needs and dosing him with lemon juice every four hours, I waited patiently by his side for any sign of improvement. After three torturously long days, the Doc and I were rewarded with Handy actually showing signs of improvement. After a few more days, Handy could actually sit up in bed and converse with the Doc and me. The same could not be said of the other three patients afflicted with this same disease. Of these, only one of them actually survived, while the others retired permanently from active sea duty!

Fully on the mend, Handy was able to get off his bed and stumble weakly across the room. This was the sign that both the Doc and I had long awaited. The Doc thanked me for my assistance and quick thinking in the matter. He made it clear to all that my help had made the critical difference in seeing two of our fellows recover. While the Captain showed no real surprise at this announcement by Doc, the rest of the crew made strong efforts to congratulate me on my success. They were simply amazed at the medical knowledge that I seemed to possess. They even started to bring their minor ailments and medical problems to me to see if I could cure them. As always, I relied on Doc's knowledge and assistance as I went about the job of tending to their specific medical needs.

The only person on the ship who did not congratulate me on my role in the scurvy epidemic was Mr. Bass. I believe that he envisioned the scurvy outbreak as his opportunity to rid the ship of his most hated nemesis. With Handy making a miraculous recovery, Mr. Bass decided to direct his internal fury in my direction. Plotting a means of extracting his revenge, he deliberately left a scuttle open ondeck that caused a crewman to tumble through. The painful result of this accident was a severely broken leg for the unlucky tar and the total blame for the open scuttle being heaped on me. My severe punishment for my forgetfulness was to see that the upperdeck was thoroughly scrubbed in order to prevent a reoccurrence of the scurvy blight.

Most of you landlubbers have probably never scrubbed a ship's deck so you would have no idea of the daunting task my punishment represented. Added to my total discomfort was the fact that I had to perform this duty under the auspices of a brutally hot and torturous sun. Additionally, I was required to carry on with all my regular galley duties as soon as my daily deck scrubbing duty was halted. After I finished each section, Mr. Bass made a point of inspecting my work closely to ensure that the deck was spotlessly clean. Because he was the judge and jury in this matter, I spent much of my time reworking sections of the deck that did not measure up to his imaginary high standards.

It took me an entire week to complete my punishment. By the end of the week, I was deeply sunburned and totally exhausted. Honestly, I might never have completed the deck to Mr. Bass' satisfaction had it not been for the assistance I received from a number of my crewmates. They helped out every time Mr. Bass was not in view to ensure that I did not expire from sheer exhaustion or from heatstroke. While the crew felt angry and upset by the brutal actions of the First Mate, they were also powerless to intervene as they were worried about their own well-being!

Chapter 19: Saint Domingue... Much Needed Rest

The aftermath of the scurvy outbreak left us with two dead crewmembers that needed to be buried at sea. Two surplus sails were utilized to wrap the bodies. Ballast stones were placed at the feet of each body to carry it down to the depths of the ocean. The Sailmaker then proceeded to stitch these burial shrouds closed with a traditional thirteen stitches with the thirteenth being sewn directly through each victim's nose. For the life of me, I could not work out the meaning of this strange ritual, especially the need to stitch the victim's nose. Handy was also at a loss to explain, telling me simply that sea burials were always handled this way. Not much of an answer from this salty tar. After the ghastly stitch job, the bodies were brought ondeck for the final ceremony. The Captain proceeded to read some passages from the Bible over the shrouded corpses, and then the bodies were dumped over the starboard side to sleep with the fishes of the deep. The crew made its obligatory sign-of-the-cross as our friends and fellow workers went for their final swim.

By this time, the crew was working around the clock making up for the sailors that we had lost along the way. After my deck cleaning ordeal, I was responsible for full-time galley duty until Handy could make a complete recovery. This duty kept me totally tied to the galley for the majority of each day. The little spare time I had was spent either with the Captain or the Doc. The good news in this labor-intensive period was that Mr. Bass was also kept very busy. Given his onerous responsibilities, he had much more important duties to attend to and pretty much left me alone to fulfill my role as Galley Master.

Having spent the last long months on the water, the ship's stores were in very dismal shape. We had virtually no fresh water and the food was running dangerously low. The only meat, fresh or otherwise, was the rat population that kept me company in the bilge. I realized that we were in desperate straights so I devised a plan to take advantage of our last remaining food resource. Making my way down to the bilge, I carefully selected and hunted the very best of the remaining rat population. Skinning and cleaning these nasty beasties took place in the bilge to prevent wandering eyes from seeing exactly what I was doing. With the unusable remains dumped overboard to serve as shark appetizers, I cooked the rat meat in a stew with rice, beans and peas. I knew that this special stew would provide my fellow crewmembers with enough sustenance to keep them alive for a little while longer. To my delight, the crew actually relished the taste of my special meal, calling it *Echo's stew* in my honor. Many of them told me that it was the most delicious stew that they had ever tasted. The Captain actually questioned me the following day where I had found meat to use in my stew. In answer to his query, I gave him a broad smile and told him simply that he really did not want to know where the meat had come from.

In addition to the lack of meat onboard, fresh water was fast becoming a serious problem. The crew's choices when it came to water were very limited. The *marsh water* stored in barrels in the bilge was all but depleted. This meant that the thirsty men were reduced to drinking their own urine, if they were desperate enough. The more creative ones mixed their urine with their daily rum ration creating a concoction they called *yellow spirits*. Lastly, some chose to actually drink seawater. This bad habit brought more harm than good for the imbibing tars, since seawater caused even more dehydration along with serious hallucinations. As Cook, I was spared these dreadful practices since a small cache of water was traditionally set aside for cooking purposes. As I performed my daily cooking duties, I was able to sneak a small sip of this cooking water from time to time as the need arose. Handy and I were lucky to have this option. All the while, I still wondered why Mr. Bass hated him so.

One afternoon, while locked in a close chess match with the Captain, I decided my curiosity needed appeasing so I tentatively broached the subject with him. I told the Captain that I had noticed some bad blood between two of my mates and was highly curious for the reason behind it. The Captain asked me to be specific and I told him the two crewmembers were Mr. Bass and Handy. The Captain seemed reluctant at first to answer but then smiled and said, *"What the hell...why not!"* His tale began on the last voyage the *Amafata* had taken. It occurred during one of the slow periods on this voyage, when several of the crew decided to kill the boredom by playing a game of cards. While the wagers were small and relatively meaningless, the participants took the game very seriously. As such, tempers continued to rise as the game progressed. The day was finally carried by Handy, but Mr. Bass, known to be a notorious bad sport, was furious with the outcome and accused Handy of cheating. Leveling this type of accusation in public was viewed as a very serious matter. Usually this kind of personal insult led to a duel between the parties involved strictly as a matter of honor. Since Handy was well aware of the usual consequences of such an outburst, he was reluctant to take the insult very seriously. Instead of reacting in anger, Handy simply laughed the matter away. Mr. Bass was not mollified one bit by Handy's reaction, and immediately challenged the accused cheat to a duel to settle the matter like gentlemen. Since he was the challenged party, Handy had the luxury of deciding the weapon choice for the duel. Thinking the matter over for a time, Handy laughed once more and chose the *curse of silence* as his weapon of choice. Mr. Bass was totally incensed by Handy's choice, but as a matter of honor was compelled to comply with Handy's choice.

The Captain sensing my utter confusion decided it best to take a moment to explain. The *curse of silence* was actually an age-old child's game. Simply stated, one youngster would challenge another that he could actually outlast the other in a duel of silence. The loser in this contest was the individual who first broke the oath of silence and spoke publicly. Mr. Bass took the entire episode as nothing more than a silly joke, but Handy was adamant about the game, and would hear no protest on the part of the First Mate as to how silly the whole duel had digressed. So began the duel with each man going mute immediately. This situation continued for a full month with absolutely no words spoken by either party. Finally one day, a lowly swab dropped a bucketful of deck cleaning sand onto Mr. Bass' right foot. Hopping around the deck in agony, Mr. Bass let loose with a full-blown scream and in a moment of white-hot anger proceeded to castigate the bucket- dropping offender verbally. Before realizing what he had done, the entire crew burst into uproarious and hysterical laughter at his tragic error. Handy became the clear winner of the duel, while Mr. Bass was supremely humiliated at failing to best his hated adversary at this childish game. From that point on, the Captain related, Mr. Bass was biding his time waiting for the opportunity to get even with Handy. I laughed long and hard at the conclusion of this story, proud of my friend for outwitting the bully.

The very next day, while the Captain and I went about our daily navigational exercises, we talked about our next port of call: Saint Domingue. The crew did not know we would be going there. This secret did not remain quiet very long at all. The crew eventually became aware of our planned stopover, causing immediate grumbling, muttering and complaining from my crewmates with some even going so far as to making the sign-of-the-cross on their forehead, lips and heart. This confused me mightily, so I decided to ask Chips for an explanation. He told me that the island was under constant threat of revolt and agitation. The reason for this reputation was the inordinate number of African slaves that had been delivered to the island to farm the many agricultural plantations. Further, he informed me that the highly outnumbered plantation owners were known to be heartless and cruel when it came to the overall treatment of their vassals. Given their barbarous treatment of the slaves, the plantation owners lived in constant fear expecting slave riots and uprisings to occur at any moment.

Chips also informed me that the island's slaves practiced a demonic form of religion called Voudou. While these religious rites were outlawed by the plantation owners, they were secretly practiced during the night in secluded locations all over the island's interior. Chips was firm in his belief that these religious rites were nothing more than a form of devil worship and an excuse for the slaves to revel in sexual orgies and other moral depredations. Chips told me that it was rumored that certain Voudou priests had the ability to turn any individual into a zombie…the walking dead! These same priests held control over these savage soulless creatures, who would do anything that the priest instructed them to do. After listening to this fanciful information, I could do nothing but laugh at the sheer ridiculousness of these claims.

Since I remained a skeptic, Chips decided to relate a story to see if he could change my view on the terrifying power of Voudou. The story centered on an unusually cruel and wicked plantation owner named Guy Beaumount. Guy was known to apply harsh and unjust discipline to his slaves without the slightest provocation. Any dissenters or lawbreakers were sentenced to cruel and painful deaths in a large pit he had filled with man-eating crocodiles specially imported from Africa. The informal slave leader on this plantation was called Bortu. He had a daughter named Silve, who was both beautiful and a gentle spirit. Like her father, Silve was also loved and respected by all on the plantation. Because of this, Guy Beaumount became extremely jealous. This destructive vice led the mean-spirited owner to devise a plan to bring hardship and ruin to both Bortu and his daughter.

Silve had a lover who was the local Voudou priest, called a *houngan*. This priest was madly in love with Silve and worshipped the ground she trod. In a malicious act, Guy moved Silve into the main plantation house to separate her from both her lover and her father. One night in a drunken stupor, Guy raped and defiled Silve. Inconsolable and unable to deal with her shame, Silve subsequently committed suicide by hanging herself in a secluded dale. While the specific reason for the girl's desperate act was a mystery, most believed that Guy Beaumount had everything to do with it. Bortu, devastated by grief and sorrow over his daughter's death confronted Guy. The arrogant plantation owner, unused to being challenged by his chattel, was infuriated by Bortu's actions and sentenced the distraught father to a swim with the crocs. Bortu was unceremoniously fed to the vicious reptiles and Guy hoped that the matter was finally settled. However, Silve's lover, the Voudou high priest had also guessed the reason for his lover's death. He knew that Guy Beaumount was responsible and began to make his own plans to extract revenge. To avenge his lover, the high priest decided to create a zombie to deal harshly with Guy. The *houngan* performed the proper incantations and rites that allowed Bortu's half-eaten and brutally savaged dead body to rise from its newly dug grave. Bortu, now acting on the will of the *houngan*, was sent on a secret mission of revenge. That very night a stumbling and dirt-encrusted Bortu made his way to the main plantation house in search of its wicked owner.

This grisly phantom's appearance went far beyond terrifying due to his recent swim with the crocs. His dead body was adorned with an extraordinary number of ragged bites resulting in massive empty swatches of flesh. The sky was dark, filled with lightning and thunder when Bortu finally made his appearance. Guy was awakened by the commotion that Bortu caused breaking into the mansion. Rising from his bed, the plantation owner quickly grabbed his faithful whip and several pistols in order to investigate the source of the clamor. Rushing down the stairs, Guy was greeted by his old adversary, Bortu. Regaining some of his senses, Guy utilized both his whip and guns to fend off the hideous creature that was shambling its way toward him. Since Bortu was already dead the whip and guns had no effect on him as he made his way slowly toward his malicious former master.

Upon reaching his target, Zombie Bortu picked up the screaming and terrified man and began his retreat from the plantation house. Once outside, Zombie Bortu stopped for a moment to launch several oil-fed lanterns into the house. These projectiles delivered enough flames to ignite the entire estate, which perished under the fire's onslaught, killing every member of the Beaumount family. With screams emanating from the upstairs windows, Zombie Bortu continued his shambling gait carrying the totally terrified Guy to his appointed destination. Reaching the croc pit, Zombie Bortu proceeded to walk directly into the pit of death with Guy hefted above his head screaming and begging for mercy. The hungry reptiles wasted no time and made their way directly toward the pit's intruders. Guy's agonizing screams continued as these voracious feeders ripped him apart devouring him in large bloody chunks. These blood-crazed beasts paid little attention to the dead slave sensing no life emanating from him. Upon completion of his tasks Zombie Bortu emerged from the blood-filled croc pit and returned to his recently abandoned gravesite. Once there, the zombie proceeded to rebury himself as he had been instructed. The surviving plantation slaves led by the *houngan* fled to the mountainous interior of the island to escape any form of retribution from the neighboring plantation owners. Chips told me that these same slave escapees often came down from their mountain fortresses to wreak destruction and death on various island plantations in an effort to help free more of their enslaved brothers and sisters.

Delivering the last statement, Chips made it clear to me that while on Saint Domingue laughing at the Voudou religion and its demonic rites could seriously jeopardize my earthly existence. He urged me to avoid any contact whatsoever with this strange theology if I valued both my life and my everlasting soul. With that he made the traditional sign-of-the-cross on his person and headed off to bed. For my part, I was nothing but fascinated by all he had told me through his Voudou tale. I was intrigued to learn more about the strange religion and vowed to do so if ever given the opportunity.

The very next morning we arrived at Cap-Francis on Saint Domingue. The harbor was both a wide and natural birth providing plenty of shelter for the many ships anchored there. There was a variety of national flags flying on the ships we spotted, including Dutch, French and English colors. A ring of brilliant white sand formed an arc around the harbor as if representing a halo around the port. We spied a fine town just beyond the harbor with shops and warehouses at the very edge of the shore. Beyond these were colorful two-story buildings with wrought-iron grillwork covering the windows and doors. These same designs also formed second-story borders for their plant strewn patios that provided a marvelous view of the entire harbor. Behind the town rose a series of steep hills that served as the home for a number of grand homes that resembled palaces. The water surrounding us was a light coral blue, deep and clear, so we were able to see the sandy sea floor clearly from the deck of our ship. There were no large breakers or waves present in this protected harbor, which gave us all pause for relief. There were a series of mountains rising up in the island's interior that formed a perfect backdrop for its surroundings. The mountains were ringed with a white fog that acted like a natural beard. We observed lush green vegetation everywhere that signaled the fertility for which this island was renowned. Mr. Bass shouted orders, which brought the ship as close to shore as caution and safety allowed. Being this close would enable work to be completed on the ship's bottom at low tide. We had finally arrived at a New World port and we were all excited to spend some time ashore…sweet liberty at last!

Chapter 20: Sweet Liberty

Liberty to make a shore visit was finally granted by the Captain, and we all scrambled to the dinghies to begin our grand adventure. Upon landing at the docks that we had spied from our ship, we were all impressed with the cleanliness and beauty of the town itself. We were also surprised at the torrential downpours that seemed to spring up randomly throughout the days and nights. These same rains also caused random flooding, which acted as a natural broom sweeping any and all refuse away from the city and into the surrounding sea.

Since the island was French-owned, there were French signs and information throughout this wondrous paradise. This fact caused much confusion and consternation among my visiting shipmates, but posed no real problem for me. Everywhere we ventured we were met with furious activity...trade and bustle was the name of the game! The majority of the buildings we passed were erected using the island's native woods with their walls slathered with a substance the locals referred to as stucco. This plaster-like covering allowed each building to be painted in the rainbow of cool tropical hues that provided uniqueness and bright color to every residence.

The great mountains in the island's interior rose to dizzying heights much like the arches inside Saint Agnes at home. The green and verdant fields and hillsides displayed before these majestic mountains attested to the natural agricultural resources of this fertile isle. The streets were laid out in a neat and precise grid-work pattern that made it hard to lose one's way as we ventured further into the town's interior. As we roamed, we noticed that the population was very unevenly divided with blacks forming its vast majority, and there seemed to be two classifications when it came to the black population.

The first of these groups was fully dressed and appeared free to roam anywhere they chose. We would later learn that this group was indeed free blacks named mulattos, offspring of the white ruling class and the black slave population. The second and more numerously populated group was the island slaves. They were half-dressed and treated in a very poor fashion by their white masters. These unfortunates were the main workforce of the island just as the orphans of London were to the workhouses and factories there. In effect, both were worked to death to appease the needs and greed of their owners.

The mulattos spoke both French as well as a strange dialect that I just could not understand at all. I learned later that this vernacular was called Creole. It was a mixture of French and a conglomeration of several African dialects. This was the language of the slaves on the island, and I knew that given enough time and study that I would be able to decipher more than just smatterings. For the time being, I was just as confused and confounded by this bizarre tongue as were my fellow shipmates.

Meandering beyond the docks and merchant establishments we encountered the homes of the island citizens. As we had viewed from our ship, the upper levels of these homes had open areas, called verandas by the locals, bordered by the iron grillwork. These verandas were decorated with vines bearing brightly colored blooms that trailed down to the ground. Further up the hillsides larger more luxurious homes dotted the landscape. The island locals also informed us that even larger homes, called plantations, dominated the interior valleys and magnificent plateaus. For the most part, we were welcomed by the island inhabitants wherever we roamed. My guess was that this fine reception would continue just as long as our coins held out!

Along the shore to the north of the city was a ragtag collection of buildings called Shantytown. In Shantytown, everyone was welcomed with open arms. There was at least one pub on every block in Shantytown, and we naturally gravitated to this section of the city. For a variety of obvious reasons, Shantytown became our new home on shore!

Roaming the streets of Shantytown, it became quite clear that this section of town housed a crazy collection of pubs, shops, whorehouses, playhouses and so much more. And have I mentioned pirates? Well, they were more than welcomed in Shantytown as they roamed the crowded and hectic streets. It is funny but while at sea, pirates were vilified by merchants as the worst sort of scoundrels and thieves. Having a first-hand view of these rogues led me to the conclusion that they tended to rob from the rich, while the merchants on land robbed from the poor and ignorant. The law protected the merchants as they perfected their trade, while pirates were forced to operate under their own protection and outright courage. However, while on shore, pirates were seldom seen as monsters. Rather they were viewed as friends and potential customers, while loaded down with gold, silver and precious gems as legal tender. Pirates also brought hordes of fine merchandise ashore to be sold at very reasonable prices. Their existence was treated in a sort of undercover manner by merchants, planters, locals and government officials who provisioned them, entertained them and kept them secretly abreast of relevant news such as military troop movements.

Taking the time to pay close attention to them, I noticed that they were a very multinational band. They seemed to have no class distinctions that I could ascertain. Many of these merry rouges were attired in ridiculous-looking outfits, including strange hats, ill-fitting wigs, multicolored stockings, expensive boots, uniforms and dress clothes, ribbons, feathers and a variety of other strange and foreign accoutrements. I guessed that much of this finery resulted from their share of plundered goods taken from prizes they had captured in their voyages. It was comical to the point of hilarity to witness these scoundrels strutting through Shantytown sporting these strange and gaudy outfits…not that I would ever dare to laugh at them in public! While the overall mood of Shantytown was ever lively and fun-filled there was a distinct sense of a danger that underlined the overt celebratory spirit and activity.

On one of the main streets, called Rue Haiti, existed a fine-looking, two-story tavern named the Palais LeMonde or simply the Palace to Us Englishmen. The Palace was much like Slugger's in layout and design but, unlike my old place of employment, had no basement, since they did not exist at all on the island.

However, like Slugger's, the Palace had a rudely constructed ring built especially for bare-knuckle battles as well as a variety of other animal contests. The ring was located behind the Palace under a large palm-thatched open enclosure. The ring was square with wooden sides that reached a normal man's midsection. Since little if any lighting existed anywhere on the island, all contests and battles took place during daylight hours. Given that I was well-versed with this type of entertainment, I spent the vast majority of my time ringside each day.

The Palace was run and managed by Monique La Montaine. She was a stout and substantial woman with flaming red hair and a friendly and welcoming manner. She acted as innkeeper, peacemaker and bouncer, all at the same time! Given her size and manner, she was hardly a woman that you ever wanted to cross. Worldly and wise, she seemed to have a nose for detecting trouble and deflected it long before it got out of hand. She was armed with a huge military saber that hung loosely at her waist to provide easy and quick access should it be required to maintain peaceful tranquility. When her saber was unsheathed, all hell was said to be unleashed.

Madame La Montaine had several assistants working at various jobs throughout the Palace. The one that immediately caught my eye was a slim slip of a girl about the same age as me, who answered to the name of Rue. She had flaming red hair trailing all the way down to her backside. Her normal duty of serving drinks kept her behind the massive wooden bar, and I was quickly informed that Rue was the only daughter of the imposing proprietress. A *hand's-off policy* was the standing order at the Palace when it came to her. A drunken slap or lustful pinch would be rewarded by a savage series of blows from Madame La Montaine's handy saber. Sailors who regularly frequented the Palace told me that you only ventured near Rue at the penalty of losing your hand, arm, privates or your life! I found Rue totally fascinating. She was fluent in French but also able to speak in the strange tongue of the slaves. I utilized my French skills to carry on a conversation with her as she went about her bartending duties. She was quite bright and full of life as she provided me an education of the island.

While I was very much aware of the baleful stare from her mother during these conversations, I acted the role of a proper gentleman the whole time I spoke with Rue. She was also very curious about my homeland. She longed to escape Saint Domingue and sail to France or England. She was bright, witty and humorous. I spent as much time as I dared conversing with her until the withering stares from her mother sent me elsewhere to conduct my business.

Rue also provided much of the entertainment for the Palace with her wonderful singing performances. Accompanied by a ragtag house band of a drum, fiddle, guitar and flute, she stunned and stupefied her adoring audiences. As we conversed, I heard a few of my shipmates boasting of my own vocal talents. Rue, intrigued by the high praise and bragging shown me by my friends, quizzed me on my singing ability every so often during our discussions. I informed her that yes I could sing but not nearly as well as her. Unsatisfied, she would simply give me a wink and tell me that I would have to prove this to her.

It was later that evening, just after she had finished a beautiful French love ballad called *Mon Coeur*, that she asked her audience if they would like to have someone else perform for them…someone who was reputed to have a wondrous voice. The audience, totally in her hands due to her latest vocal triumph, yelled and screamed a loud assent. Turning her head in my direction, she challenged me to perform in front of this drunken mob. At the start, I was a bit shy and not willing to gain such unwanted attention, but Rue was unrelenting.

Rue sensed my strong reluctance and let out a loud and raucous laugh, telling her adoring audience that she knew all along that I had no voice at all for singing, no matter what my friends had said. Well, anger and shame got the very best of me as I marched to the stage to prove exactly how wrong this beautiful angel was.

Reaching the stage, I had a short conference with the band members finally agreeing on a melody with which we were equally familiar. I relied on my memory to recreate the words and the exact rich vocal tone that I had once heard performed by a very talented French tenor. The Palace became deathly quiet at the sound of my very strong voice and remained so throughout my performance. At the conclusion of my rendition, I received huge applause from the drunken mob. Many of those in attendance, including a raft of bloodthirsty pirates, were actually brushing away tears from the corners of their eyes in a vain attempt to hide the emotional effect. Rue stood transfixed in awe as she stared in my direction. She finally rushed over to my side and planted a very tender and sweet kiss on my cheek as payment for my singing effort. In a whisper, she apologized for the embarrassment she had caused me. She also told me that I had the most wondrous singing voice that she had ever had the pleasure of enjoying. She thanked me once more before skipping off to her assigned duties behind the bar.

As I basked in my newfound fame, I noticed that there were two individuals in the tavern who were certainly not enthralled with my performance. The first was Mr. Bass, who was sitting alone at a far corner table scowling as if he had just partaken in a slice of *maggot pie*. The other was Rue's mother, who stood at the other end of the bar fixing me with a stare that would certainly stop a charging bull. Madame La Montaine was none too pleased with me, not so much with the boisterous adulations and back-pounding congratulations that I received, but more about the look on her daughter's face as she stared in my direction from her normal place behind the bar. I knew immediately that I would have to maintain a sharp lookout for trouble headed my way from either of these two sources.

The party was now jubilant and robust. Handy grabbed my elbow and steered me to the bar to both celebrate and to meet a new friend of his, a pirate he introduced as Slash Buckets. Before me stood a pirate of average height, weight and appearance except for the jagged wicked-looking scar that ran along the entire right side of his face. It surely must have been a truly savage blow that had marred this rascal's face, but his warm open smile quickly made me dismiss the external branding. With all in a lively and happy mood, I boldly inquired how he had received his name and such a telling battle reminder. Without further prompting, Slash began his explanation for his very curious audience.

Slash was quick to point out that most pirates when they go *on the account*, that is join a pirate crew, change their name for a number of reasons. First, it protects their God-given name should they ever have reason to resume its use. Second, in becoming a pirate, a man changes his complete outlook on life. Nothing of his past had any significance or importance any longer, especially his name. A true pirate lived and reveled in only the present, with the past forgotten and the future ignored. Third, as scoundrels and the spawn of the devil, Christian names had absolutely no place or use in his new pirate society. Last, he related that it was just plain fun to choose your own name rather than answer to one that has been forced on you. I agreed wholeheartedly with this rationale…after all, I had renamed myself Echo!

Slash's short tale began with a crewmate and friend named Max Liberty who he had not seen in a very long while. Both Slash and Max found themselves on the isle of Tortuga. They were both scheduled to sail on a pirate ship christened the *Lone Vulture* in search of easy prey and fabulous booty. Prior to sailing, Slash got into a minor altercation in a local tavern and was injured very badly. As a result, he was laid up nursing his wounds, including the vicious facial laceration gracing his appearance, causing him to miss the voyage. However, the *Lone Vulture* sailed the very next day with Max and a full crew of pirates aboard. With a grim look to his interested audience, Slash recounted that both his friend and his ship full of pirates were never seen again. They had simply disappeared. Perhaps victims of a storm or worse, Slash informed us that the sea had strange ways of claiming victims. A very serious look came over the pirate's face as he informed us that he had been unable to resume his thieving life at sea for fear of falling under the same curse that was responsible for the mysterious disappearance of his friend and the doomed crew of the *Lone Vulture*. With a wicked grin, he said that his injury had saved his life. Accordingly, he was both proud and thankful to sport his hideous scar as a constant reminder of his good luck!

Chapter 21: The Fight Bell Is Rung

For our continual amusement, there were events scheduled each day in the small confines of the fight ring that varied from savage human and animal battles to strange and unique contests seemingly invented on the spot by the fun-loving patrons of this pleasure house. So as to not to bore you with all the games, I will give you an example of one of the more bizarre contests. This strange game was christened the *Nick-a-Bottle Game*. The contestants seated themselves at a long table placed in the center of the ring. Four contestants were chosen from the attending throng to demonstrate their drinking skills. Each was now seated at the table with a fresh bottle of rum in their paws. The rules were very simple. Each contestant had to take one long hard swallow from their rum bottle. Once accomplished, each man was then required to swallow a small live toad provided by local children. If any contestant disgorged his reptilian meal during the course of the game, he was automatically ousted from the game to suffer the derisive jeers and taunts of the raucous spectators. The winner of this ridiculous contest was the first individual to finish his bottle without disgorging the swallowed toads.

I reasoned that the best winning strategy to employ was to consume as much of the rum as possible during each swig period, so as to limit the number of toads one was forced to consume. To add to the hilarity, the toads chosen were known to produce a very nasty effect on humans or animals. Should any creature attempt to make a meal out of this type of toad, they would lapse into a trance-like state and begin to foam heavily from their mouths. Eventually, the hapless creature would disgorge the offending toad and regain normality in a few hours time. Well aware of this danger, the contestants bravely sat down and prepared to swill as much free rum as they could!

This unique game was an instant audience pleaser, signaled by the loud laughter and hilarity exhibited by all prior to the match's start. My crewmates and I could only look on with absolute disbelief at the spectacle that was now unfolding. The contest commenced with each participant taking a long, hard swallow from their rum bottles to the frenzied encouragement of the mob. Once accomplished, the tiny toads were produced and each was swallowed along with another generous pull on the rum to provide a means to hasten the passage of the reptilian appetizer. Having completed the toad swallowing, the first round came to a noisy and clamorous end. The crowd, knowing full well the effects the toads would eventually elicit, kept a sharp eye on each contestant waiting for the real fun to start.

At a signal from the gamemaster, round two was launched repeating the previous round's steps. As the rules decreed, each successive round continued in this manner. It did not take long for the tiny amphibians to provide their horrid effect on each competitor. In fact, all were swaying in dazed states with copious amounts of white foam dripping from their mouths. By the end of the third round, two contestants had fallen out, and were on their knees retching and gagging to the savage delight of the drunken audience. Finally, after abundant foaming and disgusting salivation, a pirate named Barnacle Dan was declared the winner. He immediately assumed the kneeling position with his co-contestants retching and spewing toads. Within a few hours, even the sickest of these participants was back on his feet and had returned to the bar, showing little ill effects of the strange game we had just witnessed.

Each day, there was also a series of cockfights that particularly brought out the bloodlust in the inebriated rabble. Having spent many a night at Slugger's, I held a very distinct advantage of being able to judge each rooster's worth and skill prior to any fight. Over the next several days, I could have amassed a considerable cache of coin won by this special insight. However, I knew that attempting to hide any significant amount of money onboard would lead to trouble. Therefore, I chose very early in the winning process to share this new found wealth with my companions by purchasing round after round of drinks for them. My drink of choice was the delicious island staple…lemonade! With lemon trees in abundance, I was also able to stock up on this scurvy-fighting fruit and its wondrous healing juice.

The two people I noticed that were not at all pleased by my wagering success were Mr. Bass and Madame La Montaigne. As for Mr. Bass, my success fueled his further hatred of me. For Madame La Montaigne, I was costing the house a small fortune because my wagers were now being quickly duplicated by a slew of my associates. Madame La Montaigne approached me privately to inform me that she would not stop me from betting on the cockfights, as long as I made these bets just prior to the start of any fight. In this way, she explained, my winning choices would not influence the other bettors. My mates were not very happy, but I complied because I was aware that our liberty time was short and to cause trouble meant possible disbarment from the Palace.

In addition to cockfights, there were also a few dogfights thrown on the menu to keep the crowd's blood at a fever pitch as well as providing a bit of variety. Unlike the specially trained and bred canine killers at Slugger's, the dogs that fought in this ring were a mix of mangy island mongrels. Not suited or trained for the brutal realities of the ring, most of these nasty matches were simply one-sided slaughters. I had absolutely no interest in watching one dog butcher another helpless and cowed opponent, so I usually made my way back inside the establishment as soon as one of these barbaric contests began.

The next afternoon I was doing some exploring around the town when I literally ran into an island mongrel that had either been beaten savagely by its owner or had recently suffered a devastating loss in a dog fighting contest. I carried the poor animal back to the Palace so that I could provide it with some necessary medical assistance. Stitching up the numerous savage wounds took the better part of that afternoon. Once this was accomplished, I splinted its badly broken hind leg and then fed the poor starving beast. From that moment on, I had an inseparable friend and companion! For the next two days, everywhere I ventured, the dog followed. I needed a name for my new shadow and christened him Ding-Dong, because he would literally go crazy every time he heard a bell ring…probably a reminder of his past tragic fighting experience. Ding-Dong proved to be loyal and obedient, and I quickly became accustomed to having him right at my heels. The hound was normal in every way with the noted exception of his distinctive eye color. Unlike any canine I had ever seen, Ding-Dong's eyes were an unusual shade of yellow. On the third morning, he just simply disappeared. I looked everywhere for him but had no luck at all in my efforts to locate him. Everyone I questioned was shocked to discover that the hound had left my side. I was confused by his disappearance and actually missed his company. He had simply disappeared into the void!

Making my way into the Palace to quench my thirst with cool lemonade, I happened to notice a disturbance across the room. Rue was running away from its center with large tears streaming down her face. At the same time, Mr. Bass was issuing a slew of derogatory remarks at the poor lass as she fled from his presence. It seemed that while Rue was delivering a tray full of rum and beer to Mr. Bass and his cronies, the former had taken the liberty of pinching the poor girl's bottom. Embarrassed and indignant, Rue had made an attempt to brush the offender's hand away. In doing so, she had lost balance of the serving tray, and the entire load of drinks had found their way onto Mr. Bass' lap. Now also embarrassed and angry, Mr. Bass lashed out verbally with a myriad of crude and hateful remarks. Getting little or no support from the drunken mob, Rue fled fighting back tears of humiliation.

Seeking immediate retribution, I made a long scan of the room searching for a means to get even with the notorious bullying beast. I happened to spot a likely assistant positioned very near the enraged First Mate. My choice was a barbaric looking Turkish pirate by the name of Babar Kismet, who went by the nickname Lion. He was a fierce-looking warrior who hardly needed any excuse to start an altercation. Moving to within earshot of this terrifying foreigner, I utilized my *special voice* to imitate Mr. Bass' speech and tone to send some seriously unkindly words in the direction of Lion Kismet. Hearing my taunts clearly, Lion turned around and delivered a stunning blow to Mr. Bass' nose.

Spurting blood and seeking justice for such a cowardly and unprovoked attack, the First Mate launched himself at Lion with both his fists and feet flying. It was at this very moment that all hell broke loose in the Palace and a true *battle royale* had initiated. Chairs and tables were shattered, bodies went flying in all directions and broken rum bottles filled the air. I began to move toward the safety of the back door. About halfway across the room, a very inebriated French pirate took a wild swing at my head in a serious attempt to decapitate me. I ducked under his wild swing, and delivered a vicious elbow to his unprotected face. The blow connected perfectly and my opponent went down in a jumble of arms and legs. Protecting myself as I navigated the individual boxing matches that had sprung up virtually everywhere, I finally made my escape through the rear door but not before receiving a rash of minor injuries to my face, arms and chest along the way.

As order was being restored, I ventured back into the Palace to assess the damage I had created. Moans and groans filled the air as I made my way across the debris-strewn floor in search of my adversary. Mr. Bass had sustained a broken arm, his whip arm no less, along with a severely damaged right eye that was completely closed and leaking a viscous red fluid. The First Mate would be laid up for a time while nursing both of these severe injuries. I had attained my revenge, but knew that the whole episode would do little to assuage Rue's embarrassment and shame.

It took some time to restore complete order to the Palace. The free-flowing rum following the brawl loosened the tongues of most and I became transfixed listening to several pirate tales. One story stood out in all of its gruesomeness. It concerned a savage rogue pirate captain, who was relatively new to these waters. He called himself the Black Tarantula, which immediately conjured horror and dread at its utterance. Although he was new, it did not take this beast long at all to build a fearsome reputation. I listened raptly to his loathsome description provided by a pirate storyteller called Angry George.

Angry George related that the Black Tarantula dressed himself entirely in flowing black silk, including a voluminous ebony cape complete with hood. His voice was a hideous rasp as if originated from the very bowels of hell. He navigated from place to place like no man Angry George had ever witnessed. It could not be described as walking but rather as a skittering and scuttling gait, just like the large spider from which he had borrowed his name. The pirate informed us that the fiend did not stand straight like a normal man, but rather had a permanent hunch as if in continual supplication to some demonic entity. To navigate, he relied on the use of his two legs in tandem with his left arm to propel himself. While this three-limbed stance would be quite difficult for a normal man to achieve, the Black Tarantula had perfected his mobility to the point that he could cover any amount of ground in the blink of an eye.

Angry George stated that the pirate's black attire was made complete by a hideous black mask. This disgusting facial disguise was painted a dull black finish that gave the appearance of resembling short, spiked animal fur. Drawn on this unholy visage were two large fangs that dripped a red color depicting blood. He also told us that the mask had two red insect-like eyes painted on it. By this time, it seemed to me that the storyteller had begun to quake given the startling horrors he was describing. We also were told that this terrifying mask had the strange ability to drive a man completely mad over time. Angry George claimed that the mask had been forged in the fires of hell and subsequently stolen by this sea dog from Satan himself!

Angry George continued by testifying that the Black Tarantula was reputed to have no love at all for his fellow man, treating all with extreme cruelty and savage wickedness. He went further by giving us an example of this. Having once captured a merchantman, like our own dear ship, he assembled everyone ondeck to observe his inquisition of her Captain on the location of any hidden valuables. Upon receiving denial after denial from the terrified leader, the fiend elected to elicit answers in a most horrible manner. Securing the Captain naked to a chair that had been brought topside, the demon proceeded to deposit a handful of squirming hungry leeches directly onto the victim's lap. These blood sucking monsters immediately began their unholy feeding on the Captain's privates, incurring a series of high-pitched and pain-laden wails from the poor unfortunate. As the crew watched these proceedings in abject horror, the Captain was more than forthcoming on the exact location of every valuable hidden anywhere on the ship. The pirate horde was dispatched to collect this loot as the Captain continued his pain-filled serenade. Once all the valuables were retrieved, the abused Captain was unceremoniously dumped into the sea…chair, leeches and all!

The crew was then questioned as to their own specific duties aboard the trader. A few were offered the distinct privilege of joining this demonic pirate crew. Once completed, the remaining unlucky crew members were also thrown into the sea to join their leader. The merchantman was then stripped of any valuable cargo, medicines and tools before it was fired and sent to the bottom of the sea.

Angry George stopped at this point with his terrible tale, and winking at his audience cautioned all of us to stay far away from the insidious clutches of this deranged madman. Given the opportunity, I was quite certain that the entire group would certainly opt for this wise course of action!

The very next day, I happened to encounter the Captain in Cap-Francis. He was in quite a hurry as he proceeded about his business onshore of refitting our vessel and bargaining for additional trade goods to replace those that were lost by Jonah Jemme's incompetence. The Captain called me over to his side and asked me to join him in a noonday meal. Immediately agreeing, we retired to a quaint nearby inn to appease our appetites. As we partook in this splendid meal, the Captain divulged the secret he had been keeping about our particular stop on Saint Doningue. He told me that beyond his many trusted friends on the island, there was a trio of sisters with whom he had prior acquaintance. In fact, it was the Captain, who had delivered these same sisters to this very location. He went on to inform me that these sisters, surnamed Adams, were considered to be witches by the European members of the community. The reason for this was that these three women had actively and publicly denounced the practice of slavery on the island. They were fabulously wealthy and had also used these vast resources to assist runaway slaves whenever the opportunity arose. They were quick to point out to the island's ruling class that continuing this wrongful practice would mark their souls terribly. While the Adams sisters' strong arguments and threats of everlasting torment were incredibly persuasive, the island leaders knew in their hearts that the lifeblood of the island depended on slave labor. They all knew that without slavery, their future on Saint Domingue was doomed to total failure.

In order to rid them and the island of the sisters' destructive thoughts and ideas, the island leaders banded together and proclaimed these sisters witches. The fate of any convicted witch during this time was the inhuman practice of being burned alive. Fully aware of the cruel fate that awaited them, the Adams sisters realized that their only chance to remain alive called for an immediate evacuation to a much safer environment. Therefore, they had arranged with our Captain for hasty transport aboard the *Amafata*. The payment for their personal conveyance would be extremely generous, which provided our Captain the necessary funds to refit and restock our vessel. The Captain informed me that in return for this generous payment, we would be escorting these three ladies to the island of Jamaica, where they had friends and relatives who would gladly welcome them and see to their safety. So the deal had been struck and when our voyage continued, we would have three new passengers to carry! While I could see very little harm in the deal the Captain had arranged, I knew that my superstitious mates would feel quite differently about the entire situation. To this end, the Captain asked me to remain silent on everything he had divulged so as to not alarm my crewmates prior to our time of departure. I readily agreed.

Chapter 22: Voudou Ceremonies

Yet another unique feature of Saint Domingue was the strange religious beliefs of the slaves that had been forcibly brought to the isle. Rue became both my instructor and informer on this very sensitive subject. It was not the Voudou ceremonies that offended the island's rulers, but more the fear of revolt and reprisal. To avoid a slave revolt, the government had long ago outlawed slave gatherings of any sort, including religious meetings. However, Rue confessed the Voudou rites were still practiced in secret on a regular basis. She said that if anyone was caught practicing Voudou, the penalty was death.

Rue was fully aware of these secret ceremonies and had actually attended several to quench her own curiosity. She confided that there was a scheduled Voudou ceremony that very evening that she intended to attend. Well, I can tell you that my curiosity was peaked by her words, so I begged her to allow me to join her. Her initial reaction was to deny me this opportunity for a number of reasons, such as my telltale white skin and my inability to understand or speak the language of the slaves.

I was very persistent in my desire to attend this secret conclave. I informed Rue that I could create a complete disguise that would fool the attending zealots. I promised to adopt the island's slave dress in place of my slops. I also admitted that a mixture of tar, ashes and soot would enable me to temporarily darken my normal skin tone. I reminded her that ceremonies were held only at night, which would further mask my disguise attempt. As to the language issue, I reasoned that she could easily act as my translator for any words being spoken. Finally, I stated that I fully understood the high risks and would avoid any type of issue that might put either of us in jeopardy. Rue reluctantly agreed to my accompanying her that night. However, she emphatically forewarned me that should trouble arise for any reason at all that I would be on my own to sort out a solution. I agreed wholeheartedly with this sentiment, and we set a time for later that evening to rendezvous.

To prepare my disguise, I borrowed a set of clothes from a drunken mulatto, who was using a deserted pond to bathe. Finding some soot, tar and ash in a long abandoned shack, I made the necessary transformation from European sailor to island slave. The end result was rather stunning and I even surprised myself as I surveyed my final effort in a reflecting pool just outside the shack. While the disguise was not perfect, it was very good indeed. So good, that when I met up with Rue at our prearranged meeting site she did not recognize me at all.

The sun finally set and Rue and I made our way away from Shantytown into the wooded interior of the island. We covered a vast distance inland before I began to hear a rhythmic drumbeat announcing the secret location of the Voudou ceremony. The clearing was actually very large and there were already a large number of slaves present. Rue and I made our way directly into the throng to the persistent drumbeat announcing the onset of the ceremony. Most of the women were dressed in flowing white robes like the one that Rue sported. The men were dressed in various costumes of all sorts. In the middle of the clearing a huge roaring fire was aglow to provide light. To one side of the fire, there were several men beating an unusual rhythm on the drums that they had brought. Rue informed me that the chief priest for the ceremony was the tall individual in front of the fire. He was a self-ordained *houngan*. Like the congregation, he was frolicking and reeling around the fire in a strange ritualistic dance to the steady beat of the drums.

Rue whispered that each ceremony opened with a prayer to a spirit intermediary called a *loa*. These *loa* were not gods but rather ambassadors between the worshipers and their gods. Rue whispered that we needed to mimic the worshipers all around us, so we both began the slow stomping dance swaying to the beat of the hypnotizing drums. All at once the *houngan* held up both of his hands and all present came to a complete stop listening to his voice accompanied by the ever-present drumbeat. Rue whispered that the *houngan* was calling a *loa* named Papa Legba in order to officially open the sacred ceremony. At the same time, I happened to glance to my right and spotted my friend Ding-Dong prancing back and forth among the crowd. He seemed almost completely healed and healthy compared to the very miserable condition that I had originally found him.

But he was not alone at all! Right by his side was a very small, dark-skinned man, who was bent and crooked with age. Wearing a wide grin, this smiling dwarf had an old pipe in his mouth and a straw bag of some sort by his side. Limping and swaying to the drumbeat, the old man used an ancient twisted cane to hold himself erect. He wore no shoes and his red shirt and brown pants were tattered to the extreme. I thought this individual to be a strange companion for my friend, Ding-Dong. As the *houngan* continued his chant, which was now being answered by the surrounding throng, Ding-Dong lifted his eyes to me in recognition and bounded over to my side. I bent down to ruffle the scruff of his neck, being rewarded with licks and happy whines. The little old man was now standing right by my side smiling and gibbering to me in a language that I could not understand. Watching me intently, the old man seemed to realize that his words had little or no meaning. To my complete surprise, he suddenly switched to speaking French, again all of this going unnoticed by everyone surrounding me, including Rue. The old man told me that his name was Papa Legba and that he was very happy to make my acquaintance. He asked if I was the kindhearted sailor who had taken care of his companion. I responded that I was indeed. He again thanked me profusely for my assistance and the kindness that I had shown the creature. I answered that Ding-Dong needed the help desperately and that I was more than happy to be able to assist.

At this point, the *houngan* called out something in a very loud voice, causing the strange old man to straighten up somewhat. He then informed me that he had to leave for a while but would return later. I glanced up to see what the *houngan* was doing and when I looked back both Papa Legba and Ding-Dong were gone. It seemed to me that they had just disappeared into the crowd around me. As I directed my stare forward once again, the *houngan* seemed pleased for he too wore a huge grin as he changed his chant one more time. This seemed to be the signal for the faithful to resume dancing. Rue whispered that the ceremony was officially opened and it was time for sacrifices to be made to honor the gods.

Looking up I witnessed the *houngan*, Rue called him Boulongo, accept a black rooster from a nearby worshiper. Boulongo then twirled the black rooster by the neck over his head. The crowd seemed to sense something was about to occur, because the drumbeat got considerably louder and the dancing a bit more frantic. Finally, Boulongo stopped the chant and the twirling of the fowl. The dead, limp bird was carried over to a nearby table that had a variety of strange objects placed on it, including beads, a square cross, feathers, sticks, Spanish Moss and what appeared to me to be rum bottles. Rue whispered that Boulongo was placing the offering on the Voudou altar as thanks to the gods.

The next stage of the ceremony involved couples dancing with each other in a way I had never witnessed before. The couples formed two lines in front of the fire, with women in one and men in the other. The dance started slowly with both sexes raising and lowering their feet, successively stomping the ground, accelerating over time. Then the women danced around their male counterparts, all waving red handkerchiefs. Simultaneously, the men raised and lowered their arms with their elbows tucked to their sides with hands closed. This continued in a faster and faster rhythm that was both lively and highly animated. Then, suddenly the dance transformed back to the original two separate lines with each partner stepping to and away from each other while clapping their hands in a rhythmic and volatile fashion. This must have been the signal the crowd waited for. They immediately joined in with their own rhythmic handclapping and chanting. The dance continued in this manner faster and faster with the worshippers mimicking the speed and beat of the drums. I noticed that some of the faithful were dancing themselves into insensibility.

Finally Boulongo called for a brief respite to the hysteria, and he took a long swig from one of the many rum bottles sitting on the altar. Rue told me that the rum drink was called *clairin*, which was a very potent mixture of strong rum that had been steeped in red hot peppers. Rue told me that being so potent, the *clairin* was an acquired taste that would cause first-time drinkers to gag, cough and choke incessantly due to its powerful nature. Well, it sure did not seem to bother Boulongo, who took yet another healthy swig of the peppered rum to the roar of the faithful. Rue told me that it was now time for another ceremonial offering, a white goat. Boulongo seemed to be praying over the animal. After his silent incantations, he reached down with a huge knife and slit the animal's throat to the utter delight of his worshippers.

Dancing and clapping began once again along with more fits of frenzy, trembling, fainting and swooning. Meanwhile, Boulongo collected the goat's blood from the gaping neck wound. All at once, a storm that had been brewing broke with flashes of lightning accompanied by booming thunder, but the ceremony continued as if nothing out of the ordinary was occurring. Gusting winds and torrential rains followed, but the drums kept beating and the dancing continued. Branches were torn from trees surrounding the clearing and thrown to the ground with such force that the ground actually shook, but the ceremony continued. In the midst of all of this natural violence, I stood rooted in place seized by a strange mind-numbing fear and amazement. My entire body was shaking and shivering, and I had no power to stop it! Then with a loud whoop and a cry, Boulongo raised his bloody hands in supplication and everything came to a complete standstill, even the storm seemed to abate at the *houngan*'s firm command!

Rue turned to me suggesting that this might be an excellent opportunity to make our exit, but I was so taken by the entire experience that I begged her for just a few moments more. At the same time, I felt a strange presence nearby and looked down to find both Papa Legba and Ding-Dong back at my side. Papa Legba asked me if I enjoyed the taste of rum, knowing full well that most sailors certainly did. I answered that I much preferred the taste of lemonade, which brought another huge grin to his face. Papa Legba then warned me to relax and enjoy what was about to happen. He promised that no harm whatsoever would befall me. Totally confused by his words, something very strange ensued that even to this day I have a hard time describing and an even tougher time understanding. All at once, Boulongo emitted a shrieking wail that was echoed by all of the worshippers. Papa Legba and Ding-Dong seemed to disappear into midair, and I felt like a charging bull had driven full force into me. I hit the ground very hard, and heard Rue at my side questioning if I was all right. I answered her that I was fine in a very unfamiliar language, and she just stared at me as if I had lost my mind. Regaining my feet once again, I looked around to spot my new friends, but only caught sight of Ding-Dong, who was now tightly pressed against my leg. The faithful were now screaming and chanting some new prayer, and to my amazement I found that I had joined them echoing the exact tone, cadence and words…matching them precisely. Rue went white with fright, and her eyes were almost bulging out of her head in abject terror as she continued to stare in my direction. Then all of a sudden I began to dance…the same dance displayed by the altar couples! I could not control my movements whatsoever. It was as if someone else was in control of my body and I was a mere passenger.

I danced faster and faster and chanted louder and louder in the strange and garbled tongue of the faithful. Again, without having any control, I began to move in the direction of the altar. Rue tried to stop me from leaving her, but she had as much luck as I had trying to stop myself from proceeding…none whatsoever! I was now in full motion, arms and legs whirling with my hands clapping furiously. Shouting and screaming words that I could not understand, I made my way through the now parting worshippers moving directly to the Voudou altar. Issuing a series of unintelligible commands to Boulongo, I hefted a full bottle of *clairin* and swilled the entire bottle! At this moment, a part of me believed that this was certainly my end. I expected that any second the worshipping crowd would descend on me and tear me apart for defiling their sacred service. I was in abject shock when instead the entire worshipping congregation crowded all around me trying to reach out and touch any part of me. At this point Boulongo shouted a chant that was echoed by the congregation and answered by me. Both men and women were fainting and falling flat on their faces as I made my way to the newly slaughtered goat. I took a full cup of the goat's blood from Boulongo and proceeded to swig the entire disgusting fluid. Although totally nauseated by the thought of what I had just done, I actually enjoyed the warm salty tasting liquid.

I then raised the empty cup to the congregation shouting some kind of command to them. Whatever I actually said had to be very powerful indeed for it stopped the drums and forced everyone in attendance to drop to a prostrate position, shivering and trembling. Ding-Dong's excited barking was the only sound I heard throughout the entire clearing. Still not in control of my actions, I made my way back to the altar in a limping sort of shuffle and proceeded to gulp down a second bottle of the very potent peppered rum, while I toasted the *houngan* and his followers in the strange dialect I had somehow mastered. This act was again greeted by an almost hysterical cheering from the faithful. Gratified by their reaction, I once again danced my way back to Rue's side collapsing completely at her feet.

Prostrate in front of Rue, I felt the hot moist tongue of my friend Ding-Dong as he whined, barked and licked my face furiously. Finally I felt my normal strength and control flow back into my body. I could now move by my own volition, and I stood to find Papa Legba standing directly in front of me wearing his now familiar grin. The first question he asked me was how I enjoyed the *clairin*. I told him that it seemed very powerful but at the same time very delicious. At that point, Rue, staring directly at me asked exactly who I was talking to about the altar rum. I answered that I was conversing with my new friend, Papa Legba. That answer made her gasp in total astonishment as she crossed herself with her now trembling hand. She then asked me to describe Papa Legba to her, which I proceeded to do in great detail. After fully detailing my wizened old friend to her, I questioned her need of the description since the old rascal was standing right in front of us both. Trembling and shaking almost uncontrollably, she just kept staring at me as if I was a total madman!

Papa Legba once again thanked me for my kind assistance with Ding-Dong. He then disclosed that he had a very special gift for me, and removed a stringed necklace that he was wearing under his red shirt. Attached to this string loop was a square wooden cross which he then gently placed over my head. He informed me that this was his special symbol. He also proclaimed that the cross would always protect me as long as I kept it around my neck. He confessed that I was now very special to him, and that he would help me whenever I needed his assistance. All I had to do was close my eyes and call his name three times and he would come to my aid no matter the situation. With that he gave me one of his huge grins, winked and disappeared all over again. I searched around me but there was absolutely no sign of him or Ding-Dong. They had both simply vanished right before my eyes!

Looking over in Rue's direction, I found her lying face flat on the ground in a completely motionless state. I ran over to ensure that she was not injured in any way. As I reached her side, she slowly arose and was shaking her head as if to clear out the cobwebs from her recent fainting spell. She asked me if Papa Legba was still present, and I told her that he and Ding-Dong had just vanished from sight. Shaken and as white as a ghost, she pleaded with me to return to Shantytown, which I agreed to immediately. Meanwhile, the ceremony had resumed with drums and chants as we backed our way out through the worshippers. Nobody seemed to take notice of us as we made our way slowly back to the edge of the forest, finally melting into the thick foliage. With Rue leading the way, we headed back to town in the same manner as we had arrived. About halfway back, Rue suddenly stopped and began questioning me about my recent strange encounter. I described the experience from start to finish with as much detail as I could recall. When I concluded, she begged me to show her the good luck charm that Papa Legba had provided. Pulling the square wooden cross out from under my shirt, I let her furiously trembling hands hold and inspect the object as it dangled on the string necklace around my neck, She kept shaking her head repeating the same word over and over again…*Impossible…Impossible… Impossible!*

At this point, Rue sat us both down and proceeded to enlighten me to the mystery, but at the same time communicated information that confused and confounded me all the more. She informed me that Papa Legba was a very important *loa* in the Voudou religion. She declared that he was the only *loa* with the power to open or close the door to the spirit world. His earthly appearance was said to be exactly as I had described him to her. She also proclaimed that sometimes he was seen accompanied by a spirit familiar in the form of a mangy old mutt, just as I had described Ding-Dong. One of his significant symbols was a square cross exactly like the talisman I was now wearing around my neck.

I was at a loss to understand her explanations, but I did have several questions for her. The primary question I needed answering was what had prompted my strange behavior at the ceremony. To this query, Rue laughed and began explaining. Rue informed me that the Voudou religion held a strong belief that during a ceremony a *loa* could actually enter a person's body and mind. Once this happened, it was believed that the *loa* took total control of that individual. Having accomplished this feat, that same individual could do and say things that were totally foreign to that person's self. During this experience, an individual was trapped like a prisoner and for a short time had to abide totally with the *loa*'s whims. As she completed this last statement, I thought back to the ceremony and had to agree that it surely explained the feelings and sensations that I experienced while speaking in a strange tongue, drinking powerful rum, performing ritualistic dances and quaffing fresh goat's blood…all things that I had never done before in my life.

But her words made absolutely no sense to me at all. Rue, however, was totally convinced that I had actually experienced a Voudou spirit takeover. Beyond that, she believed that somehow I had gained Papa Legba's favor, making me one of his favorites, which would bless me with good fortune beyond any riches that I had ever dreamed! How could any of this be true? After all, what really happened was a chance encounter with a friendly old man, who merely wished to thank me for the kind assistance I had shown his mutt. In return for this favor, he had given me a good luck charm that now dangled around my neck. I shared this logic with Rue but she remained totally convinced that there was much more to the encounter than I was willing to accept. At the end of our disagreement, she asked me two very simple questions. First, *"How do you explain your ability to communicate in the right language and dialect to the assembled worshippers?"* The second question stopped me cold and gave me more than pause to consider. *"How did I enjoy the clairin, since I was known to be a confirmed lemonade drinker?"*

Chapter 23: Rue's Plight

Returning to the Palace, it seemed little had occurred in our absence. Taking the Voudou talisman into my hands, I knew that I had yet another choice to make. The choice facing me was whether or not to continue wearing the square cross. While not able to comprehend the full meaning of the *loa*'s gift, I did realize that the talisman might prove useful in the future. To tell you the truth, I had no real reason to believe otherwise. Conscious of this small weight around my neck and the warm sensation it seemed to emit close to my heart, I wore the *loa* amulet inside my shirt and tried to put it out of my mind. Handy happened to notice my persistent handling of the wooden cross and was quick to question my reason for wearing it. I informed him that a local priest had blessed the cross personally. Its sole purpose, I informed him, was to keep me safe from drowning. This brought a huge smile from my friend, who instructed me to make sure that I kept this special charm close and in my possession at all times. He congratulated me on finally acting like an *old salt*!

The good news on our return to the Palace was that Mr. Bass was conspicuously absent due to the seriousness of the injuries he had sustained in the *battle royale*. He was still nursing these injuries aboard the *Amafata*, while he supervised the mean and dirty job of careening our ship. Frequent careening was an absolute necessity for any ship spending time in saltwater. The reason for this very unpleasant chore could be evidenced the moment a ship was hauled over on its side at low tide. Various marine organisms like barnacles stowedaway on a ship's hull as it sailed the various sea lanes of the world. These clinging barnacles severely lessened any ship's nautical speed and maneuverability, if left to populate on the hull unchecked. The first step in the careening process was to scrape these stubborn freeloaders off of the hull as the ship lay beached on its side. When I say stubborn, I mean they went far beyond merely hanging onto a ship's underside…they seemed anchored in place! The second task of careening was to closely inspect the ship's beached hull for any evidence of rot caused by nasty sea worms, which could easily bore their way into even the stoutest English Oak and transform it into mushy sponge-like material. Once any damage of this sort was discovered, these mushy spots would be attended to by Chips to either be repaired or replaced with new wood. The third and last step of the careening process was to drive *oakum*, pulled and separated hemp twine fibers soaked in tar, into any visible hole, crack or crevice. The *oakum* was then sealed into place by a thick covering of hot tar in order to prevent future leaks.

Upon my return to the ship the next morning, I was alerted by Handy that Mr. Bass had graciously added my name to the careening duty roster. For the next three long days, I was totally absorbed in this backbreaking labor, battling enemy barnacles and sea worms, while forced to breathe the noxious fumes emanating from the ever-present pitch pots. Mr. Bass, his arm splinted and his damaged eye covered by a black patch, stood in the shade of a lone palm tree as he supervised our work to ensure that it met the high standards he always demanded. At the end of this duty, I was physically exhausted with many more aches and pains than I care to describe. Finally, finished with this demanding task, I was given shore leave once again. Preparing for my liberty, I took a quick sea bath, and washed my *slops* to remove the worst of the careening tar residue that had taken temporary residence. Completing these preparations, I made my way back to Shantytown to visit Rue. Striding into the Palace, I was greeted by the regular patrons, who seemed delighted to have me back in the fold. A quick scan of the first floor of the Palace produced no sighting of Rue. When I inquired about her, I was told by her mother that the girl had suddenly taken ill and was currently resting in her room upstairs. Noting the concern that must have dominated my face, Madame La Montaine informed me that I could visit with her when she next awoke. For the interim, I wandered the premises catching up on all the latest *scuttlebutt* while I waited for my chance to visit Rue.

An eternity seemed to pass before Madame La Montaine suddenly appeared announcing that the time for my visit had arrived. Accompanying me upstairs to the owner's suite of rooms, I was as anxious as a sailor about to be served his daily rum ration. Opening a small door to her secluded room, I was greeted by Rue, who appeared considerably different than the last time I had been with her. She was deathly pale and suffering from some unknown malady that left her weak and trembling. As soon as her mother left the room, Rue reached out for my hand, which I more than gladly supplied.

She informed me that our presence at the Voudou ceremony did not go unnoticed. The day following our uninvited visit, a strange package was delivered to the tavern addressed to Rue. Shakily, she pointed over to a small chest, instructing me that the lone object atop the chest was the only item in the package. She told me that it was a Voudou curse doll. She spat out that she believed that this strange-looking object was the cause of her sudden sickness. Believing the whole story to be utter nonsense, I jumped up to personally inspect the offending object. The item was rather small and was crudely fashioned out of a variety of materials. These included cloth made to resemble crude clothing on the doll's frame, feathers, beads, buttons and such. The doll had a rough hand-sculpted face with a mass of Spanish moss serving as hair. Had it not been for the abject terror in Rue's face, I would have surely burst out in a fit of laughter upon my first scrutiny of this ridiculous looking fetish.

However, Rue was in utter terror, so I waited in silence with a blank expression on my face for her to continue her strange explanation. She informed me that this curse doll represented the work of Voudou black magic. Fashioned by a high priest, this abomination served to magically represent a victim's physical form. Using magic, a *houngan* could inflict damage to this carelessly crafted image that would be transferred directly to the individual represented by the curse doll. Rue informed me that her severe pains had begun at the exact moment she had unwrapped the unholy icon. Rue also confessed that she firmly believed that this malignant curse would eventually lead to her death unless the powerful spell was somehow broken. With these words, she broke down completely into hysterical sobs that seemed to tear me apart internally!

I now questioned the hysterical girl as to exactly how this insidious curse could be broken. In a loud sobbing wail, she explained that the only way to break the curse doll's magic was to somehow force the Voudou priest to remove the curse entirely. When this occurred, the wicked spell would be broken forever by destroying the curse doll in a hot blazing flame. Realizing the utter futility of this action, Rue lapsed into uncontrollable agonizing wails just as her mother returned to the room.

Believing my presence as the cause of her daughter's distraught state, she quickly ushered me from the room and back to the company of my friends on the main floor. I spent the next several hours pondering this dilemma. I knew in my heart that I loved Rue, and would do anything within my power to see her regain her health. The question I struggled with was how exactly I might go about attaining this solution!

I needed some solitude in which to think and work out a strategy that had some hope of achieving success. Worried and fighting off sheer panic, I made my way out of the confines of the tavern and wandered aimlessly through the streets of Shantytown as I pondered every possible solution. Eventually I found the peace and solitude I had been searching for in the local cemetery. Perched on one of the larger burial crypts, I thought back in detail to the previous Voudou ceremony. Then, like a bolt of lightning, I remembered the tale about zombies that I had listened to aboard the *Amafata*! Thinking hard about this story, I hatched a very crazy idea. The more I thought about the plan that was now forming in my mind, the more I liked the insane scheme that I had devised.

Running back to the Palace, I stealthily made my way back to Rue's room to obtain more information vital to seeing my plan reach fruition. Rue was still awake and quickly apologized for her mournful outburst. Comforting her with kind words, I provided her with a brief outline of the plan I had just conceived. Buoyed by my positive outlook, Rue smiled and genuinely thanked me for my assistance. I informed her that I required the time and the place for the next scheduled Voudou rite. She told me that her slave friends had informed her that the next ceremony would take place the very next evening in the same location as the one we had both attended. So that I could actually relocate this site, Rue proceeded to draw a rough map that would lead me back to the dreaded clearing. Accepting the map, I gave my love a big kiss and promised that everything would return to normal quite soon. Wearing a mask of doubt and fear, she reluctantly wished me luck with my venture and gave me one more kiss to seal the bargain. I snatched the curse doll at her side and ran from her room to begin my lengthy preparations.

The first of my necessary steps involved following Rue's crude map back to the ceremonial clearing where the next Voudou rite would be held. I needed to inspect this site in the daylight to finalize a few necessary details. Finding the secluded glen was not too difficult given Rue's implicit instructions. Working feverishly, I completed my required tasks and by midday was back aboard the *Amafata*. I desperately needed an assistant to help perpetuate my ruse. Aware that Jonah Jemme owed me a great debt, I approached my friend and informed him of my troubles. Once he was fully briefed on the severity of the situation, I launched into the details of exactly what I had planned in order to reverse the curse and destroy the Voudou doll. I laid out the role I required him to play in the charade I had planned, and he eagerly agreed to help. Gratified by his immediate acceptance, I gave him the instructions that he would be required to follow in order to successfully play his part in our upcoming mission. He made a mental note of the things he needed to do, and was off in a flash to begin his own preparations.

Having Jonah Jemme on my side lightened my mood considerably as I initiated my final preparations. By the next morning, both Jonah Jemme and I were done with our preparatory chores and the plan began in earnest. During the day, we revisited the Voudou clearing to familiarize Jemme with its layout and the exact sequence of crucial steps each of us would enact. Just prior to sundown, we concealed ourselves in nearby hiding places awaiting the arrival of the Voudou faithful and the start of the ceremony.

As darkness fell around my hiding place the worshippers began to assemble to the steady beat of the drums. Finally, after a long intolerable wait, Boulongo made his grand entrance. Similar to my last visit, the Voudou ceremony proceeded in the same fashion. As a white goat was finally led before Boulongo to be dispatched in ritualistic offering, I readied myself for action. I was all nerves as I waited for the right moment to take action, knowing that if my ploy failed both my life and Jemme's would be in serious jeopardy from the rabid worshipers that surrounded us. Judging the time to be right, I slowly came out of concealment. I was attired in exactly the same fashion as my friendly *loa* spirit, Papa Legba, complete with blackened face and arms, brown breeches, red shirt, twisted walking cane and woven straw basket at my side. The only prop that was missing was Papa's faithful companion, Ding-Dong. Sensing a strange presence at my side, I stole a glance down and was absolutely shocked to find Ding-Dong suddenly by my side, matching my every step. Like being struck by a bolt of lightning, I suddenly had the strange sensation of being run over by a horse as I lost complete control of my normal bodily functions.

My new host was in complete charge of my person and I was now merely a spectator. As I neared the rear of the congregation, I realized that my body had once again been overtaken by the friendly *loa*, who I was attempting to impersonate. I then called out in their strange and guttural tongue that Papa Legba had decided to honor their celebration. While I was unaware of exactly what I was spouting, I guessed by the reactions of the surrounding faithful what the main messages conveyed. In a loud and thunderous voice, I made it clear that I was quite upset with their *houngan*'s behavior. By this time, the drums had ceased to beat and the wide-eyed audience was falling prostrate on their faces at my steady advance. At my pronouncement, all eyes turned to stare at Boulongo, who appeared to be quite terrified by my sudden presence. In the same unfamiliar speech, I informed the assemblage that my reason for anger centered on the black magic that the *houngan* had used to harm an innocent island child. I held the curse doll high above my head to illustrate this point. I further demanded that the *houngan* remove the evil spell he had placed on the doll to bring harm on a guiltless child. These words caused Boulongo to further quake, frozen now in utter fear. Striding up to the terrified *houngan*, I raised the offending doll over my head screaming all manner of strange threats and obscenities.

With that I shoved the doll into Boulongo's hands demanding that he remove the black magic curse immediately. Shakily accepting the doll from my hands, the *houngan* immediately began a series of incantations that would strip away the black magic he had created. Once finished, Boulongo held the evil icon out for me to accept. I took the doll from his quaking fingers, and heaved it directly into the raging ceremonial fire. This demonstrative action brought a roar of approval from the crowd, as they now raised themselves to their feet to witness any other actions I might make in their presence. I signaled the worshippers to complete silence one more time, as I once again confronted Boulongo. I continued to rant and rave at the spiritual leader who was cowed entirely by my verbal onslaught.

Suddenly, I was back in control of my physical form. While I was fully aware that Papa Legba's valued assistance had expedited the accomplishment of my vital mission, I decided to continue on with the remainder of my planned ruse out of both pure enjoyment and spite. The terrified worshippers now awaited my commands and without hesitation I shouted the words Zombie Jemme over and over. Rising from a shallow grave that we had previously dug at the edge of the clearing, Jemme shambled and stumbled his way to my side. He was totally nude except for a small cloth covering his privates. To affect his horrifying visage, I had mixed some crushed limestone with ash to form a grey-white color. This mixture had been applied to Jonah Jemme's entire body producing the death-like color of a corpse. To enhance the effect, I had used a black ash coloring directly below his eyes, which were crossed and hideous in appearance. As a final touch, I had used some red paint mixed with more ash to create huge weeping sores all over his body. The effect of this stunning disguise was truly amazing, so much so that even I shivered in fear whenever I happened to glance in Zombie Jemme's direction.

Once we had attained the full horrifying effect of the zombie ruse on the faithful, I whispered to Jemme that it was time to leave. With that I directed the stumbling Zombie Jemme to accompany my departure. Limping along with my horrifying creation and Ding-Dong still at my side, we made our way back to the edge of the forest and disappeared into its dense covering. As we disappeared from sight, I was gratified to hear the drums resume their steady beat signifying the ceremony had resumed. I knew this element was vital in order to prevent any curious onlookers from attempting to follow us.

Once out of sight, Zombie Jemme and I broke into a full run to put as much distance between us and the Voudou faithful as possible. When we were far enough away from the assemblage, we eased our pace and subsequently broke out in hysterical laughter. We continued our yelling and laughing until we reached a fast-moving forest stream that we had scouted the previous day. Here Zombie Jemme and I stripped off our costumes and completely washed off our body paint that had served us so well in the Voudou deception. Locating our *slops* that we had also previously hidden by this stream, we both got dressed. Our final act was to bury each of our disguises in a hole I had prepared for this exact purpose. Returned to a normal appearance, we made our way quickly back to Shantytown and safety. One thing I did notice was that Ding-Dong was no longer at my side when we reached the cleansing stream. He had simply disappeared somewhere along our escape route. I mouthed a small private prayer of thanks for his and his owner's assistance as well as the success we had achieved. Jemme told me that he had to return to the *Amafata* to perform a myriad of chores for Mr. Bass. As we parted, I gave him a big brotherly hug and thanked him profusely for the excellent role he had played that evening. Laughing and smiling, he told me that he was gratified to be able to assist me in this haunting endeavor.

I ran the remainder of the way to Shantytown to check on the fate of my dear Rue. Entering the Palace, I was surprised to find Rue back at her usual duties of serving drinks to the drunken rabble. Her normal color had returned and she was all smiles and laughter. As our eyes met, she halted mid-step and gave me the most entrancing smile that I had ever experienced in my life. She sprinted across the room and flew into my arms. Kissing and hugging me in total elation, she informed me that the curse had been lifted. She was curious for more detail, and I promised to provide all the particulars of the deception that I had engineered as soon as we were alone. I told her that I would meet her in the old Shantytown cemetery when she could successfully break away from her bartending duties. She gave me a parting bow of thanks and skipped her way back behind the bar to continue her customary role.

Needing some time alone to collect my thoughts and regain my composure, I made my way outside. Walking at a slow and deliberate pace, I returned to the deserted Shantytown cemetery. As I sat musing about the details of this evening's antics, I had to laugh at the deception I had masterminded.

A while later, Rue made her appearance. With a whoop of joy, she rushed into my waiting arms. We spent the next few minutes in tender embrace, trading kisses and loving words of endearment with each other. After a time, she pleaded with me to relate all that had occurred earlier that evening. Taking my time so as to not omit any detail, I related the story of the entire episode from start to finish. As I related the tale, I sensed a pronounced change in Rue. She seemed to be looking at me in a different light altogether…one of adoring love! She kissed me long and tenderly at the conclusion of my narration. Taking the lead, for I had no prior experience with the act of love, she directed my every movement as we spent the remainder of the evening atop the burial crypt. We experienced ultimate and exquisite pleasure with each other in ways that I could never have imagined. Having finally exhausted our carnal appetites, we both fell into a deep sleep in each other's arms.

Waking to the call of a nearby rooster I was a bit surprised to discover that Rue had left my side. She had probably risen earlier and returned to her home at the Palace. With a smile on my face and feeling like I was walking on air, I made my way back to the *Amafata*. Hungrily wolfing down a meal that Handy had hastily prepared at my appearance, I proclaimed that I was in love with Rue. Winking in my direction, he informed me that the strong stirrings I now felt were the most wondrous sensations that any man could ever experience. He was very happy for me, but was just as quick to point out that our layover in Saint Domingue was nearing an end. A bit discouraged by this last statement, I continued to bask in the euphoric mood that my marvelous time with Rue had produced.

Chapter 24: Anchor Aweigh

After getting some much needed rest, I was awakened by a series of loud voices and very expressive cursing coming from the topdeck. After stowing my hammock, I made my way above. My friend, Jemme, was in deep trouble one more time! This was certainly nothing new to him, but his latest incident had induced Mr. Bass into a vile and murderous rage. Jemme had inadvertently left a hatch cover open on the maindeck as he was called away to perform a quick chore for the Captain. Mr. Bass, still suffering from impaired vision due to his tussle with Lion, had not spotted the open hatch and had blindly stepped right into it. He sustained a very wicked blow to his recently broken arm. Screaming and cursing furiously Mr. Bass was helped to the Doc's surgery once again for immediate treatment. Completely paled in abject pain and suffering, he made the sailors assisting him below stop as they neared Jemme. In a terse whisper, he promised the lad a slow and agonizing death once we resumed our voyage.

Jemme approached me in a state of near hysteria begging me to help him out of this latest predicament. Unsure as to what he should do, he quickly came to the realization that he had to flee the ship in order to avoid the promised painful death at the hands of his feared nemesis. He informed me that he planned on abandoning his post in order to take refuge on Saint Domingue. The problems he faced in making this decision were many, but he was more than willing to face them compared to the ugly fate that awaited him at the hands of his evil taskmaster. I ordered Jemme to lay very low, and encouraged him to find a hiding spot in the hold until the sun went down. This, I continued, would give me time to set a plan of action in place. With these final words, he scampered off to find a hiding spot in his least favorite place on the ship…the hold!

Finishing up my onboard assigned duties, I prepared to make one final visit to Shantytown to arrange Jemme's escape. As I made my way to the upperdeck, I was greeted by yet another unexpected commotion breaking out above me. Reaching the maindeck, I was greeted by the strange sight of three unusual-looking women arriving at our ship in a small rowboat that was manned by several slaves. They were all very ancient in appearance, covered from head to toe in dark flowing robes of some sort. Bent and wizened, they slowly navigated the boarding ladder to our ship. Once aboard, they all croaked out in unison that they needed an immediate audience with our Captain. Recognizing them from the Captain's recent descriptions, I made my way over to them and introduced myself. They responded in eerie cackling laughter that they were Gertrude, Willamina and Hortence Adams. Taking the initiative, I immediately ushered these three curious crones to the Captain's quarters. Greeted at the door by our Captain, he instantaneously invited the sisters inside his quarters for a private discussion. As I swiveled to return to the main deck, the Captain stopped me and invited me to join him.

Once we were all settled inside the Captain's cabin, the three sisters launched breathlessly into the news they were so determined to relate. In a frightened and agitated state, the sisters informed us that they had been warned by nameless sources that a slave uprising on the island was imminent.

Because of this dire threat, all three sisters had opted to make the trek to convince us of the necessity to move up our departure. The Captain listened intently, and agreed at once that it was time to make our speedy departure. He instructed the sisters to return home and pack any personal valuables they wished to transport on the upcoming voyage. He informed me that I was to personally accompany the sisters and to assist them in these preparations, announcing that we would sail in a day's time. I accompanied the sisters from his quarters to assist in any way that I could. However, prior to rowing back to the docks, I paid a visit to Jemme's hiding place in the hold to alert him of these new developments. I instructed the unlucky lad to accompany me in my assigned task, which would surely allow us an opportunity to complete his planned desertion. Jemme needed no further urging on my part as we made our way back to shore with the Adams sisters.

Once we arrived at the sisters' rented abode, they hurried inside to mobilize their departure preparations. Jemme and I left immediately and made our way to Shantytown, where I arranged for the hire of a suitable transport wagon for the evening. Once this necessary chore was accomplished, Jemme and I quickly made our way to the Palace to arrange for my friend's disappearance. Instructing Jemme to remain at the back of the establishment, I made my way inside to locate Rue. My beloved was thrilled to see me enter and immediately made her way over to my side. I informed her that I desperately required her help in a matter, and she told me to meet her outside. It took a while, but eventually she joined me outside, running up to me and delivering a very amorous kiss. Enjoying the moment completely, I almost forgot entirely about my intended mission.

While both shocked and saddened by my news of our impending departure, Rue promised me that she would take Jemme into her care and personally see to his protection. I warned her that Mr. Bass would likely order a search party to be sent to recover the lad once it was discovered that he was missing. She laughed and commanded me to stop worrying because she had an absolutely perfect place to hide Jemme until the time our ship sailed. She confided that it was the least she could do to repay Jemme for the important role he played in her recent deliverance. I handed her a small leather pouch crammed with coins that I had secretly accumulated from my cockfighting wagering. Rue was extremely reluctant to accept this money. She finally relented when I pointed out that this wealth could be utilized to garner any assistance she might require from her mother in seeing to the care and nurturing of our mutual friend. Thinking hard about my argument, she finally smiled and agreed that the money would certainly smooth the way for Jemme with Madame La Montaigne.

Lastly, I expressed my concern for her safety should the rumored slave revolt actually take place. Again she laughed at my unnecessary worrying; informing me that she had numerous friends among the slave population on the island. I embraced Rue tenderly giving her a parting passionate kiss. I then promised her that I would return to Saint Domingue one day very soon to make her my wife. With tears of both joy and sadness running in streams down her face, she wished me luck and good fortune until the day that I returned to her loving arms. With our promises made, I turned and quickly made my way back to the home of the Adams sisters to assist in any last-minute departure preparations.

Back at the Adams sisters' leased residence, I was astounded to discover that the transport wagon was now fully loaded with the sisters' valuables. Without further delay, we made a hasty retreat to our ship. Upon reaching the docks, we were met by the ship's transport dinghy that transferred the sisters' goods to our waiting vessel. As we rowed out toward our anchored ship, we were greeted by an ominous sight far up in the hills that overlooked the town. A huge fiery blaze was visible to us all, proclaiming by its very existence that the rumored slave revolt had actually begun. Although a good distance away, we could plainly see a large mansion in the midst of blazing destruction.

Reaching the *Amafata*, I was not at all surprised to find the crew in full-scale madness as they made preparations to sail. Crewmen were scurrying in all directions, including into each other! I joined the melee, assisting with the loading and stowing of the Adams sisters' belongings. As we all went about our assigned duties, we would pause from time to time to view the massive conflagration in the hills above the town. At the bell sounding midwatch…midnight to you landlubbers…Mr. Bass approached me and casually inquired as to the whereabouts of Jemme. Acting totally surprised and shocked, I informed him that I had ordered him back to the *Amafata* long ago. With a narrowed glance in my direction, Mr. Bass informed me that Jemme had not yet returned to the ship. Acting totally confused and stymied, I reconfirmed that we had parted ways many hours ago.

Summoning three sturdy crewmembers, Mr. Bass ordered them to form a search party to locate and drag the missing lad back to the ship. He stated that they had only until dawn to conclude their search efforts, since our ship was scheduled to sail at daybreak with the next favorable tide. He further warned the three sailors that pain and hardship would result if they failed in their search effort. With fearful and anxious expressions, the search party was dispatched.

As I once again turned to survey the huge fire burning in the hills, the Captain made an unexpected appearance at my side signaling for a moment of my time. Nodding acknowledgment, I followed in the Captain's wake as he navigated his way back to his cabin. Apprehensive at the prospect of being questioned further on Jemme's disappearance, I was more than relieved when the Captain announced that he had a special assignment for me. He then inquired if I would act as his *eyes and ears* in the matter of the Adams sisters. Calling me a very resourceful lad, he requested that I keep a close watch on these strange passengers to avoid any difficulties whatsoever with the rest of the crew. He went on to let me know that he had had a subsequent conversation with the sisters on their return to the ship. They had voiced total agreement with the notion that I would serve as their personal attendant during the upcoming voyage. With my immediate agreement, the matter was settled, and I was summarily dismissed to resume in the process of making ready to sail.

As dawn finally broke and all make-ready preparations had been completed, I joined my fellow mates ondeck to welcome the returning search party back onto our ship. I was elated to observe that Jemme did not accompany them. Mr. Bass greeted the three sailors with a grim visage of disappointment as they made their very nervous report. They hesitatingly explained to the First Mate that they had thoroughly searched the entire town in order to locate the deserter. Having concluded their exhaustive search, they reasoned that Jonah Jemme must have made his way into the interior of the island. Rather than face the rioting slaves in the island's interior, the three decided that the best course of action was to return to the ship with this disheartening news. Mr. Bass went into a furious state of anger upon learning of the search party's failure. Promising retribution, Mr. Bass turned abruptly and headed back to his chores, leaving the fear-struck trio quaking in his wake.

To the crew's great relief, the Captain gave the much anticipated order to weigh anchor and get under way. As we distanced ourselves from this wondrous haven we had all very much enjoyed over the past few weeks, I could not help but wonder about the fate of both my young friend and my very special lover. I said a silent prayer to Saint Agnes for her intercession in protecting these two special people from incurring further harm. My final thought, as the island disappeared from our sight, was whether a *jonah* brought only bad luck to himself and those around him while at sea. Hopefully, when on land, a *jonah*'s luck would make a radical turn for the better!

Chapter 25: Witches... Witches... Witches

As we made our way back to sea, I could not stop thinking of my beloved Rue. I was quite unsure when I would get the opportunity to return to her loving arms, but knew that I certainly would make every effort to do so. Without Jemme aboard, the ship seemed deathly quiet and somber. Mr. Bass, still furious and fuming about the desertion of my friend, drove the entire crew in a maddening and brutal work routine. To make matters worse, our ship's bully was further outraged by the fact that the Captain had granted the sisters use of his cabin for the voyage. Having been given the special assignment by the Captain meant that my galley duties were taken up by a new recruit we had added just prior to our departure. What this really meant was that I was free to spend the vast majority of my time assisting and attending to the Adams sisters' needs…a full-time assignment indeed!

Gertrude was the eldest of the three, and by my reckoning the brightest of the trio. Unlike her two sisters, Gertrude was very heavyset, moving around in a slow waddling gait. While her exterior demeanor was stern and somber, she possessed a very warm and caring heart. I also found her to be the easiest and the wisest of the three to converse with about various intriguing topics. Gertrude told me that she was very much aware of the reputation the sisters had gained concerning the practice of witchcraft. The thought actually made her chuckle as she pointed out that her oversized physique would make broom riding all but impossible. Gertrude also remarked that witches were known to relish the taste of human flesh…especially that of young children. However, the fact that she ate no meat of any sort presented a huge obstacle in her acceptance as a flesh-craving initiate to any witch coven. Lastly, she mentioned that witches were reputed to be in league with the Devil…submitting to sexual congress with the ultimate evil one. This last statement brought a sudden gale of laughter and giggles as she confessed to me that she had yet remained a virgin, which would have certainly caused extreme sexual frustration to the most malevolent one.

It was her strong belief that the hysteria concerning witches abounded for a number of very simple reasons. In the first place, she explained that the witch hunts were often instigated out of pure ignorance. The existence of witches provided a perfect scapegoat for the vast sea of misfortunes experienced by the masses, which were barely eking out a meager existence given the harsh and brutal realities that faced them. She informed me that it was far easier for the suffering populace to place blame on someone else for their misfortunes. Therefore, as any natural or man-made disasters occurred, such as famine, plague, storms, floods or war, people generally found it easier and more convenient to place the blame for these calamities on the existence of witches. They singled out witches from the old, single and poor women in rural areas, who many times were acting as healers and midwives. Accusations came from all quarters, including hysterical and deluded children, desperate friends, neighbors and family members along with religious and political leaders. Once accused, these women were all but convicted, while sentenced to brutal and inhuman torture and punishment prior to the condemnation of being burned alive. Providing a quick example to prove her point, Gertrude told me that many times an accused witch was thrown into a river, lake or sea to judge whether or not she was actually a practicing witch. Should the accused sink and drown by this rough treatment, it was judged that she was actually not a witch at all! However, should the accused swim and survive this ordeal, it was believed that she accomplished this through the assistance of the Devil. She was therefore convicted of witchcraft and sentenced to the sad fate of being roasted alive in a fiery inferno. Gertrude's point was that the accused was doomed in either case to suffer an agonizing death either by drowning or by fire.

The second sound rationale she provided for witch hysteria was the ability it provided men to keep women in their place. By the nature of the barbaric treatment of accused witches, women were taught to hold their tongues or face very serious and threatening consequences. Based on the horrific fear of being accused, women learned well that silence and gentility were their only means of avoiding unholy torture and eventual death. Being a generally outspoken and potentially influential woman in any town or city could result in a very painful and pointless death. With a short laugh, Gertrude confessed that the last reason women were accused of witchcraft was that it was a very good method for society to rid itself of someone posing any sort of problem or issue by their very existence. Given the extreme temperament of the populace and the hysteria surrounding witches, it was really quite easy to eliminate potential rivals or enemies by making formal accusations as to their association with the Devil and his black arts.

Gertrude did not practice black magic, but rather only the art of healing. She and her two sisters had been raised by very unconventional parents, who had encouraged each of the daughters to pursue life careers that had the greatest appeal and interest to each. In that regard, Gertrude had spent her life studying natural cures, herbal remedies, folk medicine and other related subjects. She was very proud of the knowledge and experience she had gleaned over the years. She pointed out that mankind had utilized a multitude of indigenous plants for the treatment of various ailments since the dawn of time. As a child and young adult, Gertrude had studied a number of ancient texts on this subject, including those of Egyptian, Greek, Roman, Arabian and Chinese origins. Additionally, she had spent much time studying folk medicine and lore with various wise women in various parts of the world. While she considered herself an accomplished healer, she continually searched for additional wisdom and knowledge on this subject wherever her travels took her. She had in her possession a simply marvelous collection of plant and animal ingredients that had been amassed over her long lifespan. The many trunks that I had helped deliver to the *Amafata* for transport contained the majority of these ingredients. Thus, over the next several weeks, I worked very closely at Gertrude Adams' side sorting, cataloguing and concocting tinctures, lotions and extracts from many of these numerous natural ingredients.

As word spread throughout the ship of Gertrude's healing abilities, a number of my fellow crewmen began making appearances at the sisters' cabin in need of medical help or assistance. Many a day stopped by; Gertrude would treat as many as six or seven sailors for a variety of medical ailments ranging from stomach problems to the dreaded pox. Always by her side, I was truly amazed at the range and extent of both her knowledge and marvelous stores of ingredients. As we worked together to assist ailing crewmembers, I became more and more knowledgeable on the legions of natural herbs, flowers and plants that Gertrude held in her possession. In truth, most of the trunks holding these precious items were relegated to the hold due to the serious shortage of space in the cabin. Additionally, Gertrude was forever cautioning me on the serious dangers of many of these plants and herbs included in her medical store.

One day, a familiar face made an appearance at the sisters' cabin seeking medical assistance. My friend and crewmate, Chips, had made his way to the sisters' surgery in need of relief from a troublesome tooth, which was causing him considerable pain and suffering. Gertrude inspected the offending tooth with the extreme care and delicacy that only a woman could provide in this type of ministration. After an initial examination, she informed the pain-crazed carpenter that his offending tooth had to be removed. Chips seemed to be quite upset by this diagnosis, given his role in removing bad teeth from various individuals in the past. Gertrude, sensing my utter confusion, informed me that teeth were routinely pulled by all types of tradespeople, including carpenters, blacksmiths, barbers, hairdressers, cobblers, apothecaries, watchmakers and even jewelers. Upon listening to this extensive list, it seemed to me that just about anyone was qualified to extract a bad tooth.

She smiled as she announced that the primary responsibility of the practitioner was the ability to deaden the offending tooth and the area surrounding it in the patient's mouth. Winking at me, she pulled out a strange looking root from one of her many trunks. She told me that this particular root had quite a storied history given its strange and sometimes deadly end results. Turning to her other numerous ingredients, she quickly mixed the root with a variety of items into her well-used mixing bowl. Once completed, she was left with a thick yellow paste that she spread generously on Chips' offending tooth and nearby gums. After taking a break for a few moments to allow her mixture to take effect, Gertrude tested the tooth by hand. To Chips' great relief, he reported that his pain had virtually disappeared and now believed his problem solved. Gertrude was quick to inform the smiling carpenter that the relief he was experiencing was only temporary. She cautioned him that if the offending tooth was not removed, that the pain and agony would return shortly with utter vengeance. Nodding his agreement, Chips told us to *sail on* with the required extraction.

Chips fainted dead away at the exact moment of the actual extraction, oblivious to any further ministrations by his skilled healer. Upon gaining consciousness, Chips was overjoyed to discover the operation finished and the offending tooth fully removed from his mouth. Shakily making his way out of the sisters' cabin, he profusely thanked Gertrude for her gentle and kind assistance. Making his way slowly back to the main deck, he lauded the medical expertise shown to him by Gertrude. It did not take very long for everyone onboard to hear about the miraculous cure and tender care he had received. This news brought even more business to our new healer's doorstep from my fellow crewmates suffering from all types of medical issues…real or imagined!

Coincidentally, the Captain decided to have the crew provide a musical serenade for the Adams sisters' benefit. His motive for this impromptu performance was welcoming the sisters aboard his vessel, as well as lightening the overall mood of the ship's crew. Since our hasty departure from Saint Domingue, the sailors onboard had definitely been edgy and anxious. The ship's band was assembled on the quarterdeck and the festivities got under way. To further improve the crew's mood, a special treat of an extra ration of rum was ordered to the raucous cheering of the entire ship. Once the prized rum was distributed, the band began playing various nautical tunes to the expressed delight of all, especially the Adams sisters.

As the band performed, the youngest Adams sister, Hortence, asked the Captain if anyone aboard had the gift of song. Handy was the first to reply, confiding that indeed the ship was blessed with an extraordinary talent. Pointing directly at me, Handy continued his laudatory remarks on my behalf, which prompted all three sisters to beg the Captain for a singing demonstration on my part. At that very moment, Mr. Bass spoke up scoffing and laughing at the very thought that I had any musical talent whatsoever. He further defamed my abilities telling the sisters that drunken men do not make the most discriminating critics.

While the majority of my fellow crewmates remained totally silent due to the crippling fear that the First Mate inspired, Handy slyly answered the bully's critical assessment by suggesting that a musical trial could be conducted to ascertain the truth. He further proposed that our new guests could serve as impartial judges for this test to decide if I had any real vocal talent at all. The crew now responded their wholehearted approval of such a contest and the matter was settled. For my part, I relished the opportunity of embarrassing our mean-spirited bully once again, as I gladly accepted the challenge with total vigor.

Choosing a popular emotional ballad called *River of Sorrow and Ease,* I launched into my performance. In a deep tenor's voice, I sang the accompanying words of this haunting melody to the sheer amazement and delight of the entire ship. Did I say entire? Well let's just say everyone aboard with the distinct exception of a brooding and scowling Mr. Bass, who gained absolutely no joy from my performance. Upon finishing the number, the entire ship went a bit loony with boisterous hooting and hollering announcing my triumph. Unquenched, the audience demanded more and I spent the next hour singing song after song to their complete and total enjoyment. Finally, the Captain signaled an end to the evening's festivities and I accepted the gushing praise and appreciation from each of the Adams sisters. Hortence even made a special effort to congratulate me on my singing performance by telling me that never before in her life had she heard such a miraculous and sweet voice. Blushing now in total embarrassment, I thanked her and her sisters for the opportunity to perform and entertain them. With that, the entire ship settled back into its normal routine as I made my way down to my hammock for some much needed rest.

Chapter 26: New Recruits

We had a couple of new recruits aboard as we began this latest leg of our journey. The first of these was none other than Angry George, confirmed pirate and marvelous storyteller. I was told by Handy that Angry George had joined our voyage as a means of self-preservation. Handy related that Angry George had the serious misfortune of falling in love with an island beauty called Sugar Sally, who was also idolized by Lion Kismet. Upon discovering Angry George's intentions toward his woman, Lion promised a very unpleasant and painful death to our newest recruit. Angry George already sported a vicious knife slash across his chest as solemn testament to both the sincerity and ferocity of the offended Turk. Upon this stern warning from Lion, Angry George thought it best to leave the island that very day and sign on as a new crewmember. Although taken by surprise by these developments, I was overjoyed at the prospect of more thrilling stories from our newly signed pirate crewmate.

The following evening I was rewarded at mess with a new pirate tale from Angry George. The subject of this night's narrative was once again the feared Black Tarantula pirate demon. As usual the story ended with the Black Tarantula in control of the hapless ship and crew who were all doomed to pain, suffering and eventual death! He certainly did not ease our concerns or fears of crossing paths with this nautical madman anytime in the future. Once again, we all spent a very restless night with the Black Tarantula invading many of our dreams…or should I say nightmares!

The second new recruit we added to our company from Saint Domingue was a son of a wealthy island merchant, named Gene Fabrege. Gene's father happened to be an old and close friend of our Captain. The boy was a disciplinary problem from birth. His father hoped that the strict regimen aboard our ship would do this little miscreant some good. Owing Gene's father a huge past debt, the Captain reluctantly agreed to provide a position onboard for his wayward son. Rue had forewarned me about this nasty little imp long before we sailed. Known locally as

Catstalker Gene, this juvenile delinquent made a habit of capturing, torturing and savagely killing any small animal that he came across. The locals knew with certainty that it was just a matter of time before this demented boy would graduate to harming larger animals…including human beings! Mean, malicious and spoiled were the best descriptors for this unbalanced adolescent. He was assigned my old role of cook's assistant, and was placed in Handy's care. From my very first encounter with Catstalker Gene, I knew for a fact that Handy faced a very daunting task.

Catstalker Gene, being a proven masochist, truly reveled in scrutinizing Mr. Bass and his harsh treatment of guilty crewmembers. A natural born *cuddle up*, Catstalker Gene wormed his way into our First Mate's good graces, acting as informant and snitch in order to get his fellow crewmembers in trouble. Within a week of sailing, he had replaced Bigmouth Ajax's role aboard in all respects, constantly on the lookout for any type of infraction that would earn him some level of gratitude from his new mentor. Catstalker Gene's real enjoyment initiated whenever Mr. Bass began *walking the cat*. At the anticipation of physical pain and suffering, Catstalker Gene would get so excited that he was virtually oblivious to anything happening around him. Wearing a silly grin with eyes eager to drink in the upcoming pain, Catstalker Gene would push and shove his way to the front of any deck audience so as not to miss any part of Mr. Bass' legendary punishments.

Catstalker Gene was also a practiced expert when it came to the art of *sogering*, which is playing sick to avoid assigned duties. Forever complaining of this illness or another, Catstalker Gene spent more time in Doc's surgery than in the galley. This sad situation placed the burden of all galley work on Handy, much to the extreme delight of Mr. Bass. The Doc, frustrated in his attempts to cure Catstalker Gene of his imaginary illnesses, turned his *sogering* patient over to the Adams sisters to see if they could assist in the lad's healing efforts. After a brief examination of Catstalker Gene, Gertrude agreed with my initial speculation that any and all of his illnesses were imaginary. She decided it was high time to teach this spoiled little brat a lesson.

To do so, she decided to utilize a substance called *wormwood*. Normally this ingredient was used as a base for brewing a strong tangy tea. However, when an extract of *wormwood* was mixed with alcohol, it transformed into a very powerful concoction that had the ability to induce severe hallucinations among its users. Advising me of this so that I could keep a close eye on the lethal brat, Gertrude provided Catstalker Gene with a small bottle of *wormwood* rum that she had manufactured especially for him. He was instructed to take a small swig from the vial every day for a week. In return, he was promised that all his pain and suffering would soon disappear. Catstalker Gene greedily snatched the vial from Gertrude's hand and was off in a flash to sample his new miraculous medicine.

Having advance knowledge of the potent effects of Gertrude's special brew and fully aware of Catstalker Gene's past crimes against small defenseless animals, I devised a plan of my own to teach this miscreant a lesson he would never forget. Because Catstalker Gene had taken over my role as galley slave, I knew that he would be making regular trips to the dark and damp hold to fetch wood and food supplies for Handy's culinary concoctions. I also knew that it was unlikely that this evil lad would strictly adhere to Gertrude's *wormwood* rum dosage instructions. Instead, I guessed that he would consume the entire vial that very day. Therefore, I made my way to the hold undetected and found a very good hiding spot amid the many crates and bales of trading goods now filling the hold to await Catstalker Gene's arrival.

My wait was relatively short, for in no time at all Catstalker Gene teetered aimlessly into the hold, reeling and muttering due to the strong effects of the *wormwood* medicine. As he bounced off a variety of crates and barrels in a failed effort to keep himself standing upright, I knew it was now time to put my plan into action. This was the perfect opportunity to test a totally new talent regarding my *special voice*. I had been practicing on misdirecting this talent, so that it sounded like any noise I issued emanated from a completely different direction than the one where I was actually located. I was getting better and better at this new skill and decided that now was the perfect opportunity to test my new strategic weapon. As Catstalker Gene stooped to gather an armload of wood for the galley stove, I let loose with a dreadful cat howl that I had been saving for this very occasion. While I was to his portside, the sound I issued seemed to emanate from his larboardside. Stunned and stupefied, the drugged lad dropped the wood he had gathered, spending the next several minutes attempting to discover the source of the cat wails that I had issued. Completely unsuccessful and now muttering to himself that he had simply imagined the sounds, he returned to his wood collecting chore. Once again I utilized my special voice to unleash a bloodcurdling howl in the same misdirected method that froze the poor boy in his tracks. I followed this second howl with a low and hissing voice that sounded just like a beggar woman I had encountered once on the London streets. I proclaimed that I was the ghost of a feline that little imp had cruelly dispatched some time ago. I made it clear to him that I was very unhappy with his cruel and monstrous treatment of small animals in general. Further, I told him that I would haunt his every step from now on until he amended his mean and sinful ways.

Stumbling and gibbering from the dark hold, Catstalker Gene made a very unsteady yet hasty departure from this lower level of hell and his ghostly animal tormentor. To accent the fear I had induced, I sent a furious series of cat howls and wails in his wake as he literally flew from the hold in utmost terror. While this episode gave me some satisfaction for the cruel and nasty behavior Catstalker Gene showed toward my fellow crewmates and friends, I knew that this warped little imp would soon forget this harrowing experience and once again revert to his old devious ways. However, this incident planted a seed in the sick and warped mind of this delinquent that I knew I could nurture and grow as the future unfolded.

At the same time, I was disappointed to discover that Mr. Bass was recovering quite nicely from the beating he incurred at the hands of Lion. He was back to his old routine of prowling the ship in search of any poor soul in dire need of a firm lashing. He had been a staunch protestor when he discovered the Captain's plan of transporting the Adams sisters and continued his vehement disapproval of these ladies aboard the *Amafata*. When he learned from his new protégé, Catstalker Gene, of the latter's disastrous treatment by the sisters' ministrations, he became that much more determined to shorten their stay on our vessel. Telling anyone who would listen that the sisters were indeed witches, he proceeded to wage a one-man war to make our guests wholly uncomfortable for the remainder of the voyage. To this end, he blamed every small misfortune that occurred onboard on the *Adams Witches*, as he cruelly referred to them. Beginning to convince more and more of the crew, I knew that something had to be done to arrest his evil intentions. Meeting with Gertrude, I explained the problem in its entirety and appealed for her assistance in halting this potentially dire situation. Gertrude asked me to sort through her many crates holding her herbs and ingredients searching for a very special one she had labeled *beautiful lady*. Once I found the right crate, I freed it from its brothers and sisters and returned it to Gertrude for inspection.

As she had successfully utilized a small bit of this herb during Chips' tooth extraction, she explained that the *belladonna* plant had been discovered centuries ago and had served both good and evil purposes. Nicknamed *Deadly Nightshade*, this substance was harvested for a variety of different purposes, including medicinal cures, cosmetics and as a lethal poison depending on the dosage.

Gertrude extracted one of these strange looking roots and placed it on her workbench to begin her preparations. She advised me that *belladonna* also had very strange effects on individuals in quantities slightly larger than those considered to be normal for medicinal purposes. Under these larger dosages, an individual would suffer confusion, loss of balance, slurred speech, convulsions and significant hallucinations. She reasoned that if we somehow induced Mr. Bass to consume the *belladonna* elixir that it would incapacitate him, eliminating the threat he represented to the sisters' well-being. Thinking aloud she mused about the best method of getting the evil First Mate to ingest the right amount of the elixir. I remembered that Mr. Bass had his own private stash of rum that was usually sequestered in his cabin. Since the Adams sisters had been provided his cabin for their own use, the rum stash had been relocated to the hold for safekeeping. I notified Gertrude that it would be a simple matter to slip the dangerous *belladonna* elixir into this private rum stash on my next visit to the hold.

Over the next several days, I kept a sharp eye on the First Mate for any sign that the drug had been ingested. After keeping this vigil for a full day and a half, I was rewarded when I spotted Mr. Bass reeling and stumbling on the quarterdeck. The Captain appeared and questioned his First Mate on his health given his dazed appearance and disorientation.

In a very slurred voice, Mr. Bass informed the Captain that he was feeling fine, but was at a total loss as to the reason the ship was infested with a vicious troop of miniature Blood Monkeys. Mr. Bass pointed to the riggings of the ship and demanded that the Captain take a look because the Blood Monkeys were frolicking up and down them. At this point, the Captain ordered his First Mate to visit Doc's surgery for examination. Surprised and totally confused by the order, Mr. Bass agreed to follow the Captain's wishes, but was very insistent that something had to be done about the infernal Blood Monkeys before they overran the entire ship. With that Mr. Bass hurried over to the riggings and shouted to his imaginary tormentors to get themselves the hell off of his ship.

Seeing that his strong words had absolutely no affect on the Blood Monkey troop, Mr. Bass grabbed the nearest ratline and proceeded to scale the ropes in pursuit of his imaginary simian foes. The Captain was shocked and stunned by these actions as well as the extremely strange comments voiced by his First Mate. He could not deduce what form of insanity or illness would cause his First Mate to act in such a peculiar manner. Calling to the watch leader, he ordered a few of his tars to rescue the delusional officer before he caused serious harm to himself. The watch leader and two of his minions immediately climbed the riggings in pursuit of Mr. Bass. However, capture of the elusive First Mate was not to be a simple assignment. For nearly two hours, the pursuit team chased Mr. Bass through the ship's plentiful riggings coming close but never really capturing their prey. In the meantime, the entire crew, alerted by the screaming and wailing rants of Mr. Bass as well as the exasperated curses of the capture team, had assembled on the topdeck to partake in the fun and games.

Mr. Bass was finally snared and brought down from his high perch screaming and resisting the whole way. Once his captors reached the maindeck with their prisoner, the Captain ordered several more of us observing this farce to bind Mr. Bass in stout ropes and carry him down to the Doc's surgery for a total physical examination. Securely bound and completely immobilized, Mr. Bass continued his vociferous rants that the Blood Monkeys were now climbing all over him attempting to bite and claw him to death. The delirious fool was carried below still screaming hysterically that the Blood Monkeys were attempting to overpower and eviscerate him.

The Captain stood transfixed while watching this little drama unfold convinced that his First Mate had somehow lost his mind. Mr. Bass was tied to a bunk in the Doc's surgery for rest and observation. The mean-spirited sailor continued his rants about the antics of the devious Blood Monkeys. I knew that at least for the short term, we were all safe from the First Mate's *cat-o-nine-tails* whip as long as the much welcomed Blood Monkeys continued their reign of mischief and mayhem!

That evening's mess was very much like a raucous party aboard the ship. Every crewmember was still in a delirious and spirited mood having observed their hated tormentor trapped, trussed and trundled below for medical assistance. We were all very relieved that Mr. Bass would not be making his usual rounds in search of likely victims to assuage his wrath and vindictiveness. Needing a good story to perpetuate our unusually high spirits, Handy was called on to spin one of his *sea tales* to the absolute delight of everyone present. Giving me a conspiratorial wink, he launched into one of his sagas as we all settled down to enjoy the moment. This tale was yet another slice of his personal history, having taken place a number of years in the past. The story occurred on a ship called the *Ocean Vulture*, on which Handy had served for several voyages. It seemed that the *Ocean Vulture* had been at sea for several months returning to London from the West Indies loaded with sugar and coffee exports. With food supplies and crew morale at an all-time low, the ship's Captain needed to provide a diversion that would serve to relieve the crew's boredom as well as taking their minds off their stomachs.

To this end, their Captain, a very mean-spirited individual, invented a new pastime to relieve the tension aboard his ship. This new pastime came in the form of a novel punishment. The victim in this tale was a lowly *galley slave* named Squint McGuire. Squint was an ugly and unpopular boy hailing from a small sea town near Bristol, England. Squint was accused of the serious crime of torturing and abusing the Captain's pet feline, actually killing the poor creature in the process. At Handy's last words, I stole a glance over to where Catstalker Gene was reclining and noticed he had turned a very pale shade as well as experiencing difficulty in both breathing and swallowing. At that moment, I now understood the message in the conspiratorial wink that Handy had delivered prior to the start of this tale.

Aboard the *Ocean Vulture* the entire crew was summoned to the maindeck by the Captain, who was named Thomas Thommes... nicknamed Tom-Tom by his sailors! In full dress uniform, Captain Tom-Tom announced to the crew that Squint was going to be punished for the heinous crime he had committed against his helpless feline pet. The punishment decreed by Captain Tom-Tom was *bilging*, which caused the entire crew to groan in horror at the harsh severity of the punishment. *Bilging* was a rather new method of punishment at the time. Captain Tom-Tom explained to all that this nasty sentence involved securing the criminal in the lowest portion of the ship, the hold. Here in this dark and dank abyss, the unfortunate would be submerged entirely except for his head in the filthy, pest-infested sludge that gravitated to the very bowels of any ship. Left there totally alone in the dark for the length of the punishment sentence, the criminal would be at the total mercy of the ravenous rats, cockroaches and other filthy carnivorous vermin that ruled this nasty hellish environment.

Because of the punishment's harshness and the absolute pain and suffering it caused, Captain Tom-Tom was sure that his victim would go quite mad after even a short period of time. Squint, who was in no doubt guilty of the crime, went into an absolute screaming frenzy at the pronouncement of this formidable castigation. It took six strong pairs of hands to hold him in place while Captain Tom-Tom deliberated the length of the punishment. Even the somewhat light sentence of one full day swimming in the hellish bilge water did very little to calm the wide-eyed youth. Taken below by force, Squint's screams were more inhuman that any Handy had experienced over his entire lifetime at sea. Throughout that entire day and well into the night, Squint's wails and howls haunted the entire ship, robbing even the weariest of rest and sleep. However, an even more frightening outcome awaited the entire crew as dawn broke over the water. At this time, the guard detail that was sent down to the hold to retrieve the unfortunate youth found him long dead! In fact, there was very little left of his head when his lifeless corpse was dragged topside for review.

Handy related that since the *Ocean Vulture* had been at sea for so long, the loathsome scavengers in the bilge were just as hungry and starving as were each of the unfortunate crewmembers. These filthy crawling creatures had made a king's feast out of poor Squint, devouring most of the flesh on the poor lad's face. Staring at the gruesome remains of this unfortunate lad acted as a cure for the crew's hunger pangs for the next several days. The curious fact about the entire episode was the unspoken question that lodged in each crewmember's mind. *"How was Squint able to issue such inhuman wailing and cries without the use of his tongue or lips?"* In fact, every last bit of flesh on the lad's noggin was sorely among the missing when this small miscreant was dragged topside. This strange mystery was never really resolved nor forgotten by the crew. Some said that it was the Devil who had issued the mournful wails that all heard… while most of the crew just shivered and tried to forget the whole unfortunate incident!

At the conclusion of his tale, I glanced toward the source of the story. Catstalker Gene had turned a deathly pallor as his eyes seemed to have enlarged threefold. Handy and I shared a conspiratorial chuckle at viewing our newest enemy's consternation at Handy's latest *sea tale.*

Chapter 27: The Other Adams Sisters

Gertrude Adams was but one member of the strange trio who had taken up temporary residence aboard our vessel as we made our way to Jamaica. There were two more sisters that made up the Adams trio… Willamina and Hortence. Neither of these two sisters were accomplished herbalists. However, each pursued their own unique passions with a vengeance.

Willamina was the next oldest sister in the family. She was extremely gaunt in appearance coupled with a very stony and somber manner. She was an adept palm reader, having spent the majority of her life perfecting this craft. As I continued my herbal education with her older sister Gertrude, I was intrigued by Willamina's poise and control. She seemed totally at peace with the world around her, filtering out any nastiness or evil that might come her way. After just a few days spent monitoring this strange woman, I approached Willamina to determine if she would grace me with her talent. She was very reluctant at the onset, but Gertrude provided the necessary encouragement to spur her sister into action. Sitting down in a chair adjacent to hers, Willamina accepted my hands and began a lengthy examination.

After spending a very long period turning my hands this way and that, she began to educate me on the detailed meaning of all that she had observed. As a beginning, Willamina revealed that there were several factors to consider as a palmist prior to providing any findings. I learned that a proficient palm reader took notice of all manner of things beyond the lines appearing on an individual's palm. She instructed me that hand and finger shapes and sizes also had to be taken into serious consideration. As to the actual lines themselves, elements like depth, clarity, shapes and patterns all played an integral part in the prophesy she was soon to deliver. She notified me that there were six major lines on each human hand. These major lines included the heart, head, life, health, creativity and fate lines.

She began with my heart line, which she reported was long, clear, straight and actually doubled. This fact pointed out that I was open and warm with people, being both generous and secure with relationships. Additionally, she divulged that my particular heart line pointed to a creative approach to love bordering on the romantic. The fact that this line was doubled meant that I was extremely loyal and faithful to my friends. As she related this, I happily let her know that I was in total agreement with her findings so far!

The next line she examined was my life line, which also appeared long and clear. She announced that this was indeed fortunate in that it indicated that I was in fine physical condition and was blessed with good health. As I peered over her shoulder, I inquired if this line prophesied that I would live a long life. Willamina confessed that, while my healthy constitution indicated such, there were far too many other factors involved to issue such a bold prophesy. The next major line she turned to was the head line. She disclosed that this line was also long and clear, indicating intelligence, the ability to think and act logically along with an outstanding memory. Up to this point, I was extremely pleased with her pronouncements, but she was far from finished with her examination.

Just then, Gertrude interrupted our session requesting my assistance in fetching some needed herbal ingredients for the concoction she was brewing. As I moved away, Willamina had one last piece of information for me. She announced that I had three very unusual markings on both of my palms. The first of these markings was a star clearly formed by the lines on my palm. This rather rare marking foretold that I was most fortunate indeed since it indicated tremendous fame and notoriety would eventually come my way. But she was not quite finished for she told me that with the good there was always a balancing negative side to investigate and understand. The second special mark she referred to involved my life line. Pointing to some curious hash marks, Willamina revealed that I was sure to face many significant obstacles in my future. While she could definitely foretell that these obstacles were very real, she was unable to pinpoint exactly when these impediments would occur. She did reveal that other markings pointed out that I could rely on a powerful external force to assist my efforts in defeating these obstacles. Lastly, Willamina signaled to a section of my palm pointing to yet another star that formed there. This special marking foretold of a very major and surprising change also somewhere in my eventual future. She announced that this life-altering event was surely significant enough to overwhelm me if I was not prepared to face it directly! Just then, Gertrude called for my immediate assistance on transporting a required trunk from the hold and I raced out to fulfill her request.

The third and final member of this strange trio was named Hortence. She was the bright star of the three sisters, and probably at one time in the distant past the most beautiful. Bright-eyed and constantly smiling and laughing, Hortence quickly became my favorite of the three. Her passion in life involved all things theatrical. In fact, she had in her possession several large trunks filled with stage costumes, stage props and a variety of theatrical make-up. Her dream was to perform on the European stages to the delight and adoration of ardent admirers and mesmerized devotees. Having spent the majority of her life in the West Indies, Hortence was never really afforded the opportunity to accomplish this dream. Her admission saddened me since I realized that any such opportunity had slipped away long ago. However, it would not be long before I would realize just how very wrong I had been in this thinking.

I was very curious as to the exact talent level of this would-be actress, so I decided to approach her with a unique opportunity that would enable her to display the extent of her acting abilities. As I laid out my plan, Hortence became more and more excited about the role she was about to portray. Readily agreeing to play a key role in the conspiracy, I hurried off to procure a few needed items for our joint performance. While I was away on my mission, Hortence had spent the time with her trunks of stage make-up and accessories. As I entered the cabin and she turned around to greet me, I was totally shocked by the transformation she had achieved in my brief absence. Sitting in front of me was a close replica of Catstalker Gene, attired in woman's clothing. Handing her the sailor's slops that I had just borrowed, she retreated behind a changing screen and emerged shortly as a life-like twin of our malicious little onboard scamp. My role in the charade was much simpler since I would be playing myself.

Sneaking our way to the Doc's surgery, we planned an unannounced visit to the still delirious Mr. Bass. Reaching the door to the sick bay, I cracked it open to observe our unwary victim. Mr. Bass was sitting up in the temporary bed that had been hastily delivered to house the raving sailor. While he was still suffering the effects of the *Deadly Nightshade*, I knew that he was hardly capable of recognizing any of the minute differences in Hortence's disguise. Signaling to my accomplice, we began to act out our ruse.

In my normal voice, I announced loud enough for the First Mate to overhear that perhaps it was time to tell the truth concerning the Blood Monkeys that were beguiling our esteemed leader. Hortence, imitating a close approximation of Catstalker Gene's voice, answered that revealing the truth to the First Mate would ruin all the fun that we and the entire crew had enjoyed at Mr. Bass' expense. I responded that it was not fair to the ailing officer to continue the hoax any longer. Continuing, I announced that deceiving him any further could lead to very serious consequences and possibly a taste of the *cat* should Mr. Bass realize the serious fraud played at his expense.

Peeking into the cabin, I observed that Mr. Bass had heard our every word. I watched as his menacing scowl seemed to take a turn for the worse right before my eyes. Quietly closing the door to the cabin, Hortence and I merrily made our way back to the sisters' cabin. As I made my departure, I congratulated my accomplice on her wonderful theatrical skills, promising to never again question her acting abilities.

Making my way back to the galley to appraise Handy of the deception we had just employed, I heard the raised voice of the First Mate demanding that both Catstalker Gene and I be brought before him immediately. The Doc emerged hurriedly from his surgery in desperate search of both of us. Catching sight of me, the Doc requested that I remain nearby as he rushed off. Returning just a few moments later with Catstalker Gene in tow, the Doc hustled us both into his surgery to attend an audience with his highly delusional patient. Once we were both inside the cabin, Mr. Bass demanded that we repeat our recent discussion held just outside the cabin's door for the sole benefit of the Doc. Catstalker Gene, in a very confused and befuddled state, answered his intimidating mentor that he had absolutely no idea what he was talking about. Playing the same innocent and disconcerting role, I confessed to Mr. Bass that I was also unaware of having any recent discussions with Catstalker Gene. Maddened to the point of white hot fury, Mr. Bass verbally lashed out with utter vehemence naming us both prevaricating whelps. Continuing his tirade, he promised a visit from the *cat* if we did not end this cruel and malicious hoax that was being perpetuated against him. He ordered us to confess to the Doc that the so-called imaginary Blood Monkeys plaguing him were in fact very real. Catstalker Gene was both flustered and distraught at his mentor's demands and accompanying threats, and once again told Mr. Bass that he had no idea what he was talking about. I seconded this confession.

The Doc, believing that his patient was having a total relapse of the malady that had plagued him, quickly ushered us both from the cabin so as to not cause his suffering patient any more needless stress. As we made our hasty exit, Catstalker Gene turned to me with a look of bewilderment. I responded that I believed that the First Mate had finally lost his sanity. As we parted, I had to smile at the loud rants of conspiracy and deception being issued by my hated enemy. I also knew that it would be a very long time, if ever, that Mr. Bass would trust and confide in his malicious little assistant!

Later, I heard a commotion occurring on the maindeck. Full of curiosity and eager to earn a respite from my endless herb-fetching chores, I made my way to the maindeck. I reached the upperdeck and was greeted by my fellow crewmates who were all fixed on a particular location off the starboard side of the ship. Off in the distance, I spotted the reason for the fracas that had the entire ship in an uproar. Floating like a small cork was a ship's longboat that seemed totally deserted. At that moment, the Captain made a rare appearance on the quarterdeck, also alerted by the excited shouts and cries from his crew. Equipped with his trusty telescope, the Captain spent several minutes examining the small craft.

As we pulled alongside the small boat, the crew realized that we had been totally mistaken about this longboat being deserted. We could all now see that there were two human figures lying prone on the bottom. One of these figures looked like a small child by its size and stature. Fearing that both individuals were dead, we were ordered by the Captain to secure the longboat and inspect its human cargo. Once the vessel was brought alongside the *Amafata*, several crew members climbed down temporary rope ladders. The boarding party shouted up to the audience on the maindeck that both individuals were alive but in very bad shape. As these sunburned and nearly expired wretches were winched aboard, we were all shocked by their extremely sad and miserable physical condition. Further, we were astonished that the one individual we mistook as a child was actually a full grown man...a dwarf! Barely conscious and totally unable to talk, the two men were immediately taken to the Doc's surgery for examination and treatment. As the Doc's unofficial assistant, I was ordered to follow. For the next several days, the Doc and I treated these miserable wretches as they began their assent from death back to life. After our careful ministrations of healing tonics, salves, food and water, the pair regained consciousness and seemed on their way to a full recovery. At this point, the Doc asked me to fetch the Captain and bring him immediately to the surgery so that an official interrogation could take place.

Chapter 28: Rescued Sea Dogs

The dwarf was the first of the two to regain full consciousness. As he started to come around to his senses, the Captain informed this odd little creature that he had been rescued and was now safely aboard an English merchantman, named the *Amafata*. The dwarf, his eyes blinking in total fright, told the Captain that his bad luck had continued once more. Confused to the extreme, the Captain asked the little man exactly what he meant. The dwarf quickly responded that the ship's name that had just been uttered by the Captain had seven letters, ended in the letter A and had a total of four As in its spelling. All of these reasons, he informed his confused audience, meant certain bad luck for both the ship and its crew. The Captain, flabbergasted by this news, berated the ungrateful wretch, who had just been delivered from certain death. The dwarf quickly and profusely apologized to all of us in attendance. He informed us that he meant no personal harm in his statement as he was just spouting an old superstition.

At that point, the Doc asked the little tar for his name. Responding with a huge smirk, the dwarf told us that he answered to the name, Long Tall Willie. This answer brought a hearty laugh from us all due to its ridiculous nature. Nevertheless, the Captain proceeded with his interrogation of Long Tall Willie by inquiring how he and his still semi-unconscious partner had ended up in the drifting longboat in the first place. Long Tall Willie's eyes betrayed real fright as the miniature gnome pondered his response. Attempting to swallow, Long Tall Willie finally answered the Captain's inquiry by advising us that it was a tragic story that he would relate to us in its entirety once he had a drop of rum to loosen his prickly dry tongue. With a nod from the Captain, I ran and fetched a tankard of rum from the galley, which the thirsty little devil downed in one hearty swallow.

Momentarily satiated, Long Tall Willie launched into his story of pain and hardship. It seemed that both Long Tall Willie and his unconscious partner, named Charlie Crowsfeet, were both loyal crewmembers on a similar English trading ship called the *Flaming Dragon*. They had shipped out of Bristol slightly ahead of our own departure with planned stops in Cuba, Jamaica and Barbados. As to the voyage, all was peaceful and uneventful through their first stop at Havana, Cuba. It was upon leaving Cuba that their troubles began in earnest. A few days following their Cuban departure, a strange craft was spotted shadowing them. Believing it to be a mere coincidence, their Captain issued orders to maintain watch on this mysterious craft to determine its intentions. Still at a considerable distance, their Captain remained on course believing it only a matter of time before the mysterious ship would veer away from the *Flaming Dragon*. This, however, was not the case, as the trailing ship stayed in view for the next two full days.

On the night of the second day, the *Flaming Dragon* was attacked and overrun by a band of bloodthirsty pirate savages. Assembling the entire crew on the maindeck, the pirate horde seemed to be waiting on someone or something because nothing happened to the hapless crew for what seemed like an eternity. Finally, a malignant presence made its way from the pirate ship onto the tethered deck of the *Flaming Dragon*. Moving in a very unnatural motion, using both of its legs and one of its arms to maneuver, this creeping abomination dressed entirely in black made its way to the front of the pirate swarm and took total control of the assembly. Hiding behind a horrific facial mask that was surely painted in one of Satan's own workshops, this terrifying monster croaked out a formal greeting to the entire captured crew. This masked villain introduced himself as the evil and nefarious Black Tarantula, spawn of the Devil.

Turning his attention back to the Captain and his officers, the Black Tarantula asked for the exact location of the ship's valuables like gold, silver or precious gems. The Captain answered the savage demon pirate on the exact location of the ship's medicine cabinet, and said that he had a small purse of coins in his cabin, but that was the full extent of any such valuables aboard the *Flaming Dragon*. Chuckling in a very menacing growl, the Black Tarantula informed the Captain that he was indeed a liar and that the truth would be uncovered eventually. With these words, the Black Tarantula turned and skittered his way to the Captain's quarters calling to his henchmen to drag the Captain along in his wake. Bidding the crew to sit and rest comfortably before their own interviews, this abomination scuttled the rest of the way into the Captain's lair followed by his terrified prisoner.

Long Tall Willie ceased his dialogue at this point and motioned the Captain for another taste of rum. Nodding his approval, the Captain signaled me to fetch another tankard of rum for this very thirsty leprechaun. Once again quaffing his alcoholic offering in desperate urgency, Long Tall Willie continued his saga. He informed us that all was very quiet aboard the *Flaming Dragon* for a long period after the disappearance of the Black Tarantula and their Captain. Then, for the next very long hour, his petrified fellow crewmates were forced to endure inhuman scream after scream coming from the Captain's cabin. After what seemed like an eternity, the screams, wails and sobs ceased abruptly. The Captain's cabin door opened and one pirate scum was seen dragging a bloody bundle wrapped in sailcloth to the ship's side where it was dumped unceremoniously into the sea. He returned to the scene of the crime carrying an oaken bucket that was filled with all manner of human body parts...ears, lips, fingers, toes, hands and so much more. This gruesome sight sent a shiver of terror down the spines of all the captured observers. Like the bundle, the bucket full of gore was hauled to the ship's side and also emptied into the water. As this task was completed, a call came from the Captain's torture chamber for the next senior officer to be brought to the Black Tarantula for questioning.

Begging and pleading for mercy, the First Mate was apprehended and dragged to the den of horror to continue this unholy blasphemy. Once again a period of silence proceeded another torture session shattered by the initiation of loud agonized wails that now frightened the remaining crewmembers into a petrified trance. One young officer actually used this lull to launch himself directly into the sea, choosing drowning to the hideous interrogation that awaited him. Long Tall Willie informed us that the horrific affair lasted well past the midday hour and finally ended when all officers of the *Flaming Dragon* had their interrogation sessions with this madman turned pirate. At this time, the Black Tarantula made his reappearance onto the maindeck, whispering more instructions to his demonic minions. The remainder of the crew was then assembled in front of this bloody beast and questioned about each of their duties aboard the ship. As each crewmember responded shakily to this question, the

Black Tarantula made instant decisions as to that individual's suitability to serve his own needs in future pirate escapades. If the Black Tarantula deemed that a candidate was of any future value, that individual was then given the choice of life as a pirate or death as an honest sailor. Given this choice, all elected the life of piracy without giving the alternative a moment of thought. Those crewmembers found unworthy by the Black Tarantula were seized and thrown overboard to swim to their deaths in the open sea. Long Tall Willie was having difficulty continuing his narrative once again and the Captain signaled me to fetch yet another life-saving tankard of rum for our new visitor.

Gulping the rum down, Long Tall Willie resumed his story. He related that close to sundown, the Black Tarantula had but two sailors left to interrogate, himself and Charlie Crowsfeet. Stopping a moment to consider these two sailors, the Black Tarantula ordered a longboat launched and commanded his devils to escort both sailors to their new ship. Once they were positioned in the longboat, the Black Tarantula ordered his men to cut the small boat loose from the *Flaming Dragon*. He croaked his instructions to the two survivors to spread this tale of wanton destruction and savagery to the world at large, so that his evil reputation would flourish. With these last instructions, he turned his attention back to his captured prize. As Long Tall Willie and Charlie Crowsfeet drifted slowly away from the scene of carnage, they observed the work of the pirate crew emptying the *Flaming Dragon* of any and all of its valuable trade goods. Once completed, the two castaways eyed their fair ship being set on fire and destroyed to the distant chanting and cheering of the evil pirate horde. Spending the last week or so adrift without food or water, the hapless duo resigned themselves to death and settled in the bottom of the drifting longboat to await their final end. This statement concluded Long Tall Willie's horror story and due to complete exhaustion he passed into a deep dream state. The Captain, fearful that the dwarf's horrific saga would likely induce panic and mass hysteria among his crew, ordered the Doc and I to complete silence and forbade us from repeating or discussing a word of this tale with anyone else on the ship. He informed us that both Long Tall Willie and Charlie Crowsfeet were also ordered to remain silent on the details of their ordeal.

The Doc and I ministered to our patients for the next full day before both men were able to fully function. Charlie Crowsfeet, a tall, reed-thin specimen of a man, was almost the exact opposite of his much shorter companion. Where Charlie Crowsfeet was humorous, kind and humble, Long Tall Willie was cantankerous, mean and boastful. Having spent these long days together aimlessly adrift, these two tars had developed a strange bond. Charlie's Crowsfeet duty aboard the *Flaming Dragon* was that of Assistant Sailmaker, so he was assigned a similar role aboard our vessel. Long Tall Willie acted as *galley slave*, and he immediately replaced Catstalker Gene in this duty, since the latter absolutely refused to set foot in the hold for any reason whatsoever. Relieved of his galley assignment, Catstalker Gene was assigned to assist the recovering Mr. Bass in his onerous role of managing the everyday running of the *Amafata*. Blinking mightily in a nervous fit, this malicious brat nodded his acceptance of this surely burdensome task, since the First Mate was clearly out of his mind.

Later, Charlie Crowsfeet was questioned on the reason for his injured feet. This injury was plainly obvious to all since none of us wore shoes or stockings aboard ship. His feet resembled nothing human at all, swollen and deformed to the extreme. He explained that his injury had occurred a long time ago while he was just a lad who had been sent off to sea. As a young boy, Charlie Crowsfeet had the misfortune of signing onto a ship ruled by a Captain who was incredibly cruel and malicious by nature. Not a single sailor aboard this vessel escaped the unfair and inhuman punishments handed down for even the most minor of transgressions imaginable. All aboard knew that they were doomed to experience the bite of the Captain's *cat* no matter how careful and deliberate they performed their daily duties.

One day, Charlie Crowsfeet was assigned the duty of polishing the boots of this malicious taskmaster. Spending the entire day making sure that his efforts were perfect in every regard, Charlie Crowsfeet brought the boots to the galley to have several of his fellow crewmates inspect the highly glossed footwear for any imperfections. While being critically inspected by all, a few crumbs of hard cheese and hardtack inadvertently found their way inside the boots. When these highly shined boots were placed in the appropriate place in the Captain's locker, Charlie Crowsfeet was sure that he had done a near perfect job of restoring the boots to an almost brand new state.

What Charlie Crowsfeet did not know was that the scent of these small scraps of food would draw a starving band of ravenous scavengers. The Captain awoke the next morning from a restless night's sleep in a very foul mood. Locating his newly shined boots, he sat on his bunk and proceeded to slip them onto his feet without giving them much inspection. The cruel spirited Captain was shocked to find a large fierce rat in residence in his left boot. In fact, the offending rodent was so bold that it actually took a large chunk out of the Captain's large toe before its malignant presence was detected. Howling and screaming with rage, the Captain immediately called for the ship's surgeon to tend to his rat-riddled appendage. The Doctor, short on medical supplies, could do little except bleed the wound to attempt to avoid serious infection. Well, guess what? The Captain's toe did become infected despite the preventive medical treatment. Even worse, the offending toe turned gangrenous and eventually needed to be amputated. The Captain rewarded the bungling medical man with twenty-five lashes for his inept efforts. During this period of time, Charlie Crowsfeet lived in absolute terror and dread wondering exactly what method of punishment would be ordered for his role in the boot travesty.

Deliberating for a while on the appropriate punishment for the cause of his big toe loss, the Captain finally arrived at a chastisement that he felt truly fit the crime. Assembling the entire crew on the upperdeck, the Captain pronounced his wicked punishment on the star-crossed lad in the form of having the boy perform the *Caltrop Hop*. Confused and unsure as to the exact meaning of the sentence handed down, Charlie Crowsfeet was ordered to be blindfolded and held secure while the punishment was prepared. Two sailors were sent below to fetch the deadly caltrops to be utilized in this unique game invented by their deranged nautical commander. So that you understand, a caltrop is a finely sharpened, four-spiked iron projectile also named *crowsfeet*. It resembled a life-size replica of the child's toy named jacks. The bane of any barefooted sailor, a caltrop was ingeniously devised so that when it landed one of its lethal honed points was guaranteed to be pointed skyward. During naval sieges, these strange devices were thrown haphazardly onto the decks of troubled ships to deter boarders. Should an unlucky sailor unwittingly step on one of these barbs, he would receive a very nasty puncture wound that many times became insidiously infected.

Once the razor-sharp caltrops were distributed in quantity across the maindeck, Charlie Crowsfeet was then forced to walk blindly across these deadly dangerous and destructive devices. At the same time, several officers armed with barrel staves took positions around the caltrop pool. Their jobs were to ensure that Charlie Crowsfeet kept moving as he stepped on caltrop after caltrop as he attempted to avoid the pummeling he was receiving from the stave-wielding officers. In no time at all, he received numerous severe foot punctures, which left a trail of blood in the wake of his blind and aimless travels. Finally, unable to stand any longer, the unlucky youth fell face-first onto the deck sustaining even more punctures from his deck-diving experience. Bleeding from a multitude of wounds, Charlie Crowsfeet was hauled down to the doctor's surgery to have these serious lacerations tended to. With a sad smile, the tar related that he survived the incident but would never perform any sort of dance every again!

Since we had heard Charlie Crowsfeet's tale, Handy asked his new assistant, Long Tall Willie how and why he had become a sailor. Long Tall Willie told us all that it was a sorrowful tale that he would be more than happy to relate. As we settled down once again in the cramped and smelly galley, the little man began his narrative.

Long Tall Willie informed his rapt audience that he was once a performer for a traveling European circus. His main position as a member of this roving troop was to act as a human target in a knife-throwing act. While he told us that he was an expert at flinging blades, he was nonetheless subjugated to the role of buffoon and clown, since most people who took any notice of him tended to laugh at his diminutive size. The star of the performance was a renowned womanizer whose stage name was *The Great Ricardo*. The act's star also had a serious problem with alcohol and *drank like a hulled ship*. The star's love affair with spirits caused real issues with his knife-throwing abilities, since his hands shook like a freshly landed fish from his habitual overindulgence. In fact, Long Tall Willie confessed that he had been seriously injured on a number of occasions due to the star's inebriated condition.

Long Tall Willie further informed us that despite acting as a human pincushion, his life as part of the roving performers was really quite good. Among the company's freaks, monstrosities and outcasts, he was given both respect and acceptance, valuable commodities to one who had been shunned and laughed at his entire life. That was until *The Great Ricardo* began a secret dalliance with the dwarf's wife. Since there were really no secrets among this traveling clan, Long Tall Willie discovered the treachery and vowed to seek revenge against the Spanish drunkard. Planning to murder *The Great Ricardo* for this very personal crime, Long Tall Willie realized that he needed to bide his time and wait for the proper opportunity.

Not very long after his fateful discovery of his mate's infidelity, Long Tall Willie prepared himself for yet another knife-hurling performance. That day he noted that *The Great Ricardo* seemed more than his usual inebriated, stumbling and weaving self as he made his grand appearance. However, in studying his enemy's movements and mannerisms closely, Long Tall Willie realized that the rascal's hands were not shaking and quaking as they normally did before a truly drunken performance. The dwarf realized that this act was a ruse in order to attempt his own murder. Long Tall Willie began his own series of preparations to turn the tables on this dastardly villain.

Extremely terrified for his own well-being, Long Tall Willie happened to scan the audience as he pondered a way out of the dilemma. He had noted that seated directly behind him was the esteemed mayor of the neighboring village with a young and pretty lass snuggled beside him. Spying these two unwary assistants gave the dwarf a moment of inspiration and he suddenly realized exactly what he needed to do to escape the perilous situation. Addressing the loud and boisterous audience, Long Tall Willie made a very sincere apology for his noticeable lack in height, which would hamper the proper viewing of the dangerous performance that was about to unfold. Unceremoniously, he called out for a square prop box to be delivered to the center of the ring. The obvious intent was to utilize this prop as a means of elevating and isolating the dwarf's stature so that everyone in the audience could view the diminutive performer more clearly as he faced certain death. The boisterous audience clapped and roared their heartfelt appreciation of the dwarf's thoughtful last-minute addition to the act. With a low and steady drumbeat to announce the start of the act, Long Tall Willie waited on his specially devised platform.

Long Tall Willie knew that his philandering enemy had a tendency to aim high, normally striking the planted post against which the dwarf routinely stood. Rough, splintered marks high on this post attested to the usual placement of past misguided blades. At last the drumbeat quickened signaling the initiation of the act. Unleashing the first blade with far greater velocity than usual, *The Great Ricardo* actually parted the hair of the brave dwarf, leaving a nasty blood-welling slash in its wake. Now Long Tall Willie knew the moment was right to execute his planned deception. As the drumbeat again quickened, *The Great Ricardo* unleashed a wicked and vicious killing throw as Long Tall Willie covertly stepped down from the cube in a very stealthy manner not detected by the audience. Now considerably shorter that just a moment before, the blade whistled over his head missing the striking post entirely! Continuing on its errant journey, the knife buried itself into the sensitive *privates* of the visiting mayor. Grievously wounded and issuing a string of agonizing wails, the crazed mayor screamed for the immediate arrest of the murderous drunken swine who had tried to emasculate him. *The Great Ricardo* was escorted roughly out of the carnival tent proclaiming his innocence at the top of his voice. As he was manhandled past him, Long Tall Willie gave him a weak and brief wave goodbye. He then rushed back to his quarters, packed his few belongings and bid a cold farewell to the adulteress he had called his wife. Wishing to put the ugly past far behind him, Long Tall Willie enlisted on a merchantman headed for foreign ports of call.

We officially welcomed both Long Tall Willie and Charlie Crowsfeet as valued members of our small company aboard the *Amafata*. I remarked that we knew Long Tall Willie had experience in the receiving end of the knife-throwing act and wondered aloud how he fared at actually throwing knives. In a blur of motion, the little man hopped off the stool he was sitting on and grabbed one of Handy's sharp galley knives. The blade flew from his hands and embedded in a ship's beam that was directly over my head. I understood then that his talent was truly remarkable as the knife was no more than a finger's length from the top of my noggin, quivering furiously from the sheer velocity of the throw.

The very next morning, the entire crew was alerted by shouts and cries issued from the maindeck. Making our way topside, we were astounded when we realized the reason for the commotion. A very strange and eerie fish sighting had the entire ship in a state of near panic. As I gazed down into the clear tropical sea, I was stunned to see an enormous black shadow swimming directly below our ship. This strange fish was as wide and long as three full-grown men stacked head to toe! Handy, who was now standing at my side, made the sign-of-the-cross as he spat out the word…Devilfish. Below us was a huge winged monster that was as black as any London alley at midnight. I understood immediately how this creature acquired its name given the two large and distinctive horns that protruded from its head as well as the evil whip-like tail that trailed ominously behind the creature. Handy informed me that sailors believed that this monster of the deep spelled disaster for any unsuspecting ship.

As I stared at this enormous sea monster gliding in slow graceful movements along a seemingly aimless path, I happened to glance over and spot Long Tall Willie, who was also staring at the eerie creature white with total fear. Moving closer to the terrified dwarf, I heard him exclaim that we were all doomed. Inquiring what he meant by this claim of disaster, he swallowed back his terror and informed me that this creature was the watchdog for the villainous rogue who called himself the Black Tarantula. He confessed to me that this same monster actually served as pet and lookout for the feared sea raider that he and Charlie had the utter misfortune of encountering not so very long ago. He related that this same Devilfish usually accompanied the black rogue in his raiding efforts, acting as an advance scout and alerting his master of any potential prey.

Long Tall Willie stood at the rail mesmerized by this enormous black shadow, muttering and stuttering about destruction and ruin. His mournful state and dire warnings had shocked and frightened all now staring into the water at the gliding Devilfish. Many of my fellow crewmates were attempting to ward off this evil premonition by crossing themselves or issuing silent prayers for deliverance.

Strangely, I did not share either their absolute alarm or their certain belief that we were all doomed. While I believed that the Black Tarantula could be accompanied by such a behemoth, I did not accept or believe that this fish was that very same specter of doom. I reasoned that all of these sea phantoms would appear exactly alike, since the entire species had no true identifying markings on them in order to tell them apart. In other words, one Devilfish would appear exactly like another while traveling the ocean's lanes. In fact, I theorized that utilizing this ploy, the Black Tarantula could instill unreasonable fear and terror among honest sailors anytime a Devilfish was spotted in open waters. Therefore, I had to give credit to the very sick mind of this sea villain for creating such a strong and powerful ruse.

Chapter 29: Pirates Ahoy

Later that very same day, the topman standing watch shouted out that he had spied a ship off in the distance, which again brought the entire crew to the upperdeck. Long Tall Willie and Charlie Crowsfeet were both off to the side blubbering that the ship surely belonged to none other than the Black Tarantula, foretold by the passage of his foul pet earlier that morning. Believing our new recruits correct, the entire crew crowded onto the deck to catch a glimpse of our oncoming doom. The Captain, alerted by all this commotion, hurried from his cabin grasping his faithful telescope in order to inspect our new sea neighbor at closer range. Sighting his instrument on the far horizon, the Captain spent several long minutes scrutinizing our new arrival. Finally satisfied with his survey, he announced to all that the new ship was a schooner that sailed without a flag of any kind. While a bit unsettled by this discovery, the Captain informed us that this new ship seemed to be following a course very similar to our own. In a vain attempt to calm the crew, the Captain announced that there was absolutely no reason for mass panic, since the vessel seemed intent on its own voyage, paying very little attention to the *Amafata*. He ordered the helmsman to continue along our present course. Handing his precious telescope to me, he instructed that I maintain a constant surveillance on the distant schooner and to report any course corrections directly to him. With that he gave me a wink and a nod and slowly made his way back to his cabin.

Accepting the wondrous tool from his hands, I immediately raised the instrument to my eyes and began my ordered surveillance. I continued to monitor the situation until the fading light of day made viewing all but impossible. Returning the telescope to the Captain, I promised to resume my lookout vigil at the very first light.

Retiring to the galley for much needed sustenance, I was greeted by my fellow messmates and quizzed unmercifully as to my observations of the trailing ship. Having very little to report, I informed the nervous diners that nothing had changed since the Captain had first announced his own long-distance observations. My mates began wailing and moaning about our ill fortune and distress, convinced that the Black Tarantula had been alerted to our presence by his pet Devilfish. Further, the terrified men were also adamant that the renowned sea devil was now shadowing our every move, waiting for the precise opportunity to attack. I recounted that the ship was still a long way off and really only time would determine its true intentions. While the crew continued to mutter nervously, Angry George leapt at the chance to spin another of his *sea tales*. He waited for the groans and hisses to subside and then began by notifying all that this was not the first time in his nautical life that he had found himself in similar danger.

Angry George informed his rapt audience that the event had occurred while he served on a merchantman much like our own. His vessel had just loaded barrels of rum and sugar in Jamaica for a return voyage to England. The voyage had progressed with no major incidents and the crew anxiously looked forward to returning home to receive a promised extra bonus payment. As they made this return journey, they were oblivious to the danger that awaited them on the open ocean. One week later, a ship was spotted shark- shadowing them, neither closing the gap nor drifting away. Concern was expressed by the entire crew for both their precious cargo and their very lives should their shadow turn out to be pirate. Their Captain decided that making a run for safety was their best course of action. As luck would have it, the sky darkened as the day progressed announcing an approaching storm. The promised tempest arrived at dusk bringing both strong winds and rolling waves. Realizing that this was their moment of opportunity, the Captain ordered all sails employed to eke out the fastest possible speed in an attempt to evade their pursuers. All lights onboard were extinguished and the escape attempt officially commenced. Running blindly under full sail in very *dirty weather* the entire night, everyone onboard was confident that they had eluded disaster.

As dawn broke and the storm abated, the crew was greeted with a very startling sight. Their pursuers were spotted directly behind them and were closing the gap between them in rapid fashion. Somehow during the blackness of the night and in the midst of a raging squall, their enemies had tracked their movements and now seemed prepared to launch their attack. Being a merchantman, there was very little armament aboard to prevent their shadow from reeking utter destruction. All the hapless crew could manage was watching in horror as their adversaries bore directly down upon them. The crew fully realized the enormity of the danger facing them, but was powerless to prevent this dreaded outcome. The deck of their enemy was now filled with filthy screaming beasts intent on destruction and ruin. A black flag sporting a saber dripping red droplets of blood now flew proudly from the mainmast announcing them as pirates. The antics and animal-like behavior of the pirates struck total fear and resignation on the doomed merchantman and no fight was made to avoid capture.

The Captain was dragged forth for questioning by the pirate leader, a gaunt, sickly looking barbarian, who sported an eye patch over his right eye. This crazed animal immediately made inquiries as to the exact location of the ship's hidden treasures. The Captain, feigning ignorance, claimed that no such booty existed. Prepared for this response, the feral pirate just smiled and informed the terrified commander that he was not a very convincing actor. Calling out to his brutish horde, the pirate leader ordered that a game of *run and catch* was required to loosen the tight lips of his victim. Ordering two rogues to fetch the needed implements for the game, the pirate devil commanded that the Captain needed to be blindfolded for the upcoming festivities. Returning quickly to the captured prize, the dispatched envoys delivered several wicked-looking grappling hooks to their esteemed commander. These viciously sharp boarding instruments were then distributed to several of the pirate rabble and the fun began in earnest.

Requesting again the location of the ship's hidden treasure and receiving the same empty response, the pirate leader ordered his men to release their prevaricating prey. Shivering in absolute terror, the captured and now blindfolded Captain was given instructions on the rules of the game they were about to play. As directed, the Captain's objective seemed quite simple in scope. Should the Captain locate the mainmast and successfully ascend the nearby lines to the upper spar, the ship and crew would be released without further harm to the ship. However, if he was unable to perform this simple task then the ship would be looted, his crew marooned and he would be secured onboard to be burned alive as his ship was fired and sank. Finally, the pirate chieftain informed the poor wretch that the insidiously sharp grappling hooks would be utilized to detain his intended progress.

At a signal from the pirate skipper, the blindfolded officer was spun around several times to create complete disorientation and was summarily released. Staggering in total confusion, the bewildered Captain began his ill-fated attempt to save his ship and crew. Making very unsteady progress but assisted by the frenzied shouts from his men offering directional information, the Captain stumbled and lost his footing, slamming face-first into the deck. Rising to a kneeling position, the determined officer scuttled and crab-crawled his way across the deck in search of the elusive mainmast. As he neared his intended target, he was loudly encouraged onward by his own crew, who were overjoyed at the progress the poor soul was making. At this point, the evil pirate king ordered his grapplers into the fray. Reacting with anticipated glee, the heathens unleashed their weapons snaring the unwary Captain with the devilishly sharpened hooks. With joint heaves, the pirate tormentors dragged the blindfolded man farther and farther away from his goal.

Released once again from the sharp tines of the grappling hooks, the game was restarted with the same result time and time again. Having been pierced by the hook's barbs countless times, the pain-laden and delirious Captain was now bleeding from all ports. In his hopeless attempts at promised salvation, the suffering wretch had deposited copious blood trails across the deck. Due to this, the grapplers were now having a difficult time utilizing their weapons with any kind of accuracy as they slipped, skidded and fell into the numerous bloody pools decorating the deck. Their difficulties brought roar after roar from their pirate brethren who were totally enthralled with the *run and catch* contest.

Dreadfully weakened due to his catastrophic bleeding, the doomed unfortunate attempted one last time to reach the mainmast, but all could see that his time was quickly nearing an end. Weakened and exhausted, the bloodied lump of human meat collapsed for the final time and expired with an anguished and tortured cry. Absolutely delighted by the final outcome of their game, the pirate throng erupted in a wild celebratory spree, with rum- crazed dancing, shouting and reveling in the victory they had just witnessed. At the end of the bloody contest, the pirate Captain ordered the mutilated corpse of the valiant participant dumped overboard and the ship stripped of any and all of its valuable cargo.

The anxious and terrified crew was transferred to the pirate vessel to await their ultimate fate as their dear ship was plundered and sacked. As the numbed tars stared in dread, their ship was set afire, eventually slipping beneath the waves singing a smoking and hissing farewell. Having completed his annihilation and devastation on the captured prize, the pirate Captain ordered his crew to set sail in search of an appropriate isle to deposit his unwelcome human cargo.

The next day, the pirate heathens located a tiny atoll perfectly suited to their evil intentions. They anchored just off the isle and transferred the captured prisoners to their new home. As they sailed away, the deserted crew heard the murderous scum wishing them good fortune and luck on their marooned prison. Angry George concluded his tale of fear and terror by informing us that that the survivors had to endure a full two weeks of starvation and hardship before a passing Spanish galley came to their rescue. In that time, they had lost over half of their comrades to thirst, starvation and pure hopelessness. Concluding his frightful saga, he warned us that all pirates were in league with the devil, *Old Scratch,* and as such could track prey in the darkest of nights regardless of weather conditions! He also promised that all pirates were bloodthirsty monsters, spelling pain and suffering for any unfortunates who crossed their wake. After nervously wolfing down my meager meal, I retired to my hammock to attempt sleep knowing the following day would likely be long, exhausting and fraught with danger.

Early the next morning, I was back on the quarterdeck with the borrowed telescope trained on the yet distant transport. My careful surveillance continued for two more days with no change whatsoever! On the fourth day, our strange shadow began to close the gap between us. As they proceeded to narrow this distance, I noticed that they had raised the *Union Jack,* announcing that that they were English. Reporting to the Captain this new information and the fact that they were edging closer, he inquired if I had spotted any human activity aboard the ship. Answering no to his question, he ordered me to resume watch and to report any unusual sightings immediately. Returning to the quarterdeck, I once again trained the Captain's telescope on our pursuers and was rewarded with a brief glimpse of a few of their crewmembers prowling the maindeck. My interesting discovery involved the curious dress and the skin color of the men that I had spotted. They were hardly wearing regulation style *slops*, tending more toward rags than clothing. Secondly, two of the three crew members I spotted were black, which I also found very disconcerting.

Racing to the Captain's quarters, I provided a full report of my observations. Like me, the Captain found my report perplexing, notifying me that what I had just described seemed very much at odds with the *Union Jack* the ship was flying. He remarked that an English captain would certainly not clad his sailors in rags nor would his crew be made up of a number of black hands. He surmised that we had probably blundered into the path of a despicable pirate band. He immediately called a recovered Mr. Bass into his cabin. As Mr. Bass entered the cabin, I arose and began to make my way to the door to provide them the privacy they required, but was called back by the Captain. He announced that he wanted my thoughts in this strategy session. Earning a look of pure hatred from the First Mate, I resumed my seat as this war council convened.

The Captain was the first to speak, questioning us both if we thought we could outrun our adversaries. For the first time both Mr. Bass and I were on the same side as we told the Captain that our hold was filled to capacity with trade goods and we had no chance at all of outrunning the much swifter aggressor. The Captain then inquired about our armament, wondering aloud if we could defeat this enemy in battle if the opportunity arose. Again Mr. Bass and I both warned the Captain that we had very few weapons aboard our ship. Further, the only cannon that we carried had long ago rusted from sitting idle throughout our voyage. In addition, we had no capable gunner aboard to direct this rusty weapon against an enemy.

Caught in a serious dilemma, the Captain then probed each of us on exactly what we thought we should do given these precarious conditions. Mr. Bass, being the senior officer, spoke first informing the Captain that we should continue on our current course until such time as our sea neighbors became hostile. At that point, it was the First Mate's opinion that we should surrender and suffer the fate that awaited us. He added that perhaps I had been erroneous in my observations and that the tailing ship could in fact be English, which would pose no problems for us. The Captain nodded at the response and turned to me. Taking a moment to think the matter through, I suddenly came up with a very unorthodox idea.

Mr. Bass took this opportunity to chide me on my utter ignorance of all things nautical. Despite this objection, I slowly laid out the situation and the meager resources we had at our disposal, I talked them both through the plan I had in mind. When I finally finished, I was greeted by a loud snort of derision from Mr. Bass. He told the Captain that it was the most ridiculous plan he had ever heard. Laughing and hooting like a deranged madman, Mr. Bass announced that anyone willing to perpetuate this joke of a plan was stark-raving mad.

Angered and embarrassed to the extreme, I sat smoldering waiting for the Captain to speak. He looked at both of us and then a rare broad smile graced his face as he told me that he thought that my plan just might work. Sputtering in total disbelief, the First Mate told the Captain that my plan was utter lunacy. The Captain, directing his somber gaze toward Mr. Bass, asked if the plan was any crazier than maddened Blood Monkeys in full attack mode. This ended all arguments as the bully picked himself up from his chair and stomped noisily out of the cabin. The Captain quickly turned my way and inquired how much time and assistance I would require. I answered that it would take a good half-day to prepare everything. As for aid, I told him that all I required was the assistance of the three Adams sisters. He ordered me to begin my preparations immediately while he planned to pay the sisters a visit to enlist their assistance. Jumping up from my seat, I raced to the hold to collect a few essentials that I would require.

As I made my way back to the Adams sisters' quarters, I nearly ran down the Captain. Smiling once again, he told me that the sisters were more than overjoyed with the plan and stood ready to assist in any way they could. Wishing me luck, the Captain headed topside to keep an eye on the suspected pirate ship. Entering the sisters' cabin, I was greeted by all three sisters, who seemed aglow with the prospect of perpetuating the extreme ruse I had devised. Dividing the massive workload among us, I set about locating the right group of volunteers required for the insane performance we were about to enact. Finding Handy in the galley, I quickly laid out the scheme that the Captain had approved. He broke out in a sudden fit of laughter when I finished my summary. He let me know that the plan was certainly bold and crazy enough to work. He immediately volunteered his services, and promised to deliver the required assistants to the sisters' quarters in no time at all. Leaving him to his recruitment work, I next made a visit to the Doc's surgery. Once again relating the main points of the plan, I asked the Doc for his valuable assistance in the ploy we were about to execute. Laughing so loud that he was almost in tears, the Doc told me that this was the looniest plan that he had ever heard, but agreed that if we executed it properly that it would be a stunning victory for us all. I outlined everything I needed from him, and he promised to devote his full effort to our cause.

By the time I returned to the sisters' cabin, Gertrude was already at work brewing up a special concoction for the party we were planning. Willamina was submerged waist-deep in the large costume trunk, picking out appropriate disguises for our upcoming party. Hortence was busy collecting all the necessary make-up we so desperately required. Once she had gathered all of these, I sent her directly to the Doc's surgery, where her crucial detail work would be performed. Before leaving the room, I instructed Willamina to deliver the required costumes to the Captain's quarters, where the final touches would be affected. Completing the first round of preparations, I dashed up to the maindeck to ensure that all was made ready for the strange welcoming party we had planned.

As I left the cabin, Handy and his volunteers suddenly made their appearance. Briefing them all in a hurried manner, I sent them all to the Doc's surgery for the stage preparations that we all knew would make the difference between success and failure. Stopping briefly on the quarterdeck, I asked the Captain to give me a rough estimate on the time we had left before the rogues attacked. He informed me that our friends were moving cautiously but ever closer to the *Amafata*. He estimated that we had no more than two hours or so before the brutes would be upon us. Lastly, he informed me that a *Jolly Roger* had replaced the *Union Jack* on the closing vessel signifying that the ship was indeed pirate. Wishing me luck, he ordered all crew below deck in anticipation of the upcoming pirate raid.

Making some necessary alterations to the top deck, I ran down to the Doc's surgery to check on the status of the preparations. Doc and Hortence were busy applying the necessary make-up to each of the volunteers. As soon as each was finished, I told the Doc to send the decorated volunteers to the Captain's cabin for costuming. Rushing to the Captain's quarters, I found Willamina in full and furious activity preparing each costume for the willing actors in our little drama. Informing her that she would soon have volunteers arriving, she responded that all would be ready when each made his appearance. Lastly, I scurried back to the sisters' cabin to check on the status of Gertrude's work. She divulged that she was also almost finished. I instructed her to deliver her concoction to the Captain's quarters, where she would don her disguise and join the party topside.

Having now checked on all the elements of our fraud, I hurried back to the Captain's side to get the latest timing of the arrival of our esteemed guests. The Captain informed me that it appeared that the pirates were now ready to attack and were closing the distance rapidly between our two ships. As I watched the pirate ship drawing closer, Handy, the first of our brilliant acting troop, made his way onto the main deck. Not prepared for the startling alterations the sisters and Doc had fabricated, both the Captain and I were taken totally by surprise. Giving us both a huge wink and a smile, Handy informed me that all actors would be completely ready in just a very short while. Instructing Handy on his stage position and the final details of his role, I hurried once more to the Captain's quarters to obtain from Gertrude her special concoction. Accepting the vial with the precious liquid, I once again made my way topside to administer the *witch's medicine* that Gertrude had prepared.

Greatly relieved to find more than half of the volunteers already on the deck and in their assigned places, I circulated from man to man dosing them with the herbalist's elixir. In just a few minutes time, the actors who had imbibed the special tonic were acting out the roles exactly as I had orchestrated. They were transformed into glazed-eyed, stumbling and drooling zombies while ranting and raving about unseen but very real enemies, who were in the process of vicious attacks. At this point, I sent the Captain below to be made up by Hortence for his important role in the upcoming confrontation. At last, all was ready with the sisters each dressed in nursing outfits, the Doc in a long white surgical gown complete with blood splattered gore and our Captain also made up in a very hideous manner sporting a hailing trumpet so he could communicate with our guests from a considerable distance. Lastly, I ran to the Doc's surgery for my own preparation. Hortence quickly applied some of her make-up on my face and arms and we joined our fellow conspirators on the maindeck.

All was now in readiness, as Hortence and I made our way to our own assigned positions. At that moment we were able to hear as well as see our dear guests arriving for the party we had planned especially in their honor. Actually, they made quite a frightening sight as they quickly closed the gap between our vessels. There were about fifty prancing and dancing rum-soaked heathens crowded on the maindeck of their ship. Yelling and screaming murderous and unthinkable acts of violence, the pirate horde seemed more than ready to attack and destroy us. As they came within shouting distance, the Captain raised his hailing trumpet and shouted a very warm welcome to the savage sea dogs. His welcome was answered by additional pirate screams and shouts, but at last their Captain answered our sincere welcome with a call for complete surrender or face the nasty consequences of his blood-maddened crew.

Our Captain answered back that we had absolutely no intentions of fighting this crazed throng, but rather desperately required their assistance. The pirate leader, totally confused by this request, asked our Captain exactly what kind of assistance we required. Our Captain shouted back that a very serious and deadly plague had broken out aboard our vessel while we had been at sea. He then went on to inform the pirates that we had already experienced numerous painful and agonizing deaths at the hands of this unknown killer. At exactly that moment, I along with the Doc proceeded to drop what appeared to be a corpse wrapped in a traditionally stitched sailcloth shroud into the sea. This act and the Captain's plague announcement brought the crazed pirates to a standstill.

The pirates, who up to this point had been so intent on frightening us into total submission, took stock in what exactly was occurring aboard our ship. What they viewed shocked them into total awe. On our ship, the actors in our small drama were playing each of their roles to perfection. The Doc and the three sisters roamed from patient to patient sprawled haphazardly across the maindeck. To the pirates viewing our drama, the doctor and his three nurses seemed to have their hands full administering to the suffering plague victims in their care. As I had planned, Hortence with her skilled theatrical experience had applied make-up on each of our volunteers with startling results. Huge, weeping open sores adorned each of our sailors Handy had recruited. To add a further touch of realism to our *plague party*, we had hastily doled out Gertrude's *wormwood* elixir coupled with rum, turning each of these gruesome plague riddled victims into mindless stumbling and screaming beasts. As I stopped to take in the full effect of the charade we had assembled, I could do nothing more than shiver with fright at the horrific scene being portrayed, even with the knowledge that it was all a complete sham. The Captain and I were also made up with the same nasty and alarming weeping plague sores on our own faces and arms.

Raising his hailing trumpet once again, the Captain pleaded with the pirates to come aboard and lend their assistance to our baleful state. Well, it did not take long for the bloodthirsty pirates to make their decision. The pirate leader called across the water that both he and his crew had very little knowledge of medicine so that their assistance was of no value. Additionally, he shouted that their own medical stores were running at an all-time low level so that they had no medicine to share with us. Our Captain, keeping the ruse in motion, pleaded once more for any assistance they could offer, including our desperate need of food and fresh water for the stricken plague victims. Once again, the pirate Captain answered in the negative informing us that they were also very low on these same necessities so assistance of any kind was totally impossible.

At this point, our Captain, relishing the role he was playing, yelled across to the pirate ship that he was personally coming over to have a face-to-face parlay with the pirate Captain. Stunned by his boldness, I had to marvel at the wondrous performance he was putting on for our thieving guests. The pirate leader did not share my emotion, for he informed our Captain in no uncertain terms to remain onboard so as not to risk infecting his crew with our dreaded malady. At this point, Handy, in a completely delirious state due to Gertrude's *wormwood* tonic, yelled over to the pirates that man-eating turtles had been set loose on our ship. He informed the stunned and horrified pirates that these savage creatures were now hiding below deck waiting patiently to drag all onboard down to the hold to their everlasting doom. Well, that was the final tidbit that snapped the pirates into fast and furious action. Manning their stations in a frenzy of human activity, the pirates turned their ship away and fled the gruesome scene as if Satan and his demon army had been stationed on our ship. In a parting salute, the pirate Captain ingeniously wished us the best of luck and bid us a fond farewell.

As they made their hasty retreat and could no longer be seen through the Captain's telescope, I could do nothing but fall down laughing, remembering the horrified pirate stares as these sea devils ran out their full sail to beat a hasty retreat from our floating pit of hell. Since Gertrude's elixir was quite mild, our blubbering, stumbling and drooling plague victims began to quickly recover from their delirium. They too joined me laughing and crying with joy over the victory we won against the savage sea scavengers. The Captain raced over to me as I laid on the deck with tears of joy running down my cheeks. Waiting until I stood, he gave me a congratulatory hug and told me that I had saved the ship. To further celebrate our victory, he ordered a full hogshead of rum be brought topside to be shared by the entire jubilant crew. In the far distance, I could barely make out the last vestiges of the fleeing pirate ship. I knew for a fact that they would not return and that we had been spared sure pain and death at the hands of these monsters. Turning to thank Handy for all of his help in the drama, I noticed a scowling Mr. Bass, who had that same look of intense hatred on his face as the bloodthirsty pirates who had just abandoned us!

Chapter 30: Promotion and Advancement

Nothing was quite the same after the plague ruse. It was as if I had undergone a transformation from boyhood to manhood. Nobody really made comments of this sort, but I could sense and feel a subtle change in my mate's looks and their tone of voice when addressing me…almost a reverence toward me that made me extremely uncomfortable. I longed for the way that it had once been, but I knew in my heart it could never be again. My daily navigation lessons continued with the Captain but the time period involved became shorter and shorter. In reality, I was doing all of the navigation with the Captain acting as advisor and council on various nuances. Given the shorter duration necessary to complete these navigational duties, the time spent on our daily chess matches increased proportionally. Over the last several months, the Captain and I had become equals in our ability to play this complicated game.

While engaged in a match a few days after our pirate adventure, the Captain informed me that he planned on taking on a few operating cannons while on Jamaica. To this end, he informed me that no one onboard had any real experience with cannons. He further confided that he had discussions with the Adams sisters, who had a high-ranking military officer as part of their family on Jamaica who would gladly assist in the training of our new cannon team. Once properly trained, this team would be put in charge of all defense efforts aboard our ship. Remarking that my natural ability to quickly study and master a subject was truly remarkable, the Captain then petitioned me to take on the new role of Cannon Master.

Agreeing at once, I inquired if this new role would interfere with our daily navigational lessons or our very competitive chess matches. Smiling broadly at me, he informed me that he had thought thoroughly about the entire situation. In doing so, he related that I would be freed of my time-intensive duties to the Adams sisters once we reached the port of Kingston. Having this generous extra time on my hands would allow me to fill the dual role he had in mind for me. With the same broad smile, he announced that beyond the aforementioned duty as Cannon Master, the Captain was promoting me to the position of Ship Navigator to take effect immediately. He congratulated me on my many achievements throughout our voyage, and disclosed that it was high time that I was properly rewarded for my dedicated service to the welfare and well-being of the ship and her crew.

As Navigator, I would report directly to the Captain along with Mr. Bass. In my heart, I was sure that this new development would not please the First Mate in any way whatsoever. However, the relief I felt knowing that I would not be under the direct control of the ship's bully was both gratifying and exciting at the same time. The Captain then congratulated me on my promotion and informed me that he intended to make this announcement that very day to the entire crew, prior to our imminent arrival at Kingston.

Gratefully agreeing to the Captain's plan, he invited me to join him on the quarterdeck to formally announce my promotion. This news was greeted with a rousing cheer and congratulatory excitement by all, save a scowling Mr. Bass and Catstalker Gene, who appeared to have just partaken of a rancid slice of *maggot pie*. The ugly scowls on both became even more pronounced as the Captain announced that I would also be assuming the new role as Cannon Master, and that I would be selecting a cannon team that would be trained with this knowledge and experience. He further told the crew that we would be lingering at this new destination for the next few months to wait out the worst of the hurricane season we had now entered. This extended period of stay would provide ample time for me and my new cannon team to gain the expertise required.

The good news that we would be docked for an extended period of time brought an even greater round of hoots and cheers from the crew, who now looked forward to spending this period onshore enjoying the comforts and amenities of our new temporary home. To celebrate the news of my promotion, the Captain ordered a hogshead of rum to be delivered topside to toast my good fortune. This news made an already happy crew delirious and several more cheers were offered for my promotion as well as to the kind and generous spirit of our Captain. As the rum was distributed, Handy approached me; he put his arm around me and informed me that this was one of the proudest days of his life. Gathered around Handy were my crewmates and friends, who were waiting their turn to express their own well wishes. Noting that he had an unsuspecting audience, Handy announced that my promotion reminded him of a story. To his good-natured but hissing compatriots, he signaled for silence before commencing one of his endless sea tales.

He communicated to his now muted audience that his story took place a number of years ago, when he was but a mere lad. Looking over his cragged and leathery face, I thought to myself that it must have been an exceedingly long time ago! The subject of his latest *sea tale* concerned the promotion of an extremely popular crewmate named Gordy Blythe. As Handy continued, he described Gordy as a loyal and friendly individual, who was liked and befriended by the entire ship. For the most part, Gordy was inept at any chore he tackled. Sensing his audience as being a bit confused as to how a total incompetent could ever merit a promotion, Handy related the details.

It seemed that Handy's ship happened to sail right into the path of a band of marauding pirates. As this unfortunate sighting was announced to their Captain, he ordered all hands to their battle stations. Having absolutely no value above deck defending against the hostile pirate scum, Gordy reported to the gun crew where he was assigned the responsibility of *powder monkey*. This meant that Gordy was responsible for running shot and powder to each of the two cannon crews. Handy barked out a laugh and narrated that Gordy's *powder monkey* role was basically designed to keep him from harming any of his own crewmates.

Well, the pirates, sensing a profitable prey, maneuvered their ship to begin their attack. Their dastardly plan called for running alongside their under-gunned prey and firing a broadside with their superior firepower to force a quick surrender. Handy's Captain realized that only a miracle would save his precious ship. To that end, he instructed his Cannon Master to utilize his few cannons wisely and very selectively. As the pirate vessel neared, the Cannon Master ordered both of his cannon crews to aim their weapons at the pirate's mainmast and sails in a desperate attempt to inflict serious damage to both the maneuverability and speed of their approaching enemy. He told both crews to hold their fire until he judged the time optimal. With both cannon crews poised to unload their paltry barrage, Gordy entered the area with an armload of cannon shot. Oblivious to a slow match that had dropped down on the deck, Gordy stepped directly on this burning cord with his bare feet. At that same instant, the Cannon Master ordered his two gun teams to fire. As the gun crews touched the powder pans that would ignite the charge and fire the loaded shot, Gordy, howling and screaming in absolute pain from his burned and pain-wracked feet, dropped the shot he carried further injuring his aching appendages.

Hopping around in abject agony, Gordy managed to knock into both cannons changing their intended trajectory. Since the cannons' fuses had already been lit, there was nothing the stunned cannon crews could do to stop their weapons from firing. With a loud and thunderous clap, both cannons unleashed their powerful blasts. Running to the gunports, the cannon crews scrambled over one another to judge if their errantly jarred shots would have any chance at all of striking their attackers. To their extreme shock, they realized that each of the misdirected shots hit the bow of their enemy directly at the pirate ship's waterline. Both shots caused massive and crippling damage to the pirate sloop, which immediately broke off its attack. As Handy and his crewmates assembled on the main deck, they were greeted by the sight of their feared enemy mortally wounded and taking on water at a prodigious rate.

As the pirate sloop slunk away, the Captain, refusing to show any mercy to the nautical thieves, ordered his crew to maintain their present course in total disregard to the sinking pirate scum. The Captain then called his Cannon Master forward to explain why his direct order had been disobeyed. The nervous Cannon Master sensing trouble from his Captain, pointed to the injured tar telling the Captain that Gordy alone was responsible for altering the aim of both cannons. The Captain was a bit surprised by this news. When he regained his composure, he called Gordy forth. Nervously inching his way to the Captain's side, it was now Gordy's turn to be shocked as the Captain wrapped his arms around him and announced to the crew that Gordy had just saved both the ship and their lives. Smiling and clapping Gordy heartily on the back, he proclaimed that from that moment on Gordy was promoted to Cannon Master. Calling for rum, the Captain ordered a celebration in honor of their newest ship's officer and hero…Gordy!

In the days that followed, Gordy's promotion went directly to his head.

Abandoning his old friends, Gordy gained an inflated opinion of himself and began to order around his old crewmates, who were well aware of the lad's exploits when it came to the real story behind the cannon shots. Initially believing Gordy's new role as well as his idiotic orders to be nothing but a joke, they refused to obey the commands of their newest officer. Embarrassed and enraged, Gordy sentenced two of his oldest friends to ten lashes of the *cat* to garner their attention and obedience. Once both old friends were summarily punished, the rest of the crew went about their assigned duties, knowing that something had to be done to revenge the unjust punishment that Gordy had just delivered.

For the next full day, Handy and his shipmates made plans to revenge their comrades. Well aware that Gordy was not much of a drinker, they proceeded one night to ply him with round after round of drink until he was blind-staggering drunk. At this point, their plan began in earnest. Coaxing the drunken officer to the maindeck for one last toast, they all fell upon Gordy and bound his arms behind his back and then blindfolded him. Once incapacitated, a call was made to make ready the new officer's bath. In actuality, the bath ordered for Gordy was a dip in an overflowing *piss tub*. I believe I have failed to inform you of these nasty devices. You see, *piss tubs* were nothing more than urine tubs usually situated in seldom-used corners of a ship. These noxious devices served as temporary latrines during nasty weather as well as receptacles for disposing unwanted tobacco juice. However, an overflowing *piss tub* was the foul and disgusting device that suited this revenge-minded crew just perfectly!

Carrying their bound and blindfolded victim over to his promised bath, they proceeded to dunk Gordy head first directly into the vile *piss tub*. Sputtering, gagging and choking, Gordy was dunked again and again until he vowed to amend his ways around his crewmates. Finally screaming his agreement to their demands, Gordy's hands were untied. Before his captors could remove his blindfold, Gordy took off in a drunken, stumbling run to get far away from his malicious friends. Running at a full rate of speed, Gordy collided with the ship's rail and his forward momentum carried him directly over the rail into the dark and turbulent sea. Calling the dreaded alarm of man overboard, they all raced to the rail to catch sight of their old friend. Alerted by their terrified cries, the Captain appeared and ordered the ship brought around so that a proper search could be conducted.

Launching the ship's two longboats, the Captain conducted a search for his newest officer. The remainder of that night was spent in a fruitless search for Gordy. By dawn, the Captain realized that Gordy was lost and ordered all search efforts ceased. When questioned on how Gordy managed to fall overboard, the contrite conspirators answered that he had stumbled over a *piss tub* that was up on deck to be dumped and fell over the rail into the sea by accident. The Captain, well aware of Gordy's past accidents, accepted the explanation and the matter was closed permanently.

In finishing his tale, Handy turned to me and communicated that the moral to his story was *"do not let success go to your head because it can lead to nothing but trouble."* With that he laughed and slapped me on the back, telling me that I had much more common sense than Gordy ever had. At the same time, I took his ominous warning to heart.

As expected, all three Adams sisters were also thrilled and excited by my good news. Gertrude informed me that their nephew was the commander of Fort Charles on the island. She promised that they all would see that the necessary arrangements were made to provide me and my new cannon team the proper training and experience needed. Wishing me the best of luck in my new role, they excused themselves and returned to their cabin to begin preparations for landing on their home island.

I retired to my hammock for some much needed rest but before I slipped into sleep I thought about the likely candidates for my new cannon team. I realized that I needed to select sailors who I could not only trust but who could also train effectively. While I really wanted Handy to be a part of this team, I understood that the selection of my friend was just not possible. His missing appendage would pose a serious hindrance in making him an effective cannon crew member. I finally settled on Long Tall Willie, Angry George and Creeping Jeremy as my best options. Satisfied with these choices, I settled down for a few hours of sleep made extremely difficult by the anticipation and excitement that coursed through my body!

The very next day, I informed the Captain of my crew choices. Each of these crewmembers was called to his quarters, where the Captain and I announced our plans. Each of my new team was excited and promised that they would work hard at becoming an excellent cannon team that the entire ship would be proud to call their own.

Soon after, the island of Jamaica was spotted on the horizon and activity aboard became furious, as we began our landing preparations. As we neared the southeast coast of the island, we were all treated to a spectacular view of Kingston's harbor, surrounding beaches and the town itself rising up from the beach before us.

Chapter 31: Jamaica... Sugar Sweet Port

As the center of English trade, Jamaica served as a vital redistribution point for most goods arriving in the Caribbean. As we neared Kingston's harbor, we were greeted with several different wondrous sights. The most impressive of these were the lushly vegetated Blue Mountains that rose to form a backdrop to the town. Additionally, as we neared the harbor entrance, we were able to spot the submerged ruins of old Port Royale in the clear aqua sea. Once named the Wickedest City in the New World, all that now remained were these underwater burial ruins that we were passing. Handy had told me that when the devastating earthquake plunged this settlement into the sea, an estimated two thousand individuals met their maker. As we passed over this nautical gravesite, we were all very somber and respectful for the dead souls buried beneath us.

Kingston presented itself as a very colorful and beautiful city from our seaward vantage point. As with any port, the buildings directly off of the white sand beach were made up of trading warehouses and offices. Behind these trading establishments, the remainder of the town sprung up in the form of shops, inns, entertainment edifices and colonist homes.

Like Saint Domingue, the interior of the island contained huge and sprawling plantation estates that were situated on the higher fertile plains of the island at the base of the spectacular Blue Mountains. As was the case on other islands, these gigantic farmsteads were powered by slaves. The port itself was a hive of activity as trading ships were constantly being loaded and unloaded. The majority of this backbreaking labor was being accomplished by a multitude of slave gangs. The island slaves went about their hard labor from dawn until dusk driven by whip-wielding overseers, who, like Mr. Bass, were not shy about putting their instruments of encouragement to good use. In all, Kingston appeared to each of us to be both a haven of prosperity and at the same time a den of iniquity…a true magnet to sailors bent on carnal fun and recreation!

As we prepared to drop anchor, I was called down to the Adams sisters' cabin to assist in their final preparations. As I entered their lair, I was not the least bit surprised to find that virtually all of their belongings were packed and ready for unloading. Questioning my overall usefulness at providing a modicum of assistance, the three sisters smiled and told me that all they really wanted was to say farewell and to thank me once again for my invaluable assistance and friendship during the voyage. To this end, each had a small gift that they wanted to present. Gertrude, being the oldest, went first presenting me with one of her herbal trunks that was filled to capacity with priceless ingredients from her own precious stores, including two large *belladonna* roots.

Willamina gave me a slender golden ring, which she informed me would certainly make for a very handsome earring to ensure luck and good fortune in my future travels. She explained that the golden ring was in fact the wedding band of a very famous and powerful Gypsy Queen, named Zarina. Finally, Hortence was given the opportunity to speak. She informed me that my marvelous singing voice coupled with my budding acting talents were the highlight of her voyage. To repay me for my kind assistance, she furnished me with a trunk filled to capacity with make-up and various theatrical props that also might come in handy in the future. Speechless at receiving these three marvelous gifts, I had a very hard time holding back tears of joy. At last, I regained my voice and I thanked each sister profusely for their wondrous gifts. They made me solemnly promise to visit them on a regular basis over our time in port. With a parting modest kiss for each, I swore to pay them a visit at my very earliest opportunity. Waving a brief goodbye to my new friends, I made my way to the topdeck to assist my fellow crewmates on arrival duties.

After what seemed like an eternity, we were securely anchored and the unloading effort began, including the transport of all the sisters' numerous trunks and crates to the nearby shore. When all these duties and responsibilities were completed, the crew was given its long awaited liberty to begin exploring our new haunt. When on liberty, my crewmates were interested in three things...good food, strong drink and loose women!

As was the case on Saint Domingue, pirates strutted through town dressed in all types of finery and sported expensive dazzling jewelry. They looked absolutely ridiculous to us in their fine and fancy clothes. Their dressing up efforts had much the same effect on the island's population, who seemed amused and entertained by their outlandish appearance. The other noticeable pirate fashion was the number of different weapons each carried from swords to pistols to every kind and type of weapon imaginable. These colorful roosters were also considered very dangerous reprobates, who needed only the slightest provocation to set them off on a wild killing spree. As such, we tended to avoid any serious confrontations with these iniquitous rogues as we meandered our way through Kingston exploring and scouting out a hospitable entertainment establishment. Handy kept insisting that we locate a tavern known for its food, fun and sporting events, called Fat Dog's Pub. This saloon was owned and managed by a former shipmate…appropriately named Fat Dog. It took us several hours of exploration, but we finally found our intended target and made plans to enter and enjoy this establishment's renowned depravities!

Chapter 32: Fat Dog's Pub

At first sight, Fat Dog's Pub was a bit of a disappointment to all. Like all of the buildings we had come across in Kingston, Fat Dog's was a low-slung edifice, consisting of only one level due to the prevalence of earthquakes the island was cursed to endure. The exterior of the establishment appeared battered and bruised since it had withstood the brunt of numerous tropical storms, severe earthquakes and the continual abuse of its nefarious patrons. The only interesting feature of this edifice was the large unique sign that carried the pub's name coupled with a picture of an extremely fat hound with a barrel around its middle, as if the obese canine had got stuck in the barrel and could not extricate itself.

Entering the infamous pub, we were all very astounded to discover that it was much larger internally than its appearance from the street. A huge bar dominated the center of the room with tables and chairs ringing it sides. The grogshop was crowded, noisy and filled with noxious odors. We searched for a place to sit. Just then, Handy called to an unfamiliar rogue, who responded immediately by shouting Handy's name while he pushed and shoved his way over to our group. Upon reaching us, he clapped Handy on his back, introduced himself and welcomed us all to his temple of depravity. Chasing away a few drunken patrons from a table toward the pub's rear, Fat Dog got us settled and comfortable, signaling for the nearest serving wench to answer to our needs.

From the name given to his pub, I expected a rotund individual sporting nautical tattoos and dress. Instead, I was stunned to discover that Fat Dog was a gaunt, rat-faced individual dressed from head to toe in somber black attire of the type normally worn by funeral undertakers. I noticed that peculiar scars criss-crossed the entire surface of Fat Dog's face and arms. From the look of these ancient wounds, he appeared to be a survivor of a vicious attack by some strange savage beast! Sporting a self-sure perpetual sneer, Fat Dog seemed totally out of place in this island funhouse. Once our order was taken by the dim-witted trollop, Fat Dog announced that we had arrived at just the right time to enjoy the day's events. Inviting us to relax and enjoy our meal and drinks, he promised a very special dessert for all of us. With that he asked Handy to fill him in on his adventures since last the two had parted, which seemed to represent a good number of years.

As the two old tars were catching up on past history, our drinks and food were delivered. We attacked the offerings with voracious appetites that spending any time on ships will certainly produce. At one point in their reminiscing, Handy asked Fat Dog a very strange question concerning the welfare of his monkeys. Giving Handy a wink and a huge lopsided grin, Fat Dog informed him that all was well in that regard, as we would soon see. With that, he bid us a renewed welcome and bustled off to referee a brawl that had suddenly erupted between two inebriated tars. As he hurried off, I turned to Handy with a questioning look in my eyes. Handy recognized my confusion and answered my silent question with a nod and a hand gesture of his palm facing me, which indicated a need for patience on my part.

We were all laughing now, enjoying the sumptuous fare and, other than I, the strong spirits that accompanied it. After our wonderful repast, our host reappeared at our table and inquired if we were ready for some very unique sporting events. In unison, we spouted to our congenial host that was exactly the reason we had chosen his fine establishment in the first place. With a wave of his hand toward the rear of the pub, he informed us that all events occurred out back during daylight hours, so we needed to make our way there now to secure a good viewing position. As we and most of the pub's patrons made our way to the rear door, Handy leaned over to tell me that I was in for a rare treat. Holding my tongue, I pondered silently how any event could surpass the brutal animal and human contests that I had personally witnessed in Slugger's basement of horrors.

As we made our way out the rear of the establishment, we were not at all surprised to find a large thatched enclosure that in every way reminded us of the Palace on Saint Domingue. Much like the Palace's events, the first several animal matches involved either roosters or dogs in mortal combat. While I watched these events with mild interest, I really hoped that there was something different on the afternoon's agenda that would spark my interest. No sooner had my silent plea for a unique match passed than Fat Dog took the center of the ring and announced that the next event was as unique an offering as anybody could find anywhere in the New World. As I watched, two stout and upright cages were delivered to the ring. Once both cages were properly arranged in two opposite corners, the doors were opened and to my amazement two apes emerged from these holding pens. These monkeys were of a species of which I was not at all familiar. They were both black-furred creatures about the size of a young adolescent. Snarling and screeching, they now faced one another across the ring. Handy informed me that this breed of ape was called a chimpanzee, and that these creatures were found only on the African continent. Fat Dog, renowned to be consummately fascinated with monkeys, had paid dearly to visiting slave galley captains for the capture and delivery of these hairy man-like creatures. Handy further confided that Fat Dog had personally trained these apes to battle each other in the ring. With Handy's admission, I realized instantly the source of the scars sported by our host.

As the chimpanzees were being prepared to face one another in combat, I noticed that a commotion had begun on the opposite side of the ring. As I strained my gaze to understand its origin, I was finally rewarded by spotting our very own Mr. Bass right in the midst of things. He appeared to be moving in a disorientated manner, stumbling into patron after patron as he pushed his way closer to the ring. As he finally managed to gain access to the very front row, I could see that his eyes had an extremely crazed appearance and he seemed to be drooling copiously. He also seemed to be shouting something directed at the upcoming combatants that was impossible to understand over the tremendous crowd noise. At last, I was able to distinguish his words as he issued a thunderous roar concerning the Blood Monkeys who were about to engage in battle. I reasoned that he must have sampled a wee bit more of his personal rum stash aboard ship that still contained the *belladonna* elixir that I had introduced into it.

In any case, his bizarre actions and speech brought disapproving stares and shouts from the crowd around him. Fat Dog, realizing the danger this crazed sailor represented to the success of today's entertainment program, sent two of his larger henchmen over to remove this distraction before he could create any more disruption. When they reached Mr. Bass, he put up a massive fight as he continued to sputter and slobber his dire warnings of attacking Blood Monkeys. After a vigorous struggle, the raving madman was finally subdued and was carried bodily from the ring by several more of Fat Dog's assistants. As they made their exit, I could distinctly hear my sworn enemy frantically issuing warning shouts to anyone in the near vicinity that Blood Monkeys were indeed very real and dangerous creatures. His maniacal cries brought nothing but nervous laughter from the surrounding crowd, certain that the poor soul had lost his mind, and as such posed a real danger to himself as well as everyone around him. As Mr. Bass was dragged roughly from the entertainment enclosure, I experienced a brief moment of satisfaction that my elixir was still causing my enemy problems. I was also aware that Mr. Bass would be issued no hospitality or courtesies anywhere on the island due to his outlandish behavior. After all, it was a very small community and word spread as fast on this island as any *scuttlebutt* aboard a sailing vessel!

With the distraction properly handled, Fat Dog entered the ring and made his way over to one of the simian combatants, who, recognizing his master, gave him a big affectionate hug. Fat Dog whispered something into the chimpanzee's ear before repeating the same procedure with the other fighter. Remaining in the ring with his snarling and human-like pets, Fat Dog announced that the battle would commence with the ringing of the bell. To the thunderous roar of the spectators, Fat Dog further declared that the match would continue until one of the contestants ceded the fight by pounding its fist three times on the floor of the ring. He also informed us that both of the apes were female, answering to the names of Bountiful Betty and Sorrowful Suzy. With all ready, he signaled the bell keeper to begin the match.

Well, I can honestly report that I was not at all prepared for the furious and savage battle that ensued. At the sound of the bell, both chimpanzees seemed to go completely insane and flew across the ring at each other in a flurry of screeches, fangs and claws. Barreling into one another, the two furry fighters unleashed a series of vicious blows and savage bites to their opponent while hooting and shrieking the entire time. While I had previously witnessed a good many bare-knuckle fights, none of them compared to the pure primal savagery that I was now viewing.

As the battle raged, never once waning in animalistic fury, Sorrowful

Suzy seemed to be winning. She had bitten the left leg of her opponent, and it continued to bleed profusely. Grievously wounded, Bountiful Betty finally slammed her paw three times on the ground signaling the end of the match. At that point, Fat Dog pulled out a whistle from his pocket and blew several shrill notes. Both chimpanzees came to a full and complete stop, standing facing each other as if waiting for further instructions. On cue, Fat Dog blew one continuous screech from his whistle and both chimpanzees turned and made their way back inside their cages, which were then quickly extricated from the ring. As the cages were hauled away, Fat Dog announced that the culmination of the afternoon's entertainment agenda had not yet arrived. As I waited for the next contest, I thought back on the savage battle I had just witnessed. I was thoroughly awed by the feral power and ferocity that these two unique combatants had demonstrated. It was also my fervent wish to never have to face these powerful and murderous animals in battle!

Well, my former plea for unique entertainment was answered once more. Fat Dog again took his position in the center of the ring and announced that the day's final event would pit animal against reptile in the pub's infamous *Gator Gobble Game*. Calming the delirious crowd with furious hand signals, Fat Dog called for the combatants to be delivered to the ring. With this announcement, a very large and stout cage was dragged into the ring by several massive slaves. Once in position, the gate at the front of the cage was slid open to allow the beast within to emerge. We were all stunned as we observed a ferocious looking alligator of sizable proportions slowly crawl out of the cage and into the center of the ring. As the cage was roughly dragged out of the enclosure, the reptile hissed and snarled at its retreat. At the same instant, several assistants on various sides of the ring released the different animals that had been placed in their care. These creatures were all very young and skittish given the loud noise level generated by the excited crowd and the gruesome fate that awaited each of them. There were four different animal varieties in all…chicks, ducklings, piglets and baby goats. Further, there was five of each type of animal totaling twenty in all. These tiny and helpless creatures shivered and took a few tentative steps inside the enclosure exploring their new surroundings while instinctively avoiding any contact with the reptilian monster waiting in the center of the ring.

Before I continue my narrative, I believe it only fair to instruct you on the rules of this barbaric contest. The *Gator Gobble Game* was in effect a betting contest at heart. Each animal that had been released into the ring of death represented a different numerical value. The larger the baby animal the smaller the point value attributed to it. Therefore, the baby goats were valued at two points apiece, the piglets at three points, the ducklings at seven points and the chicks at eight points. If one did the necessary calculations, the total point value of the baby animal population came to a grand total of one hundred points. As the hungry reptile gobbled up a quick meal of any particular animal the point value assigned to that type of animal was then added to the total. After a period of thirty minutes, the animal casualty list was summed up to arrive at the final numerical count for the match. Should the reptile finish off the entire baby animal population, the total number of points would equal one hundred. However, should the alligator choose to ignore the small delectable morsels surrounding him then the contest's point value would be zero. The spectators were allowed to place multiple bets on the contest as long as these bets were placed prior to its initiation. Since the outcome of this bloody spectacle was always different, the house was the winner on all bets except those rare wagers that pinpointed the contest's exact total. Those few bets that were actual winners were then paid on a ten to one basis, which was a huge payoff. Judging from the riotous mood of the crowd, I was unsure whether the prospect of winning was more important versus the overall butchery that was about to occur. If I had to guess, I would have bet soundly on the butchery aspect!

As the event commenced and a fat piglet was snatched and gobbled down the beast's maw, I confirmed that the true fascination with this hellish contest was definitely one of bloodlust with the gambling aspect serving a distant second place. The baby animals were running haphazardly around the ring trying to evade the reptilian demon out to devour them. Squeals and screeches could be heard on a regular basis as these terrified, helpless infants were subjected to brutal and bloody deaths. The snapping and crunching of soft bones was a continual partner to the baby animals' screams and cries as the event unfolded to the absolute delight of the blood-maddened mob. Unlike my fellow spectators, I was totally disgusted with the proceedings as the ravenous reptilian monster continued to roam the ring enclosure devouring the squealing babies. Thinking about the utter brutality of this event was indeed difficult, but I reasoned that it certainly provided a welcomed diversion from the harsh and vile conditions we all faced on a daily basis.

The alligator was totally oblivious to my objections as he continued on his brutal dispatching of his sacrificial victims. Once the time had mercifully ended, the alligator was noosed and dragged from the ring so a final tally could be made. Unless an animal was totally devoured, it could not count toward the final tally. In other words, crushed and mangled babies left in the ring counted for nothing but a meaningless death! The final result ended up with the brutal gobbling of four goats, five piglets, two ducklings and one chick for a total point value of forty five. Since nobody had chosen this number, the house collected on each and every bet wagered. This meant that everyone in the audience was a loser. However, I viewed absolutely no remorse or regret on the faces of those all around me. Rather the bloodthirsty mob was deliriously content and sated!

Fat Dog entered the ring for the last time of the day to announce the day's entertainment was at an end. He invited his patrons back inside his punchhouse to partake in the sumptuous fare and even stronger spirits. The mob was cheering, screaming and yelling, as we made our way back inside the pub while the sun began its decent in the west. As Handy and I joined the human caravan of bodies returning to our island watering hole, I accidentally bumped into a well-dressed gentleman. After giving me a cursory appraisal, the scoundrel proceeded to give me a hard, vicious shove that sent me tumbling head-over-heels. In my wake, he called me a filthy smelling pirate and ordered me to keep my distance from men of honor such as himself. Jumping up to reciprocate with fury written across my face, I was grabbed from behind and pulled back outside the tavern. Turning quickly, I found myself face to face with our host, Fat Dog. Cautioning me to keep a cool head, Fat Dog steered me even further away from my tormentor.

When he finally stopped pushing me away from the conflict, Fat Dog informed me that it was very fortunate that I did not respond to the taunt of this so-called gentleman. Fat Dog then informed me that the name of my harasser was none other than Sir Jonathan William Brisbane

III, one of the most feared and powerful plantation owners on the island. Fat Dog went on to inform me that Sir Jonathan was unbeatable in any type of gentleman's duel, having dispatched a staggering total of twenty-three men. Understanding completely Fat Dog's intention of preventing any type of nasty retort on my part, I quickly put my anger in check and began to cool off considerably. Handy soon joined us questioning Fat Dog on his interference in the potential conflict. Laughing, I explained to Handy that his friend was merely attempting to keep me from ending up as victim number twenty-four!

Back inside the pub, we joined our crewmates who were in an animated and preoccupied discussion on the unique contests that we had all witnessed. As this discussion proceeded, I stole a curious glance around the bar to locate my newest nemesis. He was regally seated at a table on the opposite side of the room resuming the card game that had been temporarily abandoned in order to watch the animal extravaganza. As I observed Sir Jonathan from a safe distance, I detected that he was just a few years my senior. While not portraying a daunting physical form, he nevertheless conducted himself with an air of superiority and aggression. He was a few inches taller than I, and wore a continual scowl of disapproval and indifference. Elegantly attired in a fine suit of clothes, he carried two pistols in a sash at his waist along with a jewel-hafted saber at his side. His cronies at the table treated him with the utmost courtesy and respect as they bowed and scraped to his every whim. Realizing that no real harm had come to me, short of the bruising of my pride, I turned back to my friends who were still raving about the wonderful spectacle we had just witnessed. Entering back into the conversation, I turned my back on Sir Jonathan and wiped the whole foul encounter from my mind.

As the evening wore on and Handy was in the midst of yet another of his never-ending *sea tales*, a commotion broke out on the other side of the room. As I glanced over to discover the source of the ruckus, I was not surprised to find Sir Jonathan right in the thick of things. From where we were sitting, we could just barely make out the shouted words being exchanged due to the thunderous roar emanating from the inebriated pub patrons. However, as the commotion strengthened, the entire pub quieted, as all eyes were now trained on Sir Jonathan's gambling table. From our distant vantage point, it appeared that Sir Jonathan was distinctly at odds with one of his fellow gamblers. As the crowd hushed, I was able to hear the young man, who had been gambling with Sir Jonathan, call him a miserable card cheat.

This serious insult brought an instantaneous and furious reaction from Sir Jonathan, who proceeded to slap his accuser across the face with a pair of fencing gloves that he had retrieved from the sash at his waist. At this point, everyone in the pub knew for certain that the master duelist had chosen victim number twenty-four. Stunned by the slap, the poor youth looked bewildered and terrified. Taking a moment to regain his composure, the frightened youth told the murderous plantation owner that he accepted the challenge and chose pistols as his weapon of choice.

Calling for assistance from the nearest curious onlookers, Sir Jonathan instructed these unwary volunteers to clear away the closest tables and chairs so that the duel could be conducted right there inside Fat Dog's. Dutiful to the extreme, several of these volunteers jumped to their feet and began to relocate the offending furniture as ordered by Sir Jonathan. The boy by this time had turned a ghastly white shade and was trembling violently from head to toe, but seemed intent on participating in what in all likelihood would be his demise. Once the furniture was moved, Sir Jonathan placed his two pistols on a table in front of the challenged youth, asking him to select either of the pistols being offered. In an almost dreamlike trance, the young man reached down and made his selection. Announcing the rules of this gentleman's dispute to the gathered crowd, Sir Jonathan informed all that he and the challenged party would stand back-to-back, pace ten strides and then turn and fire at each other. Each party would be allowed only one shot, so he advised his young adversary that careful aim was of the highest importance. Barely nodding his agreement, the boy stumbled over to Sir Jonathan, placing his trembling body back-to-back with his feared challenger. Sir Jonathan called Fat Dog over and requested that the proprietor vocalize the count so that both parties could concentrate on their aim. Fat Dog agreed to play the role of Master of Ceremony for the duel.

Prior to starting his count, Fat Dog pleaded with the lad to beg for forgiveness so as to avoid his probable death. In a halting and high-pitched voice the lad expressed his most sincere apology, but the so-called gentleman laughed cruelly and announced that he did not believe or accept the apology as being genuine. Sir Jonathan went on to explain that nothing the lad could say would appease his defamed reputation. With this declaration, he ordered Fat Dog to commence counting. By the time Fat Dog actually began counting, the pub patrons had physically moved clear of the line-of-fire of both duelists. However, they refused to vacate the premises in anticipation of enjoying the bloody spectacle that was about to occur. Fat Dog counted one, and both parties took a long step away from each other. And so the mournful count continued until Fat Dog reached the number ten at which point he ordered the duelists to turn and fire.

As I watched the boy make his turn, I could see that he was terrified to the extreme, with copious sweat running down his blanched face and arms along with his entire body shaking like a freshly landed fish. As he looked up to observe his adversary, he was greeted with the same cruel, sarcastic scowl that I had received just a few hours previously. Shakily raising his dueling pistol, the lad attempted to take aim at the scowling visage of death that stood calmly awaiting his effort. Having absolutely no luck at calming his frayed and tattered nerves or the incredible tremors they produced, the lad pulled the trigger and fired his pistol at his tormentor. The lead ball shot from his trembling hand and missed Sir Jonathan by a very wide margin bringing a wolfish grin to the plantation owner's face. Informing all of us that he was now prepared to make the youth pay dearly for his insult, he fired his own pistol striking the boy squarely in his stomach. Issuing a dreadful wail, the lad dropped his pistol and clutched his wounded abdomen as he crumpled to the pub floor. All spectators of this mismatched fight knew that Sir Jonathan could have put his shot directly into the youth's heart delivering an instant killing blow. Instead, the villain had chosen to mortally wound the lad, consigning him to tremendous pain and suffering. This dark deed cast a black pall on the evening's fun and entertainment. The majority of Fat Dog's patrons decided it was time to vacate the premises. My crewmates, also reaching this unhappy conclusion, finished their drinks, and we all left the pub to return to our ship for the night. As we made our hurried departures, we were treated to the mournful wails and yelps of the dying youth that would stay rooted in our memories for a very long time thereafter!

Before my return to the ship, I decided to pay a visit to the Adams sisters to ensure that their homecoming had been well-received. After I bid my crewmates a good evening, I made my way in the direction of the Adams' mansion, since the sisters had previously provided me explicit directions. Upon locating their home, I was happy to observe that a celebration of sorts was under way with candles and oil-fed lamps lighting up much of the mansion's interior. Knocking on the front door, I was received by an ancient manservant, who inquired as to the reason for my presence at the home. I informed the decrepit vassal that I was a friend of the sisters from their recent voyage, and that I was merely checking on their well-being following their return home. He asked my name and then requested my patience as he announced my presence to the household.

My wait proved very short because Hortence Adams happened to be nearby when I related my name and intentions. Gliding to my side, she dismissed the disgruntled servant and swept me into her arms, giving me a kiss on both cheeks. Ending her warm greeting, she grabbed my hand and hustled me into a very large room that held a number of guests, including our very own Captain. As we entered, her two sisters jumped up from their chairs and hurried over to my side also planting several more kisses on my face in unabashed gratitude and welcome. Turning then to face the rather large group assembled in the room, they announced in unison that their savior from their recent voyage had graced the evening's festivities with his presence. The entire room broke out in spontaneous applause, which embarrassed me to no end causing me to blush a very deep crimson hue. Strolling to my defense, the Captain shook my hand and welcomed me to the homecoming party in honor of the sisters' return. Stopping for a minute to scan the crowd, the Captain signaled to a tall, thin military officer in full dress uniform, who quickly made his way over to us. Before the Captain had the chance to introduce us, the sisters once again in unison told me that this fine-looking officer was indeed their illustrious nephew, Captain Ronald Shuster Adams. Executing a perfect gentlemanly bow, this impressive specimen of a man shook my hand in greeting and clapped me firmly on my back. He informed me that his aunts had been extolling my virtues and exploits the entire evening. He graciously thanked me for the heroic deeds at thwarting the attacking pirates, as well as for the kind assistance I had shown his aunts throughout our very eventful voyage. Well, if I thought I was embarrassed before, I was now thoroughly abashed and my face turned an even deeper shade of red!

Since I was the hero of the moment, the sisters dragged me from person to person introducing me to all. After an hour or so of all this demonstrative attention, I made my escape and found myself outside the mansion in a rather spectacular garden collecting my thoughts. As I reminisced about the eventful day I had experienced, I was surprised to glance up and spy Captain Adams approaching me. He quickly put me at ease by apologizing for the hero treatment and informed me that the Captain had requested his assistance in training our ship's new cannon team. To this end, he promised that he would personally see that my squad was properly trained to the finest degree possible. As we made our way back into the house, he related that he owed me a great debt, and would happily and proudly provide me any favor I might require. I immediately thanked him for his kind words and promised to come to him directly should such a need ever arise. Smiling and again clapping me on my back, he led the way back inside the mansion to enjoy the ongoing festivities.

As we entered the party room, Gertrude rushed over to my side expressing her relief that the sisters' extreme exuberance had not frightened me away. She took the lead as usual and inquired about my initial impressions of the isle of Jamaica. I told her honestly that it was indeed a beautiful sparkling gemstone set into the fabric of the West Indian Islands. I also told her that Kingston's harbor was magnificent and an absolutely safe haven to rest and replenish our stores. I further lauded the natural beauty of their island and the generous and friendly nature of her populace. Once I finished, I received a rousing ovation from the entire room, who had been quietly listening to my every word without my knowledge. On the verge of repeating extreme embarrassment, Hortence came to my rescue by inquiring what I had done on my first day ashore. Utilizing this opportunity, I launched into a detailed account of the day's experiences ending with the brutal one-sided duel I had the extreme displeasure of viewing.

As I finished, Gertrude informed me that on my very first day I had the unfortunate luck of running into the vilest and most evil scoundrel on the entire island. She continued that she and her sisters had known Sir Jonathan since he was a very young boy. During his maturation, they had the distinct displeasure of watching this monster evolve into his present hideous form. Gertrude confessed that Sir Jonathan was nothing more than a maniacal killer, who treated all in his path with hatred and disdain. Further, she told me that he was also a drunkard and a sadist, treating his slaves in the very worst possible manner. While he was now credited with killing twenty-four men in cold blood, she told me that he probably had murdered at least triple that number of slaves in his possession. She spat the last several words out in true vehemence, displaying an utter hatred for the despicable brute. At the end of her graphic description, she made me promise that I would stay far away from the clutches of this demonic murderer. Having no real choice at the time and sensing the sisters were truly concerned for my well-being, I made a promise that I would do everything in my power to steer clear of this dangerous individual while on their beautiful and wondrous island. Little did I know at the time that some promises are very difficult to keep!

Chapter 33: Cannon Practice

The very next morning the *Amafata*'s cannon team reported to Fort Charles for training. We were cordially escorted directly to Captain Adams' office where we met with our training instructor, Sergeant O'Toole. After we had all introduced ourselves and were seated comfortably in the roomy office chairs, Captain Adams opened the discussion by outlining his objective for our limited learning span. To start, he ordered his subordinate, acting as our tutor, that the daylight hours should be wisely spent, holding off any detailed instruction and study that normally occurred in every military training exercise until well after sundown. This, he reasoned, would provide us the maximum amount of time to actually practice firing the cannons put at our disposal.

Additionally, he commanded Sergeant O'Toole to ensure our proper training so that we could compete as a team entry in the upcoming *Cannon Challenge* planned for part of the festivities of the Founders Day Celebration scheduled in just three short weeks. The sergeant, appearing a bit challenged at the daunting task assigned him, just nodded a weak assent and an even weaker salute to the order. Before he dismissed us, Captain Adams asked where our fifth member was hiding. A bit surprised by his request, I answered that this was the total number of members for the team our Captain had ordained. Captain Adams seemed a bit perplexed, but in a moment's time that familiar Adams smile came to his face as he sternly commanded that Powder Monkey be assigned to our team until further notice. This command seemed to bother Sergeant O'Toole more than the daunting order to train us adequately…something that was worth keeping a keen eye on in the future! With a crisp salute of farewell, we were sent off to learn how to fire cannons with the expressed assistance of the mysterious individual named Powder Monkey.

Sergeant O'Toole wasted no time and drove us at a crisp pace to the cannon tower, actually an elevated platform that allowed an open sea vista for firing cannons. Arranged at the furthest edge of the platform facing an open expanse to the water were the cannons we would soon be firing…a great many indeed in all shapes and sizes. From our vantage point, we could see groups of soldiers scrambling all around the various cannons in what appeared to be some sort of cannon firing drills. Marching us over to a medium-sized gun that coincidently was the farthest away from all the other teams, we were introduced to our new toy of warfare. With that, Sergeant O'Toole waved his hands in a circular motion over his head while he shouted for Powder Monkey to report for duty.

His shout was answered by a crouching, filthy form that appeared entirely black as a crow's feathers, except for a pair of blinking brilliant green eyes set in a clear white sea. I could immediately read a hidden intelligence in those eyes. I could also understand the looks of scorn and disgust the creature received from my fellow cannoneers since this ball of filth was truly disgusting. He gave each of us a welcoming snarl as our instructor prepared to issue his orders. Sergeant O'Toole began by commanding Powder Monkey to act as the supplier of shot and powder, water, slow matches and countless other things. What the sergeant failed to do was actually speak these orders to the wretch. Instead, he utilized a series of crude hand and body signals to express the words he had spoken. Turning back to us, Sergeant O'Toole informed us that Powder Monkey could not hear nor speak due to the lad's many years of service in the Royal Navy on a *Man-o-War* serving as a *powder monkey*. The frequent firings of the guns had robbed the small imp of his hearing and had scrambled his eggs leaving him a dullard. As with any animal, he was taught to recognize simple signals in order to follow specific orders. Lastly, Sergeant O'Toole informed us that Powder Monkey was the property of Sir Jonathan William Brisbane III, who had loaned his slave to Captain Adams at his expressed request.

As I gazed over to Powder Monkey and observed his expressive eyes, I understood quite a different message. At that instant, Sergeant O'Toole informed us that we needed to be assigned specific roles, each as a functioning member of the unit. Angry George was assigned the role of *plunger*, responsible for plunging the powder charge and shot into the cannon's barrel, and swabbing the same completely clean after firing. Creeping Jeremy and Long Tall Willie were assigned to be the *powdermen* and *tacklemen*, responsible for priming the weapon and aligning and hauling the cannon back and forth as required after each firing. Lastly, my assigned role was *gun chief*, responsible for targeting and firing the cannon. With that, Sergeant O'Toole impatiently walked us through the individual steps that we needed to perform each time we fired the cannon. He then pointed to a distant floating raft with a painted bull's-eye identifying it as our intended target, and he ordered us to fire the weapon. Prompted continuously by Sergeant O'Toole, we painstakingly went through the many different steps required to ready the gun for actual firing. Once finished, I touched the slow match to the powder primer and in an instant the big gun roared and spat out the shot we had stuffed down its throat. Our first attempt fell woefully short of the target to the snide snickering of our tutor. As he swiveled his body to take leave, he commanded us to continue practicing until the sun disappeared from the sky.

To be perfectly honest, none of us could actually hear his parting instructions due to the incessantly loud ringing sounds each of us experienced. In watching our instructor striding away, I motioned for Angry George to swab the barrel clean to prepare for our next shot. Before we again fired the weapon, I realized that we needed some sort of hearing protection to enable a semblance of communication between team members. Thinking back, I remembered a trick Gertrude had taught me to cure ear pain. She had shown me that her herbal ear remedy could be sealed in a patient's ear utilizing simple candle wax. Motioning to Powder Monkey, I signaled that we required candles, and he was off in an instant to comply with the order. At the same time, I turned to my team and shouted that until Powder Monkey returned we would continue to practice each of our duties until we became extremely proficient at performing them. For the next hour, we ran through these cannon steps over and over until we had all thoroughly memorized the procedures. Powder Monkey returned with the required candles and we melted the wax from them into a pliable substance, which I then gently inserted into each member's ears.

We then aimed, fired and missed our target once again…our only consolation was that the candle wax allowed us to fire round after round without rendering us completely deaf. While the candle wax corrected our hearing problems, nothing seemed to work when it came to aiming the thunderous beast. We missed our target time and time again, either long or short as well as landing on all sides of it. The other purpose the candle wax served was to block out the laughter and snide remarks of the other cannon teams sharing the platform with us. Near sundown, with our derisive audience gone for the day, we were prepared to fire our final round. As I carefully made my aiming preparations, Powder Monkey happened to catch my eye and he shook his head from side-to-side indicating that something was amiss. To be sure of his meaning, I signaled that my aim was set to which he immediately responded with the same sideway shake of his head. Signaling to him that I wanted him to aim the cannon in the proper direction, he immediately signed a very pronounced no!

Walking over to the lad, I signaled in a way only he could see that I desperately needed his assistance in aiming the cannon. Further, I signed that I alone knew that he was not a simpleton, and that I believed that he was quite intelligent. Blinking in surprise, he walked over to the loaded cannon and made several adjustments to the aim. He then turned and signaled that the aim was now correct. Touching the primer with the slow match, the cannon barked for the last time of the day while delivering a direct hit on the elusive target. With a surprised cheer from the entire team for our success, we all turned in unison to Powder Monkey, offering our heartfelt thanks and praise for his accurate assistance. As my team broke up for the day to answer the extreme hunger and thirst built up over their daylong cannon practice, I motioned to Powder Monkey that I would like to speak to him privately for just a short while. Nodding his assent, we watched our fellow cannonmates in the lingering twilight hustling off to appease their raging appetites.

Sitting with Powder Monkey, I signaled that my name was Echo and that I was very pleased to make his acquaintance. Smiling for the very first time that day, he motioned that he preferred the name Powder Monkey and was also very happy to meet me and to be a part of our team. I asked him in the strange sign and signal language, how he had learned to aim cannons so accurately. He answered that he had learned this trick by simply watching cannons being fired over and over. I then asked him if he would be willing to assume the aiming duty in addition to his procurement responsibilities. He signaled that he would be more than honored to do so. I then questioned why he hid his intelligence from the world. He answered that most people just accepted the notion that he was a dullard so he simply went along with the ruse. I understood his message implicitly since I also followed this same path with my special ability. We continued with our conversation for the next several hours until he indicated that he had to take his leave to attend to his other assigned duties, and we signaled goodnight to each other. Before he skittered away, he asked me if I would keep his secrets to myself and I answered immediately that indeed I would.

Before my return to the ship, I decided to stop once again and visit my friends, the Adams sisters. Arriving at their household, I was immediately ushered into their salon and warmly greeted by the sisters and their nephew, Captain Adams. Bidding all a good evening, the sisters inquired when I had last eaten. Once I answered that that meal had been breakfast, the sisters hurried out to see that something was arranged for me. The stop gave me the opportunity to question Captain Adams on the history of our newest member, Powder Monkey. Stopping for a moment to collect his thoughts, he spun a sad tale. It seemed that the lad was orphaned as a tot, spending his early years in a harsh and brutal workhouse for young children. Sold into a life as an indentured servant to the Royal Navy, he made his first voyage at a very young age. Assigned to the miserable life as a *powder monkey*, the unfortunate lad lost both his hearing and his senses due to the thunderous detonations of the booming guns. When the Royal Navy realized his impairment, they offloaded the muddled youth to Sir Jonathan for a very paltry sum. Since then, Sir Jonathan had taken his sadistic tendencies out on the child.

When the miserable situation came to Captain Adams' attention, he bargained with the evil plantation owner for loan of the lad, given his experience and knowledge around large guns. Since then Powder Monkey had been housed at the fort, performing a multitude of tasks assigned to him. Captain Adams concluded by informing me that the scamp was a frequent surprise visitor to their household, whenever he was able to sneak off undetected. The sisters soon returned with a veritable feast, and I hungrily attacked their fine offerings. Exhausted and sated to the extreme, the sisters insisted that I spend the night in a guest room that had been prepared for this very purpose. As I lay in the luxurious bed that had been arranged for me, I could only wonder what the future held, but I knew in my heart that I would find out in no time at all!

The next morning, after enjoying another sumptuous meal, I was back at the fort awaiting the arrival of my team. The military cannon teams were also present and there was a smattering of jokes and snickers from them as I stood waiting. Ignoring their crude jests and remarks, I spied my team returning to the fort and we immediately gathered to plan the day's routine. I informed them of my decision to promote Powder Monkey to be the target master of the team, which was met with rousing approval by all. We once again donned our protective ear wax and readied ourselves to proceed. Now prepared, we loaded our cannon and aimed it at the newly delivered target. To our astonishment, we proceeded to blow it straight out of the water on our very first attempt. This feat brought our haughty audience to an awed silence as they now stood and watched our preparations in a whole new light. Well, we spent the remainder of the day along with the next several weeks destroying target after target. After the first week, Sergeant O'Toole ordered a significant reduction to our target's overall size in an attempt to increase the difficulty level. These smaller targets were dispatched just as quickly as their predecessors as our team's abilities sharpened to a very acute degree. At the end of the three weeks of practice, we had become a concisely functioning team ready to compete in the *Cannon Challenge* scheduled for the very next day.

The day of the match was yet another perfect tropical morning with bright sunny cloudless skies. The match itself hosted ten teams in all. Besides our team, there were seven teams from the fort along with an additional two independent teams from town. These latter two teams were badly disguised as retired soldiers in ill-fitting and tattered old uniforms. There was not a person present at the event who did not recognize these two teams as being pirate, but absolutely nothing was mentioned given the festive mood that pervaded the celebration. The throng of spectators was quite large as it seemed like just about everyone on the entire island was in attendance. In the midst of the crowd, I recognized the Adams sisters escorted by our Captain along with several of our own crewmembers, including my close friend, Handy. Among the more illustrious guests, I spotted Sir Jonathan, who wore his traditional look of contempt and hatred. Further down from Sir Jonathan was our amenable entertainment host, Fat Dog.

Long Tall Willie had previously informed me that huge wagers were being placed on each team in the competition. Our team was a distinct dark-horse at a substantial fifteen-to-one margin. Given these lucrative odds, I placed the remainder of my significant hoard of coin on our team to win the entire event. Should we somehow be fortunate enough to win the contest, my winnings would amount to a very sizable windfall. The military band from the fort played several tunes to the absolute delight of the entire audience. Banners, streamers and various other decorations could be viewed everywhere adding to the overall celebratory mood. The air was filled with excitement and frivolity as this very special celebration got under way.

The Governor of the island was introduced and droned on and on about various topics. Mercifully, he ended his meandering discourse by announcing the introduction of the fort's commander, Captain Adams. My new friend's address was much more abbreviated, welcoming all of the town's guests and explaining the rules for the upcoming *Cannon Challenge*. As Captain Adams explained, there would be a series of three rounds conducted in order to narrow the field down to an eventual champion. The first of these two rounds would occur that very day with the final round scheduled to be completed the following morning.

In the first round, each team would be allowed a carefully timed period of ten minutes to conduct their cannon firings. Accuracy and speed were the two measures being utilized to determine success versus elimination. The six teams that demonstrated the most accuracy and fired the most number of times during the ten-minute time span would advance to the second round. These same measures would prevail for the next two rounds. By process of elimination, the last team remaining at the end of the second day would be declared the winner of the contest.

As teams, we drew lots to determine our order of fire for the first round. Our team drew the seventh position, so we had over an hour wait and decided to closely observe our fellow competitors. Having scrutinized our competitors from a comfortable shady spot, I judged that we needed to score either a direct hit or a very close approximation, while firing our flame-belching beast at least four times to remain in

240 / Bilge Rat

the competition. I informed my team that we did not need to strive for perfection during the first round. Instead, I insisted that we fire no more than four times and that we perform a direct hit no more than once. I was supremely confident in my team's abilities, knowing that we could easily best these objectives that I had just announced. However, I knew that this competition would not be won in the first round, and I really wanted to save our best effort for the two succeeding rounds.

The handgun signal was finally sounded and we went to work as a team in a blur of action. Taking no risk on our accuracy score, Powder Monkey sent the first shot directly on the target destroying it completely. As a new target was moved into position, we fired an additional three more times to the roar of the spectators. As the first round came to a close, we were among the top teams advancing to the next round. While a short recess was called, we regrouped and I instructed my team to avoid imbibing the rum that was being offered freely to the competitors so as to not impede our efforts in the second round. Creeping Jeremy expressed his sincerest disapproval but a stern look from me ceased his grumblings almost immediately.

The start of the second round was then signaled for the six remaining teams, which included Sergeant O'Toole's team along with the two pirate entries. Once again we drew a position toward the end and calmly sat in the shade awaiting our turn. During this round, the teams firing before us fared a bit better than the first round with Sergeant O'Toole's team and one of the pirate teams scoring a direct hit along with each firing a full five times. As our turn approached, I again called for a team rendezvous to discuss our strategy for the round. Once again, I reasoned that we needed just one direct hit and five firings to advance to the finals. Nodding their approval, my team prepared for the signal to start. As was the case earlier, the signal sent us into furious motion and we again enjoyed success!

At the end of the second round, we were actually the leaders with only Sergeant O'Toole's military team and a pirate sharp-shooting team advancing to the finals along with us. Captain Adams announced the end of the day's competition and the festive throng of spectators disbursed to partake of food and drink and further celebration. In dismissal, I cautioned my team to be circumspect in their alcohol consumption that evening. The Adams sisters appeared at my side offering their heartfelt congratulations along with an invitation for me to join them for a sumptuous supper. Agreeing immediately, I escorted my three benefactors to their home and the promised fare.

After partaking of their fabulous meal, I made an excuse of exhaustion and retired to the guest room that they had graciously offered. As I was lying in bed slowly drifting off into a peaceful slumber, I heard a scratching noise at the room's window. Glancing over, I was shocked to spy Powder Monkey's face just outside the window. Signing that he had important news, Powder Monkey came in and informed me that Sergeant O'Toole was not happy at all with our success thus far in the contest. To ensure our certain demise, Sergeant O'Toole planned to sabotage our cannon by pouring enough molten lead down our barrel to misdirect any of our future shots. Since the small amount of lead required to affect this result was rather minuscule, it would be almost impossible for anyone to detect its presence.

Thinking quickly, I asked Powder Monkey when this dastardly deed would be perpetuated on our gun. Powder Monkey informed me that he had read the lips of our adversaries and knew that midnight was the appointed time. Surprised, I signaled that I did not realize the lad was capable of understanding speech by merely studying someone's face. Smiling broadly, he signed that he had reluctantly forced himself to learn this trick after losing his hearing many years ago. While he told me that his first efforts were both clumsy and difficult, the following years spent perfecting this craft had enabled him to understand spoken words perfectly. Nodding my understanding, I focused on the new problem that faced us. I asked him how difficult the task would be to rearrange the cannons to solve our dilemma. Smiling with a wolfish grin, he signed that most everyone at the fort would be celebrating that evening so that no guards or sentries would be posted tonight. He continued by signing that with the assistance of three men, we would be able to switch the sabotaged cannon rather easily. Understanding the task that awaited us, I signed that I would find the required manpower and meet him at the start of morning watch…four o'clock in the morning for you landlubbers!

Now fully alert and awake, I made my way downstairs, finding Gertrude hard at work brewing one of her never-ending elixirs. I quickly filled her in on the latest ill news from Powder Monkey. While her first thought was to involve her nephew, I told her that with scant proof available there was very little that Captain Adams could actually accomplish. Instead I filled her in on the plan I had devised. After a moment's deliberation she agreed that my scheme seemed the best course of action. Quizzing me on how she could assist the endeavor, I answered that I was in need of a few strong men who could help in completing the cannon switch that I planned to make. Gertrude asked me why I required these men since my very own cannon team could easily perform the task at hand. I informed her that I believed my teammates were currently celebrating our success and would therefore be in no condition to assist in the effort!

With a look of understanding, she reached over and rang a small bell positioned on the desk near her. At once, her manservant answered the summons and she questioned him on the availability of two strong men whose services were required later that night. The servant nodded and told her that he knew the perfect candidates and was off in a flash. About an hour later, he returned with two of the largest men I had ever witnessed. It turned out that they were brothers, who were distant relatives of his. He then informed me that both were available the remainder of the night to assist in any matter I chose. With that, he introduced the pair and silently slid out of the room. I told the brothers what I had planned and they were more than glad to lend their help, especially since Sergeant O'Toole had treated them both very badly in the past.

A little before the agreed meeting time with Powder Monkey, I made my way to the stable and collected my assistants. Treading carefully, we made our way to the fort's entrance, passing unmolested. Once we reached the cannon tower, we were joined by Powder Monkey, who seemed exceedingly calm given the dangerous task we were about to perform. Making our way to our doctored cannon, the two behemoths dragged it over to Sergeant O'Toole's gun and the swap was made. Now that the cannons had been switched, I instructed Powder Monkey to see that all the evidence of the rearrangement was obliterated. Signing that he would see to this chore, I turned and gave my thanks to the brothers for their kind assistance. They both grinned at the anticipated result of the deception and immediately took their leave.

The next morning I was not alone when I arrived on the cannon tower.

Both of the competing teams were already in place making preparations for the final match. Carefully but unobtrusively, I inspected our cannon and found it to be free of any lead. As I turned, I was greeted by the remaining members of my team, who appeared to be in relatively good shape given the prior night's celebrations. Creeping Jeremy, in answer to my surprised expression, informed me that all three members of our team had retired early after consuming a wondrous dinner. As a group, they had decided to delay their celebration until after we had won the challenge. Thanking them for their foresight and abstinence, I asked them to begin preparations for the last round of the match.

As we went mechanically about the duties of checking and rechecking our armament, the spectators began to slowly assemble. Within an hour's time, we had completed all of our preparations. During this time, the crowd of spectators had grown to even greater numbers than the previous day. At last, Captain Adams addressed the multitudes explaining that the final round of the Cannon Challenge would proceed in the same manner as yesterday with one exception. By design, the targets that we would be firing on had been positioned much farther away, making the possibility of a direct hit quite improbable at best.

Once the crowds had arrived, the three team captains drew lots to determine the order of firing. This order was announced to the crowd with the disguised pirate squad leading the way, followed by Sergeant O'Toole's military team and leaving us in the very fortunate position of dead last. With everyone ready, the signal was given to commence firing and the pirate team leapt into action. In furious frenzy, this team proceeded to score several near misses while firing a hefty seven times. Elated with the results of their efforts, the pirate team broke out in smiles and slapped each other's backs as the crowd went absolutely wild in their expressed appreciation of their excellent effort. As the crowd quieted, the signal was given once more and Sergeant O'Toole's team went into action. As their first shot went very wide of the target, I had to stifle laughing outright. Stunned and uncomprehending, the team scurried to send a total of six shots not even close to the target. As their time expired, I could read defeat on each and every one of their faces except Sergeant O'Toole, who was staring at me with a hardened and malevolent expression. During the course of their turn, Sergeant O'Toole

244 / Bilge Rat

had figured out that somehow their cannon had also been sabotaged, not yet realizing the switch we had made in the wee hours of the morning.

Calling my team together for the last time, I informed them that we needed to fire a total of seven times and score at least one direct hit to win the day. Confident yet anxious, my team resumed their assigned positions as the signal to start was finally given. Leaping into a more frenzied routine than the previous day, we sent our first cannonball on a true path, destroying the target to the riotous roar of the crowd. From that point, we proceeded to fire a total of seven more times in the time allotted…scoring three more direct hits! At the conclusion of our awesome display, the spectators went absolutely wild, storming our position and offering their boisterous congratulations. Mobbed by the crowd, I happened to glance over and spot the ugly scowl worn by Sergeant O'Toole at his failure to win the *Cannon Challenge*. Realizing now that we had switched the sabotaged gun in place of their weapon, his temper was at the extreme. I knew that I would need to keep a sharp eye out for future troubles from this humiliated military man.

At the conclusion of the awards ceremony, the Adams sisters invited our Captain and his entire crew to their mansion to celebrate our marvelous victory. Smiling, he told the sisters that he and his crew would be delighted to attend the celebration. Turning to his new cannoncrew, he thanked us all for our hard work and practice over the past several weeks. He announced that he had recently purchased two new cannons for our protection on the remainder of the voyage. This news was met with a mighty roar of approval. Signaling us all to silence, he clasped his arms around my shoulders and with a huge grin informed me that he was now convinced that he could not put these new weapons in more capable or knowledgeable hands. Well, this statement incited the crew to an almost delirious roar as they descended on me and my small team hugging and congratulating us in hysterical fashion.

When I finally managed to extricate myself from the celebratory bedlam, I knew that I had one more mission to accomplish. Striding over to the spot where Sir Jonathan was standing with his wealthy and aristocratic friends, I petitioned the arrogant plantation owner for a moment of his time. I explained that over the course of the last several weeks, his indentured servant, Powder Monkey had become a valued member of our team and a close friend. Impatient for me to get to the heart of the matter, he demanded to know exactly what I wanted from him. I informed him that I had wagered all the money I owned on our team in the *Cannon Challenge* and was now quite wealthy. Continuing, I told him that I would be honored to buy Powder Monkey's freedom out of these substantial winnings if he would agree. A sinister mask stole over the sadist's face as he prepared his answer to my proposition. Sneering once again in my direction, he spat out that Powder Monkey was not and never would be available for sale no matter the price offered. In his most insulting manner, he donned an evil-looking smirk and chided me that even if Powder Monkey were available for sale, I would be the last person on earth that he would sell the miserable wretch to. With these words, he stomped off with his high and mighty friends, laughing loud and hard at my utter embarrassment!

Chapter 34: Powder Monkey's Redemption

With the embarrassing sting of Sir Jonathan's abrupt refusal coupled with the hoot and jeers from his cohorts, I decided to take my immediate leave. Wandering the Kingston streets aimlessly, I found myself in close proximity to the Adams' manor and decided to stop and pay a visit to the celebration party. As I was warmly greeted by the sisters, they questioned me on my obvious sullen mood. I related my agitating confrontation with Sir Jonathan. When I concluded, Gertrude was the first to speak. She informed me that my failed attempt to liberate Powder Monkey from the ownership of this fiendish monster did not surprise her. While neither she nor her two sisters had any suggestions on solving my predicament, they nevertheless commiserated with my plight and promised to provide support in a solution if one could be reached.

Since the celebration was fully underway, they pleaded with me to set my dilemma aside and partake in the sumptuous fare they had prepared for my crewmates and me. Although still quite upset, I agreed to their invitation and managed to pick my way through the staggering amount of delicious treats that were arranged on various tables. As I was enjoying a particularly delicious piece of lemon cake, a ruckus broke out at the back of the house. One of the serving girls hurried into the room announcing that a beaten and bloodied youth had arrived at the mansion requesting an audience. Intrigued, I made my way out back and discovered my new friend, Powder Monkey, who appeared to be in very serious shape. Gertrude arrived at my side and taking note of the nature and severity of the wounds, she mobilized the entire household into frenzied action. Gertrude promptly took Powder Monkey to an upstairs bedroom and proceeded to minister to her newest patient.

Once the majority of the serious wounds were cleaned and bandaged, she managed to get some hot tea and broth into her patient. Gertrude questioned him on the source of his injuries. With his saddened eyes peering up at us, Powder Monkey signed that Sir Jonathan was the fiend responsible. It seemed that following my failed attempt to purchase his freedom, Sir Jonathan had taken Powder Monkey back to his estate and proceeded to beat and berate him mercilessly. After his brutal treatment, Powder Monkey had fled the home of his evil owner. As I gave him my assurance that I would continue my assistance, Gertrude dosed him with a strong pain-numbing elixir that had the boy sleeping in very short order. Exiting the room with the lad now resting peacefully, Gertrude and I made our way downstairs to discuss the situation. As we entered the parlor, I was a bit surprised to find that the celebration had abruptly ended with the arrival of Powder Monkey. My shipmates had quietly taken their leave so that the sisters could attend to the beaten boy. Captain Adams had remained and immediately requested answers for the sudden and sad appearance of the lad. After listening to our story, Captain Adams expressed his keen desire to teach this vicious ingrate a hard lesson. I interjected that any retaliation by any one of us would surely result in further pain and injury to Powder Monkey. At that instant, an inspired thought came to me and I knew what needed to be done to accomplish Powder Monkey's liberation.

Turning now to Captain Adams, I asked him to relate all he knew about Sir Jonathan's gambling habits. Taking just a moment to collect his thoughts, Captain Adams answered that Sir Jonathan was a renowned gambler, who favored the card game *One-and-Thirty*. He explained that this game was played with three cards dealt to each player. Starting with the player to the dealer's immediate left, one card was discarded face up after that player picked up the top card from the remaining deck. Play continued with each player opting to keep or discard a card chosen from the top of the deck. The cards each had a numerical value with aces representing eleven points, any face card at ten and the remainder equal to their actual face value. The object of the game was to be as close to the value of thirty-one with only cards of the same suit. Additionally, he informed me that three of the same card, three kings for example, garnered a total of thirty-and-a-half points. In this game, play continued in this fashion until one player, confident with his hand, knocked three times on the card table announcing to his fellow players that they had but one more turn to improve their hands before all the cards were revealed. As each hand progressed, bets were made by the participants so that really close matches could mean a very large pot for the winner.

A few savvy islanders suspected Sir Jonathan of cheating, usually only chanced when the pot reached large proportions. I questioned Captain Adams how his cheating was accomplished. He smiled and informed me that Sir Jonathan usually enlisted the assistance of a beautiful woman, who would provide some sort of distraction at a critical juncture of the game. It seemed that these distractions were varied, providing Sir Jonathan with an opportunity to switch cards, thereby improving his hand.

Lastly, Captain Adams added that Sir Jonathan seemed to bet on a rather large scale when he was in possession of three of a kind, usually a winner in any situation unless one of his opponents managed to land a perfect score of thirty-one. Smiling for the first time that evening, I told him that the only way to beat a card cheat was to figure out a way to cheat better than him!

I bid a cheerful thanks and good evening to my hosts. Captain Adams informed me that he would accompany me back to Fat Dog's Pub in order to watch the fun in person. We both took our leave to the sincere well wishes of all three Adams sisters. As I entered the pub, I spotted a familiar group of my crewmates crowded around Handy, who was in the midst of yet another of his *sea tales*. I joined the group and blended into the fabric of their conversations as the celebration of our cannon exhibition victory was under full sail.

As I enjoyed the familiar company of my fellow mates, I had ample opportunity to observe all that was occurring inside the pub. I noticed that Sir Jonathan was seated at a card table gambling in a carefree manner. Seated on the opposite side of the room were Sergeant O'Toole and a group of his soldiers, who appeared glum and despondent while consuming copious quantities of rum. Seated to the extreme right of the soldiers was my sworn enemy, Mr. Bass, who was also imbibing in a sullen mood alongside his *cuddle up*, Catstalker Gene. Having taken the time to assess all of my enemies, I realized that I might require some additional assistance in case any of these foes decided to do me harm. Peering over to my cannon team, I selected Long Tall Willie as the best choice and signaled him to join me outside for a breath of fresh air.

Once outside, I informed the questioning dwarf of my plan to beat Sir Jonathan at his own game. I asked him to keep a watchful eye on both Sergeant O'Toole and Mr. Bass. Long Tall Willie then told me that he had heard Sergeant O'Toole ranting about being cheated and planning to even the score between us. Deciding that Sergeant O'Toole was a far more dangerous opponent at the moment, I begged Long Tall Willie to keep a very close vigil on him while I attempted to outwit Sir Jonathan. Nodding, Long Tall Willie informed me that he knew exactly what had to be done should Sergeant O'Toole attempt any sort of retaliation. Thanking him for his loyal assistance, we both returned to the manic atmosphere inside. On the way to our table, Long Tall Willie made a detour and headed straight for Mr. Bass' table. As he reached the First Mate, he stumbled and proceeded to fall face-first into the First Mate, knocking him and his table over completely. I watched as Catstalker Gene lifted him roughly off of his mentor, savagely shoving the intruding dwarf away from him. Returning to our table, Long Tall Willie gave me a conspiratorial wink and flashed a glimpse of Mr. Bass' prized dagger, which was now hidden in the waist of his breeches.

I kept a very close watch on my intended victim, Sir Jonathan. Finally a spot at the table opened and I knew that the time had arrived to set my plan into motion. Excusing myself from my friends, I made my way across the room. Petitioning in my most humble and polite voice, I asked if I could join their game. Sir Jonathan was quick to point out that the table was reserved for gentlemen, of which I certainly did not qualify. This witty response brought a loud roar of drunken laughs and snickers from his fellow tablemates. Captain Adams suddenly appeared and announced in a rather loud voice that if the winner of the *Cannon Challenge* was not good enough to join their table then who exactly was good enough?

By now everyone in Fat Dog's establishment had heard the exchange, and they all were in sympathetic agreement with Captain Adams. Sir Jonathan and his cronies had little choice other than to allow me to enter their game. Sir Jonathan was quick to inquire if I had enough coin to gamble with gentry. Plopping my overstuffed coin purse on the table, I politely answered my nemesis that I believed that I had more than enough coin. Nodding in acquiescence, Sir Jonathan proceeded to deal the next hand of *One-and-Thirty* without taking his malicious eyes off of me. Realizing that I had plenty of coin and ample time, I settled into my seat and began my premeditated stratagem. As play progressed, I slowly amassed a huge pile of coins in front of me. In fact, my coin stacks soon outgrew my hated enemy's across the table.

At one point in the game, Sir Jonathan asked maliciously if I had recently seen my team member, Powder Monkey. Answering that I had not, I inquired why he had asked in the first place. He waved my query off as insignificant, but then provided a response. In a drunken leer, he stated that his slave deserved a harsh beating that was sure to be administered once our friendly game of chance ended. Keeping my temper and rage under control, I responded in my most innocent voice that I was sure that this would not be the first time that the lad was severely punished. This statement brought a snicker or two from the many interested spectators observing our play, while at the same time eliciting a fierce spark of anger from my opponent. Visually upset by my passing comment, Sir Jonathan questioned what I meant by this last remark. Appearing quite confused, I responded that I was sure that Powder Monkey was a continual disciplinary problem that more than likely required his owner's constant attention. Unaware of the irony I had employed, Sir Jonathan merely grunted and resumed his card playing.

As the evening ground on, I continued my winning ways to the detriment of everyone else at the table. The time I spent at this gaming table allowed me a very close inspection of Sir Jonathan. I had noticed earlier that whenever this mean-spirited brute felt he had a promising hand, he would take a long deep breath prior to drawing a card or placing a wager. Confirming these suspicions on one particular hand, I neatly dropped out of the hand early, watching Sir Jonathan eventually prevail with three Kings! However, that was the last hand that he actually won, and as the evening got later and later his losses grew greater and greater. I realized that his desire to end the evening on a winning note was becoming distinctly less and less likely to occur. I also knew that in his current state of drunken desperation that he would likely resort to his cheating ways sooner rather than later.

At one point, I noticed Sir Jonathan smirking, which signaled a favorable hand and possibly a chance to employ his cheating methods to ensure victory. The hand was also favorable to several at the table and betting increased significantly and the winner's pot hit staggering proportions. With much on the line, I knew we had arrived at the crucial moment.

Just before he drew for the third time, Sir Jonathan signaled over to one of the more attractive serving wenches to fetch him a fresh tankard of rum. As she delivered his drink, Sir Jonathan whispered something quietly in her ear. With a nod of acknowledgment, she collected his empty tankard and inquired if any other player required a refill. Several players, captivated by her beauty, spoke up and requested refills, which brought an evil grin to my enemy's face. I knew the time and size of the wagered pot were both right for his attempted manipulation.

Glancing at my cards, I was aware that I desperately required the Ace of Hearts to complete a perfect score of thirty-one. Since I had dealt this hand and had taken the opportunity to peek at the bottom card in the draw pile, I knew with certainty where my needed ace resided. I was not surprised in the least when the serving girl returned and accidentally spilled a fresh tankard of rum on the player to my right. Jumping up immediately and slapping the poor lass across her face, all eyes in the tavern turned to this ugly scene as I secretly watched Sir Jonathan slip a card from the discard pile in exchange for an unwanted card from his hand. With a sneer of smugness plastered across his face, Sir Jonathan raised the bet to an unprecedented level. I knew the time was now and utilizing my *special voice*, I created my very own diversion. Throwing my voice fully across the room, I imitated a woman's bloodcurdling scream of pain and agony, which immediately drew every eye in the room in that direction. I used this diversion to neatly pluck the needed ace from its hiding place. With the required card now resting safely in my hand, I was more than ready to execute my plan. I then upped my bet by pushing in all of the remaining coins sitting in front of me.

This bold move forced the other two players to fold their hands, leaving only Sir Jonathan and me in the game. Realizing with some alarm that he did not have enough coin on the table to cover my large bet, Sir Jonathan inquired if I would be kind enough to accept his personal word to cover the shortfall. Grinning fiercely, I informed him that while I trusted his word as a gentleman that I would rather accept the ownership of Powder Monkey in its place. He did not hesitate at all, and readily agreed to wager the ownership of his slave to make up for his coin shortfall. Having agreed, he triumphantly turned over his cards revealing three Jacks to the jubilation and cheering of his cronies. Smiling modestly, I informed him that thirty and a half was a formidable hand, but it still did not beat a perfect thirty-one as I turned my cards over revealing my winning hand.

I was being noisily congratulated by the throng as Sir Jonathan rose from his place and pointed a shaking finger in my direction. Seeing this occur, the jubilant mob quieted. In a loud and menacing voice, Sir Jonathan accused me of cheating throughout the evening. In my most humble voice, I responded that I certainly did not need to cheat to best such a poor card player. Fighting back his rage, Sir Jonathan surprised me when he removed a glove from his waistcoat and proceeded to slap me across the face. Clearly enraged, he informed me that the matter would be settled by our participation in a gentleman's duel. Since I was the challenged party, Sir Jonathan informed me that it was my right to choose the weapons to be utilized in our duel. Still in a dazed state of shock and surprise, I responded that I required a moment to ponder the choice.

Laughing as though my request was ridiculous, Sir Jonathan sneered at me to take all the time I required, but not to plan on running away. In the strongest voice that I could muster, I informed the bulling beast that I had no plans of running away and looked forward to facing him in our upcoming duel. With these words, I strode out of the tavern into the quiet and empty streets.

Finding a deserted stairwell adjacent to Fat Dog's Pub, I sat down to deliberate my options. I shut my eyes to close out the world around me so I could fully concentrate on the problem at hand. Then a very strange thing seemed to occur. As my eyes remained closed, a vague but somehow familiar image started to form in my mind. As this vision cleared, I was surprised to find that the image was of my true love…Rue!

As I concentrated on her image, I realized that my love was actually blindfolded and smiling sweetly at me. My love then vanished but her brief appearance had sparked a nugget of an idea. Remembering back to the story of Handy's duel with Mr. Bass, I determined what was required to survive my dreaded predicament. Silently offering thanks to Rue, I made my way back inside Fat Dog's Pub.

As I entered, I was greeted by looks of worry and dismay on the part of my friends and shipmates. Striding directly up to their table, I asked

Handy if he would be kind enough to act as my second in the duel. Grimacing with worry and anxiety, Handy answered that he would be honored to accept the position. With his agreement, I turned and made my way over to the gaming table where Sir Jonathan was still roosted. Reaching the table, I announced that I had decided on the weapons for our duel. Haughty to the extreme, Sir Jonathan inquired which I had finally chosen. Matching his smirking grin, I informed him that I had settled on a *Blind Man's Dance* as my choice. Confused to the extreme, Sir Jonathan questioned what in hell I was talking about since this was a duel and not a church social. I then filled him in on exactly what I had meant by my words and he reluctantly agreed to my choice. A time was set for dawn of the following day on a deserted beach south of town. With our agreements in place, Sir Jonathan rose abruptly and stalked out of the tavern.

You see, I had gotten him to agree to participate in a blindfolded duel utilizing swords as weapons. While highly unconventional, this bizarre choice would provide me a sliver of an opportunity to actually best my skilled adversary. As my nemesis stalked out of the pub, he stopped momentarily at Sergeant O'Toole's table and signaled the military man to follow him outside. I judged this development as very curious, but decided that I had far greater things to concentrate on before the sun showed her glowing face the next morning.

As agreed, we arrived on the deserted beach about a half an hour before dawn along with half of the town's population. Included in this highly subdued gathering was the vast majority of the *Amafata* crew, including our Captain and Mr. Bass. As Handy and I approached Sir Jonathan, I was a bit surprised to find that Sergeant O'Toole would be acting as the plantation owner's second. Also standing nearby our First Mate was my cannonmate, Long Tall Willie, who gave me a knowing smile and a wink as I gazed in his direction. As the sun broke through the hazy horizon, I realized that the fateful time had finally arrived.

Before the start of the match, I attempted to relax and control my thoughts. I realized that one wrong move with this master of the blade would cost me my life. We were both securely blindfolded by each other's seconds. After what seemed like an eternity, Captain Adams fired the starting signal and our duel was officially commenced. At the sound of the gun, Sir Jonathan's sneering voice announced that I had very little time before I would meet my end. Hearing his voice, I pinpointed his exact location, and moved yet further away in order to extend our dueling time in the hope of achieving ultimate success. In order to keep him talking, I utilized my misdirected *special voice*. I heard his blade whistling through the air as he lashed out in the exact location where I had just thrown my voice. His breathing sounded clear and effortless, but I trusted that time and strenuous exertion would significantly change his tone. Already beginning to show signs of frustration, Sir Jonathan called out once more telling me that he intended a quick, painless death for me. Again, I misdirected my *special voice* and answered that I did not want to die. I placed my voice directly behind the position he occupied, and I listened to him shift positions to attack the area where he had heard my voice emanate. Since I was blindfolded, I could not accurately judge the reaction of the spectators to my diversions. However, I judged by their silence that my ploys had thankfully gone unnoticed!

As I executed this tactic, I navigated closer to his position and at the last instant lashed out with my blade making solid contact with his backside. My unexpected attack earned a grunted, surprised yelp from my startled foe. I immediately pivoted away from his position as I distinctly heard the whistling of his blade slicing air in the exact position I had just vacated. At the same time, I detected his breathing becoming more and more ragged. I could clearly hear him spinning in wide circles with his blade slashing out harmlessly as it met no resistance. As he realized that his efforts were nothing more than futile, he curtailed his wild flailing in an effort to relocate my position.

Throwing my voice once again, I moved toward him to take advantage of his confusion one more time. As I prepared to strike, he suddenly spun his body around and lashed out with his blade. This effort proved successful as his sword found me and sliced deeply across my chest inflicting a very serious wound. Realizing my error, I feinted to my right and then moved quickly to my left circling around my adversary to safety. Taking a moment to assess my injury, I ran my free hand over my chest to inspect my wound. While the cut was deep, it did not seem like it was immediately life-threatening. Nevertheless, I could feel a steady flow of blood. I realized that I needed to put an end to the duel soon or face the prospect of slowly bleeding to death.

Aware that his strokes were all aimed high, I got down on my knees in the sand. This position would severely limit my mobility should I miss with the attack that I had in mind, but I also understood that unless I took this calculated risk I would surely die with my blood drenching the white sand beneath me. Remaining perfectly calm and holding off the panic that was creeping up my spine, I waited for the right opportunity and once again misdirected a call to him directly forward of me. After failing to contact solid flesh with his wild slashes in the area of my voice, I distinctly heard my opponent shift his position to slash the air directly behind him, exactly as he had done in our previous skirmish. Knowing that the time was now right, I tensed and delivered a swift upward stabbing thrust that skewered Sir Jonathan as he continued his misguided attack. Pulling my blade free of his flesh, I executed a rolling turn and was quickly once again up on my knees ready to strike once more. As I executed this movement, I could hear his labored breathing and his whistling sword slashed the space I had just occupied. Tensing one last time, I sent another furious thrust that met nothing but flesh and bone! With a pain-laced groan, my opponent toppled face-first into the sand cutting off the agonized sounds that he was now emitting. At that moment, Captain Adams called a halt to our duel and I reached up and removed my blindfold to assess the situation.

Sir Jonathan was laying face-first in the sand with gaping and ragged holes punched into his backside that were oozing copious quantities of blood. His breathing was very ragged as he lay directly in front of me dying. As I moved closer, I could see the anguish and fear written on his face, as he desperately attempted to breathe life back into his shattered frame. Leaning over him, I whispered that I hoped he enjoyed his next home in Hades as Satan was surely delirious with expectation over his immediate arrival. Grimacing, he whispered that I was certainly no gentleman to fight in such a cowardly fashion. Leaning closer, I whispered to the dying monster that he was definitely right on two counts. In the first place, I informed him that I never pretended to be a gentleman, since that dubious title was reserved for odious characters like him. Secondly, I informed him with a huge smile on my face that I did indeed cheat him at cards and life. With that I wished him a speedy voyage to hell!

As I staggered to my feet, there was a huge roar of approval from the spectators, who had long prayed for justice to be served to this malignant and deranged murderer. Handy was the first at my side and he inspected my wounds, which he declared to be nasty but certainly not fatal. As he congratulated me, I heard a commotion directly behind me. Turning, I spied Sergeant O'Toole preparing to unleash his drawn dagger in my direction. Just as he was about to throw his deadly projectile, another dagger appeared out of nowhere striking the military man squarely in the chest. Totally shocked by this new development, Sergeant O'Toole flinched at the pain, and the resulting movement caused havoc in his aim as he released his dagger in my direction. His blade whistled right past me and instead found a home in my old friend, Handy! The blade caught Handy directly in his throat and he stumbled and fell facedown at my feet. Reaching down to my friend, I gently turned him face up, but could plainly see that his wound was mortal. As I cradled a dying Handy in my arms, he sighed and told me to take special care from now on since I would be journeying on without him. His final words had a devastating effect on me as the overwhelming grief and sorrow at losing my best friend sunk firmly into my entire being!

As I ministered to my dying friend, I was totally unaware of the activity going on around me. Our Captain was the first to reach us, and he too was shocked and numbed by the loss of his close friend. After a moment of silent prayer, the Captain turned his full attention to the murder that had just been committed. Joining Captain Adams, they both made their way over to Sergeant O'Toole's corpse. A quick inspection revealed that Sergeant O'Toole had joined his compatriot on a speedy voyage to the underworld. When Captain Adams and our Captain turned Sergeant O'Toole's body over, they had a clear view of the murder weapon. Our Captain blinked in surprise as he recognized that the blade belonged to his First Mate...Mr. Bass.

As soldiers surrounded their suspect, a totally surprised and sputtering Mr. Bass shouted out his innocence to anyone who would listen. Looking over to Long Tall Willie, who had now moved farther away from the arrested First Mate, I receive another conspiratorial wink indicating who the real knife thrower had been. Nonetheless, Mr. Bass was summarily arrested and led off to an awaiting prison cell. As his frenzied cries of innocence faded into the distance, I looked up to find three friendly faces staring down at me. My protectors and friends, the Adams sisters, took full control of my situation and ordered a few of my shipmates to hoist me up and carry me to their awaiting carriage. Once inside, Gertrude began her skillful ministrations on my wound. She informed me that I was extremely fortunate that Sir Jonathan's sword slash did not do major harm to any vital organs. I responded that I just felt damned lucky to still be alive. Upon making this pronouncement, I must have passed out for the next time I gained consciousness I found myself in the guest bed of the Adams' mansion neatly bandaged from stem to stern!

As I regained my senses, Gertrude was right by my side welcoming me back to the land of the living. I had remained unconscious for three straight days. I questioned her on the deaths on the beach and she informed me that Sir Jonathan, Sergeant O'Toole and Handy were all pronounced dead by the island's authorities. Further, she informed me that Mr. Bass was under military arrest and awaiting trial for the murder of Sergeant O'Toole. The trial date was set for the following week, which meant that should my recovery proceed normally, I would certainly have the opportunity to attend the official proceedings as a prime witness to the event. Happy with that bit of news, I questioned the sisters on the fate of Powder Monkey, who was no longer a slave due to the untimely demise of his owner. The sisters smiled in unison and told me that several witnesses had stepped forward to confirm the terms of the wager that the late Sir Jonathan had made while gambling. Powder Monkey was now my property to do with as I wished. I inquired as to the whereabouts of the little scamp, and was told that he had been at my bedside for the past several days, praying for my recovery and aiding the sisters with anything they might require.

Slipping out the door, Gertrude signaled for my new property to enter. As he came into the room, I almost did not recognize him due to his neat and clean appearance. The first word he signed was the word master. I held up a restraining hand and told him from that moment on he was a free man and not subservient to anybody. Smiling and grinning in his own strange way, he signed that he understood and was totally grateful for all that I had done to allow him to escape the evil clutches of his sadistic owner. He further signed that he was very pleased to pledge the rest of his life acting as my faithful attendant and servant. Appraising him as he stood before me, I signed that I did not require that kind of service. This announcement brought a bleak and crestfallen look to his face, as his lifelong plan was scuttled before it even had a chance to start. Smiling now, I signed that while I did not require the services he offered I was always in need of a good friend and ally.

Understanding my meaning, he once again began to beam as he signed that he would be willing and able to fulfill that role with the greatest of pleasure. Nodding my agreement, I asked him with our rapidly developing nonverbal communication if he would like to return to the life of a sailor, with the important responsibility of being a member of our new cannon team. His face lit up in pure bliss and he signed that he had long dreamed of just such an opportunity, and he pledged to fulfill the role in an exuberant and zealous manner. Clapping his hands vigorously and performing a sailor's jig, he signed that he would relish the opportunity to be my side for the rest of his life. I could judge by his manner that he was wholly sincere in this statement, and I was touched deeply. I informed him that his first chore was to purchase proper sailing slops as I slipped him some coins from one of the purses sitting at the bedside table. With a curt nod and wink, he was off in a flash and I once again marveled at his natural speed and agility.

I spent the next several days entertaining a parade of visitors. Captain Adams was the first of these, and he disclosed that he was present in an official capacity. He explained that he had been sent to take a report on my recollection of the events surrounding the beach murders. I divulged all that I had witnessed that morning, which in truth was very little since I had been blindfolded most of the time. He listened to my statement intently, and then thanked me for my cooperation and made his way out of the room. As he was exiting, he turned and appraising me, proceeded to let me know that I was a truly remarkable young man. I thanked him for the compliment, and he exited smiling all the way.

The next visitor was my Captain, who seemed quite pleased with my recovery. Full of grief and sadness, I expressed my overwhelming sorrow over the loss of our mutual friend, Handy. I confessed that life aboard the *Amafata* would never again be the same. With a doleful nod, the Captain commiserated with my pain-laden sentiments! Attempting to diffuse our mutual grief, he confided that our loss was indeed tragic since good cooks were hard to come by. Laughing for the first time in quite a while, I stated that I was certain that Long Tall Willie could adequately fill the role with the assistance of Powder Monkey assigned my old role as *galley slave*. Smiling now, the Captain agreed wholeheartedly and wasted no time in informing me that he would be delighted to add the lad to the ship's crew.

So as to not rekindle our grief, the Captain then pulled out his trusty chess set, which was tucked securely under one arm and proceeded to arrange the men on the board as we silently reminisced over the strange events of the past week. As the match opened, he confided that all indications pointed to a guilty conviction for our former First Mate. To this end, he asked if I had any recommendations in that regard. I responded honestly that I knew very few souls on the island but was absolutely certain that Captain Adams could provide the names of a few worthy candidates. Grinning, he agreed with my thinking and we launched into a furious fought match.

The last notable well wisher was my savior, Long Tall Willie. The smiling dwarf bounced into the room informing me that he was totally disappointed in my power of recovery. He blamed this weakness on the fact that I did not imbibe spirits to hasten my recuperation. As he put it, if I was a rum drinker then I would be up and dancing a hornpipe jig by now. I sadly informed him that my injuries and recuperation had not driven me to thirst for spirits of any kind. Smiling sadly, he informed me that no human being could ever hope to be perfect! After we both stopped laughing, I became serious and thanked him sincerely for my life. Waving my statement off as if it were of no great importance, he seemed anxious to forget the entire tragic episode. Not to be daunted, I told him that I considered his actions to be very noble and vowed to pay him back one day for the huge favor he had granted me. Becoming deadly serious once again, he questioned if I had told anyone else of his participation that morning on the beach. Quickly, I retorted that there was absolutely nothing I could report since I had been blindfolded the majority of the morning. Winking, he thanked me for my silence and merrily skipped toward the exit. At the door, he paused for a moment to inform me that he had a huge favor to ask. Nodding to him to proceed, he licked his lips anxiously and inquired if I might spare a coin or two to appease his strong thirst. Snatching the smaller of the two coin purses on the bedside table, I tossed it to him and appointed him keeper of the *Amafata* treasury. He responded that he would take very good care of the cache of coins and with a parting bow and wicked smirk, danced out of the room!

After the dwarf's merry departure, my thoughts turned toward the future. I firmly resolved to do everything in my power to hasten my healing so that I could play a pivotal role in the upcoming trial of my enemy, Mr. Bass. I was also consumed with the burning desire to reunite with my true love as soon as possible. Thinking ahead, I was certain that I would face many daunting challenges before my ardent dream could be realized. For now, I needed to concentrate on getting well in order to achieve my forthcoming desires and aspirations!

Chapter 35: Growing Older and Voyaging On

Ahoy landcrabs, I am currently forced to beg for a brief respite at this point in my narrative for a number of critical reasons. Most importantly, I am in immediate need of reestablishing a much safer...higher and drier...position on this floating scrap of oaken debris. The sole objective of which is to avoid the gnashing jaws of death that currently surround me. Every so often I am reminded of my perilous predicament when a plaintive yelp or a desperate whimper reaches my ear. These pitiful sounds are routinely followed by an eventual splash along with the instantaneous roiling of the sea's surrounding surface as the flesh strippers perform their frenzied feeding. This brief respite will also allow me the distinct opportunity to gather my thoughts to provide you a succinct and complete recounting of my life's adventures.

As I have indicated previously, our time period was both extremely harsh and exceedingly brutal. I can genuinely proclaim that I have already been directly responsible for the ultimate demises of several miscreants such as Scarf Rockingham, Bigmouth Ajax and Sir Jonathan Brisbane. I justified these malignant situations mentally as forced self-defensive actions.

I am certain that as you continue to follow my life's story, you will see that future choices and conduct regarding proven enemies as well as strangers harboring harmful intent will take a dramatic course change. My actions to combat and defeat these maniacal and nefarious threats will result in cold, calculating and savagely harsh behavior on my part! I believe wholeheartedly that I did not revert into some sort of unfeeling and rabid monster as my life unfolded. However, I am certain that you will discern that I dealt with these mortal threats and dangers with a firm and calculating purpose in order to merely survive in a world loaded with cutthroats and degenerates of the highest order.

My adventures are so very far from over! I promise that the continuation of my tale is fraught with a veritable slew of precarious situations and maniacal villains, which will require ingenious planning and implementation on my part in order to merely survive. Therefore, please excuse me for just a short time while I dodge my relentless predators while putting these continuing memories in order. I promise you it will be worth the wait!

To be continued in Book Two...Scurvy Scoundrel

CHARACTERS AND NAMES

Book One: Remarkable Rascal

London, England
William Echo Eden-orphan and narrator
Toby Eden-Echo's younger brother
Arch Deacon Williamson Archibald (Old ghost and Uncle Arch)-
    Echo's elderly uncle
Vicar Walters- superior of Saint Agnes of Agony Basilica
John Block-Master Builder
Scarf Rockingham-vicious bully
Brutus-John Block's hound

Slugger O'Toole's Sport Emporium
Slugger O'Toole- owner/operator of pub
Yankee Sullivan-bare-knuckle fighter
Frenchie Flook-bare-knuckle fighter
Lipless Billy Winder- Scarf's young assistant
Big Jack Masters-Slugger's head bouncer
Bloody Beast-canine champion
Poxy Mary- pub doxy
Gwen Corder-street hag

Amafata
Jedediah Potts (Handy)- Galley master and Echo's friend and mentor
Achilles- Handy's former ship in seatale
Edmund Spriggs- black cat victim in Handy's seatale
Creeping Jeremy- storyteller and mate
Beloved- ship in Creeping Jeremy's seatale
Samuel Conway-Captain of Amafata
Mr Bass-First Mate
Matt Pyewicket (Stuttering Matt)- whipping victim of Mr. Bass
Jemme Buttons (Grommet Jemme)- suspected jonah and dullard
Ajax Rowe (Bigmouth Ajax)- Mr. Bass' cuddleup
Shipboard Band:
        Handy-triangles
        Nasty Cornelius Marr-squeezebox
        Fighting John English-fiddle
        Muttering Moses Hart-fife

Grommet Jemme- spoons
Geovanni Perilli (Doc)- shipboard physician
Moses Hayes (Chips)- shipboard carpenter
Baron George Wren- notorious traitor and hanging victim in Chip's tale
Pablo Cruces- jonah in seatale on *Flying Duchess*
Phillip Watson-victim of greased riggings murder attempt
Monkey Faced Bill- mate

Saint Domingue

Guy Beamount- cruel plantation owner in Voodou tale
Bortu- informal slave leader in Voodou story
Silve- Bortu's daughter and suicide victim
Cap-Francis- Saint Domingue's major city
"Palais Le Monde" (Palace)- Saint Domingue's house of pleasure
Monique La Montaine- Palace owner and operator
Rue La Montaine- Monique's daughter
Slash Buckets- pirate storyteller
Max Liberty- mate on "Lone Vulture" in Slash's tale
Tiny Eyed Pete- nick-a-bottle winner
Ding-Dong- injured island mutt
Babar Kismet (Lion)- Turkish pirate
Black Tarantula- pirate scourge of the Caribbean
Angry George- pirate storyteller
Papa Legba- Voodou loa
BouLongo- Voodou high priest
Zombie Jemme- Grommet Jemme in disguise
Adams sisters:
  Gertrude- naturalist and healer
  Willamina- palm reader
  Hortence- aspiring stage actress
Rene Normand- brutal island plantation owner
Big William- Rene Normand's tormented slave
Sugar Sally- prostitute love of Babar Kismet
"Trident"- Black Tarantula's transport ship renamed "Spider's Web"
Gene Fabrege (Catstalker Gene)- miscreant and small animal torturer
"Ocean Vulture"-ship in Handy's seatale
Thomas Thommes (Captain Tom-Tom)- Captain of "Ocean Vulture"
Squint McGuire- galley slave on "Ocean Vulture"
Long Tall Willie- rescued dwarf knife expert
"Flaming Dragon"- ship in Handy's seatale
Charlie Crowsfeet- rescued mate of Long Tall Willie
The Great Ricardo- villain and attempted murderer of Long Tall Willie
Gordy Blythe- Handy's seatale pisstub victim

Glossary of Pirate Terms

Bilge.....The lowest internal portion of a ship located far below the waterline. This dark, dank and dreary location was the collection point for all manner of liquids (seawater, oil, urine, etc.) that continually leaked down from the decks above on any sailing ship. This noxious, filthy and disgusting "liquid soup" was home to a wide selection of pesky and nasty vermin including rats, fleas, lice and an army of other annoying and disease-ridden pests.

Chanty.....This was a work song used on all manner of sailing ships to take their crew's minds off of the hard labor they were forced to endure. Chanty's simple rhythms and words allowed work crews to operate in a coordinated effort on strenuous and repetitive tasks aboard ship. Chanties were usually performed without musical accompaniment for work based labor rather than for pure entertainment.

Caltrop.....A life-sized jack with four protruding sharpened spikes, that when thrown upon a ship's deck always resulted in one of its deadly spikes pointed menacingly pointed in an upward direction. These nasty devices were spread on the decks of ships in combat situations to deter and injure barefooted intruders. Beyond their short termed intended purpose, these weapons inflicted a painful and debilitating puncture wound that could easily lead to eventual infection and ultimate death.

Careening..... The process of beaching a ship in a protected location then heeling it on its side to perform necessary cleaning and maintenance below the waterline. Tropical warm waters abounded with "freeloading varmints" such as barnacles and the insidious Teredo worm that caused great destruction to the stoutest of ship building materials. In addition, these clinging leech-like invaders caused a huge drag on their victim which could dramatically slow a ship and impair critical maneuverability. Once a ship was scraped free of these unwanted pests, the hull was repaired as required and seams were tightly caulked with pitch, tar and oakum (untwined rope soaked in tar) to prevent leakage.

Crow's Nest.....This term refers a crude structure on the upper portion of the mainmast. The position of with was high enough to enable a lookout clear vision of the surrounding sea to watch for hazards, other vessels and landmasses. The name was derived from the traditional naval navigators who utilized actual crows as an essential part of early navigation. These common and large black birds were carried onboard to help navigators find land when dirty weather impinged on visibility. Released from the ship's upper reaches, these easily visualized birds would instinctively head for the nearest land thereby allowing the navigator to plot a correct course. Since the birds were released from above, they were also caged there thus providing the name to this lookout berth. Given the considerable distance from the center mass of the vessel, the crows nest was subjected to intensely amplified movements made by the ship. It certainly was not a location for any tar subjected to owning a weak stomach or prone to seasickness!

Cutlass..... A short, slashing sword and a pirate's favorite weapon. Strong enough to repel enemy swords and spikes yet short enough to allow effective close-quartered combat, these versatile weapons also served as vital tools to hack cable, sail or wood aboard ships. Usually these weapons had a curved sharpened blade with a hilt equipped with a closed guard to protect the wielder's hand. Easy to mast and essential in any shipboard attack, their flat blades also served as a powerful pain inducing club to induce captives to divulge the specifics of hidden booty.

Dogwatch..... This was a vital period between 4 PM and 8PM that was split into two equal two hour segments to allow the crews of sailing ships to stand different watches on a daily basis. In effect, this divided watch provided an odd number of daily watch periods (a standard of four hours each) that allowed for this natural rotation. This crucial period was also the time supper was served aboard ship for each watch crew in two hour increments.

Doubloon..... This highly sought after pirate booty was the Spanish coin of the realm which was utilized for fair trade throughout the Caribbean. It was also widely known in pirate vernacular as "pieces of eight". The word originated from t the Latin "duplus" meaning "double" because it was originally valued at

two escudos or dollars. It was eventually minted in denominations of one, two, four and eight escudos from where the pirate name sprung. Minted in Spain, Mexico and Peru the front of the coin featured members of the Hapsburg royal family, such as king Ferdinand and Queen Isabella. On the reverse side several images were routinely utilized including the Crusader's cross, a lion or a castle. These coins were minted by hand so perfecting a precisely round coin was quite impossible!

Draft/Draught..... A word with many meanings, Draft can refer to the depth of a vessel's keel below the water line, especially when loaded; very important if you are Captain of a pirate ship, this is the minimum water depth necessary to float a ship, Draft could describe the creative process of writing a document, or; to be selected for the crew. Of course, another important Pirate use of the word indicates the amount taken in by a single act of drinking, i.e., the drawing of a liquid, as from a vial, cask or keg.

Figurehead..... Nearly every sailing ship was equipped with a decorative carved and painted wooden image facing down upon the sea at the prow. These images were specifically designed and created to embody the spirit and essence of its vessel. Many of these nautical icons took the shape of a partially undressed female to appease an old sailor's superstition that believed that "a woman baring herself to the waters would appease the gods of the sea and allow for a safe and calm voyage". Figurehead design was handcrafted and varied to the extreme including depictions of beautiful women, mythological creatures, famous historical personalities or even the ship's owner. The prevailing thought of the time was that the ship's figurehead would lead the vessel's voyage and watch out for troubled waters or dirty weather.

Galley..... This was simply the area designated in a vessel where food was prepared and consumed. Since space was always a constant constraint, tables were wooden devices much like doors that were hinged to the hull's side and drawn up and out of the way when mealtime ended. Chairs were a makeshift of barrels and overturned pails and tubs which were also secured at meal's end. The galley included a large wood-burning stove...a potentially dangerous necessity on a vessel constructed entirely of wood...which carefully monitored and tended by the head cook. Since meals at sea oftentimes lacked fresh ingredients and provisions, the men at these times chose to eat in the dark rather than face their rancid fare.

Grog..... This liquid was a sailor's name for any watered rum. For reasons of necessity, it was invented aboard sailing ships which allowed their crew a daily ration of rum. Many sailors saved up their daily rations of rum to drink in one sitting to get a larger bang from their alcohol, abject drunkenness and disciplinary problem naturally arose. By diluting the rum with water, spoilage was accelerated...given that water turned and spoiled much faster than rum...which prevented hoarding and the problems associated with it. Not to mention that water rum is far less of a powerful consumable spirit! Sometimes citrus juice was added if available to mask the foulness of spoiled wa-

ter also unknowingly acting as a strong deterent to the insidious disease...scurvy. This custom may have led to the British sailors being nicknamed "limey's due to the juice they consumed in their grog.

Hardtack..... This was a simplistic cracker or biscuit cobbled from flour, water and salt...when available. Cheap to produce and having a long shelf-life devoid of spoilage and ruination over more perishable provisions, these hardened crackers became a staple for long sea voyages. The name originated from the British navy's slang word for food...tack. Nicknamed ship biscuit, pilot's bread and sea biscuit, it also carried several pejorative labels such as worm castles, tooth breakers and dog biscuits. Baked on purpose top a crusty hard surface, it could last for years if it remained dry. Hardtack also served as the home to freeloaders like weevils, maggots and worms. Any salty tar learned early on to rap this standard fare against a strong wooden beam or post to drive out some of these unwanted vermin. Eaten al;one or dunked in hot coffee or water, hardtack was a sea staple for any long voyage! The dilution ratio was normally two parts water to one part rum! On land, pirates and sailors alike favored a similar drink named bumboo which included nutmeg, cinnamon and sugar not likely to be found in plentiful supply at sea.

Holystone..... This was a large soft, brittle and white sandstone used for scouring a ship's deck. It received it moniker because it's shape and appearance resembled a printed bible. It was also speculated that it was tagged as holy because toiling tars were always on their knees when using this cleaning aid. The vessel's decks were

272 / Bilge Rat

cleaned in a very precise and prescribed manner. The first step was to wet down the deck area to be cleaned with seawater followed a generous sprinkling of sand. The next step was to scrub the wet sanded deck with the holystone on your knees. Lastly, this dirty aftermath mixture was swabbed up with the use of a mop and clean seawater.

Idlers.....A sailing vessel's crew was divided into three categories...officers, watchmen and idlers. While the term seemed to denote a lack of initiative and effort, the reality of the situation was vastly different. Idlers were individuals whose specific assignments precluded them from fulfilling regular watch duties. This vitally important group included the ship's doctor, cook, carpenter, sailmaker, cooper, navigator, musicians and other ship specialists. The term was coined because this group usually worked all day but were idle at night.

Keelhaul..... This was a vicious and oftentimes fatal punishment of dragging a guilty sailor under his ship either from side-to-side or from stem-to-stern. Under this punishment, the victim's ands and ankles were secured by ropes with a stout cable attached to either bound location. At a signal from the presiding officer, the victim was launched from the ship and summarily dragged under the vessel. Since most sailors of the time lack the simple ability to swim, this harsh treatment usually resulted in death by drowning. In addition, the hulls of these ships were generously adorned with pesky barnacles who'd sharp shells cut, abraded

and tore apart the human invader as they were dragged across their domain.

Lagoon..... Simply stated this was a small body of water separated from a much larger one by reefs, spits of land and barrier islands. Normally shallow and salty in nature, lagoons provided a perfect hiding place for much smaller pirate ships from the much larger military ships sent out to chase and destroy them. Derived from the Italian word...laguna...referring to the waters surrounding the city of Venice. Naturally developed inlets cut through reefs and barrier islands permitted tidal flow into and out of lagoons.

No Quarter..... This term signified a 'fight to the death". It received its meaning as the polar opposite of "giving quarter" which was a sailing custom of officers offering a fourth of their pay upon surrendering to pirates as ransom. It came to be known in pirate terms as showing no clemency, mercy and refusing to spare the lives of surrendered or vanquished opponents. A no quarter command meant that no prisoners would be taken and all enemies would be slaughtered. it was basically an ordered death sentence on any foe deemed worthy for complete destruction!

Salmagundi..... A zesty pirate dish...either a salad or a stew...that was comprised of a hodgepodge of cooked meats including that of turtle, seafood, vegetables, fruit, eggs, flowers, leaves and nuts and flavored with oil, vinegar and a variety of available spices to add flavor and cover the scent and taste of any rancid ingredient. This pirate's dish never followed a single recipe as cooks utilized anything hand to concoct this popular dish. Basically it was a mishmash that pleased its pirate consumers like no other meal could hope to do!

Scuttlebutt..... This informal title bestowed upon shipboard gossip, rumor or unofficial news. The term originated from the name of a large cask...scuttle butt... of fresh water usually placed in a central position on the top deck in easy reach of all crewmen so they could quench their thirsts with a quick drink. It was the only place onboard where watchmen could gather and trade talk and information during their watch. As crewmen crowded around the scuttle butt for their drinks of water, they traded gossip, opinions, rumors and the like which spawned the term.

Skedaddler..... This is a name for a crewman who devises methods to shirk his assigned duties at every opportunity. In many instances, this hated and despised individual would routinely feign illness to avoid harsh physical labor. This unwelcome nautical label was also levied on cowards who turned tail and fled during armed combat. The punishment for such a distasteful act usually resulted in a death sentence.

Slops..... Sailors required practical working outfits to accomplish their assigned shipboard duties. Therefore, the clothing worn was suitable to enable them to do their obs. Nicknamed "slops", derived from the generous knee-length pants popular at the time. The sailor's slops ensemble included wide and flowing pants that ended at the knee, a short jacket to

ward off cold weather, a neckerchief to act as a sun blocker for the neck and a sweat rag, a linen or hemp shirt, a hat of varying designs and no shoes. As old and discarded sailcloth was readily available, a majority of seagoing slops were fashioned from this unwanted material.

Scurvy..... An insidious disease that attacks victims who experience a pronounced deficiency of Vitamin C. Scurvy victims initially suffer through a lethargic state of misery which is followed by depression, bleeding and receding gums, spots on the skin especially on the legs and partial paralysis. At the end, victims lose teeth, become jaundice, experience dangerously high fever and an eventual horrible death. Epidemic in nature, this blight usually claimed multiple shipboard victims, weakening crew numbers and making the ship vulnerable to further disasters from weather or aggressive enemies. Alcoholism can foster the onset of this dangerous pestilence. Since most pirates were hardly "dry gobs" by nature, they were prime candidates to contract this ugly and lethal disease.

Yardarm..... This is a long horizontal spar tapered at the end and used to support and spread a square sail or lateen, often a square yard in size. Most commonly it would be the place to fly the ship's flag, although was an inviting place to call attention to other things you might want to display on a more temporary basis. Hence you occasionally heard expressions like "Hang him from the yardarm!"